The Last Alchemist

by Erik Hamre

The Last Alchemist

Copyright © 2015 by Erik Hamre

Most of this book is fiction, the rest is not. Characters, corporations, institutions and organisations in this novel are the product of the author's imagination, or, if real, are used fictionally without any intent to describe their actual conduct. Some of the historical events in this book are, however, real. For a list of documented events head over to the author's website.

Cover art by Twinartdesign
Edited by Mike Waitz
Interior design by Erik Hamre

www.erikhamre.com

Give feedback on the book at:
eh@erikhamre.com

First Edition

Printed in the U.S.A

To mum, for unconditional support.

Part 1

– 1 –

Bundesbank, Frankfurt, Germany
Monday, 22nd of September 2009

The canteen at Bundesbank was buzzing with life. Hans Baumler, a senior auditor from Bundesrechnungshof, Germany's Federal Audit Office, was picking at his salad.

He was sitting alone. Most of his colleagues ventured out to eat. They would find themselves a reasonably priced restaurant where they could spend their lunch break in silence, without anyone annoying them. Hans Baumler on the other hand enjoyed the attention. He had worked as an internal auditor, in various international banks, for as long as he could remember. And he had finally arrived at the conclusion that he appreciated detecting errors and faults in protocols and processes. Most of all he appreciated discovering human errors. Not innocent mistakes, but deliberate attempts to circumvent the banks' protocols. Deliberate attempts of fraud.

He didn't mind that people sometimes made mistakes. He himself did the occasional blunder. What he detested was the human tendency to never admit one's mistakes. Instead of coming clean, people tried to hide and conceal what they had done.

And in that process, without exception, they all got themselves further into trouble. Hans Baumler almost felt like an investigative detective when he was working. It was a given that no one tried to sit down next to him at lunch. If they did, they would be scrutinised with extra caution. People always had an agenda.

Like the person who had been seated at the next table for the last twenty minutes. He had tried to be discreet, but Hans Baumler had noticed him almost immediately. He had been sitting there, hardly touching his food, just observing Hans Baumler. Hans Baumler assumed he was working up his confidence, working up his confidence to approach Hans Baumler. Hans Baumler took notice of the guy's facial features. He would go through the employee files later that night and find out who the guy was. And when he found him he would put him under the magnifying glass, find his every little dirty secret.

Maybe he had managed to figure out what Hans Baumler had discovered during the audit of the Bundesbank? For Hans Baumler the auditing work he had completed over the last few weeks was the culmination of a long and successful career. If he was right, something he already knew he was, he had discovered the biggest fraud in the history of Germany.

Hans Baumler rose from his chair and carried the half-eaten salad over to the garbage bin. He adjusted his glasses and wandered out of the canteen with a firm grip on his briefcase. He took the escalator down to the reception and exited the main entrance. He felt like a stroll and some fresh air. He felt like clearing his mind before he put the finishing touches on the report.

He turned left outside the Bundesbank building. The sun caressed his face and sent warm shivers throughout his body. It felt nice. He hadn't really gotten a lot of sunlight the last few weeks, consumed as he had been by his work. And he had started to feel the onset of sleep deprivation and vitamin D deficiency on his body. Maybe he should stop by a travel agent? See if he could find a deal for a long weekend trip to another European capital? London, maybe? Just he and his wife. Her parents could look after Oliver, his four-year-old son. They loved to babysit anyway. He smiled. Life was good.

As he was waiting for the traffic light to turn green he got that peculiar feeling he had experienced so many times over the last few days. It was as if someone was watching him. He turned around. On the stairs of the entrance of the Bundesbank, the person from the canteen stood and stared directly at him. There was something strange about his stare, as if he didn't care to avert his eyes even though Hans Baumler looked straight back at him.

What can he possibly want? Hans Baumler thought before he felt his legs almost cave in beneath him. An indescribable pain rushed through his chest. What the hell was that? The first wave of pain had hardly subsided before the next arrived. It felt like someone had just turned on an electrical switch and sent thousands of watts through his body. He hunched forward and had to lean against the traffic light to avoid falling over. When the next jolt came he was at least more prepared, but this was also somewhat different from the first two. The third jolt didn't disappear. Instead it was as if a python had curled around his chest and slowly started to apply pressure. Just started to squeeze harder and harder.

"Do you need any help?" An elderly lady, probably more than eighty years old, gently put her hand on Hans Baumler's left shoulder.

He managed to squeeze out a smile, all while his sweat glands were working overtime. It was as if his head had been dunked in a bucket of water. "I'm ok," he muttered.

He just needed to rest. He was so incredibly tired. He leant towards the traffic light. In the corner of his eye he could see that the man from the stairs had disappeared.

Who is he and what does he want? Hans Baumler thought as the world got darker around him. It was as if all the traffic came to a halt, it was so silent and peaceful. A new electric jolt shook him out of his dreamstate. The pain in his chest was extreme and he realised that he was about to die. This wasn't a sign that he had pushed his body too hard and needed a rest. This wasn't a vague pain in his jaw nor a tingling feeling in his arm, the early signs of a heart attack that his doctor had told him to be vigilant for, now that he had turned forty years. This was no drill. He was in the middle of a massive heart attack, a widowmaker. To his great surprise he realised he wasn't scared. He had just made the most important discovery of his career. He had been allowed to finish something that was worth living for, something bigger than himself. His colleagues would find his briefcase. They would find his report, and they would realise that he singlehandedly had managed to uncover this fraud. Martha, his wife, would be proud. He would receive a proper funeral. He would be remembered.

His face unwillingly made a grimace from the sheer pain that again rushed through his chest. He forced his eyes open; maybe there still was hope? Maybe there still was a chance that he could survive? Heart attacks weren't always deadly. He tried to hold up a hand towards the person who was approaching him. He tried to stay upright, but the legs wouldn't listen. He could feel that he was falling forwards, and he wanted to raise his arms, to protect his face from the fast approaching concrete below, but his body had shut down. Nothing worked as it should.

As he tipped forward, and was preparing to feel the pavement meet his face, he felt a couple of strong arms grabbing him mid-air. The arms lifted him up and placed his body gently on the ground. A rush of joy went through his body. He would be saved.

He could feel the same strong hands now rolling him over on his side. He was being placed in a recovery position. The person had placed him in a safe recovery position. The Bundesbank building was located in the middle of Frankfurt CBD. It wouldn't take many minutes before the ambulance arrived. He would be able to see his son Oliver grow up. He would be able to experience Oliver's first day at school, the awkward moment when he brought his first girlfriend home.

He would be saved.

In front of his eyes a sea of shoes and legs materialized. They belonged to all the people who had gathered around him. Like a wall of people, there to help him, there to save him. He was about to smile when he felt a sting of fear rush through his body. Someone was releasing Hans Baumler's grip on the briefcase. Someone was removing the precious briefcase from his hands. He wanted to tell whoever it was to be careful, to take good care of the briefcase. He would have no idea what it contained, what information it held, how important it was.

But no words came out of Hans Baumler's mouth. Instead he tried to tilt his head up a little bit. He wanted to get a glimpse of the person who now held his briefcase. To look him in the eye, to give him a sign, to make him understand that he had to get that briefcase to the authorities as soon as possible.

With a shock he realised he wasn't even able to lift his head.

The sea of legs and shoes seemed to disperse, and in the

corner of his right eye he recognised his own briefcase. A man in a dark suit was carrying it, he was carrying it away from Hans Baumler. Suddenly the man in the dark suit turned his head, and for a short moment Hans Baumler could see his face. He thought he could see a smile, and he wanted to scream with all the air in his lungs.

He recognised the face. It was the man from the canteen, the man with the eyes that didn't divert.

A teardrop appeared in the corner of Hans Baumler's right eye, making the figure of the man with the briefcase harder to see.

With sadness Hans Baumler realised he wouldn't be remembered after all.

I won't be remembered, was his last thought as he felt someone pressing down his ribcage.

And a face above him leant closer, ready to kiss him, ready to give him the kiss of death.

-2-

CIA HQ, Langley, USA
Tuesday, 26th of June 2013

The CIA director, Mark Green, sat down at the large mahogany table. He felt like his hair had become visibly greyer over the last few days.

"Status report," he said with a firm voice, studying the faces on the fifty-inch screen in front of him. They were supposed to be two of the most experienced agents from the London office. The Winkelvoss twins from the Facebook saga, that's what came to Mark's mind when he looked at them. Identical haircuts, identical smiles - like two human robots in suits.

"There's no change. Germany remains firm in her demands," one of the agents replied. The other agent raised his cup of coffee and had a sip. To test how hot it was, it appeared. It was obvious that it was hot because his face twitched a bit before he put the cup back onto the table. At least that proves they are human, the CIA director thought with a sigh.

"And Operation Aurum. What's the status?"

"Operation is proceeding according to plan. Phase one has been initiated," the other Winkelvoss twin answered.

"Give me immediate feedback if anything changes. This

operation is our number one priority going forward," the CIA director said before he pressed the button on his remote and watched the screen turn black.

He leant back in the black leather chair, and put his feet on the table. Maybe it was time to think about something else to do with his life? The job wasn't what it used to be anymore. It had been so much easier with conventional enemies. The CIA director had enjoyed the Cold War, the cat and mouse hunt for Soviet spies. He had even enjoyed hunting Al-Qaida terrorists and Bin Laden. At least they were known enemies, physical enemies. Enemies a person could respect even though he disagreed with their ideologies, motives and actions. But mankind lived in a new world. The Chinese didn't spy to get their hands on military secrets; they spied to get their hands on the latest commercial technology. Who ruled the world wasn't determined by who had the strongest defence army or controlled the largest fleet of warships. What mattered was who held the economic power in the world. What mattered was who had the biggest financial muscles, the biggest financial guns. And this balance of power was about to change in a significant way.

The US was still in an acceptable financial shape. They still had a large home market and a proven culture of creating global market leaders. Out of nowhere Steve Jobs and Apple had taken over the global mobile market in less than five years at the end of the 2000s. But now even Apple was under threat, by a South Korean company called Samsung, by a bloody fridge maker.

Something had drastically changed over the last few years. The Asian companies had evolved. They weren't content with only being suppliers to American brands anymore. They had started to innovate, to adapt.

So much so, that the top brass in Washington was starting to get concerned.

They worried that the US had outsourced too much of their technological competence over the last decades.

The engineering know-how wasn't located in the US anymore.

It was situated in Asia.

But there was something even more serious going on. Something that had worried many Republicans since the early 1970s, when an important decision had been made.

The Republicans had warned that the US at some stage would have to pay the price for that decision, and over the last few months this band of Republicans had gotten a lot more supporters.

It was the CIA director's task to ensure that this whole thing didn't escalate into a crisis, a crisis they didn't have any weapons to fight back against.

− 3 −

Bond University, Gold Coast Australia
Thursday, 28th of June 2013

"David, you're up." The Indian classmate poked David in the shoulder. David Dypsvik turned around and shot him an annoyed look. He knew it was his turn. He was just trying to postpone the unavoidable as long as possible. The whole morning he had procrastinated and suffered from bad conscience because he hadn't prepared for the day's lecture. He had no excuses. There had been plenty of time. There had been plenty of opportunities. Nevertheless he was now sitting in auditorium 14 with nothing but a couple of blank pages in front of him. David was a full-time student in the MBA program at Bond University on the Gold Coast in Australia. The class was relatively small, only 32 students, and the course in entrepreneurship was generally recognised as one of the easiest of the MBA curriculum. Despite all this he could feel the heart race in his chest when he got up to speak.

"Professor Grossman. Unfortunately I am unable to hold my presentation today. I am still awaiting an authorisation from my employer regarding divulging confidential information to this class without requiring all students to sign a strict confidentiality agreement."

Professor Grossman coughed. "I understand your predicament David, but we are now four weeks into the semester. It is hard for me to give you any constructive feedback when I don't know what you are working on."

"I will get the authority signed before the next lecture," David replied.

"Make sure you do that," Professor Grossman quipped.

David had just bought himself another week, but that was all. He couldn't continue to procrastinate with this project. He had to make a decision, and he knew it would hurt.

As a replacement for David's presentation one of the American students entered the podium and started on his well-rehearsed speech. David didn't bother listening. He had heard it all before. Not exactly this presentation, but a variation of it. The American was a typical eager-beaver. He followed the book from beginning to end. He hadn't prepared a business plan for a ground-breaking new invention or idea. Instead he had chosen the safe route. He had prepared a strategy for how an established American producer of diapers could enter the Australian market. Yeah!

With a slick smile on his face, the American described the approach his client would take in order to rape the Australian diaper market. Yes, those were his exact words. Rape the Australian diaper market. David had to listen twice before he believed it.

Well, David thought, packing up his blank pages, things could have been worse. He could have been standing up there on the podium talking about raping the Australian market for diapers.

On the way out of the auditorium he heard someone call out his name. He turned around and looked straight into Professor

Grossman's chiselled face. The professor didn't look like a typical academic, more like a retired mountaineer with his flashy white teeth and sunbaked face.

"Do you have five minutes?" Professor Grossman asked.

"Of course," David replied, feeling a bit ambushed.

"Let's go have a coffee," the professor suggested, and gave David a friendly pat on the back.

David bit his lips together. He had forgotten to wear sunscreen the previous day, and three hours of surfing at Burleigh Heads had left a back that was as sensitive as the new iPhone from Apple, even though it was still winter on the Gold Coast.

"Sounds great," David answered, uncertain of the professor's true intentions. He quickly assessed it could only be one of two possible reasons the professor wanted to have a talk with him outside class. The first one was obvious: The professor had seen through David's little acting performance. He had realised that David didn't work on a business plan that required an authorisation from an imaginary employer. And he had realised that the excuse this morning had just been a badly executed ploy to buy David some more time. The other alternative was more serious: Professor Grossman also taught the financial investments course. And last week David had been pulled aside after class. The essay he had written, about how management's purchase of shares in their own company could affect the share price, didn't adequately refer to sources. It had in fact zero footnotes. Professor Grossman had told David that the essay was being investigated for plagiarism. David hadn't really worried too much. It was true he hadn't referred to any sources. But he hadn't copied anyone either. Now he started to worry. Did Professor Grossman suspect David of cheating?

"You probably know why I would like to have a chat with you,"

Professor Grossman said, breaking the eerie silence between them.

"I'm not entirely sure I do," David replied.

"I don't get you. You are obviously among the smarter people in my class, but it doesn't seem like you care much about your grades. It almost seems like you have a secret wish to fail. But you don't have the guts to go through with it." Professor Grossman looked David in the eyes while they walked towards the campus coffee shop.

David had entertained the same thought himself. If he failed a course then his return back to Norway would have to be postponed, and the job offer he still had from his old employer back home would be declared invalid. The scenario would definitely buy him some more time. And maybe it was just that extra time he needed to come up with an idea that could change his life forever. He couldn't make himself go through with it, though. He couldn't make himself fail a course. Even if he hadn't been financially successful he at least had an impeccable academic record. He didn't want to let go of that bit as well.

"I do my best. Even if I might not seem like I'm interested in the lectures I am always paying attention," David said, struggling to keep up with the professor's rapid walk.

"I know that's bullshit David. I see you every week. You sit back there, all the way in the back of the classroom. You are present, but that's only a physical presence. You act like you're still in high school for Christ's sake. You pay what? Fifty thousand for this MBA degree? Yet you seem keener to be at the beach than in my classroom. And I don't believe for one second your story about not being allowed to divulge information about your business plan."

They had now arrived at the coffee shop and Professor Grossman reduced the tempo. David was lost for words. He had been totally caught off guard and had no idea how to respond. The professor talked to him like he was a five-year-old kid.

"How do you take your coffee?" the professor asked, unaffected by the rant he had just unleashed on David. It was as if the conversation had never taken place.

"Just tea for me. Earl Grey and a glass of water please," David replied. His mouth suddenly felt incredibly dry.

"Janine, could I have a flat white and a mug of Earl Grey?" The professor flashed his white teeth to the waitress and grabbed the little number tag she handed him.

"You'll find water over in the corner," he said to David, pointing to a large water container with two rows of paper cups placed directly beneath. "Could you find a table as well?"

David nodded and headed towards the water container. Luckily there were hardly any students in the coffee shop. David had never enjoyed having personal conversations in public, and he sure as hell didn't look forward to this one.

A few minutes later the professor joined David at the table in the corner of the coffee shop. He placed his own cup of coffee and David's mug of tea onto the table.

"So, have you thought about what I just said?" the professor asked.

"I didn't think it was a question," David answered.

"Is it a question you want?" Professor Grossman asked, slightly raising his left eyebrow. "Well, tell me David, tell me why you spend fifty thousand dollars, plus lost income and one and a half years of your life wandering around here at campus if you don't like it."

David stared at the bottom of his tea cup, the bag of Lipton Earl Grey slowly dispersing a stream of brownish colour into the clear water.

"Change, I wanted change."

"And have you got change?"

"Yes."

"But not the change you wanted?"

"No."

"So tell me what you want, David. It is frustrating for me to try to create enthusiasm in the classroom when it is clear as daylight that you really want to be somewhere else."

"I wanted to change. I thought that if I travelled to the opposite side of the globe, to a place where nobody knew me, then I could change. That I could become the person I'm supposed to be."

"And who exactly is that?"

"I don't know. I only know that I'm not meant to be stuck in a job where I work from nine to five every day. Trapped in a job I don't even like. Everyone I know is making fortunes on real estate, shares and God knows what. And still I'm stuck in a job where I work from January to May to pay tax, and the next seven months to pay the other bills. I'm tired of being measured on everything I do in my job. I live like a modern slave and I hate it." David's voice almost broke as he spit the words out. He had never before told a living soul what he really felt about his own life. And now he sat here, spilling his innermost secret to a total stranger. This hadn't gone as planned.

"You're not that unique, David." Professor Grossman looked straight into his eyes. He had a look that wasn't intrusive, but it still was as if he saw straight through David.

"Most of the bright students I talk to feel the same. They don't however arrive at this realisation until much later in life. So consider yourself lucky, David." Professor Grossman adjusted his slim and slender body in the seat. "I have a suggestion for you, David. You won't get much time to consider. This is a proposal you either say yes or no to. And that decision will have to be made here today, before I finish my coffee." Professor Grossman took a large drink of his cup.

David didn't know what to say. He was confused.

"I have a job offer for you," Professor Grossman started.

"A job offer? Thanks. But I'm not interested," David replied.

"Don't you want to know what you are saying no to?" the professor asked.

"Of course," David replied, a little embarrassed. "I didn't mean to be so crass. It's just that…well, I came here to change my life. When I start working again, when I finally graduate, then I'm back where I started."

"Maybe this job offer is different from what you expect," the professor said. "It is correct that you worked as a journalist a few years back, isn't it?"

David hadn't noticed, but Professor Grossman had placed a copy of David's CV on the table in front of them. He must have gotten it from the admissions office, David thought. "That's correct. I worked a year and a half for a Norwegian newspaper, focusing on business news."

"Did you like it?"

"Yes and no. I enjoyed meeting people, learning how they had built their business and succeeded in their careers. It was inspiring. The other side of the coin was that those stories didn't sell any papers. I had to write stories that people would read, but that sometimes ruined good people's lives. I guess that's why I quit. In the end I couldn't stomach it anymore."

"I have just concluded a study, David. A study about wealth. A study into the reasons why some people make fortunes while others struggle financially their whole lives."

"What's the conclusion? Is there any hope for me?" David said with a cheeky smile.

Professor Grossman ignored the ill-attempted joke. "I believe I've found some shocking connections," he instead began. "This study will force radical changes to the education system and open a lot of people's eyes on how great wealth is actually created. But as it is almost impossible to convince the established academic world about long-needed changes to the system, I have devised my own little plan. I have written the draft for a new book, David. A book about ten simple principles that lead to great wealth. And that is why I need your help."

"My help? To do what?"

"To help me market my book," Professor Grossman replied.

David adjusted his back. He felt uncomfortable in the hard plastic seat. "Why me? I don't have a marketing background, and I'm sure there are other students with better grades," David said. It came out a bit harsher than he had expected.

"I don't need somebody with straight A's," Professor Grossman said. "I need someone with the right attitude."

"I still don't understand why you want me," David replied, staring down at the bottom of his tea cup.

"Well, first of all I would strongly advise you to never talk yourself out of a job offer before you know what the job is. I can still change my mind, you know. But you are entitled to a proper explanation," Professor Grossman said before adjusting the glasses on the tip of his nose. "I've conducted a small search of your library activity. It might not entirely be in line with the official privacy policies of the university, but sometimes you have to do what you have to do. And the result speaks for itself. In April and May you borrowed half a dozen books about real estate, investing in shares and boring biographies about successful people. You may not be best in class David, and you may not read all the prescribed reading material or prepare for every lecture, but you do something much more important; you choose what you want to learn more about. And still, you seem to be able to stay somewhere near the top of the class in most of the courses you take. I come from a business background, and I have no problems admitting that most of the MBA curriculum is overly theoretical and holds limited value in the real world." Professor Grossman put both his hands on the table and leant in closer to David. "What value do you think an MBA degree has to a prospective employer?" he asked, peering into David's eyes. It was clear to David that he might as well be honest.

"I believe that an MBA degree shows that I have ambition. That I have a thirst for knowledge, and that I'm willing to sacrifice something today for a better tomorrow."

"Exactly, you've hit the nail on the head, David," Professor Grossman said enthusiastically. "The important thing is not what you learn. The important thing is that you learn to learn. That's what's important for an employer: Ambition and a hunger for learning." The professor removed his hands from the table before continuing. "An MBA degree is in other words nothing but a paper confirming that you had the willpower to spend a year and a half of your life to study and memorize theories with little practical value, because you wanted to climb the corporate ladder. It is abundantly clear that such a person could be an asset for any company, but not necessarily for me," Professor Grossman said. His eyes narrowed before he continued. "I need someone who wants to contribute. Someone who seeks the true answer to the eternal question of why some people get rich, while most others struggle financially their whole life. The fact that you choose to spend your personal time investigating how people really make their money tells me that you have a secret wish to break out of the life you are currently living. A life where you work for a pay check every month, a life most of your MBA colleagues are destined to live."

"It doesn't sound like you are too impressed by the standard of my MBA colleagues," David said, studying Professor Grossman's face for his reaction.

"It's not that I'm not impressed," Professor Grossman said. "There are some very smart people in your class. Some a lot smarter than you. But being good at academics can only take you so far," he said, stretching his arms out to the sides to illustrate his point. "To succeed in life you need something more to offer. I have worked at some of the very best universities around the world, and something that never fails to astound me is what happens at the ten-year anniversary of my students' graduation. I always have scores of students coming up to me, telling me that their years at university were the best of their lives. That's nice to hear. And it makes me happy that they enjoyed their time at uni. But I also always have this thought in the back of my mind, this thought that won't go away. I believe that a lot of these people think back of their student years as the best of their lives because they still had opportunities back then. They still had dreams back then. Ten years after graduation your life is pretty much set on a course. You have chosen a career. You may have started a family. You definitely have commitments and responsibilities. And what many realise on this night of celebration is that life has not turned out the way they thought it would ten years earlier. They catch up with old friends, and even though they may have established themselves with a nice life and a good career, they realise that others have done better. Other people who were inferior to them at university. A lot of my students leave these anniversary gatherings with a sour feeling in their stomach, a feeling that life isn't fair. They have worked hard and made lots of sacrifices, yet others seem to have just fallen into wealth. It is quite frankly upsetting to me that so many of my old students leave what should have been a pleasant gathering with old friends, feeling that they have failed in their lives. So David, it is not that I'm not impressed by your MBA colleagues; I just don't think they are using all their abilities – because nobody has told them what is really required when they leave the university grounds and enter the real world. We can help these people, David, we can help them get another perspective on the world, so that the years after university may be the best ones for a lot more people."

David nodded. Professor Grossman had just pointed out the exact thing David was fearful of. "It sounds interesting, but when you say help with marketing…what is it that you really want me to do?" David asked.

"Everything will be explained, David. Meet me at my office tomorrow at eight am, and I will give you some more information. You have an exciting week ahead of you. You will be introduced to Yossar Devan."

And with that comment Professor Grossman rose from the table, grabbed his empty coffee cup , and left. David remained seated at the table, left in solitude, with only his half empty cup of tea and his thoughts as company. He couldn't really fathom what had just happened. He had never heard about a professor named Yossar Devan at Bond University, but something told him the following week would not be an ordinary one.

– 4 –

The sun had struggled to break through the thick layer of clouds the whole morning. Professor Grossman was unsure whether it would rain or be a sunny day. Truth be told, he didn't really care. But he was sort of wondering whether today's races at the Gold Coast Turf Club would be cancelled if the clouds didn't soon evaporate. If so, he might have to change his dinner plans. He closed the drapes and sat down in his office chair. He leant forward and started tapping the tip of his foot against the floor. He had been born with a restless leg. David on the other hand was slouching casually in his chair, almost falling off it. He had made sure that he got up early so that he wouldn't be late for the meeting, and now he was sitting there, regretting that he hadn't eaten any breakfast. He had been up for three hours already and his stomach was making embarrassing sounds. At least that was what he imagined. He also regretted not wearing something more appropriate for the meeting, trousers and a shirt maybe? Instead he was wearing a T-shirt from Quicksilver and a pair of well-worn shorts. The flip-flops didn't really contribute to lift the bar of his outfit.

"Do you know what I do for work, David? When I'm not lecturing about entrepreneurship and finance?"

"No, I can't really say that I do," David answered.

"I study economic history," Professor Grossman said. "Most

people, academics included, don't understand that economies move in cycles, and that everything that goes up must eventually come down. That's why governments around the world scramble to solve this financial crisis that has evolved. A crisis they should have seen coming a mile away."

The professor was referring to the ongoing global financial crisis, which was now going on its fifth year.

"It is however surprisingly few people who want to listen to my theories about economic waves. Instead they listen to self-proclaimed experts, who are good at explaining the reasons for economic events only after the events have actually occurred. I have, therefore, for the last few years, concentrated on something very different. Namely, the study of wealth. In the world today there are more than fourteen hundred billionaires, and the number is growing rapidly. The richest one percent in the world own more than fifty percent of the world's total wealth. And contrary to most normal people these billionaires have increased their wealth substantially during the financial crisis." Professor Grossman stopped for a brief moment, to catch his breath and clean his glasses, before continuing. "Over the past five years I have successfully interviewed a large portion of these billionaires. This is quite unique as most of them avoid the media at all cost. Many of them have in fact never before given any interviews. The study started off as a mapping of their qualities. What were their attitudes towards wealth, family, climate and so forth. The results were quite interesting and it is worth mentioning that the ultra-rich seem to worry about the same things as most other people – such as illness, kids and the future. There are many things that undoubtedly become easier with money, but great wealth can also have its drawbacks with increased stress and responsibilities."

David couldn't hold back a yawn, and was a second too late

to cover his mouth. The professor's eyes narrowed as he looked at him. "What has been the most interesting find though is that every single one of the billionaires has had a virtually identical set of 'life rules' that they attribute as the main reason for their financial success. It is these 'life rules' I have used to develop a set of ten principles for the accumulation of wealth. The study clearly shows that students who incorporate most of these principles in their life have a many times greater probability of getting wealthy. We have in other words, for the first time in history, documented a clear connection between wealth and a set of principles that in theory are accessible to anybody."

"That sounds fantastic," David exclaimed. "Why don't you publish your results straight away?"

"Well, there are a few things that have to be double-checked before I can release my final data and results. The academic societies are traditionally not that happy about the prospect of change, and this study will bring about a much-needed change in teaching methods. Something not all academics will be pleased about."

"What do you mean?" David asked.

"I have, for a long time, been frustrated about the state of the Western education system. The whole system is based on the presumption that there is only one correct answer to every question. My experience is that the world is much more complex than that. Maybe this is the reason why so many of the top students decide to remain at university, pursuing academic careers or additional degrees. Here at university they are shielded from the real world and they can always get a perfect answer. Out in the real world they have to make mistakes. What differentiates the best from the average in the real world is how they deal with their mistakes."

"You mean how they learn from their mistakes?"

"Yes. The problem is that they are so afraid of making mistakes that they only see threats. Never opportunities." Professor Grossman peered out the window, before letting his eyes rest on the great artificial lake that constituted the centre of Bond University's campus. The sun had finally managed to break through the clouds. It appeared he didn't have to change his dinner plans. "It is with great sorrow I have to admit that many students who walk out of these gates to a certain degree are ruined by the system when they graduate. We have taught them how to become good employees and how to make sound decisions for the large organisations they will work for. But we haven't taught them how to nurture their own financial wealth, how to make the right financial choices for themselves. That is the main reason so many students come up to me at their ten-year anniversaries and tell me that their university years were the best of their life."

David nodded. He knew the feeling. He was extremely good at giving advice. But he very seldom followed his own advice. "So how can you change any of this?" he asked.

"Regardless of whether one agrees with my arguments or not, it is a fact that the best here at campus most likely won't become the best out there in the real world," Professor Grossman said, pointing out the window. "Maybe some of them would even have had a greater chance of financial success if they had never sat a foot inside the university gates. I'm a great believer in education and knowledge, but when knowledge becomes a hindrance to success there is something wrong in the way we convey that knowledge to our students." Professor Grossman sat down, swirled around in his office chair and fixed his gaze directly at David. "If we can give students a proper introduction to these principles of how to accumulate wealth, then we can change many lives. Ralph Waldo Emerson once said something like 'There are millions of methods, but few principles. The person who understands principles can himself choose which methods to use.' And that is exactly what I've found, David – some universal principles. The person who truly understands these principles of wealth will have millions of different methods to acquire wealth. By understanding these principles my students will be given opportunities previously only available to an exclusive elite of rich people. They will acquire knowledge priceless to their ability to accumulate wealth throughout their lives." The professor caught a long breath before continuing. "Ayn Rand once wrote that you could either be a person being pushed around by life, or you could choose to be a person who pushes back and moves the world. I assume that you don't want to be an extra in your own life, David. I assume you want to be someone who makes his own decisions. I will give you a chance to do exactly that, David, but I want something back."

"What do you want me to do?" David asked. He was intrigued, but still hadn't quite yet understood why the professor needed his help.

"I want you to find Yossar Devan."

"Yossar who?" David asked. The first time he had ever heard the name Yossar Devan was the day prior, when Professor Grossman had casually mentioned it in conversation. David had thought Professor Grossman was talking about a colleague.

"Yossar Devan was one of Europe's richest persons more than thirty years ago. He built up his vast corporate empire from scratch and it is rumoured that he owned more than half of London's real estate when he disappeared, aged only forty-four."

"Disappeared?"

"Yes, Yossar Devan is one of the great unsolved mysteries of economic history. We don't really know a lot about him. The only thing we know for sure is that he never existed."

David was now completely confused. What was Professor Grossman talking about?

"When Yossar Devan disappeared, it turned out he had been living under a fake identity most of his life. The name Yossar Devan was a fictitious identity he acquired when he immigrated to England, and London, in the late 1940s. Who he really was, and where he originally came from, nobody knows. The only thing we know for sure is that he probably was the greatest investor to have ever set foot on earth. Nobody, and I mean nobody, has ever been close to achieving the same returns on their investments. Even Warren Buffet looks like a schoolkid compared to Yossar Devan. Then one day, more than thirty years ago, Yossar Devan went out for a morning walk, and he has never been seen since. He was single, childless, and left no will. As he had been living under a fake identity since he arrived in London, authorities for an extended time had no idea what to do with his vast business holdings and assets. To this date several of Yossar Devan's companies are owned by the estate of a man who never lived."

David was surprised. He thought it was strange that he had never heard about Yossar Devan before, but then again Yossar Devan had disappeared before David was even born.

"The really interesting matter however is that Yossar Devan held a series of lectures at Oxford University, in the weeks leading up to his disappearance. The lectures, 'The Principles of Wealth', are relatively unknown and I only came across them by coincidence, when an Oxford alumnus told me about them over a beer one night. Yossar Devan completed nine lectures before he disappeared and what astonished me was that those nine lectures were about the exact same principles I had developed as part of my independent study. Yossar Devan thus possessed this knowledge more than thirty years ago."

David nodded. "But where do I fit into this picture?" he asked.

"This is a once-in-a-lifetime marketing opportunity for me," Professor Grossman replied. It is not necessarily the content that sells a book in today's market. It is the packaging and the story around the book that sells. An attention-grabbing title and an exciting story around the author is really what you need. And let's be honest, I don't fit the criteria to get a lot of press coverage. Who wants a middle-aged professor in economic history on their talk show? It doesn't really scream high viewer ratings. If I however can link the mystery of Yossar Devan's disappearance to the launch of my new book, then maybe I can get the attention and coverage I need to get my message out there."

"I still don't understand where I fit into the picture," David said.

Professor Grossman leant back in his chair. A change swept over his face. He didn't look comfortable with what he was about to say.

"David, I have reviewed your finance essay from last week's class. I have to suspend you for plagiarism. I have no choice."

"What?" David almost fell out of his chair. He could hardly believe his ears. "I didn't copy anyone. It was all my ideas."

"Well, then your ideas are unfortunately too close to the ideas of some published authors. Unfortunately, you didn't include a single footnote in your document. It was just not good enough. But let's move on to the good news. As you have now been relieved of the requirement to attend lectures for the next eight weeks, I want to hire you as my assistant. I want to hire you to find Yossar Devan's real identity."

David could hardly believe his own ears. This was beyond

comprehension. First Professor Grossman suspended him. Without any real evidence that he had actually done anything wrong. And now he wanted to hire him to be his copyboy.

"I don't think so," David said. "I'll appeal the decision."

Professor Grossman immediately went on the defensive. David could see it in his facial expression. He had expected David to accept the suspension without any argument, without any fight.

"You can't buy me with an assistant position. I've done nothing wrong. My essay wasn't plagiarism and I will appeal the decision," David repeated.

"You're not focusing on the important issue here David. The important issue is that your return to Norway has just been delayed by one semester. Your return to a life with a traditional job has just been delayed by a couple of months. Wasn't that what you wanted?" Professor Grossman asked.

David was more angry than disappointed. He hadn't cheated.

"But what will prospective employers think when I tell them I had to use an extra semester to finish my degree?"

"It sounds to me that you are still looking for excuses, David. You wanted a chance to change your life. Here it is on a silver plate. Seize it," Professor Grossman said.

David was struggling with mixed emotions. The unfairness of the suspension, and the excitement of a possible opportunity to change his life.

"What do you mean by finding Yossar Devan's real identity anyway?" he finally said. "What is it that you really want me to do?"

"I don't have the opportunity to take any time off until at least nine months from now. It is impossible to find a replacement for the courses I teach on short notice, and to be honest I don't really have the skill set required to find out who Yossar Devan really was. I'm an economist, for good and for bad. You have worked as a journalist, David. You are from Europe. You have the abilities and skill set required to find out more about Yossar Devan's background. And together, David, together we can write history."

David realised that the professor was only trying to flatter him, but he couldn't help feeling good. And Professor Grossman had a point; David had been exceptionally astute at locating people hiding from the press or the police when he worked as a journalist; it had been his specialty. Yossar Devan wasn't hiding. He was probably dead if he disappeared more than thirty years ago. Especially if he left behind a billion-dollar fortune. But David could use the same skills to find out what had happened to him, and who he had really been. He gave Professor Grossman a small nod, a signal that he wanted to hear more.

"Because my study could have major consequences for academic institutions I would like you to familiarise yourself with the data and the methods I've used. At some stage I may need your help."

"Help to do what?" David asked.

"I would like you to brush up on your statistical knowledge and go through the raw data of my study. I can't ask any of my colleagues as they could very well have a conflict of interest, and to be honest I don't really trust them. You seem to have acceptable grades from your undergraduate courses in statistical analysis. Hopefully I won't see any more students walk up to me at the next ten-year graduation anniversary, because it was first after graduation that they really blossomed," Professor Grossman said.

David hadn't even had time to make up his mind of what to do. But life consisted of random events that lead to opportunities. In the past he had never been brave enough to jump on any of them. Maybe it was time he changed his ways? "If I accept…. When do I start if I accept?" he asked.

"Tomorrow," Professor Grossman replied. "And you don't have to worry, David. I have followed all the procedures for random selection and sample sizes. The fact that I want my data double-checked doesn't mean that I doubt its validity. I have followed all the relevant protocols for handling the data, but I wouldn't mind being on the safe side as there will be lots of people who won't appreciate my conclusions."

"Ok, I accept," David said, secretly wondering if he had just taken upon himself a bigger task than he could handle. He wasn't exactly an expert in statistical analysis, it was more than seven years since he had last taken a course. He had admittedly done quite well, but that was more due to his uncanny ability to cram in knowledge just before the exam. Like a 100-meter runner would be planning his whole season to reach peak form right at the final run in the world championships, David had developed his own method to reach peak knowledge at the day of the exam. But unlike a 100-meter runner, who most likely was in pretty good shape an hour after the race, David's brain was drained of any subject knowledge ten minutes after the exam had finished. If he enrolled in a subject he didn't believe he would need after graduating, he didn't see any particular reason to retain that knowledge in his brain. And as he didn't have any immediate plans to construct tunnels, or whatever it was one needed to know statistical analysis for, that knowledge was now long gone. He hoped he could invite it back as it had already been there before. This was the opportunity he had been waiting for. While everything had been at its darkest it had surfaced. He really had no choice.

"I'll take the job," David said. "On one condition though."

"What's the condition?" Professor Grossman asked.

"Drop the 'assistant' title."

"I've got no idea what a title has to do with it, but if that's your only condition it is ok with me. What do you suggest I call the position?"

"I don't care, as long as you don't call me an assistant," David replied.

"We have an agreement," Professor Grossman said, and extended his hand. David's hand met Professor Grossman's and they gave each other a proper shake to seal the deal.

-5-

Wen Ning lowered his body into the basic wooden chair in the hotel room. A cheap copy of the Picasso lithography Blue Nude was hanging on the wall next to him. Wen Ning studied the back of the naked blue woman while he poured himself a glass of eighteen-year-old Johnny Walker whiskey. Wen Ning was no whiskey connoisseur, but he knew that this was a good drop. It was a suitable day for a good drop. Wen Ning raised the glass to himself, hovered it underneath his own nose for a few seconds, and took a large sip. As usual he couldn't taste a thing. It was now more than thirty years since he had lost the physical ability to smell and taste, and it still annoyed him. There were so many things he hadn't managed to taste and smell before the accident, and whiskey was one of them. Thus he had no memories he could draw on when he let the expensive liquid circulate in his mouth. His thoughts wandered back to the fateful night. Wen Ning put down his glass and swallowed.

For a long time Wen Ning had believed he would make a full recovery. Truth be told, he had received a major blow to his head, and it wasn't even clear whether he would survive the first few weeks after the accident. His skull had been cracked in two different places and he had been held in an induced coma for three weeks. But gradually he had recovered, and the doctors had told him that he most likely would regain his sense of smell and taste within a few months. That was now more than thirty years ago. He had never regained any senses, he had never recovered.

Wen Ning had however found comfort in the fact that humans through evolution had grown to rely less and less on smell and taste, and instead started to rely more and more on vision. Even though humans had the same number of genes for smell as other primates, only half of them were still active. The rest had mutated in ways that prevented them from working properly. Scientists thought this could be explained by the historic evolution of the human brain. Over time vision had gradually become more and more important for a human's ability to survive. It had become more important to be able to recognise friend or foe, prey or predator, than to enjoy food and smell the flowers.

The world hadn't changed much, he thought.

He raised the glass, and emptied it in one single drink.

He knew the taste well.

It was the taste of success.

–6–

Professor Grossman's office was tiny and looked almost unused. David had expected to see stacks of books and paper lying around everywhere – like the offices of the other Bond Uni professors. But there was hardly a paper in Professor Grossman's office.

Professor Grossman noticed David's confused look.

"An old habit from when I ran my own business. I always clean my desk before I leave the office in the evening. It forces me to never postpone any unpleasant tasks or decisions by hiding them underneath a stack of paper." He laughed and pointed towards an empty chair. "Please have a seat. Do you want anything to drink?"

"A glass of water would be nice," David replied. He hadn't had time to eat any breakfast. The surf conditions had been perfect down at Burleigh Heads this morning so he had gotten up at four am, and arrived directly at Professor Grossman's office from the beach. He had however put some more effort into his attire than he had the previous morning. A white short-sleeved shirt from Country Road and a pair of brown shorts, that hadn't been purchased from any of the surf clothing shops, was the best he could muster in this weather. Professor Grossman collected two bottles of water from a small bar fridge in the corner of his office, and handed one to David.

"I thought we could start off with a little introduction of my study. What I hope to get out of it, and where you fit in. Does that sound ok?" the professor asked.

"Sounds like a plan," David replied. He was quite frankly looking forward to learning more about the study, and leant back in his chair.

Professor Grossman cleared his voice, turned his laptop so that it faced David, and started on his little presentation.

"What we know about Yossar Devan is frustratingly little," he started. "He surfaced out of nowhere in London in the late 1940s. It is unclear how he really started up, but we do know that he built up a small fleet of fishing boats before he moved on to other ships, including oil tankers and container ships. He bought at the right time and took massive risks. He sailed in war zones and continually devised new methods for cutting down travel time and costs. In a relatively short timeframe he became a titan of the shipping industry. It was an extremely volatile market in those years. Several times his ships paid themselves back in a few hauls, while at other times he had to sail with continuing losses for several years. The money he made he reinvested in real estate, supermarkets and natural resources. In due time he became a very big landowner."

Professor Grossman adjusted his back in the chair, cleared his voice, and continued.

"The Swedish Wallenberg family has an expression – esse non videri – to be, but not be seen. You could say that Yossar Devan lived his life under the same motto; in time he gained an immense amount of power, power he wasn't scared of utilising to achieve his goals. But very seldom did people realise it was Yossar Devan they were dealing with. He utilised a multitude of tax havens, secret trust structures and straw companies to conceal who was really at the receiving end of any deal. He was a master of using other people's money, and financed shipping investments by contracting oil and iron ore deliveries for ships he still didn't own, or financed real estate investments by signing leases for properties he still hadn't built. There exist only a few pictures of Yossar Devan, and they are all of poor quality, but at the height of his business career, at the end of the 1960s, hardly a deal of significance in Europe went down without Yossar Devan having a hand in the pot of honey. He was involved in everything, and nobody knew about it. Not even some of his closest associates. To quote the French poet Charles Baudelaire: 'The greatest trick the devil ever pulled was convincing the world he didn't exist'. Nobody knew they dealt with Yossar Devan because his name was never on any contract. But in reality they all dealt with the devil. They all dealt with Yossar Devan, they all dealt with the devil's merchant."

David's thoughts immediately went to the cult classic The Usual Suspects and Keyser Soze. A man nobody had seen, but everyone feared.

"Why do you call him the devil's merchant?" David asked.

"Because that was what they all called him when he disappeared." Professor Grossman looked straight into David's eyes when he continued. "On the sixth of October 1973, Syria and Egypt launched an attack on Israel. Everybody knew that this would have a dramatic effect on the price of oil, and on the sixteenth of October, OPEC decided to increase the price of crude oil by seventy percent. Then things unfolded rapidly; on the nineteenth of October the US declared their support for Israel with several billions in aid, and as countermeasure most Arabic countries initiated an oil embargo against the US. The price of oil went through the roof and it didn't take long until the world had their biggest financial crisis on its hands since the Great Depression in the 1930s. What then unfolded nobody expected; it turned out that Yossar Devan had sold his entire fleet of oil tankers to the Norwegian shipowner Hjalmar Hjorting and the Greek shipowner Socrates Vlachos. The deal had been finalised just days before the invasion of Israel. Did Yossar Devan know about the impending hostile attack on Israel? Did Yossar Devan know what was about to happen, and choose to ignore alerting the US and the UK governments, Israel's allies? Unfortunately we will never know the answer to this question, because on the twentieth of October 1973 Yossar Devan vanished from the face of the earth. He became a ghost. The unfortunate investors and industrial tycoons who had been stupid enough to buy his ships and properties at record high prices went bankrupt within months, and the name 'the devil's merchant' arose." Professor Grossman cleared his voice. "Any questions to what I've just gone through?"

David shook his head. "Not really. But I do wonder how you intend to use Yossar Devan to market your principles of wealth. The picture you paint of him is not a nice one."

"Exactly," Professor Grossman said. "I want you to find the positive sides of Yossar Devan. Who was he? Where did he come from? What really happened when he disappeared? There are too many unanswered questions. Something is not right about the official story. I want you to find the real Yossar Devan, the true story. Are you ready for that?" the professor asked.

"I can give it a try," David answered. He thought the story about Yossar Devan sounded interesting, and he had always liked to pursue the truth when he had worked as a journalist. But what he really wanted to do was to learn more about Professor Grossman's principles of wealth.

"By the way. I also have a hot new lead for you," Professor Grossman said. He handed David a piece of paper with a single name and an address.

"Peter Swarkowski is an alternative history, slash conspiracy theory historian. He claims to have come across some new information, but he doesn't want to discuss it over the phone. He probably thinks he is being bugged by the government," Professor Grossman laughed. "He's a bit strange, but harmless."

David quickly glanced at the piece of paper, before looking at Professor Grossman with a confused look. "But the address is in London."

"Oh, yes. My apologies. I forgot to give you the tickets. You leave tomorrow. Pack lightly, but bring warm clothes. Summer in London isn't the same as summer down here," he laughed, handing David an envelope.

Still confused, David accepted the envelope containing a credit card and a ticket for return flights to Europe. He hadn't envisioned this when he got up in the morning.

Professor Grossman reached for a Kindle ebook reader at his office desk.

"You'll find the manuscript for my book in the documents folder. On two conditions you can be the first one to ever read it."

"Ok, what are the conditions?" David asked hesitantly.

"The first condition is that you take good care of the manuscript. Don't make any copies and don't let anybody else read or even know about the manuscript. The second condition is that you promise to only read one principle each day."

David nodded. "Can I ask why I am only allowed to read one principle each day?"

"If you don't give the principles sufficient time to mature in your mind, then you will not grasp the full value of them. Obey my conditions and you will understand what I mean. Actually, to be certain that you follow this rule I will only send you one principle a day," Professor Grossman said, and led David to the door.

David couldn't help smiling. He looked forward to learning more about the principles of wealth and the mysterious Yossar Devan.

– 7 –

The speed of the ceiling fan increased. David relished the cold air streaming down in the bed where he lay, eyes half closed, staring at the blades of the rotating fan. He rolled over to the side and put away the statistical analysis book that had been on top of his chest, neatly turned to page one hundred and eleven for the last hour or so. Oh my god how boring it was, he thought. He didn't have any other things to do though. There was no point reading the semester curriculum. Professor Grossman had told him he had been suspended for the next eight weeks. He could head down to the beach or go see a movie. Do something fun. But he didn't feel like it. He needed to do something to quash this feeling of unease in his stomach, something productive. He had felt better after the meeting with Professor Grossman earlier in the day, but then he had started to get cold feet. What would his mother say when he told her what had happened? It was embarrassing, that's what it was. He had just realised the gravity of what had happened. He had been accused of cheating, he had been suspended.

He had experienced a small upper at the meeting with Professor Grossman. The meeting had been inspiring and he had felt that he could hardly wait to learn more about Yossar Devan and the professor's principles of wealth. The Kindle reader was however still on his nightstand. He hadn't turned it on yet. He was growing increasingly unsure of whether he should go ahead or pull out of the offer Professor Grossman had given him. He was afraid. Afraid of what his fellow students would think of him when they heard he had been suspended, afraid that friends and family would learn about what had happened. David chewed on the nail of his left thumb. A drop of blood appeared from the open wound he had managed to bite himself to over the last few hours. He should appeal the decision, that's what he should do. They couldn't suspend him without even having heard his version of the plagiarism case.

He rolled over on his side and reached for the Kindle reader. He could at least read the first principle before he made his decision. He slid the 'on' button to the side, and in the upper left corner he read 'David's Kindle'.

David smiled. The professor had registered the Kindle to him. There were only two pdf documents on the Kindle: The raw data of the professor's study, and the first principle. David clicked on the first principle and started reading.

Dear reader,

There have been written numerous books about wealth and money, some by self-made millionaires and others by charlatans. The disappointing reality is that most of these books have minimal value for the average reader. Perhaps the inspirational message provides a brief boost in your optimism? But this boost is soon gone when the reality of life hits you in the face. In real life most things aren't as easy as three hundred pages of glossy paper pretend to portray them.

Most people intuitively understand that if someone really knew a secret way of getting rich, then he would try to keep this secret for himself as long as possible. One thing is for sure, he wouldn't try to share it with the rest of the world for a paltry few dollars. If such a secret really existed, and was shared with the masses, it would by definition become common knowledge and worthless. The secret of most authors of 'get-rich-quick' books is simply to sell books and courses. Those authors have no secrets to share. They are only out to get your money.

This book is based on some principles developed more than thirty years ago, by a man who was both a billionaire and a charlatan. A man rich enough not to worry about money ever again. A man rich enough to share his wisdom with the rest of the world without fearing someone would steal his ideas. The principles he launched over a few lectures at Oxford University in 1973, just before he mysteriously disappeared, are as relevant today as they were back then. I learnt this firsthand when I started interviewing a carefully selected group of successful businesspeople. It turned out that they all were proponents of this man's principles of wealth. And that they attributed their own success and wealth to the understanding and practice of these secret principles.

"Get a solid education, good grades and find yourself a stable and secure job" is advice most parents give their kids. But even though this advice may have been sound advice some generations ago, the world has progressed since then.

There are no secure jobs anymore.

A good education is no longer a guarantee for a good job.

And a good job is no longer a guarantee for a life without financial struggles.

The problem is that most students who exit the gates of a university have never been taught how money really works, how money can be both a damnation and a salvation.

Yossar Devan wanted to share his wisdom on how money really works. He held a range of lectures at Oxford University in the autumn of 1973. The following chapters are based on those lectures.

Dr Evan Grossman
Bond University, Gold Coast

Principle 1: Desire

I was lucky and had an epiphany when I was relatively young. I saw how my dad struggled financially his whole life. He worked hard, he had a good academic background, and he was well respected within his profession. Still we were always only one pay check away from the poor house. Every time he got a miniscule raise, that extra money went straight to pay off old debts or cover increased bills. We were never able to get on top of things. I decided early that my life would be different, and different it became.

As far back as I can remember I always wanted to get rich. In the beginning it was to avoid ending up like my dad. Later, money became a goal in itself, and finally I realised that money in itself wasn't important either – it was what I could do with money that mattered. With money I could create jobs and make dreams into reality.

But one thing never changed; the underlying need to become financially independent, to never have to beg for a job like my dad had to.

Most people have a misconception about what wealth is. The usual way to determine a person's wealth is to add all their possessions and then subtract what debts they owe to the bank and others. With this procedure you end up with a net value, a net financial worth. But this net worth doesn't really tell you anything. What was important to me was to not have to depend on a monthly pay check to live. My financial goal was quite simply to have enough passive income every month to cover all my expenses. And thus my definition of wealth became how many days I could survive without a regular pay check. The day that my monthly passive income finally surpassed my monthly expenses I, for the first time in my life, felt truly rich. I have made a lot of money since then, but I have never felt as rich as on that particular day. The knowledge that I had achieved my goal of becoming financially independent was indescribably satisfying.

But it is easy to state that you want to get rich. The important thing is how to get there, how to achieve that goal.

The first principle of wealth, or for success in general, is desire. You need to figure out what you are really passionate about. What you really want to do with your life. If you are working with something you are passionate about, then everything becomes much easier.

Don't despair if you still don't know what this is. In some strange way life already knows what you are supposed to do. You just have to be willing to let it guide you there. Make the choices that feel right. Let the invisible hand of life lead you to the life you are meant to live.

For me that life was shipping. I grew up inland, and I always dreamt about running away as far as possible. The ocean was therefore an obvious dream. It always seemed so far away. It became a symbol of the unknown.

I sailed around for a few years as a deck hand, before realising that I wanted more. I knew it would have to be something related to the ocean, but I didn't know what. To own a ship seemed like an impossible dream, my salary as a deck hand hardly covered my living expenses. Even though I felt free out on the ocean I was never really a free man. I was a hostage of my spending habits, a prisoner of my monthly pay check.

I went ashore with one determined wish; I wanted to own a ship, not work on it. After a few years of hard work I managed to buy myself a ship, and then another one. To my surprise my dream was no longer only a dream.

But then came the realisation: I was still not a free man. I was now a hostage of the bank, always one mortgage payment away from losing my life's work. And I finally understood what so many people had realised before me; you will never be free of all your worries, you just replace them with new ones.

But I felt better about my life, now that I did what felt right for me. If I lost everything tomorrow I could always just start up again. I had already done it once, the dream was no longer impossible.

The most important thing was that I was doing something I loved.

I truly loved owning ships. I loved being out on the ocean and I often sailed with my ships to different ports. The fact that desire makes everything so much easier was my most important realisation when I finally became financially independent. And desire is the first principle you have to master if you want to succeed. You need to ask yourself what it is you really want to do with your life. What is it you would regret not having tried if you died tomorrow? If you are content with your current life, if you go to work every day and can't imagine a different life, then you are one of the lucky ones and you should continue doing what you do. But if you most days feel unhappy about your job, if you most days secretly would like to do something completely different, then you should take a good look in that mirror and think through what you really would like to achieve with your life. You only get one chance, you only have one life. Seize it! Because if you are truly passionate about something, if you are willing to take a risk, then life will give you a chance.

David had been concentrating on reading the first principle. It wasn't as he had expected. Professor Grossman had portrayed the principle as being written by Yossar Devan, and that wasn't right, was it? But as the professor had said in their first meeting at the coffee shop, the goal was more important than the means. If these principles could help people, stuck in the same situation as David, to break out of the rat race, then it didn't really matter if they hadn't been portrayed truthfully. Did it?

The problem was that David didn't know what he wanted to get out of his life. He just had this continuous feeling of not living the life he was meant to live. It was hard to explain; he wasn't depressed or unhappy. He just felt there was something missing. Maybe the professor had a point. Maybe he should let himself be guided more by his own intuition and see where those decisions took him. David had always had a tendency to postpone important decisions and not take risks because he was afraid of failing. But what was he really afraid of? He had never really sat down and looked at the consequences of following his own dreams. Maybe the worst outcome really wasn't that bad? He grabbed his notepad from the nightstand and started to scribble down some notes. What do you want? (1) To become wealthy enough to not have to worry about my pay check coming in every month. (2) To be able to take time off when I want and to travel more. (3) To create something by myself.

He looked at what he had written on the page and pondered

whether he should be more specific. How much money did he need? He needed to cover his living costs and have some extra for travel. That would mean he needed between eighty and a hundred thousand dollars in yearly passive pre-tax income from investments. Something that meant he would need about two to two and a half million dollars in the bank. What are you willing to sacrifice to follow your dreams? Everything, he thought. What is the worst that can happen if you go for your dream? A black hole in my resume, maybe some more debts, he thought. Nothing irreparable.

David reviewed his notes and wondered why he had never done this before. The amount, two to two and a half million dollars, seemed high, very high, but not unachievable. And the worst outcome didn't seem that scary.

But he realised what he really wanted to do was to find out more about the mysterious Yossar Devan. Professor Grossman had piqued his interest. How had Yossar Devan managed to build himself such a massive fortune in such a small timeframe? How was it possible that he had vanished without a trace? And had he really possessed the knowledge of "the principles of wealth" more than thirty years ago?

To read the first principle had motivated David. He did have a strong reason. He did have a strong desire. He wanted to find out why some people got rich while others struggled financially their whole lives. He had wanted to find the answer to this question his whole life and now he had been given the opportunity.

This was the opportunity of a lifetime for David, an opportunity he simply couldn't say no to. It was time to take more risks, it was time to be braver and bolder. There was no point in trying to appeal the University's suspension. One extra semester and a bit more to pay off his student loan was a price he was willing to pay to get the opportunity to solve the mystery of how people got rich.

– 8 –

The sun was baking the hood of Wen Ning's blue Hyundai Getz, the rental car he had been using the last few days. Like a handful of other motorists Wen Ning had parked on the shoulder of the road, a couple of hundred meters out from the garage complex of Brisbane International Airport. His fellow motorists had parked there to save a few bucks when picking up their loved ones from the airport. Wen Ning had parked there to think.

He enjoyed lurking in the shadows, being invisible. It was just a shame that was almost impossible these days. There were cameras everywhere. George Orwell's nightmare about a society where big brother knew everything about its citizens hadn't just become a reality, the reality had become much worse, and especially in an airport like Brisbane International. There weren't many places you could walk without having a camera fixed on you, observing your every movement.

He turned his wrist so that the TAG Heuer watch became visible underneath his shirtsleeve. He could wait another ten minutes, he had plenty of time to return the rental and check in.

He pulled out an old Nokia mobile from his pocket, removed the SIM-card and tossed it onto the road. A second later a Toyota Kruger, fully loaded, presumably with a family on their way to a holiday, crushed it into the asphalt. He had acquired the mobile from eBay a few months ago. One of the real ancient ones with numeric keyboard and long batterylife. They were still the best ones if you wanted to be sure nobody could listen in on your conversations. He looked at it for a moment before breaking it in two, wiping it clean for fingerprints and placing it in an empty paper bag from McDonalds. He would toss it in one of the dustbins at the airport.

It was time for phase two.

–9–

David arrived at Brisbane International Airport early in the morning. He walked straight over to the closest bookstore to find something to read on the long trip ahead of him. He had already decided not to watch any movies on the flight, as he always regretted having watched a good movie on a tiny screen when it was finally released on video. He therefore found himself a book with a catchy title: The 4-Hour Workweek, by Tim Ferriss. He fished out the Kindle reader, with built-in 3G network that Professor Grossman had given him, and looked up and bought the book for a third of the price advertised in the store. The book was downloaded in a couple of seconds. This is the death of the book industry, he thought, exiting the bookstore.

He proceeded to the check-in and asked for a seat near the exit. He was quite tall and was normally given the extra leg space if he checked in early. More importantly, it also reduced his chances of being seated next to a screaming child or an overweight passenger. The emergency exit seats were normally reserved for people who could provide some assistance in the case of an emergency. The Qantas staffer confirmed his exit seat and David started to look forward to the trip.

Well-placed in his seat, David reflected on what had occurred over the last few days. He had been moping in an entrepreneurship lecture at Bond University, feeling miserable about his own life. And then out of nowhere this opportunity of learning how people got rich had presented itself to him. For some reason, he still wasn't entirely sure why, Professor Grossman had decided to employ him to find out more about the mysterious disappearance of Yossar Devan, the billionaire.

While he was sitting there, pondering these matters, the exact thing he had wanted to avoid came wobbling down the mid-aisle – an overweight Pacific Islander who most likely wouldn't even manage to squeeze into a business-class seat. I hope he doesn't sit down here, David thought as he observed the big person, huffing and puffing, closing in on his row of seats. David wondered whether the professor's principles of wealth were like a diet. If there had been an idiot-proof diet, then nobody would be overweight. But a fail-proof diet didn't exist. Most diets required more than following a prescribed eating regimen; you had to put some effort into them as well, although most people seemed to want the simple solution, to eat themselves fit.

A formula to get fit without having to do anything.

A pill for everything.

Maybe he himself wasn't too different from all those fat people? He was so frustrated with the lack of progress in his financial situation that he had almost given up. He only had hope left. He hoped that he would win the lotto, or that something totally outside his control would bring him back on route to the life he was supposed to live. A life that didn't involve working himself to death, a life that didn't mean turning into an old and bitter man because of all the missed opportunities.

He realised that he did want a simple solution, a pill for wealth.

He quickly dismissed the thought. He was willing to sacrifice a lot to become rich. He just wanted to know if it was possible for him. If it was possible for people like him to get rich or if he should settle with the life he already had, a life he didn't particularly like.

The overweight Pacific Islander passed the row of exit seats and the air stewardess started reading the instructions in case of an emergency landing. David closed his eyes and relaxed.

"Do you want something to drink?" David woke to a soft poke in the shoulder.

He realised that he must have fallen asleep before the plane was fully boarded because there was now a beautiful blond woman sitting next to him. And when he glanced at his watch it revealed that they had been in the air for a few hours already.

"Yes please, a glass of red and a glass of water please," he replied.

David tried to wipe the tiredness out of his eyes as he forced a smile to his new side passenger.

"I hope I didn't snore too loudly," he said.

"No, you were in fact very quiet," the blond woman replied. She waited a moment before turning her head to face David again. "To be honest I was waiting for the air hostess to come around so that I could check that you were still alive. I couldn't hear or see you breathe and it bothered me. I couldn't really relax."

David laughed. "My apologies. I will make sure that I snore loudly the next time, so that there is no room for misunderstandings I mean." He extended his hand to introduce himself. "David," he said.

"Sophie, Sophie Masson," the blond woman replied. She looked like she was in her early thirties, with nice friendly eyes and a cheeky smile that curled up in the left corner of her mouth.

She was a woman whom David could easily fall for. But he knew that he gradually deteriorated on long flights, so there wouldn't be any immediate risk that he would be joining the mile-high club anytime soon.

"Nice to meet you. Are you on your way to holidays or work?" she asked.

"I'm on my way to London for a few days. I guess you could call it work. What about you?"

"Work. I'm on my way back to Turkey."

"Are you from Turkey?" he asked. She didn't look at all Turkish.

"No, I'm originally from France. But I work at a Turkish University."

"So what brought you to Australia?" David asked to keep the conversation going.

"I attended a physics conference in Brisbane. A whole week with only theoretical physicists. No wonder I'm drinking vodka," Sophie Masson replied, shooting David a smile.

"What's the suit about anyway? You look like you work in the City, and quite frankly shouldn't be seated back here in economy class."

David had noticed that he was the only one dressed in a suit. "Looks can be deceiving," he said. "I'm a poor student. The only reason I travel in a suit is that the airlines have a tendency to think like you. If they have available seats in business class they may be more inclined to upgrade someone who looks like they belong there and would appreciate the gesture by flying with the airline again. Unfortunately the plan didn't work."

"Sorry to burst your bubble," Sophie said. "But I have in fact worked for an airline, and we never made judgements based on our passengers' clothing. What matters is the colour of your card. If you travel often you will get upgraded. It doesn't matter whether your suit is made by Prada or H&M. If you don't have a gold card you will be seated back here with us," she said.

David felt a bit stupid, sitting there in his cheap suit. He might as well have been travelling in sweatpants and flip-flops. It would have been a lot more comfortable.

"You learn something new every day," he said, and raised his glass of red wine. Sophie raised hers too.

Forty minutes later the conversation was still flowing nicely. They had both had some more to drink and Sophie had already given him her phone number. It was however unlikely that he would ever get a chance to ring her. He had no immediate plans to travel to Turkey. Even though his family owned a small vacation home there, it would most likely be at least a couple of years before he would he get a chance to go back.

When the lights in the passenger cabins were turned off, and people started to go to sleep, David pulled out his Kindle reader. He quickly flipped through the book he had purchased at the airport and decided instead to read the second principle. He had loaded it onto the Kindle when he turned on the 3G network at Brisbane International Airport.

Principle 2: Faith

I am certainly not a religious man, but sometimes I wish I were. It would be nice to believe in a life after this one. I suspect that religion is one of the main reasons many people endure the hardship of their lives, the belief that there is something better waiting for them on the other side.

A side effect of not being religious though is the understanding that you only have one life. There is no second act. You have to live your life the best way you can, because when it is over

— it is truly over. Thus for me death is not scary, it is my best motivation. Death is nature's own change agent, it cleanses all the old stuff out and replaces it with new. With death as a perspective everything else becomes unimportant. You have to do what you feel is right because you will not get a second chance. I therefore choose not to believe in a God, but rather believe in myself. To believe that there is a meaning behind the fact that I have been given the gift of life.

That I have a purpose.

However small, I have a purpose. There is something I am meant to do.

The same way blind faith or a belief in an afterlife can help people endure incredible suffering, faith can also help you achieve your dreams. There are no free lunches, you have to give in order to receive, but if you have great faith then everything becomes much easier.

I didn't believe I was going to achieve everything I eventually did. I didn't have enough imagination. But I always believed that my life would be on the ocean. That I would live off the sea. That I would become a shipowner. There were many times I doubted myself, but instead of giving up, I listened to my heart. And in my heart there were never any doubts.

The second principle of great wealth is therefore faith. Faith in yourself and your own abilities.

When it comes to wealth almost all people are driven by fear and greed. We all want to become wealthier, and most of us are scared of losing money. The secret is to learn how to control this fear and greed. To be able to do this you have to first acknowledge that money isn't real. Money is an illusion. Money is something humans invented to make it easier for us to trade between ourselves. A twenty-dollar bill only has a value because we have made a decision that a twenty-dollar bill is worth exactly twenty dollars. Nothing more, nothing less. When you learn to view money as not having any intrinsic value in itself, then you are on your way to learning how to handle fear and greed.

And it is only when you have first learnt how to handle fear and greed that you can learn how to handle money. If you can't handle fear and greed, then all the money in the world wouldn't make a difference to your life. Most people who are given more money only end up with more debt. They are stuck in a hamster wheel where life consists of getting up in the morning, going to work, making money and paying bills. More money doesn't stop the hamster wheel, it just increases the speed.

When you finally let go of the fear of failing, the fear of losing money, the fear of becoming the laughingstock of family and friends, only then are you ready. Ready to follow your dream.

And in order to follow your dream you will need faith, because you will have setbacks. Days where you don't want to get out of bed, but just curl up under the bed sheets and hide. But you will also have wins. Small victories where you feel that you are moving in the right direction. Great wins where you feel you are on top of the world.

I don't know if this is true, but I have always felt that life is trying to test me. Most often I succeeded just in that final moment before I was ready to give up. When I had no money left and everything seemed to work against me, I would bite my teeth together and in some miraculous way everything solved itself.

In the same way, you need to find your own faith. The belief in yourself, the belief that you can achieve anything you set your mind to. If you are surrounded by people who are negative to everything you do, then I suggest you find yourself some new friends. Because surrounding yourself with negative people is the same as surrounding yourself with fear, and it can stop you from achieving your goals in life. Because remember: faith can move mountains, faith can cure or cause illnesses, and faith can change your life.

Envision the person you want to become, envision the life you want to live, and jump into it. It is only your own mind that constrains you. Believe in yourself and life will reward you.

Exercise: Be honest. Is it your thoughts or you that control your life? Decide when you get up tomorrow morning that you will decide the outcome of the day by controlling your thoughts. Use ten minutes every day to visualize the person you want to become. Visualize the life you want to live.

David thought about what he had just read. Could it really be that simple? Could it be that his own thoughts controlled what happened in his life? If he sat in his seat and feared that the airplane would crash, would his thoughts increase the probability of this actually occurring? And would it matter how many in the plane sent out the same thoughts? He shrugged it away. He couldn't see how his thoughts could have an impact on the physical world. That was pseudoscience. But he did agree that you could probably choose how your day would be by either being negative or positive. So maybe you could choose whether to become rich or poor by having the right attitude. He didn't really know if he could visualize the person he wanted to become. He wanted to become rich, but it wasn't really about the money. He wanted a purpose with what he did, and financial freedom. For all he knew he might even turn out to be an asshole if got into money. You never knew how money might affect you until you got it.

He closed his eyes. He envisioned himself sitting on a grassy area with a view of the ocean. A surfboard leant against a palm tree, and a hammock swayed in the wind. Sophie Masson came walking down to him with a strawberry margarita in her hand. David opened his eyes. Had he just dreamt about the woman next to him? The woman he had only met a few hours ago? He had to be a bit tipsy. He peered over at Sophie. She was sound asleep in her seat. She looked so angelic and peaceful. David turned on the entertainment screen. He should probably try to stay awake. He didn't want an embarrassing episode where he woke up with an arm around Sophie.

-10-

A short, stocky guy with a beer belly, red eyes and a pint in his hand, was singing the Red Hot Chili Peppers' song "Under the Bridge" from the stage in Jon Berthelsen's favourite pub. Jon Berthelsen thought he sounded better than the original, Anthony Kiedis. It must be tragic, to have such a good voice, to be so good, but still never be able to show off your talent to a broader audience, he thought. To never be able to live your dream.

X-Factor, American Idol and other TV competitions had made it possible for people like the guy on stage to chase their dreams. But Jon knew that the guy on stage would never be able to play for more than a handful of people. He saw it in his eyes. He seemed content. He was stuck in his zone of comfort. Jon on the other hand was definitely not in his zone of comfort. He wanted more, much more. But it was bloody hard. He took a large drink of the Guinness he had been sipping on for the last half hour. He was waiting for David Dypsvik. It was almost five years since he had last seen him, and he looked forward to heading down memory lane. Jon and David had first met at the Norwegian Business School where they earned their respective bachelors. They had clicked almost immediately and had shared a small apartment the last two years of studying. If Jon was completely honest,

David was probably his best friend, but still they had hardly had any contact over the last five years. Neither David nor Jon was good at keeping in contact on phone or email, and that was not how their relationship was, either. But Jon knew that the very second David entered the pub, it would be like he had never been away.

"Hi mate!" David came through the door of the pub with a large smile on his mouth.

"Long time no see," Jon quipped, and walked over to give David an uncomfortable Norwegian man-hug.

"What are you drinking? And what brings you to London?" Jon asked as they walked towards the bar.

"A pint of Stella, please."

"Still into Stella?" Jon laughed, ordering two beers from the bartender.

"You don't forget an old flame that easily," David replied.

Jon returned to the table with the beers and looked at David. It had been five years, but he looked the same.

"You didn't answer me. What brings you to London? I thought you were back at uni," Jon repeated.

"You know me. The eternal student," David smiled at his own comment. "But yes you are correct. I am actually a student again. In Australia of all places. I thought I would get all the partying out of my system before the life a job, a station wagon and two dogs start."

"Well, just get a job here in the city and you won't have to worry about those things for a while. I party more now than I did as a student."

"We'll see. I am starting to get a bit tired of all the partying," David said.

"So why are you really here? You mentioned something on the

phone about a missing billionaire?"

"What do you know about Devan?" David asked.

"Yossar Devan?"

"Yes."

"Not much. He is both a legend and a pariah. There isn't much official information about him around, and he disappeared before I was born. I do however work with several companies related to the conglomerate of business he started up before he vanished, and I have heard a few rumours about him."

"How did he start?"

"That's a good question. The legend says he arrived in London without a cent in his pockets, and a few years later he owned factories, companies and ships. Nobody is going to tell me that is possible without seed capital or an established network. Especially not in London, the world's hardest city to succeed in. If you ask me I think there was somebody behind Yossar Devan. Maybe it was the mafia. I don't know. What I do know is that Yossar Devan didn't do it all alone. Someone was helping him. Someone with very deep pockets."

Jon looked satisfied with his own argument. "And you can bet your arse that is why he disappeared without a trace. He was taken care of."

"You believe he was killed?" David asked.

"It is not a question of believing. Yossar Devan was a front man, a window-dresser. A window-dresser who got too much power."

"What do you mean?" David asked.

"Look at what has happened to some of the Russian oligarchs. Nobody in the west cared when the richest man in Russia, Mikhail Khodorkovski, was arrested for tax fraud and shipped off to Siberia a few years back. Nobody lifted a finger when the

Russian Government nationalised all his assets. To us here in the West Mikhail Khodorkovski was just another Russian criminal who had made his fortune buying up state property for nickels and dimes. The episode, however, sent shockwaves into the Russian community here in London. They had assumed that as long as they acted like respectable businessmen the West wouldn't allow Putin to use KGB methods to repossess the assets they had acquired. So how could they protect themselves against something similar happening to them? They had to get a public profile. They started buying soccer clubs and mingling with high society. Putin can't touch Roman Abramovich, millions of Chelsea fans would simply not allow it. In much the same way Yossar Devan started to get too big already back then. Even though he avoided the press, people started to notice his influence. He owned half of London, for Christ's sake. He donated money to Universities and hospitals. And more importantly – he started to collect art on a grand scale. There were even rumours that he was planning to open up his own museum and name it after himself. If he had done that it would have become impossible for the mafia to get him removed. And he was truly removed. The day after he disappeared it was discovered that there hardly existed a picture of him. Even though he had been the owner of one of Europe's largest private companies he had managed to totally avoid mainstream media's attention. And when they finally started to dig into his past, it turned out that even his name was fake. He was a constructed person, a ghost."

"But what did the mafia gain by getting rid of Yossar Devan? I understand most of his companies were nationalised or taken over by charitable trusts when he disappeared."

"That was his genius. He must have known that his days were numbered, and in secret he must have had his lawyers draw up plans for what should happen the day he disappeared. I'll bet he went out with a smile on his face. He got the last stab."

Jon tilted his head and studied David.

"What is it you that you are not telling me? Why are you interested in Yossar Devan?" he asked.

David wondered for a second whether he should tell Jon about Professor Grossman's principles of wealth, but he decided not to. The professor had told him to keep the principles secret and it was best not to create expectations about something that couldn't be shared.

"Oh, it's nothing. I have taken up a part-time job for a professor at Bond University this semester. He had some money left over in his budget and wanted to find out what really happened to Yossar Devan as part of a study he is conducting. You know how it is; if he doesn't use this year's budget he won't get the same amount for next year."

David knew that a comment about the waste of money in the public sector would divert Jon's attention from the original issue. As soon as Jon heard about misuse of public money he wouldn't ask any more questions, but instead he would start on his well-practised speech, his defence of capitalism. Jon didn't know that Bond University was a private university and that exhausting the year's budget funds had no impact on the level for next year's funds.

"You're kidding me. And this is what I pay taxes for? You have to get back to the private sector David, before the system ruins you."

David had avoided a long and tedious interrogation, but he had also set in motion something that would have to run its course. He straightened his back on the barstool and waited for the usual spiel about capitalism.

Still he was satisfied with the outcome of the evening thus far. He hadn't learnt too many new things about Yossar Devan, but he was looking forward to a nice and pleasant evening with his old friend. He therefore changed the subject as soon as possible and they talked about women and how life had been since they graduated from the Norwegian Business School.

Jon told David about how he really disliked his job. He was tired of pretending to be rich. He hardly made enough money to pay his rent, but since he was a stockbroker everybody expected him to behave in a certain way. Thus he always ended up paying when his friends went out partying, and he would wake up with regrets and anxiety the day after. The job he'd once loved had become something he had to do. Most of all he wanted to return to Norway, but he had realised that that was never an option. He wanted to return to Norway as a success, not a failure. He was tired of making everybody else rich. What had once been respect had almost turned into hate. He felt that he was smarter and more clever than most of his clients, but still he had to bow his head and scramble for the crumbs they left at the table. He couldn't even give them the advice he wanted to, because no investment bank in the City rewarded a broker who didn't do trades. Thus he had to push stocks on his clients, even in a bear market, and he had gotten quite used to listening to abuse on the phone.

They ordered a new round of beers, and a couple of shots.

"I just don't get it," Jon said. "Everybody except me makes a ton of money."

"You're doing well, Jon. Don't be too hard on yourself," David said. He studied his friend where he sat, downing tequila shot after tequila shot. "Focus on what you have, not on what you don't have."

"What do I have?" Jon asked. "I have nothing. I live in a rented flat, and I have no money left, no money whatsoever left at the end of the month."

Jon told about how he was always a bit too late with his investments. Recently he had read about investors making millions of dollars on buying and selling domain names. Trying to cash in on the craze he had taken the rest of his savings and bought a bunch of domain names. As most good domain names had been taken more than a decade ago, he had ended up with a ridiculous portfolio of names. It was one of many bad investment decisions he had made. He took a big sip of his beer and sighed. He felt sorry for himself.

David realised that he wasn't alone in thinking like he did, and he wondered whether Professor Grossman could be right in his suggestion that you could make your own luck by the way you thought. Jon had a tendency to be negative. It was as if he expected all his investments to tank before they did. He made lots of money for his clients, but nothing for himself. He never followed his own advice.

David decided to become more positive going forward, to visualize the person he wanted to become.

But first he needed to find out more about Yossar Devan. His knowledge could be what people like Jon and he needed. David decided to cut the night short.

He wanted to read the third principle while he was still somewhat sober.

-11-

The draft from the open window sucked all the air out of the room, and the hotel door slammed shut behind David's back. He peeked over at the red numbers, flashing on the digital alarm clock, before he threw his jacket down onto the bed. He kicked off his shoes. One of them hit the curtains, which still hadn't been closed.

The alarm clock showed 03:15.

It hadn't been as easy to leave the pub as planned. Jon Berthelsen was obviously unhappy about his life as a prestigious stock broker in London. And in a somewhat strange way that made David happy. It wasn't the fact that he didn't want the best for his friend, because he did. It was just that he felt a little less like a failure knowing that other people felt the same way he did. David was thirty years old and still a student. He had no ambitions of becoming the CEO of a large corporation. His ambitions were really just to become his own boss. Something he found almost impossible to achieve, as it required that he start his own company. And he had no idea what he wanted to start up.

If he was to be totally honest, he didn't even know if he would have the balls to start up a company by himself, even if he came up with a brilliant business idea the very next day. He was thus locked into a life living pay check by pay check, and it made him a bit less depressed that someone who appeared so successful from the outside was struggling with the same issues he struggled with.

He grabbed a bottle of Evian from the mini-fridge in the room, and finished it in two drinks. The water made him feel a bit better. He found the Kindle reader and started to read the third principle: Planning.

Principle 3: Planning.

I have gone through the first two principles, desire and faith. These two principles are essential if you want to become rich. Nobody has ever achieved great wealth without having a strong desire to succeed and a great belief in his own abilities.

But faith and desire are not enough. Action is required. And the first step before action is planning. I am no proponent of elaborate business plans that are outdated the second they are printed. With planning I simply mean that you need to sit down and think through your strategy, and make a plan for how you will achieve your goals.

When I was running my businesses, it was a blessing to compete against business-educated people. They were so focused on developing perfect services and products that they never brought to market something truly innovative. I, on the other hand, I tried and failed, and tried and failed. I let the market be my litmus test. If the customers didn't like what I served I just changed the recipe. I failed more than I succeeded, but my mistakes didn't cost that much. To make a mistake early is a lot cheaper than to make it after you have developed a perfect product.

So start your planning now. Set yourself goals and deadlines for when you want to achieve those goals. When you write something down on paper it becomes real. So plan for your dreams to become real. Write them down and commit to a plan for how to achieve them. Don't procrastinate, start now.

David put away the Kindle reader even though he wasn't even half way through the principle. He was tired, but forced himself to stay awake. It would have been nice to be able to write down his goals on a piece of paper, if for nothing else than to make them more real. But David didn't know what he wanted. He was still on something like an eternal search for what he was supposed to do with his life. He read big stacks of books every year in the hopes that he would figure out what it was he was supposed to do, but nothing seemed to stand out. For years he had browsed through books mentioned as sources of inspiration for important people, but he himself had never been overly inspired. And he had realised that there were some things you couldn't find the answer to in books. Some things you had to learn through living life. Some things you had to figure out by experiencing the world.

The Yossar Devan project had arrived at the right time. It wasn't his dream to find out what had happened to Yossar Devan. But for the first time in a very long time, he had the feeling of doing something important. The hunt for Yossar Devan's real identity was something that interested him. Ever since high school he had been more than averagely interested in rich people. The fascination had diminished over time. His time in banking and journalism had provided him with an understanding of how most rich people had really made their money. And surprisingly often great wealth was simply a result of willingness to take risk, good timing and dumb luck, rather than impressive business skills. But this respect for, this idolisation of rich people had never really lost its grip. He still read the financial papers before he read the tabloids. David wondered if this was a result of his upbringing.

He had always looked up to his uncle who had made a fortune developing shopping centres. While his dad had struggled to pay his bills, the uncle had always arrived at family gatherings in the newest Mercedes and seemed so happy. Life had always seemed so easy for him, and David had wanted the same life for himself. And then there was the Norwegian mentality: Public display of the annual personal income figures and article after article about who was making money and who was not. What had supposedly started off as a socialistic principle of transparency – that everybody should be able to know how much money their neighbour made – had turned into the exact opposite; it had become an eternal focus on how much money people made and who was successful or not. It had become abundantly clear for David, in those periods he had been living outside Norway, that the focus in his native country was different from most other places. It seemed like the most important question in all Norwegian papers always was how much money people had. It didn't matter whether you had played in a movie, written a book or started a company. People needed to know how much money you had made. David had, after a while, understood that this focus wasn't exactly healthy, but he hadn't been able to shed it. He was still fascinated by rich people and wanted to become rich himself.

Even though he felt he should probably go to bed, he decided to use the third principle to get some structure on the investigation of Yossar Devan's past, and mysterious disappearance. He had to make a plan for what he was supposed to do the following day. Whom was he supposed to talk to, and how was he supposed to organise the story?

He grabbed his laptop and started typing.

Background story; Who was Yossar Devan? Where did he come from and how did he manage to become a billionaire in just over twenty-five years?

Interview friends and family for a balanced picture.

Possible sources;
The university where he held his lectures.
The Chief Inspector of the missing person case.
Close friends/colleagues/family.
Competitors/critics.
Professor Grossman's source; Swarkowski.

David reviewed his list. He had sufficient material to keep him busy for the next few days. Hopefully he would also be able to grab another beer with Jon before returning to Brisbane in five days. But he had a busy week ahead of him. He put the list to the side and turned off the lights.

Wen Ning stood outside the hotel and stared up at the windows of room 302, where the lights were just turned off. He looked at his watch: 03:40. It was late, but he wasn't tired. He hardly needed sleep anymore. It was one of the benefits of getting older. He needed less sleep, less food, less everything. A taxi passed by, and some young kids were hanging out of the windows screaming at Wen Ning. He couldn't hear what they yelled, but he took a step backwards, into the darkness. Young kids without any purpose in their lives, out binge-drinking every night. A world in decline. He shook his head. It was time.

Up at room 302 David was staring down at the man dressed in black. David had just turned off his lights and walked over to the window to close it. There had been something strange about the way the man in black moved. As if he was trying to avoid being seen. As if he had stood down there staring up at David's window. David opened the window to get a better view of the street.

But it was too late.

The man was gone.

Disappeared into the darkness.

-12-

The landscape raced by on the outside of the train window, while the sound of metal against metal, and chatting passengers interfered with David's attempt to listen to Sade's "Smooth Operator" on his iPod. Even though he had turned the volume up to full, he couldn't shut out the world. He took another bite of his bacon and avocado sandwich, and glanced at his watch.

Not long now.

He didn't particularly like trains, he was more of a car man. It wasn't the travel experience he disliked, because he found it quite comfortable to travel on a train. It was the fact that he couldn't feel himself move closer to the goal when he was on a train. He had no influence on how fast they would get there, he had no feeling of moving forward. In a car, at least when he drove himself, he could always feel himself getting closer to the goal, closer to the destination.

He decided to rent a car when he arrived at Oxford University, it would make him less dependent on taxis as well. There was no point fighting it, it was just the way he was built. Without access to a car he sometimes felt trapped. There could be days between each time he used his car and the next, but he always needed access to it. Was it kind of a phobia, he wondered. He did have problems being dependent on anything and anyone. It shouldn't therefore have come as a surprise to him that he wouldn't love his previous jobs in journalism and banking. Jobs where you were dependent on almost everyone. If he ever wanted to become his own boss he had to start up by himself. It was the only way he could achieve true happiness, he thought. He would do it. When he had finished this MBA degree. No more delays, no more procrastination. But first he had to complete this assignment for Professor Grossman. He felt that it was right, he felt that this was something he was meant to do.

The train rolled onto Oxford train station and stopped with a long sigh. David flagged down a taxi and headed towards the university straight away. He had been successful in tracking down the person responsible for admissions to Oxford University, James McIntyre, and had an appointment with him at nine o'clock. He didn't expect that the meeting would give him a lot of useful information, but at least it was a start, a promising start.

James McIntyre's office could have benefitted from some more light, David thought as he tried to keep the conversation going. David had been able to secure the meeting on the basis that he was visiting from Australia and was conducting some research on one of the benefactors of the university. James McIntyre had been willing to meet with him on short notice.

"I've heard that Yossar Devan, one of the UK's great industrialists, was a guest lecturer at Oxford one semester. Is that right?" David asked.

James McIntyre smiled. "I must admit that this is probably the first time someone has referred to Yossar Devan as a great industrialist in my office."

"But he was a great industrialist, wasn't he?" David asked.

James McIntyre shrugged his shoulders. "Depends on how you define industrialist, I guess. But yes, he did hold some lectures here. In 1973 if I'm not mistaken. Not many people know about them though."

"Why not?" David asked.

"That's a good question. One thing that has remained a constant in society throughout time is people's ability to shy away from confrontation. You refer to Yossar Devan as one of England's great industrialists. Not many do that these days. Yossar Devan was in his time almost looked upon as a traitor. The fact that he had used a fake identity ruined his credibility overnight. Then the bankruptcies of the people who bought his companies started to hit the press. Nobody knew what was true or false anymore. Yossar Devan was being portrayed as the devil himself, and then the rumours started circulating. Had he been involved with the mafia? Had his whole business empire just been a house of cards?" James McIntyre took a deep breath before continuing. "And then the strangest thing happened. Normally when rumours start flying around, it is almost impossible to stop them. But the strangest thing about the Yossar Devan scandal wasn't that he had been operating under a false identity. It was the sudden silence about the case. Newspapers, which normally would have had a feast on a case like this, stopped reporting about it. Rumours circulated for a few weeks, but then they also died away. All that remained was silence, and in light of this silence most people with political ambitions or business interest cut their ties to the fictitious person Yossar Devan. In this light it is not that strange that we changed the name on the library Yossar Devan had donated the year before. We could however not change the fact that he did hold a couple of lectures here in the weeks leading up to his disappearance."

"Do you have any copies of the lectures he held here at the university?" David asked.

"No, I'm sorry. This was before PowerPoint and data, so the university doesn't have any copies. Your best chance is to locate one of the students who attended the lectures."

"Do you have a list of the attendees?" David asked.

"No," James McIntyre replied.

"If there is no list, how am I supposed to figure out who attended?" David asked, a bit confused.

"Look in the yearbook. Find the most successful students from 1973. I'm sure they were all present," James McIntyre replied.

David used the remainder of the morning to go through the 1973 yearbook. Some of the names and faces looked familiar, but he didn't know where he knew them from, and it didn't necessarily mean that they had been successful anyway. He realised he needed someone with local knowledge to help sorting through the pages. David walked over to the university library and scanned the pages with business students from the yearbook. He knew that selecting only business students was a gross simplification. A lot of English businessmen graduated with degrees in everything from history to philosophy, before pursuing their careers. But David didn't have time to go through all the names. And he assumed that a lecture given by a businessman like Yossar Devan would appeal mostly to business students. It was time-consuming to scan the pages from the yearbook, and David tried to utilise the time reading what students had written about where they envisioned themselves in ten years' time. Most were ambitious and envisioned international CEO jobs or political positions where they could make a difference to the world. David wondered how many of them had actually ended up living their dreams. How many had achieved the high goals and aspirations they had entertained when they were barely twenty years old?

He smiled. There were also the occasional students with more modest and realistic goals. A young, dark-haired girl, who wanted to work with people so that she could make a difference in ordinary people's lives, a young Asian who wanted to become an accountant so that he didn't have to work more weekends in his parents' restaurant.

David put away the yearbook. He had scanned approximately one hundred names and photos. That should do it. He uploaded the file to Dropbox and sent a link to Jon via email, asking whether he knew if some of the students had been successful later in life. He knew that Jon would define success as who had the most money, which was a very narrow scope. But it would have to do for now.

David had hardly finished his lunch before he got a reply.

Interesting prospect list.

Top ten:
Ryan Mortimer, net worth GBP 1.4B, finance (missing)
Ralph Ferguson, net worth GBP 700M, technology (deceased)
William Candy, net worth GBP 400M, retail
Chris Walsh, net worth GPB 1.4B, media (deceased)
John Mitchell, net worth GBP 1.5B, real estate
Michael Jones Smith, net worth GPB 800M, inheritance
Vijay Singh, net worth GPB 600M, retail
Li Ka Sun, net worth GBP 900M, software (deceased)
Mary-Rose Whitton, net worth GBP 1.1B, retail (Deceased)
Ivana Sampa, net worth GBP 1.1B, fashion

This is an A list of some of London's richest self-made millionaires and private investors. You'll have no chance in hell of getting through to any of them unless you know someone who knows someone. Sorry, but can't help you. I have tried calling every single one of them at one stage in my career and no one has ever returned my calls.

And further complicating your work, only five of them are still alive.

Good luck catching the big whale!

Jon

David perused the list. Jon was right. These people most likely received several hundred phone calls every single day from people who either wanted to sell them something or wanted them to invest in something. It was unlikely that David would even get through the gatekeepers and personal assistants if he didn't have something special to offer. Something he could use to make himself more interesting.

When he had worked as a journalist he had found situations like this challenging. But most times he had been able to come up with an angle that worked. Something that made people want to speak to him. This was different, however. These people were in a different league. How was he supposed to get a meeting with any one of them? How was he supposed to be able to even get through to one of them?

David reached for his Kindle reader. Professor Grossman had sent him the raw data to the study. On the pdf file all the interview subjects would be listed. Professor Grossman had told him that the billionaires he had interviewed had utilised his ten principles for wealth. Principles that Yossar Devan had been lecturing about thirty years earlier. Were some of the students from the Oxford yearbook also on Professor Grossman's list of interviewees?

He scrolled through the names. He immediately recognised several names. All the ten names Jon Berthelsen had sent him were on the list, and several of the other names from the Oxford yearbook. Had Professor Grossman simply interviewed the students who had attended Yossar Devan's lectures, and compared them with the ones who hadn't attended? It almost appeared as if this was the case. This was getting interesting. David took the list of millionaires whom Professor Grossman had interviewed, and emailed it off to Jon Berthelsen. He asked whether Jon could dig up some more information about them. He got a quick reply:

The markets are tanking today. Rumours about the US defaulting on their debts. I might as well take a break from being verbally abused by clients who have lost money – so you'll get a reply by tomorrow morning.

Jon.

David packed his things. He needed to do a more proper review of Professor Grossman's study before he made any definite conclusions, but he had a feeling something wasn't right.

On a positive note, he now knew his angle.

Professor Grossman was his angle.

-13-

David was worn out. He had spent the whole morning calling people on Professor Grossman's list. Jon had answered the email earlier than expected. It was clear that he didn't love his job because it looked like he had put a fair bit of effort into the list David had sent him. David knew the feeling well. When your job didn't really interest you that much, and you just longed for an opportunity to use some of the talents you never got to use in your regular job. He acknowledged he could also be wrong. He had, after all, provided Jon with a list of potential clients and an angle on how to get a foot in the door. They had all been students at Oxford University and perhaps also attended Yossar Devan's lectures about the principles of wealth. David, however, held another ace up his sleeve. He knew they had all been interviewed by Professor Grossman. He could call, claiming he was working for the professor, and see how many meetings that would get him.

Instead, something strange happened. David had been able to get through to a few of the billionaires on the list, but none of them had ever heard of Professor Grossman nor the study he was supposed to have conducted. David was confused. He had a copy of Professor Grossman's study on the Kindle reader. And there was no doubt, he was talking to the right people. Had Professor

Grossman made up all the interviews? Had he never met anyone of them face-to-face?

First David had discovered that it wasn't just a random selection of millionaires whom Professor Grossman claimed to have interviewed for his study. It was a very specific group of students who had all attended Oxford University in 1973. And after the day's phone conversations David had started to wonder whether Professor Grossman had ever met any single one of them.

David had tried to call Professor Grossman several times. But the calls went straight to message bank. He had even completed a few Google searches on the professor. To check him out. But it appeared that he had a spotless career. There was simply nothing that indicated that he would have cheated in his study.

The only positive was that one of the billionaires, the real estate tycoon John Mitchell, had agreed to meet David. John Mitchell had never heard about Professor Grossman nor his study, but he had become interested as soon as David mentioned Yossar Devan. John Mitchell had said he was willing to have a chat, but it would have to be the following day. Thus David had achieved his goal, and had an appointment with one of the billionaires from the list. David hoped that his next task would be easier: to get an appointment with the detective who had led the investigation of Yossar Devan's disappearance.

David hadn't made an appointment with Neill Flynn, the retired chief investigator of the Yossar Devan disappearance. A lot of David's colleagues in the banking industry used cold calling to attract new clients. They conducted a brief background check on a company, found out who was the owner or general manager, and then they called, asking for a meeting. This kind of prospecting typically had a very low success ratio. Maybe one of twenty phone calls led to a meeting and one of ten meetings to a new customer. Most sales managers, however, loved the strategy because it showed the right attitude. It signalled that you were hungry. David's comment to his last boss was that he couldn't understand the point of showing he was hungry if he knew that the strategy wouldn't make him full.

Instead, David preferred to just show up, unannounced, outside the business he wanted to target. It still wasn't normal that a banker acted as door-to-door salesman without an official appointment. And most months this unconventional method had landed him a meeting or two every week. The great advantage was that people found it a lot harder to dismiss a person when they stood there at the front door. People could be tough on the phone and even tougher in an email. But when they stood face-to-face with David it was hard to reject his charm.

Now he was standing outside the retired chief police investigator Neill Flynn's door, and tried to man himself up. To be confident and persuasive when he asked for permission to have a chat.

He buzzed the doorbell and an older woman opened the door.

"Who is it?" a deep voice shouted from the living room.

"My name is David Dypsvik," David said and extended his hand to the elderly lady. "If it is not too much of an inconvenience, I would like to have a chat with Mr Flynn about a case he was involved in many years ago," David said.

"There's a journalist here to see you," the older lady called out to the voice from the living room.

"I'm not ....." David started, but he was cut off by a tirade from the voice inside the house.

"Tell him to bugger off. "I'm not interested in speaking to a bloody journo."

"I'm a student," David started off again. "I have just flown in from Australia. My professor at Bond University is writing a book about a person named Yossar Devan. A person who disappeared about thirty years ago, while your husband still was the lead investigator of most missing persons cases. If it is not too much to ask, I would just like a word with him about the case."

"Why?"

"Because Mr Flynn was the lead investigator of Yossar Devan's disappearance in 1973. It would be incredibly helpful to get his view of what happened to Yossar Devan the day he disappeared."

"I don't think Neill will be of much help," the older lady said. It was obvious she was his wife. "He hasn't been himself the last few years. Alzheimer's."

David nodded. "I understand, Mrs Flynn. Would you mind asking him anyway?"

"I must warn you. He'll probably say yes, but you won't be able to get anything useful out of him. It's not one of those days."

David was asked to follow Mrs. Flynn into the living room. He secretly started to wonder whether she looked at this as a small opportunity to get a bit of a break from her husband. It had to be hard to live with a person suffering from dementia.

The conversation went almost exactly as the wife had warned. Neill Flynn remembered nothing from the Yossar Devan case. But David felt sorry for the older guy and kept him company for more than an hour. They mostly talked about soccer. And when it came to soccer there was nothing wrong with Neill Flynn's memory.

He was like a living encyclopaedia when it came to Manchester United and their past achievements.

Mary-Rose Flynn walked David to the door after he had said goodbye to her husband. She stopped and gave him a hug on the stairwell.

"Thanks for taking the time to speak to him like a human being today. We have visitors, but most of them ignore Neill or roll their eyes when he says something stupid."

"It was nothing. I enjoyed myself. I can tell your husband must have been a very knowledgeable man before this….before this thing happened," David said.

Mary-Rose Flynn smiled, and wiped a tear away. "He was," she said. "I'm sorry, but it's hard to see him wither away. The hardest is to see the sadness in his eyes the few days his mind is still clear."

David didn't know what to say, so he just kept quiet.

"You're a good person. Give me your card and I will get Neill to give you a call if he has a clear moment," Mary-Rose said.

David smiled, embarrassed. "Thanks for the offer, but it's not necessary. Enjoy any good moments together."

Mary-Rose gave him another hug, while insisting to get his number.

David was on his way down the stairs when Mary-Rose asked him to wait. He waited next to his rental car for ten minutes before she came back.

"These are Neill's notes from the Yossar Devan case. He was a good policeman, and they should never have done what they did to him." Mary-Rose handed David a box of folders.

"I don't understand," David said.

"Neill had his own theory about what had happened to Yossar

Devan. But his bosses wouldn't let him investigate. That case ended his career," Mary-Rose said. "Maybe you can find out what really happened?"

"I'm not an investigator, Mrs. Flynn. I'm just looking into what happened; the information will go into a book."

"You're a good man," Mary-Rose said. "You'll do what is right."

-14-

ohn Mitchell, the founder of Mitchell Properties Ltd, stood staring out the floor-to-ceiling window of Mitchell Properties Ltd's elegant boardroom. He seemed lost in his own thoughts as David was led in by a very attractive and blond secretary. The secretary cleared her voice. "Mr Dypsvik is here for his appointment. I'll bring some refreshments."

"Thanks Laura," John Mitchell quipped as he turned around to face his guest. He had a warm and welcoming voice. David hadn't known what to expect. He had met a lot of successful people through his previous jobs in banking and journalism, but this guy was in a different league. He didn't come from a rich family. He hadn't inherited a fortune or a company. He had worked himself up from rock bottom. The biography on Mitchell Properties Ltd's website said that he had started off renovating a small two bedder outside London, and used the profits to buy a three bedder. Then he had just continued. All profits he made were reinvested in the next project, which of course was always bigger and better. The real growth had begun when the banks had started to compete for his business. He had used the appreciation in value of his existing properties as security to raise funds for ever larger and larger projects. When everyone else had been scared of soaring interest rates John Mitchell had just kept investing. And this contrarian strategy, of doing the opposite of what the rest of the market did, had served him well. Even though he had been close to bankruptcy, both in the late 1980s and mid-1990s.

"Hi David," John Mitchell said cheerily. "Welcome to Mitchell Properties."

"Thanks for taking the time to see me," David replied. "I know you must be a very busy man."

"No problem. I love my job and I love buildings. But we all need a break sometimes. To stimulate our intellect with conversations."

John Mitchell moved away from the window and over to a small seating group. He indicated with his hand that David should follow.

"So, what can I do for you?" he asked, after having followed his own advice and seated himself in a white leather chair next to David. "You mentioned on the phone that you were working on a project about Yossar Devan."

David had decided not to lie. But he didn't want to tell the whole story either. He quickly came up with a cover story. "Yes, one of the professors at Bond University is working on a book about Yossar Devan. I'm basically trying to learn as much as I can about Mr Devan so that I can portray him accurately in the book."

"And now it turns out nobody is willing to talk about him?"

"Correct. It seems like everyone wants to distance themselves from him."

"Welcome to politics and real life. Unfortunately that's often how it is. There is no upside in being associated with Yossar Devan anymore. He is dead and buried."

"But why this fear of talking about a man who has been gone for more than thirty years? I just don't get it." David said.

"Well, I don't think Bond University is very proud of still being associated with their founder Alan Bond," John Mitchell replied.

David understood that John Mitchell had done his homework. Alan Bond became a national hero in Australia in 1983, after winning the America's Cup and putting an end to New York Yacht Club's continuous victory stretch from 1851. The longest victory stretch in modern sports history. When Alan Bond founded Bond University in 1987 he was the pride of the nation. But everything changed overnight when he in 1992 was responsible for the biggest bankruptcy in Australian history. After a string of failed acquisitions Alan Bond ended up with a seven-year jail term, and Bond University with a challenge of how to market the university to students.

"But you don't have any objections to talking about Yossar Devan?" David asked.

"Well, that's not entirely correct. I am not prepared to give you any official comments. What I say here today stays between us. You can't quote me on anything."

"Fine by me," David said. He didn't need to use John Mitchell as a source in Professor Grossman's book. The most important goal was to learn as much as possible about Yossar Devan.

"So, can you tell me why Bond University has decided to write about Yossar Devan? He disappeared several decades ago. What interest does he have now?" John Mitchell asked.

"One of our professors, Evan Grossman, has conducted a study into the life-long question of why some people become rich while others struggle financially. The work has resulted in ten principles that lead to wealth. During his work he discovered however that Yossar Devan had developed some very similar principles."

"Yossar Devan's lectures about the principles of wealth?" John Mitchell asked.

"Correct," David replied. He studied John Mitchell's facial expression, looking for any signs that he knew of Professor Grossman. But John Mitchell's face was almost emotionless. If he had ever met Professor Grossman he didn't want to reveal it.

"So, what do you know about Yossar Devan's lectures?" John Mitchell asked.

"I know that he completed nine lectures before he vanished in 1973. I haven't heard nor seen them myself, but Professor Grossman has interviewed people who attended the lectures."

"Nine," John Mitchell mumbled to himself. "So, you haven't seen the content of the lectures yourself?"

"No," David replied.

"And why did you contact me?" He asked.

David wasn't sure what to reply. Initially he had contacted John Mitchell because Professor Grossman had claimed to interview him in his study. John Mitchell had however refuted this claim in their phone conversation.

"You're a successful businessman. You attended Oxford University when Yossar Devan held his lectures. And I assumed that the lectures may have played a vital role in your great success."

"So, you want to trivialise what I have created. Explain my success by saying I attended a couple of lectures in 1973?"

"No, no. I don't mean to trivialise what you have achieved. But it is a remarkable fact that many of the 1973 graduates have amassed great wealth. Does this have anything to do with Yossar Devan's lectures? That's the question I want answered."

"I have been successful on my own accord," John Mitchell replied. "And I don't appreciate that you, or anybody else, imply that my wealth is the result of some principles that Yossar Devan, a traitor of England, blabbered about back in 1973. What you see here," he said, and pointed to a table filled with miniature models of high-rises and other buildings, "is my work. I have done this all by myself, without the help of anyone." John Mitchell abruptly got up from his chair. "This meeting is over," he said, and pressed a button on his desk. In less than a second the beautiful blond secretary appeared in the door entrance of the boardroom.

"Could you please follow Mr Dypsvik to the elevator," John Mitchell said.

"I'm sorry. Did I offend you?" David asked.

"No," John Mitchell replied, without offering any further explanation.

"Then why do you throw me out?"

"I'm not throwing you out," John Mitchell replied. "I have simply changed my mind. I don't want to contribute to the book. I just don't like the way you attempt to trivialise my work. It is hard work that leads to great wealth. Not a few cheap principles."

David was obstructed from commenting as John Mitchell disappeared out a side door of the boardroom.

While studying David on the security monitor, John Mitchell dialled a familiar number on his phone.

"It's me," he said. "It doesn't seem like he knows anything, but we can't be sure. Buy everything you can and increase security. I'm afraid our secret isn't as safe as we thought it would be."

He hung up and looked out the window.

Slowly he started to count the buildings he was responsible for.

Counting the buildings always calmed his mind.

-15-

David was sitting at a restaurant, drinking a glass of iced tea. He didn't understand much of what had just happened in the meeting with John Mitchell. Why had John Mitchell agreed to the meeting if he didn't want to answer any questions? David had run through the conversation in his own head several times already. And he was certain that he hadn't said anything that could possibly offend John Mitchell. The only plausible conclusion was that John Mitchell had cut the meeting short because he had been afraid that he would reveal something to David, something that had to stay secret. What was John Mitchell hiding? Why would a wealthy and powerful man fear being locked in a room with David for more than ten minutes? He had asked whether David knew about Yossar Devan's principles of wealth. But David had only read the professor's principles, the first three of them. Professor Grossman, whose credibility at best was in doubt, after David had revealed that all the interviewees originated from the Oxford University class of 1973. What was it with this particular group of students? David pulled out the business card James McIntyre had given him and dialled his number.

The phone rang four times before James McIntyre answered. "Ahh, the young man interested in Yossar Devan. What can I do for you?" he asked.

"When I asked you how I could find out which students had attended Yossar Dean's lectures you told me to locate the most successful students from the class of 1973. What did you really mean by that?"

There was a moment of silence before James McIntyre finally answered. "There weren't that many students attending the tenth and last lecture of Yossar Devan. It was held on a Saturday evening. And I guess only students with a special interest chose to attend. The rumours are, however, that the students who attended this last lecture have done exceptionally well afterwards. Devan's disciples they were called."

"Devan's disciples?"

"Yes, there was something about them not being willing to share the last principle with the other students. Understandably the students who didn't attend the last lecture got upset. There has always been an unwritten law here at Oxford that you share information, but these students chose to ignore that rule. And of course, if you keep something secret the stories begin to grow. Especially since Yossar Devan disappeared just days after the last lecture."

"Do you think there could be a connection between the disappearance of Yossar Devan and the last lecture he held?"

"No, no, no. I'm only saying that everything that is illegal or secret has this tendency of being coveted by people. Suddenly a lecture, held by a boring businessman, became a mystery. Everybody tried to find out what was being said at that last lecture. It was as if they believed Yossar Devan had shared a secret formula for wealth. It was crazy."

David thought back on John Mitchell's behaviour. He had totally changed character when David had denied reading Yossar Devan's principles of wealth. Did John Mitchell have a secret?

Did the students who attended the last lecture learn a secret principle on how to get rich? Knowledge that they didn't want to share with anyone else? Was there a tenth principle?

"Thanks for the help," David said. "You've been very helpful."

"No problem. It has been a pleasure."

David stood there, lost in his own thoughts for a moment. There was something strange going on. It wasn't a coincidence that Professor Grossman had hired him to look into the mystery of Yossar Devan. There were simply too many things that didn't add up.

He needed a break and pulled out his Kindle reader. He had made a deal with Professor Grossman, he had to read one principle every day. Even though he felt that Professor Grossman hadn't been honest with him, he could at least honour his part of the agreement. He started to read.

Principle 4: Imagination and integrity

'You are never too old to dream.' I still remember the day my dad said those words to me. He almost had his own dream within his grasp. His dream wasn't big. It was just the dream of a better life for himself and our family. Unfortunately he couldn't keep his integrity if he wanted to achieve his dream. He had to take an assignment for money only, an assignment for blood money.

And it ended in horror.

But his saying has been with me since that day. It has been one of the pillars of my life. You are never too old to dream. The only amendment I have done is that I have added a word. You are never too old to dream big. Because dreams are free so you might as well dream big.

But your dreams and your integrity must never come in conflict. Money will come and go, but your integrity is forever. It requires great courage to do the right thing in any situation. Regardless of what the consequences will be. Regardless of who is watching.

I've always kept my word. The reputation I built as a businessman you could trust was priceless when I started my career. And if I, at any time, had breached my integrity I could have ruined what I had spent decades building. Thus I never chased quick money. Instead I did what was right. What I felt was right in my little world. What enabled me to sleep well at night.

I remember I one time criticised one of my staff for buying a lotto ticket. "Why did you buy that? It's money straight down the drain. It's the poor man's tax. You're paying eighty percent tax on money you have already paid tax on."

"I have no illusions that I am going to win Mr Devan," he replied. "But for the next week I will go around dreaming about what I will use the money on if I win. So, it's not money down the drain for me, Mr Devan. It's a small payment for a week of big dreams."

And he was of course right. It is the anticipation of something that is the greatest feeling. When you finally achieve a goal, or buy something you have wanted for a long time, you often end up with an anticlimax. You end up feeling empty. An emptiness I have felt numerous times in my own life. An emptiness I used to feel before I realised that it wasn't the money I made that was important, it was the journey. And that's why it is so important that you choose to do something you like, not just something you want to make money on.

The problem is that these two goals often are conflicting. Let's say that you as me, are fascinated by the ocean. So you decide to make a living out of the sea. Let's say you decide you want to be a fisherman. You can invest in a small fishing boat, be the skipper and make a good living. But your income will always be constrained by how many fish you can catch with your boat. If you want more income you need to invest in a bigger boat or in more boats. But this investment will also mean that you won't be able to fish that much yourself anymore, because you now have new commitments. You have to make sure that all permits are in order and so forth. Suddenly you are not a fisherman anymore. You are a boss. A boss with an office job.

You should therefore think hard about what you want to do before you start up your own business. You need to know what you want, but you also need to understand that your passion might not be compatible with great material wealth.

Regardless I would ask that you have big dreams. And important dreams. Even so big that your friends believe you have megalomania. Because it is only when you view the world as an abundant source of wealth that you can truly achieve your potential. And it is only when you believe you can make a difference that you can actually do it.

Most people receive a wakeup call when they lose or quit their jobs. They may have thought they were irreplaceable, that the business or organisation they worked for would run into massive problems as soon as they left. Reality is different. To replace a worker is part of daily business. Nobody is irreplaceable.

The only thing that can't be replaced is your imagination. It is unique. There may be thousands of workers with the same skills as yourself, but there is nobody with an identical brain and imagination. Your brain, your thoughts, ideas and imagination are unique to you. And thus no one can really replace you.

Walt Disney once said, "if you can dream it, you can do it.'

And he was right. The world is our playground. We can either stand on the sideline and watch everybody else play. Or we can join in.

Be a child again and dream that you can conquer the world. Let's all be children again.

David put his Kindle away. He had a problem. He didn't know what he wanted to do. As many of his friends he had chosen an education that would give him a lot of options in the future. There was a reason they called business students potatoes – they could do a lot of different jobs. David had envisioned for himself a future where he worked for a couple of fun and exciting businesses for a few years. He would pick up some good skills, get himself a good network, and then he would launch his own successful business. Time had, however, passed him by. He had commitments. The massive student loan and the miniscule apartment he had mortgaged to the hilt were worries that never ceased to plague him. If he had been a potato he could have been hiding in a nice and comfy hole in the ground. But life wasn't that easy.

David had to get up every morning. He had to get up to make money.

He grabbed his notepad and a pen. He thought about how the billionaires in Professor Grossman's study had made their money.

-Retail.

-Real estate.

-Technology.

Boring. Boring. Boring.

There was nothing that stood out. David still had no clue what he wanted to do. He still had no clue what he wanted to achieve in life.

He closed his eyes and hoped that an idea would appear in his dreams. After ten minutes with closed eyes, and without any heavenly revelation of what he was supposed to do, he grabbed the box of folders that Chief Inspector Neill Flynn had given him.

On top there was a folder marked Yossar Devan. It was relatively slim, and it only contained three grainy pictures of Yossar Devan, a short summary of body identifiers and an even shorter biography. There was also a bigger folder marked company structure in the bottom of the box.

David opened it. It looked like it was incomplete. The first page had a myriad of arrows with question marks. It appeared that the police had struggled to understand the true nature of Yossar Devan's company structure. David skimmed through the information, chewing on a packet of chips.

Neill Flynn's wife had said that the Chief Inspector had come up with his own theory on what had happened to Yossar Devan. But that someone higher up in the organisation had stopped him from pursuing this theory any further. David wondered what this theory could be. But he couldn't find any trace of it. Maybe Neill Flynn had thrown out some of the information? Maybe he had never even had a theory?

He had however tried to make an overview of where the money flowed. And this was in line with David's thinking. The quickest way to get to the bottom of these cases was almost always to follow the flow of money. The problem in this case was that the money seemed to flow to a holding company in Cyprus, and from there to a trust in the Caribbean. No financial information was available, and it was impossible to find out who was the real owner of the trust.

In the margin, someone, David assumed Neill Flynn, had written; 'why so many transfers to Turkey? Suiris Export and Import.'

David continued to flip through the pages in the report, but there was no theory there. When Flynn's wife had given him the box of folders he had gotten such high hopes. He had almost anticipated that Neill Flynn had discovered something important. That he had figured out what had happened to Yossar Devan. Instead there was nothing.

David still didn't know who Yossar Devan had been or where he had come from. He hadn't been successful in getting any information from John Mitchell or Neill Flynn.

He had tried to contact old competitors, friends and acquaintances. But no one wanted to speak to him.

He had nothing, absolutely nothing.

This was not going as planned.

He only had one chance left.

Swarkowski.

The guy with the new lead whom Professor Grossman had talked about.

The conspiracy theorist.

-16-

A black VISA card was lying on the polished dining table and a stripe of white powder surrounded its chipped edges. A cigarette was sending its last breath of deadly fumes into the air as the glow approached the red lipstick mark. Small glimmers of light crept through the room every time the wind pushed the curtains to the side. The massive penthouse in the Hyde One building seemed abandoned. Outside people were busy hurrying to lunch meetings or shopping for luxury goods. Wealthy Arabic wives, dressed in full covered Burkas, carried shopping bags from Versace and regular bags from Louis Vuitton. Professionals dressed in expensive tailor-made suits scurried past, chatting with their mobile phones.

The city was buzzing.

Inside the apartment there was something else buzzing. It was the sound of the air-conditioning system going on full machine. It was freezing cold inside the massive apartment that covered the upper floor of the Hyde One building.

Wen Ning closed the window. It would be at least a few days before the smell got so bad that someone would consider calling the police. But he didn't have much time. The reality was that this one had gone really bad.

He had planned it well. And everything had seemed to go

according to plan. He would make it look like an accident. Like she had slipped on the bathroom floor and hit her head. Instead she had survived the fall against the bathroom tiles when he had kicked her feet from underneath her. She had hit her head hard against the floor, and he was sure she would eventually die from the cracked skull and bleeding on the brain he had imposed on her. But he had been too rough with his kick. He could see it on her legs. She would bruise up before she died. A clever detective would notice immediately, and this one wouldn't be written off as an accident in the home. The most dangerous place to be if you disregarded hospitals. This one would be investigated as a murder. And that meant he had to change his plans. He had to make it look like a murder.

To complicate things he didn't know whether she had a maid or other staff with their own keys. He didn't know whether she had appointments that would be broken or not. But time was about to run out and he needed to complete what he had started. With firm steps he walked back into the bathroom where the naked woman lay stretched out on the floor. He studied her from the door entrance. She was quite a distance away. The bathroom was bigger than his apartment. He walked closer. Oh, how he missed the smell of a woman. He had realised several decades ago that he was one of the few lucky ones who could survive without material things. His willpower was his biggest strength in life. He had taught himself to sacrifice most things, to not want for anything. But he did miss the smell of a woman. There was no hiding that fact.

He leant over the body and took a deep breath.

Nothing.

He reasoned that it was a good thing. The loss of smell and taste made him capable of completing his mission without getting distracted, without getting tempted. Without feeling.

He was the chosen one. The only one strong enough to go through what was required. He couldn't trust anyone else.

Leaders in the Party had started to ask questions. Criticised that he was getting bolder. What did they know? They lived in their own bubble, corrupted by power and money desires. No willpower whatsoever.

Wen Ning rolled the dying woman onto the plastic.

Willpower.

Self-control.

It was those two things that differentiated them from the Americans. And it was those two things that would ultimately lead them to victory. Wen Ning had read about the so-called marshmallow test that Walter Mischel from Stanford University had developed in 1968. Mischel had tested the ability for self-control in children between the ages of four and six, by giving them a marshmallow, a Pretzel or an Oreo biscuit. If the kids wanted to they were allowed to eat the marshmallow straight away. But if they waited for fifteen minutes, and didn't touch the marshmallow, then they would be rewarded with a second marshmallow. Mischel tested the same children later in life. It turned out that the kids who chose to wait to eat the marshmallow scored better on university tests, and became more successful, popular and respected in adult work life. The ability to postpone the satisfaction of a need was a better predictor of later success in life than any IQ test.

To postpone the satisfaction of a need.

Wen Ning had postponed the satisfaction of all his personal needs the last twenty years. He had sacrificed everything.

But at last the reward was now finally soon within his grasp.

The plastic crackled when Wen Ning rolled the woman onto her side. He had to set the scene as quickly as possible.

There was no room for errors.

-17-

Dark clouds hovered over the streets of London. David had taken the tube into the city and everybody seemed to be busy. Everyone seemed to be late for something. Maybe he had been damaged by staying on the Gold Coast, because he felt stressed by all the busy people. They all seemed like they had some important meeting to go to. People they needed to see.

David was in no rush. He had plenty of time.

A bus honked its horn, passing only centimetres from his face. He retracted to the pavement. His shoes were soaked by the stream of water the bus had stirred up.

Wet, clammy shoes. Suddenly he longed to be back on the Gold Coast and wearing his thongs.

He was, however, glad to be back in London. Even though he couldn't imagine ever living there it was a city he loved. And he had been there several times to watch his favourite soccer team, Chelsea, play. Nothing tasted like a pub meal after a soccer match. David put his hand to his left temple. Come to think of it, a visit to the pub didn't seem that appealing. The late night with Jon Berthelsen had done some serious damage. Even though it was now three days ago David was still struggling with a headache.

Getting older was a bitch.

A taxi drove up alongside him and David stretched his arm out. He had realised that it was much easier to get around without a car in London and had returned the rental car a few days earlier than expected. The door of the taxi opened.

"Where to?" the Indian driver asked.

"Pimlico. 22 Chesterwore Street," David answered.

He had Peter Swarkowski's address. But that was also all he had. He didn't even have a phone number or a description of the guy. If Peter Swarkowski wasn't home, he didn't have much other choice than to leave and try again another day.

"Jump in," the Indian driver said.

David wondered how Peter Swarkowski would react when David arrived at his door. He didn't know if the professor had warned him that David would be coming.

There was no point worrying about it, though. He had to take the chance that Peter Swarkowski would talk to him. The taxi driver seemed confused and kept calling a colleague. David assumed it was to ask for directions, but the driver refused every time David asked.

The metre climbed steadily, and on the radio a reporter talked about the rising price of gold and the difficult economic times. When David, for the fifth time, leant forward to ask whether they were on the right way he looked straight into the Indian's white teeth. He had finally located the street and was obviously proud of himself. David paid forty-two pounds and mumbled something about an expensive ride.

"It's the petrol prices," the Indian said. "It's not cheap to drive a taxi anymore."

David handed him forty-five pounds, told him to keep the change and stepped out.

He stood waiting as the taxi took off down the road. Most people in the streets had opened up their umbrellas, but David relished the feeling of rain tingling on his skin. It was one of the few things he had missed living in Australia. Rain and cold made David feel alive; it was only the amount he couldn't stand in Norway.

On the other side of the road a middle-aged man stood staring at him. An Asian. David looked up and met his gaze. There was something familiar about him. The man pulled out his mobile phone and started to talk, walking away from David. David realised he must have been wrong.

He walked up the staircase and pressed the doorbell.

An unwelcoming man's voice answered.

"Yes, who is it?"

"I am here to talk to Peter Swarkowski. Professor Grossman has sent me," David replied.

There was a silence from the other side of the intercom. "It's regarding Yossar Devan," David shot in.

A couple of seconds went by before the door opened.

David took the elevator up to the third floor. The hallway was covered by a carpet and David was unsure whether he should take off his wet shoes in the elevator or wait until he got to the door. He chose the door. Large wet prints on the carpet bore witness of his choice. The door was half open. David knocked and stuck his head inside the crack.

"Come in'" a voice called out from the living room. David obliged the order. He removed his shoes and followed the sound of the TV. The wet socks sucked themselves to his feet when he wandered into the living room of Peter Swarkowski.

Peter Swarkowski sat in a wheelchair in front of the TV. David looked at him with genuine surprise in his eyes. The professor had called Swarkowski a conspiracy theorist. David had fully expected to meet a longhaired geek in an X-Files T shirt and a dirty basement full of computers, with open wiring hanging from the ceiling. Peter Swarkowski was an old handicapped guy and he lived in a luxury apartment.

"I assume you are David Dypsvik?" Peter Swarkowski asked.

"Yes," David confirmed.

Peter Swarkowski looked at him with small, suspicious lizard eyes. He was wearing a dark red smoking jacket and a white shirt that was partly unbuttoned. The greying hair was combed back and accentuated his red face.

"An accident playing polo, when I was fifteen," he said, tapping his fingers on the wheelchair. He preferred addressing the elephant in the room early. "So, what is the good professor up to these days?" he asked.

"He is working on a study about wealth," David replied.

"Can't help you there," Peter Swarkowski said. "With all the price hikes on utilities it isn't easy to get by on the pension these days. The old advice of always spending less than you earn is kind of worthless when you hardly have an income," he laughed.

David nodded politely. "Professor Grossman said you may have some new information about Yossar Devan."

"Slow down, kid. We have hardly met each other. You don't jump straight to second base on the first date."

David sat down in the couch, next to the wheelchair. Peter Swarkowski turned the TV off.

"The good professor called," he started. "He said you had a quick head, and were helping him out with a study."

"Did he say that? That was very kind of him, but I have only worked for Professor Grossman for a few days," David said, trying to conceal the fact that he appreciated the flattery.

"The professor is a nice and generous man. I have known him for many years. If he vouches for you that is good enough for me."

David didn't mention that the professor had called Peter Swarkowski a conspiracy theorist. He was however happy that the professor had high hopes for him. Or had expressed high hopes for him was probably a more correct assessment. David assumed that the professor was a well-experienced manipulator. He had even managed to get David so excited about the assignment that he had travelled to the opposite side of the globe, in the middle of his expensive MBA education, to search for a man who had disappeared thirty years prior.

"So, what brings you to London, David?" Peter Swarkowski asked.

"Curiosity," David answered. "The professor told me about Yossar Devan, and I am interested to learn more."

Curiosity is a good quality, but in moderation. There was a reason I insisted that the professor come here to London. There are many people who have searched for Yossar Devan since he disappeared thirty years ago, but no one has ever found him. I'll tell you what I was supposed to tell the professor. But I ask you to think long and hard about what you want to do with this information. There are many people who spend their lives searching for treasures on the bottom of the sea. It doesn't mean that they will ever be found."

"I know," David replied. "I only want to learn more about Yossar Devan. Who he was and why he disappeared without a trace."

"Horseshit," Peter Swarkowski spat out. "You're driven by a desire for money. I can see it in your eyes." Peter Swarkowski's narrow lizard eyes turned, if possible, even more narrow. "To get rich. That's what you want. Isn't it?"

David sighed. "Don't we all? The fact that I want to get rich doesn't mean that I believe I will ever achieve it though. I play lotto every week, even though I know the odds of me winning are less than being struck in the head by a meteorite. But I don't give up. The only thing that is certain is that you will never win unless you're in the game. If I don't do what I can to find out who Yossar Devan really was, then I will never be able to figure out how he was able to get so rich."

"Ok. That's an honest answer. But what you do with this information is your own responsibility. Because it will affect your life."

"Shoot. My life needs something new," David said.

"How much has the professor told you about Devan?" Peter Swarkowski asked.

"He has told me how Yossar Devan arrived in London in the late 1940s. And in a relatively short time he managed to become one of the wealthiest people in the world. He was declared a business genius because he never seemed to make a bad deal. And suddenly one day, he vanished off the face of the Earth. After he disappeared it turned out he had been living his life under a fake name. Yossar Devan had never existed."

"Until now," Peter Swarkowski said.

"What do you mean?" David asked.

"I suspect the good professor has told you that I like to read about conspiracy theories and alternative history. The story about Yossar Devan's disappearance never excited me though. To me he was just another rich guy who disappeared. Not very interesting. That was, until I found the picture."

"Picture, which picture?" David asked.

Peter Swarkowski rolled his wheel chair over to the cabinet next to the TV. He pulled the door open and grabbed a blue folder. When he returned to David he produced a black-and-white picture, of a young man, and placed it on the table in front of them.

"There exists only one official picture of Yossar Devan from his young days. And that is from when he was around twenty years old and had just arrived in London. When I first saw the picture I knew I had seen him before, but I didn't know where. Not until a month ago."

Peter Swarkowski started to tell his history.

"I was supposed to hold a lecture about the secret weapons programs of Nazi Germany. The architect behind this program was a little-known officer by the name of Dr Hans Kammler. Dr Kammler was the officer in charge of a range of weapons programs during the Second World War, amongst others the development of the V2 bombs that caused so much damage here in London. He was also in charge of the development of concentration camps in The Third Reich. Some conspiracy theorists, or alternative history scientists, which we prefer to be called, have written extensively about Dr Kammler's weapons programs. Most of these authors, like Joseph P. Farrel, base their work on sources with limited credibility though. For example, the Polish Igor Witkowski claims that he in 1997 was shown printouts of interrogations of the SS general Jacob Sporenberg. In those interrogations Sporenberg claimed that Dr Kammler was about to develop a new secret weapon, Die Glocke. I found the story interesting, because you have to understand that even though most of these theories sound crazy, they have to be viewed in conjunction with the Third Reich's interest in the occult. And where there is smoke there is most often fire. The Third Reich spent enormous resources on occult science in addition to their conventional research projects. So one day I was bored and I sat down, pun intended, and started to dig a bit deeper into Dr Kammler's background. And by total accident I found out that he had been involved in an excavation accident in Turkey in 1944." Peter Swarkowski took a deep breath before continuing. "I found it strange that one of the most highly commended SS officers, responsible for several of the most important weapons projects in Nazi Germany, would be attending an excavation in Turkey during the most intensive fighting of the Second World War. What was it with this excavation that was so important that Adolf Hitler sent Dr Kammler, a four-star general, to oversee it? I didn't find out very much about the accident. What we know is documented in Dr Kammler's recently declassified report where he simply records the loss of eleven SS soldiers. Dr Kammler's report does not, however, explain the reason for the trip to the excavation nor what happened there. It only states the bare facts. Dr Kammler was attending an excavation in Turkey, an excavation collapsed and eleven of his men died in addition to several local workers. So I asked one of my contacts in Turkey to look into the accident. Even though people think you can find all the information on the internet these days there are many newspapers that have never been digitalised, and therefore only exist in their original paper version. He sent me this article."

Peter Swarkowski opened a pdf file on his computer.

"The article is not that exciting in itself. It only reports that a delegation from Germany arrived to attend the opening of an excavation at the Tumuli Heights."

Peter Swarkowski clicked on the picture in the newspaper article. Next to a tall, blond SS general, who was identified as Dr Kammler, there was a young kid. Peter Swarkowski double-clicked on the picture again and the face of the kid filled up most of the screen.

The kid had a scar on his left cheek. Peter Swarkowski held up the picture of Yossar Devan from his arrival in London.

"Tada. I give you Yossar Devan," Peter Swarkowski said with pride in his voice.

David looked closer at the picture. "Who is he?" he asked.

"I don't know," Peter Swarkowski answered. "And that's why I wanted this meeting with the professor. Sending information over the net is not safe these days."

"But you have a theory," David said.

"Always," Peter Swarkowski smiled. "Always a theory. I believe that Yossar Devan was Dr Kammler's son. It makes sense with regards to how he managed to build himself up from nothing to become one of the richest men in the world. If he was Dr Kammler's son he could have had access to parts of the enormous wealth the Nazis smuggled out of Germany before the end of the war. It could also explain why Dr Kammler chose to keep the trip outside all official channels. It was recorded as a trip in relation to the Glocke project. Something that would ensure it was classified. As a father he wanted to be there for his son when he opened an historic excavation, even though it was in the middle of a world war where he himself was a crucial player. He kept the trip secret because he had to avoid anyone finding out that he had a son. It shows the arrogance of Dr Kammler when he takes the time and effort to travel to an excavation in Turkey for personal needs. Dr Kammler had the power to do whatever he wanted to in the Third Reich."

"So what happened to Yossar Devan?"

"Well, there is no evidence that Dr Kammler ever had a son. I believe that Dr Kammler intentionally kept his son's existence away from public knowledge. As a backup plan if the Third Reich failed and someone else had to rebuild it." Peter Swarkowski caught his breath and adjusted his glasses. "By removing his son from all public records, something he could have easily enough done in his position. He had a person without any links to Nazi Germany, a person who could be used to rebuild the Third Reich if it failed on the first try."

David didn't look convinced. "Do you have any more information or do you base everything on this one picture?" he asked.

"I know it isn't much," Peter Swarkowski replied. "But this is how all theories start out. Now the work to confirm or refute my theory begins. And this is where you and the professor enter the picture. As you can imagine I'm not very mobile." He tapped his fingers on the side of the wheelchair. "To get further in this case you will have to travel to Turkey. That's why I asked the professor to come here. If he was here in London right now a trip to Turkey wouldn't seem that bad. It's worse when you sit in an office in Australia, and look at the globe." Peter Swarkowski laughed. "But then he sent you instead. Life chooses its own route."

David remained sceptic. The story just didn't seem credible. "Let's assume that Yossar Devan was Dr Kammler's son, and built his business empire by using money stolen by the Nazis during the war. Why did he disappear so suddenly? Why did he disappear without a trace?"

"I believe that the authorities in the US or England figured out the same thing I did. And to avoid the scandal it would be if it was revealed that the son of one of Nazi Germany's worst killers had built himself a fortune on stolen money from the war, they simply decided to get rid of him. If there were more people from the Nazi era involved they would be best off staying hidden. Sure they would have been pissed off that that all their money ended up in the hands of the UK government, but if they had said anything they would have revealed themselves. The choice would have been easy." Peter Swarkowski tapped his fingers on the wheelchair again.

"But Yossar Devan was only a kid during the war. He wasn't responsible for the atrocities committed by the Third Reich."

"It's not important who pulled the trigger. If Yossar Devan used money, stolen from Jews sent to the concentration camps, then he was just as guilty as all the other war criminals."

Peter Swarkowski pounded his hand at the table. And for the first time it struck David that Swarkowski might be a Jewish name, and that Peter Swarkowski most likely had lost family members and friends during the war.

"I'm sorry," David said with a humble voice. "What do I do now?"

"You go home to your hotel. Call Professor Grossman and tell him that you have several promising leads, and that you will return in a week's time. Then you book a ticket to Turkey. You find this village." Peter Swarkowski turned the picture of the SS general and the unknown kid, the kid that he claimed was Yossar Devan, and scribbled an address and a phone number on the backside. He then handed the picture to David. "David, you have the opportunity to become the first person to identify Yossar Devan. You have the opportunity to rewrite history."

David nodded, said thank you, and walked out of the apartment.

His head was aching from all the information he had received over the last few days. Was somebody playing him? He felt like he was a contestant on a hidden camera show. The whole story sounded too fantastic.

What had started as a research project about some principles of wealth had turned into a global conspiracy involving Nazi money and unknown sons.

On the other hand he had decided to take more risks in his life. There was a striking resemblance between the picture of Yossar Devan and the kid from the excavation in Turkey.

And what was it that Chief Inspector Neill Flynn had written on the page with money flows from Yossar Devan's companies: Why so many transfers to Turkey?

David had to follow the money.

He had to go to Turkey.

PART 2

-18-

The Lufthansa airhostess leant over David as she interrogated the passenger next to him whether he wanted tea or coffee with his meal. David had already started his breakfast, which he gulped down in a few bites. The movie he was watching was paused and the captain's lax voice filled the cabin. The captain reported that the weather forecast was good and that arrival would be as scheduled in Ankara, Turkey's capital, in less than three hours. The movie started up again, but David had lost interest and turned off the screen.

He was unsure what he would find in Turkey. David wasn't religious, far from. But over the last few days he had increasingly felt that he had been led by an invisible hand. He needed to make a decision. He needed to decide whether to follow his intuition or his brain going forward, gut feeling or logic. Because those two alternatives seldom led to the same answer. If David had listened to his brain, which he would normally do, he wouldn't be on a plane, thirty-two thousand feet up in the air, on the way to Turkey, on the hunt for the identity of a man who had never lived. If he had listened to his brain, he would have been back in Australia, writing his appeal. But David had changed over the last few days. He had gradually realised that once you started to make choices that weren't only based on logic, then it became easier over time. He had already flown to London, with nothing more than a name on a piece of paper as his best lead. In light of this, flying to Turkey didn't seem as such a big stretch.

David decided that he liked the new David. The new David who took chances the old one would never take. The new David who seized the opportunities.

He pulled out his Kindle reader. Three hours to Ankara. He should probably do something more useful than watching a movie. He should read the next principle of wealth.

Principle 5; Other People's Help

I find it quite comical that a lot of the people who have made money, like myself, become ridiculously arrogant and narcissistic. The reality is that I could never have done it all on my own. My best skill is that I am a good people person. I have been good at employing and listening to the right people.

If you surround yourself with the right people it will radically increase your chances of success. I believe that my father's biggest problem was that he came from an academic background, and therefore mostly surrounded himself with other academics. I never heard him discuss money apart from when we had too little of it, and had to be even more cautious than normal. I don't believe denial of anything is good. In an ideal world we wouldn't have to worry about paying rent or putting food on the table. But we don't live in an ideal world. Most of us are dependent on making money to survive. It is therefore extremely important that you find friends and acquaintances who discuss investments, ideas and money matters if you want to become wealthy. Because you have to talk about these things to identify opportunities.

Many people who want to start up their own business, or

have a dream, choose to keep it to themselves. They don't want to involve too many people in their plans. There can be several reasons for such a strategy. Some are of the opinion that others could steal their idea if they share it too widely. And this could be a valid concern. History is full of examples of people or companies that have stolen other people's ideas. With limited resources there is very little an inventor can do if a powerful corporation chooses to run over you. Others are afraid they will never follow through with their grand plans. If you don't tell anybody about your plans, you can't fail. You're not a failure if nobody knows you even tried.

I would, however, like to propose an alternative strategy. Involve people in your plans, but select them carefully. And be specific about what you want from them. Your friends can either help you reach the next level, or they can hold you back for the rest of your life.

I played soccer when I was younger. I was the top scorer on my team along with my friend Hasan. One day we received an offer to play for a team, one age group above our own. We both accepted the offer. But I quickly re-joined my old team. I didn't like the feeling of not being best anymore. Hasan on the other hand continued to play with his new team, and one year later I got to play against him. It was an eye opener. Hasan had improved so much that he was running circles around me. After the game I asked how he enjoyed playing with the older boys, and I got the most surprising answer. He felt that he had had a bad year, he was struggling to make the team and didn't feel like he was as good as the other players. I was dumbfounded. The reality was that he had developed much more than me because he had been given the opportunity to play against kids better than him. I had stagnated because I had nobody to compete against anymore. That summer taught me that to get ahead, I would always have to challenge myself and make an effort to surround myself with people who were stronger and smarter than I was. People I could learn from.

Just the same entrepreneurs can't afford to be afraid of listening to advice or hiring people smarter than them. That is the only way to improve.

Most successful entrepreneurs therefore surround themselves with a handful of advisers whom they listen to. And it is a fact that several minds think better than one. The art is to know when to listen and when to follow your own intuition. Because if you always listen to others you will never become wealthy, and if you never listen to others – ditto.

The well-known author Napoleon Hill described this principle as 'The Mastermind' in his work Think and Grow Rich, which was published in 1937. With this expression he wanted to shed light on the fact that several brains pondering about the same problem are more effective than one single brain. Napoleon Hill interviewed successful entrepreneurs like the steel baron Andrew Carnegie, the founder of Ford Motor Company Henry Ford, and the inventor of the lightbulb, Thomas A. Edison. They all surrounded themselves with a small group of trusted advisers. Even though they always made the final decisions themselves, they had at their disposal a range of intelligent opinions that could be utilised in reaching the final conclusion. Instead of only their own mind, they had a 'Mastermind' at their disposal.

But it is not only other people's knowledge an entrepreneur should attempt to utilise. A lot of successful entrepreneurs raise money from external investors to establish or grow their company. Not everyone has wealthy parents, and often you need capital to get an idea from the drawing board to the market. By using other people's money you reduce the risk, but you also have to share the profits. The thought is that it is better to share a big cake than to hold on to a very small cake for yourself. And if you are not willing to share, there will most likely never be a cake at all.

David skimmed through the last pages of the principle. It was interesting, but it didn't give him any 'aha' experience. He didn't really know what to expect. But he knew he expected something more. Every time he started on a new principle he had this unrealistic expectation that he would learn something amazing. That somehow Professor Grossman had stumbled across Yossar Devan's secret and shared it in his manuscript. But it wasn't like that. Not at all.

Professor Grossman's principles of wealth were sound, and David didn't doubt that he would benefit from following all of them. But they wouldn't lead to any rapid change in his financial situation. And David wasn't patient enough to wait until he reached sixty-five before becoming a millionaire.

He wanted a change now.

He wanted to get rich quickly.

He did, however, feel a little bit better after having read the principle. Maybe this was one of those opportunities he should grab. He was often very quick to dismiss anything that didn't stack up on all levels. This could be a good quality for a conservative bank manager, but not always the best option for your own life. If David only made safe choices he would never know what could have been. Maybe the hunt for Yossar Devan's identity was one of those choices that could have a great impact on the rest of his life? Most successful people spoke about a couple of important crossroads in their lives. A couple of important decisions that truly changed the direction of their lives, and had tremendous impact on where they ended up. David decided to keep a more open attitude the next couple of days, to think larger, and focus on opportunities instead of threats.

He knew it would be difficult.

It was against his nature.

The airplane bumped and the captain's voice yet again filled the cabin, advising the passengers to fasten their seatbelts. David put down the Kindle reader and looked at his watch. He had no idea what he would discover in Turkey, and felt that he was on sketchy ground. What was he supposed to do when he landed? He needed to come up with a plan.

David had a growing suspicion that Peter Swarkowski hadn't been totally honest with him when telling the story about the picture of the kid he claimed was Yossar Devan. David could, to a certain degree, understand that Peter Swarkowski wanted to be cautious. After all he only knew David through Professor Grossman. But it was still frustrating. What was it that Peter Swarkowski hadn't told him? What was he hiding?

-19-

The Nikon watch on David's left wrist informed him the time was five past nine in the morning. It didn't feel like breakfast time though. David adjusted the time two hours forward - to local time Turkey. Almost time for lunch. It felt more appropriate. For the first time in his life David was struggling with jetlag. He just had to cave in and order a coffee even though he had stopped drinking coffee several years ago. He wondered if the small hotel he stayed at had a coffee bar. It had been the only half decent hotel near Yassihoyuk, the place where the fatal excavation had occurred in 1944.

Yassihoyuk was located an eight-hour drive from Bodrum, where David's dad had bought himself a vacation home some years ago. David's dad had, however, never been able to use the vacation home as planned as he died in a tragic car accident, only six months after having bought the place. It was then David decided to move to Australia and become a student again. You never knew what life had in store for you. The purchase of the place had greatly affected his dad's mood. For years he had been talking about getting himself a writer's lodge when he retired. And when he had finally made the step it seemed like his life had blossomed. He was only halfway into his first year as a retiree when he most likely fell asleep behind the wheel of his car. The car had veered off a cliff and ended up in the ocean several hundred meters below. David's mum hadn't handled the situation very well. She had been home in Norway at the time of the accident, and David had done his best to comfort her as he struggled with his own grief. One day, however, his mum had told him that she was finished crying, life had to go on. She had rented out their house in Norway and moved to Turkey, permanently. David was shocked, but understood that this was her way of handling the loss of her husband. Everyone grieved in their own way, and she wanted to be at the place that had made his dad happy again. She had lived there ever since. David had moved to Australia shortly after.

David checked his watch again. He had changed his mind. He wanted to head straight to the excavation site to see whether he could get some work done before it got too dark. He jumped into the rental car, a tiny red Toyota Prius he had picked up from AVIS, and keyed the address Peter Swarkowski had scribbled on a piece of paper into the car's navigation system. He turned on the engine and hit the road. It was a surprisingly comfortable car, although it was hard to hear that it actually had an engine. Not that he cared much about cars anyway. True, he had looked up to his uncle because he always drove the latest model of Mercedes, but that had been many years ago. He had changed since then. Over the years he had almost totally lost his interest in cars, especially the interest in spending money on cars. The few cars he still liked were not regarded as symbols of status and wealth anyway.

He actually just had one dream car. If he ever managed to get so wealthy that money didn't matter, then he would buy himself a Ford Mustang Shelby GT 500, 1967 model. A sight for the eyes, without being show-offy.

But it was unlikely he would be able to afford that anytime soon.

The drive took half an hour. When he arrived he noticed that the area was closed off to tourists, which there were none of anyway. Instead the area was riddled with Turkish soldiers. David walked over to one of them, who looked like he was more asleep than awake.

"Is it possible to take a closer look at the excavation?" David asked.

"No," the soldier replied. Leaning against the fence that sealed off the area where the excavation had occurred back in the 1940s. A concrete bunker was placed squarely in the middle. But there didn't seem to be any activity there.

"I just want to take some pictures in relation to an article I am working on," David said.

The soldier recognised the accent. "From Norway? Ahh, magnificent Norway. I speak Norway," he said.

David used the opportunity to try to build some rapport with the soldier and nodded interestedly when the soldier told David how easy it was to bed Norwegian women in Alanya. He claimed to have slept with fifty-seven of them. And he wasn't all that bad in Norwegian, so David reasoned that he must at least have had a few conversations with them. But David's ass-kissing left little result. The soldier, Antonio, explained that the whole area had been closed off to tourists many years ago, and was now primarily used by the military. It was unthinkable to let any civilians into the area.

David sat down on a rock and opened his backpack. He pulled out a few pages he had copied from the folder Neill Flynn's wife had given him in London. Neill Flynn had constructed a detailed overview over the funds flowing to Turkey from Yossar Devan's UK operations. The money seemed to have ended up in Suiris Export and Import, or Gordion Export and Import, which it had later changed name to.

The strange thing was that the Turkish company had never made a single cent. Still Yossar Devan had kept wiring tens of millions to it in the early 1970s.

The excavation site was obviously off limits so he thought he might as well go and have a look at what Yossar Devan had spent so much money on. According to the map Yossar Devan's old company was located only a few kilometres from the excavation site.

David returned to the rental car and started driving in the direction of Yossar Devan's old company. He had tried to Google the company in London, but nothing had come up. It appeared that the company had been shut down several decades ago.

When David finally arrived at the entry point of an ill-kept dirt road, he realised that he had been right. A rusty steel boom blocked the road. And the area was surrounded by a tall metal fence that seemed to stretch for several kilometres in every direction. It didn't look like anybody had opened the gate for years. It had rusted straight through. David exited the car and attempted to lift the boom. The endeavour was futile. Two massive locks kept the boom down. Slightly frustrated he parked his car on the side of the road, and filled up his backpack with two bottles of water, a flashlight and a couple of bananas. A shot-out rusty sign hanging on the fence warned that the area was private and supervised, but given the state of the place David considered the threat empty. He ducked under the gate and started to walk towards Yossar Devan's only money-losing business.

It took him almost forty-five minutes to reach the top of the hill where an enormous building rose up from nowhere. It was an almost surreal sight. A massive industrial building in the middle of no-man's land. From his previous jobs in banking and journalism, David was well-versed in visiting industrial areas. And most often he managed to quickly assess whether a business was going well or not, just by inspecting their premises. Busy or idle, clean or dirty, happy or frustrated workers, inventory or empty shelves. There were always a million small signs that could reveal how your business was doing. Here there were no signs. The building just didn't seem to fit into its surroundings. It was as if someone, with more money than brains, had built something though they didn't really know what it was supposed to be. A bumpy dirt road, minimal parking space, only a gigantic building in the middle of nowhere. It went against everything Yossar Devan stood for. David increased his pace and jogged up to what appeared to have been an entrance at some point in time. He grabbed the handle.

To his great surprise the door opened.

He entered.

A bird got scared and flew up to the ceiling. The echo from the wings bounced off the walls. David stepped over some empty beer cans and understood why the door had been open. This was an ideal place for young teenagers wanting to be by themselves.

He peered into the darkness of the empty building, and wondered why Yossar Devan had built it. Why had a brilliant man, a man who never made a bad decision, built this massive building?

The next hour or so was spent thoroughly inspecting the premises. David consumed two full bottles of water, but he didn't become any wiser. There were simply no clues as to what the building would have been used for back in the 1970s.

Frustrated, he decided that it had been enough sightseeing for the day. He only had one more thing to check out – the area surrounding the premises. He started off with the front of the building, but didn't find anything out of the ordinary. It wasn't until he arrived at the back of the building, the side that faced a small hill, that something caught his attention. There was another dirt road leading straight into the mountain, almost as an entrance to a mine.

He glanced at his watch. His stomach was making growling sounds and he regretted not having brought any food except for the bananas he had already eaten, but he didn't want to return the next day either. If he was going to check out the mountainside, he needed to do it now.

–20–

When he approached the hill he realised that it wasn't a mine he had seen. It looked more like the entrance to a bunker. Like one of those he had seen when he completed his mandatory military service in Norway. They usually contained large halls where the army could store materials and ammunition. He pushed the rusty steel door aside, and entered. Armed only with his flashlight he entered a narrow tunnel. It was dark and David felt uncomfortable. There had been empty beer cans everywhere in the abandoned building. What if someone was inside the mountain? It was an ideal hideout if you wanted to be left alone. What if someone had an illegal operation going on with the mountain gallery as a base? What if he fell and hurt himself? Nobody knew where he was, he would never be found.

David contemplated turning around, but decided to proceed a bit farther into the tunnel. He swiped his flashlight along the walls and what he saw made his blood turn to ice. The walls were covered with black ash, as if there had been a fire inside the tunnel. Why had Yossar Devan constructed the building? Why had he dug into the mountain? Why were there all these burn marks on the walls? David's curiosity got the better of him. He couldn't turn around now. He had travelled half across the globe to find out who Yossar Devan had been. Right now he was pursuing the hottest lead he had, the only lead he had. He had followed the money and that lead had taken him here. It was the abandoned building and this hole in the mountain that Yossar Devan had spent enormous amounts to construct. Why? David wiped some sweat off his forehead and pointed the flashlight forwards again. His rental car was parked by the steel boom. Somebody would find it and add two and two together if he didn't return to his hotel by nightfall.

They would find him.

Nobody disappeared without a trace.

Nobody except Yossar Devan.

After a couple of minutes of slow pace walking, which actually had felt more like an hour, David finally arrived at what he had expected to find inside the mountain. A hall. It was smaller than David had anticipated, maybe because he only fifteen minutes earlier had been inside one of the largest buildings he had ever seen. But it was still an impressive construction that revealed itself in front of him. If he hadn't known the area had belonged to Yossar Devan's old company, Suiris Export and Import, then he would have thought this was a military installation. It was hard to get a proper overview, with only a small flashlight as the only source of light, but David estimated that the hall was about a thousand square metres, with a ceiling height of about six metres. Everywhere he pointed the flashlight he could see the same burn marks he had seen inside the tunnel. It was impossible to guess what Yossar Devan had used the hall for, though. Initially, David had thought that it could have been for storage. A more secure alternative than the large building outside. But when he was standing there, inside the main hall, he had a distinct feeling that it had been built for something else. The burn marks on the walls, the apparatus to seal the room. It was almost as if it was a military test room. A room where someone had been conducting experiments.

David had nevertheless seen what he wanted to see: The massive building and the gallery inside the mountain. Nothing brought him closer to the real identity of Yossar Devan though. An indication that Devan hadn't been perfect, maybe? Evidence that he sometimes had been wrong and made bad investments. But nothing that could clear up the mystery of who Yossar Devan had really been.

Unless Peter Swarkowski had been right in London. Unless Peter Swarkowski had been right about Yossar Devan being the SS General Dr Hans Kammler's unknown son. If that was the case, he could have been using this site to experiment on new weapons. If Yossar Devan's ultimate goal had been to re-establish the Third Reich then this place could quite possibly have been part of that plan.

If that was the case David was glad he had disappeared. The world was a much better place without the Nazi ideology.

It took David almost an hour to return to his car. He was tired, hungry and thirsty. He had originally planned to return to the hotel, but then he had realised that he probably wouldn't last that long. He needed food as soon as possible. So he stopped at the first restaurant he saw on his way back.

He started to wonder whether he had chosen a too-local restaurant when he saw the clientele, but he decided to enter anyway.

The average age was about eighty-five, and most of the patrons sat around wooden tables, playing chess and drinking tea. David knew that looks could be deceiving; he had eaten some of his best meals at restaurants where his expectations had been low. Eat at the most popular local restaurant and choose the most popular local dish. Then they know how to prepare it and will use fresh ingredients, his well-travelled dad had always said. The trick had worked so far in David's life and the afternoon's meal turned out to be no exception. The food was amazing and David started to get some of his optimism back. He paid for the meal and rose from the table. As he was pushing his chair back underneath the table he accidentally dropped his backpack on the floor. The Kindle reader and Chief inspector Neill Flynn's file on Yossar Devan spilled out on the floor. An older woman, dressed in a full-covered black dress, bent down to assist David in retrieving the content. As she picked up the Chief Inspector's file, one of the pictures of a young Yossar Devan fell out. She blinked twice. Then she shrieked and fell backwards. It was almost as if she had received an electric shock. For a moment she just sat there with a face as pale as a ghost. Then she started screaming. "Seytan! Seytan!" she cried before storming out of the restaurant and into the kitchen. David had hardly gotten back on his feet before an aggressive man arrived from the kitchen, knife in hand. In seconds David was ushered out of the restaurant.

As he stood outside, uncertain of what had just happened an old man bumped into him. "Follow me," he whispered before continuing his walk. David was confused and didn't really know what he should do. The rational choice would be to return to the hotel. But he wasn't the normal, boring David anymore. He had made a commitment to be bolder, to make gutsier choices. He decided to follow the old man. With rapid steps they walked through narrow streets and dark back alleys. David had totally lost his sense of direction. Confused, he squinted at the grey house walls that curled around them like snakes. It was as if the streets became narrower and less populated with every step they took. The blood pumped through his veins. What the hell was going on?

Then suddenly the old man stopped in his tracks. He turned quickly, so that he faced David when he started speaking. "Why are you here?"

"I'm a student. I'm doing some research on an excavation back in 1944. It was done close by, on the Tumuli Heights."

"What is your article about?" the old man asked.

"It's a documentary about a German general," David lied. If he really was on the trail of Yossar Devan's true identity, he would have to keep that secret to himself. Nobody else could know. If the secret spilled out before Professor Grossman could reveal it in his book, the whole marketing stunt would be worthless.

"And why do you carry a picture of the Alchemist?" the old man asked, pointing at the pictures David still held in his hand. He hadn't had time to put them back in his bag since the incident in the restaurant.

"Who?"

"The Alchemist. Why do you have pictures of the Alchemist?" the old man asked impatiently.

A few seconds passed before David's brain managed to process the information. The old man was referring to the picture of a young Yossar Devan. He was actually confirming that he recognised Yossar Devan.

"This kid?" David asked holding the picture of a young Yossar Devan, having just arrived in London in the late 1940s, up in front of the old man's face.

"Yes," the old man answered, slightly irritated. "Why do you have pictures of the Alchemist?"

"He was at the excavation I'm interested in. He was there, along with a German general by the name of Dr Hans Kammler, in 1944," David replied, and pulled out the picture of Dr Hans Kammler and the young kid with the scar. The picture Peter Swarkowski had given him in London. "Same person?" David asked.

The old man nodded. "Come with me. I can help you."

David followed the old man, uncertain about what was about to happen.

"The kid in the picture caused a lot of trouble for us. After he disappeared a curse has rested over us all." The old man spit on the ground.

"A curse? What do you mean?" David asked.

"I'll explain later. Not here."

They walked through narrow roads for almost twenty minutes before finally arriving at an old chalkstone house. The old man opened the door and went inside. David waited outside. Seconds later the old man arrived at the door and invited David inside. "You'll have to excuse the mess. I'm an old widower and cleaning isn't the biggest priority when you're arriving at life's end," the old man said. They entered a spartanly decorated house. A square wooden table was placed up against one of the walls. A lonely plate and an empty glass rested on top of it. The old man pulled out one of the two chairs and indicated for David to sit down. "I've waited for the day someone would come asking about the Alchemist," the old man said.

"Why do you call him the Alchemist? What was his real name?"

"Nuri Turan, Nuri Turan was his real name. But nobody called him that. Not after he disappeared. The Alchemist arrived here with his father and mother in the early 1940s. I call him the Alchemist because that is what he and his family were, alchemists." The old man scratched his chin. "His father was an archaeologist. When he started digging in the ground it was the beginning of the disaster."

"You mean the accident where four locals and eleven German soldiers died?" David asked.

"The accident was nothing. It was what happened afterwards that was truly terrible."

"I don't understand," David said.

"You say you came here to write about the German general. Don't you intend to write about what he did?"

David stared at the old man. "Tell me what happened. Tell me everything," he said.

David was then told the story about how Yossar Devan's dad had led an excavation on the Tumuli Heights in 1944. The Tumuli Heights consisted of a multitude of graves from different time eras. Yossar Devan's father had been working on the excavation of what was believed to be the grave of a king. Not because of the size, but because of what they had found inside the grave. The Tumuli had been around sixty metres high and about three hundred metres in diameter. Something that strongly indicated that it had belonged to a person of importance, someone of stature. It was however inside the Tumuli they had made their important discovery. Inside the grave they had found some drinking cups from the Iron Age, and some basic wooden and bronze items. Things you would expect to find in any grave on the Tumuli Heights. The inner chamber had been relatively spacious, six by six metres wide and four metres tall. Placed on top of the remains of a wooden chest they had found the skeleton of an old man, estimated to be about sixty when he had died a violent death. Nothing out of the ordinary. A grave like many others on the tumuli Heights. But in one of the corners of the grave they had found a door. A door with an ancient Phrygian inscription that the archaeologists suspected read 'Mida'. "That discovery was what unleashed our hell," the old man said. "Although it was never confirmed, there were rumours that they had located King Midas' grave. Not long after the rumours started the German general arrived with his platoon of Nazis. The excavation was shut down, and only a handful of locals were allowed to continue working on the excavation. Nobody knows what they discovered in there, but there were of course rumours."

"What sort of rumours?"

"There were rumours that the hidden door led to King Midas' grave."

"I thought King Midas' grave was discovered in 1957. They advertise guided tours at my hotel."

The old man laughed. "It's all a charade. A distraction from the truth. The grave they opened in 1957 most likely belongs to King Midas' father, Gordias."

"So what did the Nazis find in the real King Midas' grave?" David asked.

"Nobody knows. When the excavation collapsed the grave took its secrets with it."

"You refer to the accident?" David asked.

"Yes. When the grave collapsed there were eleven German soldiers inside, and five local workers, including the Alchemist. Everybody died that day. Everyone except the Alchemist."

"How did Yossar Devan survive? I mean how did the Alchemist survive?"

"It's hard to say. He was found unconscious several kilometres from the grave, lying on the banks of the river. Some local gold diggers brought him to the local doctor." The old man stopped. It appeared that he was considering what had happened to Yossar Devan. "There are lots of underground caves in this area. Somehow he must have managed to escape into one of them, and followed it all the way to the river."

The old man coughed. David leant in to check that he was ok. He was swiftly brushed away.

"The German general was very interested in talking to the Alchemist. But he must have seen something that he knew would be dangerous, because he ran away from the doctor's house that very night. And he has never been seen since. Not until you pulled out those pictures," the old man said, pointing at David's backpack. The old man glanced over at David. It was obvious that it was hard for him to talk about this.

"As revenge, the general gathered all youths between the ages of sixteen and twenty at the city square. He threatened to execute them all unless someone told him where the Alchemist was hiding. Of course, nobody knew where the Alchemist was hiding. So the general had a crane towed into the middle of the city square. It was one of the cranes they had been using for the excavation. Some of the German soldiers attached a steel beam to the crane and tied a noose around the neck of four young kids. They got one minute to tell him where the Alchemist was hiding." The old man was on the verge of crying. "How could they possibly know where the Alchemist was hiding? Nobody knew where he was. The general kept going for more than an hour. Mothers and fathers, friends, brothers and sisters. They were all forced to witness twenty-two young kids hang that afternoon. They were forced to witness that their kids were hanged by their necks until there was no more life left in their tiny bodies. The kids that were standing in line had to first witness their friends be executed before they were hanged themselves." The old man collapsed, crying. "Write this story. Write the truth about what happened here in Gordion." The old man rose from the table, and walked into his kitchen.

David was almost paralysed by the shocking revelations. He was lost for words. Peter Swarkowski had been wrong. Yossar Devan was definitely not Dr Hans Kammler's son. Yossar Devan was the son of a poor Turkish archaeologist. The boy had happened to stumble across a secret grave here sixty years ago. A secret grave that had led to the blood of twenty-two innocent children being spilt.

"What happened to the Alchemist's family?" David asked, after having pulled himself together.

"His family's fate was sealed the day he disappeared. The father and mother, Hakan and Adja were executed together with the kids. They were shot in the head."

"Is it possible to find out some more about what happened the day the grave collapsed? Are some of the locals who assisted with the excavation still alive?"

"You can try Samet Erkin, he was only fourteen at the time and thus his life was spared."

"Thanks for the help. I promise you that I will let the world know what happened here," David said, before he quickly exited the old man's house.

He wanted to speak to Samet Erkin.

-21-

Samet Erkin had just received a delivery of three whole lambs, and was well into the monotonous work of making them into sellable products. He enjoyed the systematic work. First he split the carcass in two, along the spine. The metal saw screeched as he gently pushed the carcass forward.

Then he split it in two, just below the sixth rib. He was well into dividing the carcass into lamb chops when a young foreigner entered the shop. Samet Erkin turned off the electric saw, washed his hands, and walked over to the counter.

"How can I help you today my friend?"

David perused the selection at the counter. He always felt compelled to buy something from people he was going to ask for information. But he couldn't really see a point in buying meat only to throw it away. So he dove straight into it. "I'm a student. I'm working on a story about a crime committed here during the Second World War, and I was wondering if you would be willing to help me out by answering some questions."

Samet Erkin shrugged his shoulders. "The past is the past. Sometimes it is best to leave it as it is."

"I would really appreciate if you could spare five minutes," David said.

Samet Erkin was already back at the metal saw. The ear-ringing sound of metal against frozen meat made it almost impossible for David to let himself be heard. David waved to Samet Erkin. "I need some information about the Alchemist," he yelled.

Samet Erkin turned off the saw and removed his earmuffs. "Did you say the Alchemist?" he asked.

David nodded. "Yes, I'm trying to figure out what happened here that day the grave collapsed."

"The coward ran away. That's what happened."

"Why do you think he ran away?" David asked. He had to keep the fire burning. He had managed to get Samet Erkin talking.

"He only thought about himself. That's why he ran away."

"How could he have known what the German general would do? How could he have known the consequences of his actions?" David asked.

"They found something special in that grave. Something the Alchemist knew would have consequences. Still he chose to flee. He chose to leave everybody here helpless. He was as guilty as the general who ordered the executions."

David was surprised by Samet Erkin's strong reaction. There was something more lurking behind all this aggression. Something David had to lure out. "Well, then that's how I will portray it in my article. The Alchemist was a coward who left all the kids in the village to die." David turned around. Ready to leave the shop.

"He was never a coward," Samet Erkin shrieked.

"I don't understand. You just said he ran away. That he left everybody to die." David looked straight into Samet Erkin's eyes when he made his accusations. The effect was immediate. Samet Erkin suddenly seemed uncomfortable. He started to pace back and forth behind the counter.

"There is something I need to show you," he finally said. He threw his bloodstained apron over the electric meat saw, and waved for David to join him behind the counter. David followed him up a set of steep stairs that ended up in what David assumed was Samet Erkin's living room. Old and grainy black-and-white pictures of Samet Erkin, shot at various mountain tops, decorated the walls. A lamp hung from the ceiling and gave the room a simple and moody glow, like an underexposed Polaroid picture. "If you are really going to write about what happened back then, you might as well get it right," Samet Erkin said. He walked over to an old desk, located a key, and opened one of two drawers. The old wooden drawer creaked when it was pulled out. "The truth is that the Alchemist didn't know what had happened in Gordion until months later. He sent me a letter where he asked for forgiveness for all the pain he had inflicted upon us. He thought that he would do least damage if he left the village." Samet Erkin handed David an old, and yellowish letter. "He never gave me the chance to forgive him," Samet Erkin said with a voice on the brink of breaking. "I didn't lose one brother that dark day in 1944, I lost two. Don't portray the Alchemist as a coward. He brought a lot of grief to this village, but he was never a coward."

David handed the yellowish piece of paper back to Samet Erkin. Why had the Nazis been so interested in the excavation of a grave in Turkey? This happened at the height of the Second World War. Why had this grave been so important? Was it possible that it could have been King Midas' grave? David was intrigued. Dr Hans Kammler was the key. David realised that in order to find out what had been inside that grave he needed to learn more about Dr Kammler.

Wen Ning crossed the road with firm steps. In the corner of his eye he could see the Norwegian exiting the butcher shop. Who was the old man? And what had he told the Norwegian? Wen Ning hardened his grip on the knife in his pocket. But it didn't give him the relief he sought.

He had been fighting the urge for a long time. He had been so patient. But he couldn't stop what was coming.

The Norwegian disappeared around a corner. Wen Ning stopped and looked around. Nobody was watching. He observed the old man where he stood inside the butcher shop, staring out into space. Wen Ning slipped the knife back into his pocket.

It wouldn't be necessary.

A butcher shop.

So many sharp tools.

So easy to have an accident.

-22-

David keyed in the phone number to Peter Swarkowski. He answered on the third ring. It sounded like David had woken him up.

"How did it go, David? Have you found out who Yossar Devan really was?"

"Yes," David replied. "But it is not as you thought. Yossar Devan wasn't Dr Hans Kammler's son. Dr Kammler killed Yossar Devan's family."

"What are you saying?" Peter Swarkowski bellowed.

"Yossar Devan was the son of a local archaeologist involved with the botched excavation on the Tumuli Heights. I haven't been able to confirm all the details yet, but I have two independent sources verifying Yossar Devan's true identity. His birth name was Nuri Turan, son of Hakan and Adja. When the excavation site collapsed Yossar Devan was the only survivor. And he must have seen something special. Something that was important to Dr Hans Kammler and the Nazis. Because he chose to run away. As revenge Dr Kammler executed his parents and all kids between the ages of sixteen and twenty in the village."

"Oh my god," Peter Swarkowski exclaimed. "What did they find in that excavation?"

"Nobody seems to know for sure. But it appears that they

were looking for King Midas' grave."

There was a moment of silence on the other line. "Are you still there?" David asked.

"I'm still here. I'm just considering what this could mean," Peter Swarkowski replied.

"Why were Dr Hans Kammler and the Nazis interested in this old grave? I thought the story about King Midas was an old myth from ancient Greece. Why would Dr Kammler be interested in a myth?" David asked.

"There are a lot of things I don't fully understand with regards to Dr Kammler," Peter Swarkowski replied. "The deeper I dig, the stranger it gets."

"What do you mean?"

"The four-star SS general Dr Hans Kammler is hardly mentioned in the established story of Nazi Germany. But it appears that he had almost unlimited power by the end of the war. His Kammlerstab, the secret laboratory where they conducted research into the development of new weapons systems, had virtually no restrictions. They were free to do whatever they wanted."

"What sort of research did they do?" David asked.

"It's hard to say. All documents and drawings were destroyed in the last few days of the war. But it appears that a project named Die Glocke was the main priority of Kammlerstab during the latter part of the war. And that's the oddest thing. When England invaded Nazi Germany in 1945 they chose to attack Pilsen and Prague before they headed towards Berlin. I've always wondered why the Allied Forces took this detour. From a tactical point of view there was nothing to gain. Except that it was in Pilsen, in the old Skoda factory, that Dr Hans Kammler and his Kammlerstab kept one of their largest research sites."

"So you are proposing that the English took the detour to attempt to catch Dr Hans Kammler?"

"It can appear that way. Whatever Dr Hans Kammler was up to in Pilsen, it must have been pretty dangerous stuff, so dangerous in fact that the Allied Forces deemed him a greater threat than Adolf Hitler and his Berlin."

David wiped some sweat pearls off his forehead.

"I'll try to find out some more. Is it ok if I continue to call you on this number?"

That will be fine. Call me anytime," Peter Swarkowski said before hanging up.

David remained motionless, just staring out on the barren landscape in front of him.

Who was Dr Hans Kammler? And why had he been so important to the Allied Forces?

-23-

Professor Evan Grossman packed his suitcase, placed it on the bed, and sat down next to it. He was stressed. He studied himself in the mirror. The chiselled face didn't have its normal sparkle. It was pale. Dark rings encircled his bloodshot eyes. The three-day beard hardly improved his look. He looked more like a homeless man than a respected university professor. The doorbell rang and Professor Grossman jumped up from the bed.

They were here.

They had found him.

He sat down on the bed again, hands folded in his lap. How could he have been so stupid? All his problems could have been solved. The solution had been there, right in front of him. Instead everything was now over.

So close, and now it was all over.

He rose. With brisk steps he walked over to the nightstand. He pulled out the top drawer and stared at the gun he had purchased in Upper Coomera two days earlier. The heavily tattooed Maori had told him it was an ok gun for self-defence; he just had to be close to his target when he pulled the trigger.

When Professor Grossman looked at the small Glock he regretted not buying a bigger gun.

-24-

D avid surveyed the note on the wall next to the broken Starbucks sign. Free wireless internet. Exactly what the doctor prescribed. He ordered a cup of Turkish tea and sat down to work. Many years in open offices had taught him to work structured and block out his surroundings. He started with Wikipedia.

General Dr Ing Hans Friedrich Karl Franz Kammler was born in 1901 in Stettin Germany. In 1919 he volunteered for military service in the right wing Rossbach Freikorps, and in 1932 he was awarded his Dr Ing title after completing studies at the Technische Hochschule der Freien Stadt Danzig, and some years of practical work in building administration. This background in building administration would become beneficial later in Dr Kammler's career as he by the end of the war was responsible for both construction of concentration camps and Germany's secret weapons projects. In addition he was also in charge of more conventional projects like the construction of V-2 rockets. He was infamous for his extreme focus on delivering projects within unrealistic deadlines. Human casualties didn't seem to matter.

David stared out into street. Dr Kammler was evil reincarnated. But why would such a person have been interested in the excavation of a grave in Turkey? Why would he have travelled to

Turkey when the Second World War was at its most intense? This was in 1944. The weapons race with the Allied Forces would have been at its peak. Why go to Turkey? What was it that had been so important about this excavation that one of the most senior SS officers in the Third Reich had travelled there personally to witness the opening of the grave?

The Wikipedia article didn't reveal any clues. But it did have some references to the authors Peter Swarkowski had mentioned in London. The authors had however limited credibility, as they had based their theories on relatively few and questionable sources. But as David's father had always said, where there is smoke, there is usually fire.

David therefore continued to search for clues. Hidden details that could explain why Dr Kammler had been interested in an excavation of the possible grave of King Midas.

David decided to read about the concentration camps Dr Kammler had been responsible for constructing. Auschwitz wasn't one large concentration camp, but rather it was a network of forty-eight different concentration camps. The three largest ones, Auschwitz I, II and III, all had different functions to perform. Auschwitz I, base camp, was the location for the administration, while Auschwitz II, Birkenau, was the largest extermination camp. More than 960,000 Jews and 75,000 Poles were killed in just this camp. Auschwitz III, Monowitz or The Buna which it was also called, was a work camp for the German chemical company IG Farbens. The strange thing was that the largest of the Buna factories had been totally empty when the Allied Forces took over the area. It hadn't only been empty. It appeared that it had never been used. This massive building, covering an area of fifty-three thousand square metres, had been the recipient of great attention by the Soviet troops, who closed off the surrounding area for days before moving on. The massive empty building belonged to Dr Hans Kammler's Kammlerstab. Surviving Jews told about rumours of a new weapon that Dr Kammler had been developing inside the building, a Wunderwaffe. A new and revolutionary weapon. A weapon that could change the course of the war.

David blinked. He wasn't sure why. But he thought this Buna factory could be important. He bookmarked the Wikipedia page before rubbing his eyes. They were dry and tired after many hours of staring at the computer screen. He knew he soon needed a break. He looked away from the screen.

Dr Kammler had worked on multiple secret weapons projects and David had problems understanding the relevance to the possible burial chamber for the ancient King Midas. Rightly the Nazis had been obsessed with the occult, but the story about King Midas was just an ancient Greek myth about a king who had possessed the ability to turn everything he touched into gold – an alchemist. What did this myth have to do with the weapons race towards the end of the Second World War?

With regret, David decided he had to do some more research before calling it a night. He opened up a new folder in the web browser and wrote 'change lead to gold'. Eight and a half million hits popped up. Most of the hits were about alchemy. David started the monotonous work of going through the pages. He filtered out the pages that seemed unprofessional, and started the tedious work of getting an overview. This was the problem with the internet. There was so much information that you could easily spend several days trying to find what you were looking for. Search engines like Google and Bing used relatively similar algorithms to rank their searches. That meant that the pages that linked to a lot of other pages always would rank high on relevant hits. David, however, wasn't just after the most popular or conventional theories. He had to be open to the fact that the answers might not be obvious. That they most likely weren't obvious.

He therefore needed a source. Someone who could help him navigate through all the irrelevant information. He pulled out his wallet and located Sophie Masson's business card. She had been seated next to him on the flight from Brisbane, and she had told him to give her a call if he ever found himself in Turkey. Well, he was there now. Hadn't she said that she worked as a physics professor? That meant she would have contacts in the academic world. Maybe she could be of assistance? It was also a convenient excuse to give her a call, he thought. He had enjoyed their conversation on the plane. He put the card back in his wallet. He would give her a call later. First he wanted to eat something and read another 'principle of wealth'. One principle each day, the professor had told him. At least that gave him some stability in his life.

He rose from the table and exited the Starbucks café. He didn't need to venture far. The smell of freshly cooked kebab reached his nostrils and led him to the neighbouring restaurant.

After having ordered a kebab and a local beer, he pulled out his Kindle reader. In the beginning he hadn't been so excited. He still felt that a book should be something that was made out of paper. But gradually he had grown fond of his Kindle reader. It was practical that the professor could send the principles directly to him, and it was so tiny that he could bring it everywhere. He slid the power button to the side, and the grey-font screen came alive.

David started to read.

Principle 6: Let your money work for you

The most important lesson I got from my years at sea was how money really worked. At first I was content. I didn't spend anything when I was at sea fishing, so I had a fair amount of money available whenever I was on land leave. But I was never able to save anything. What came in went out. Sometimes even more.

One of my colleagues seemed to be in a worse situation. He occasionally joined the rest of us for a beer. But he always left early. One evening I asked him whether he needed to borrow some money. He laughed. "The problem isn't that I can't afford drinking with you guys. The problem is that I don't have time. I have to get up early tomorrow morning. I have to go to work."

"Go to work?" I asked, confused. "We don't have to be back on the boat until Monday."

"I mean my real job," he answered. He told me that the fishing gave him enough money to cover his living costs. But he wasn't a fisherman.

"Not a fisherman? Then, what are you?" I asked

"Come and see for yourself tomorrow," he said, and told me the name of a building.

After a long and hard night out with the boys I was neither in the mood nor shape to go see him. But an appointment was an appointment.

I met him at the address he had given me. He had his hands full, and was busy stitching up fishnets. "Have you got two jobs?" I asked. "No, this is my building," he replied. I looked around. It couldn't be true. The building was at least two hundred square metres, and expensive equipment was scattered around on the floor. "How can you afford all this?" I asked. "You never have any money when we go out drinking." "I've got money to go out drinking," he replied, "and this costs me nothing. On the contrary I make money on this," he said. "I have a disease called Parkinson's. I am healthy now, but I don't know how long it will last. I try to put my money to work so that it can work for me when the day comes that I can't work for myself anymore."

He explained that he rented out equipment to fishing boats. So every month, day and night, his money was working for him. My money on the other hand was left at the nearest pub.

I felt so incredibly stupid that day. I had thought I was a hotshot who would be buying a poor colleague a beer. And then it turned out I was the poor one. I was the one who didn't understand how money worked. How you either could work for money or let money work for you.

That day I decided to let money work for me. I realised it was the only way I could ever achieve my goal of becoming financially independent.

David put down the Kindle reader and considered his own situation. His biggest, and only investment, was the tiny apartment he had back in Norway. Previously he had always felt slightly richer when there had been reports of rising property prices, and slightly poorer when the property prices were dropping. Now, as he rented out the apartment instead of living in it by himself, he understood how this feeling of wealth had been illusory. The important thing wasn't how many percent points the property market rose or dropped every quarter, the important thing was how much money he was paid in rent each month. How hard his money worked for him.

He needed to invest more.

He needed to let his money work harder.

Why did it take so long? Why hadn't he revealed himself yet? He had to understand that he had been found out, that there was no point in still hiding.

Wen Ning had no respect for weak people. People who gave up at the first sign of resistance. For many years he had looked up to the man with the secret. The man with the many faces.

The man they had called the Alchemist.

The man they had called Yossar Devan.

But who was it he had looked up to? Yossar Devan had been weak. He hadn't been anything to look up to. He never had what it took. Wen Ning was the right one, the chosen one. Didn't he see that? Didn't he understand that everything that had happened was destined? That everything had led them towards this?

Wen Ning firmed his grip on the knife handle. He immediately felt calmer. He studied the Norwegian where he sat eating a kebab and drinking a beer. The Norwegian was weak. He resorted to alcohol when he was stressed. He seemed confused and nervous where he sat, surveying everything around him. But he hadn't discovered Wen Ning.

Wen Ning was too good to be exposed by this amateur.

He was however a useful amateur.

A useful idiot.

A useful idiot who would lead Wen Ning straight to his target.

-25-

Sophie Masson pounded the palm of her fist on the table.

"It's not fair," she cried. "It's not fair." She glanced at the letter on the table in front of her. It was another rejection letter.

"Why do they only want String Theory researchers? Don't they understand it is a gigantic mistake?"

She looked over at her colleague Franz with genuine frustration in her eyes. He had grown accustomed to her outbursts a long time ago. He was the vent for Sophie's anger with the allocation of research grants. He wasn't unfamiliar with rejection letters himself. Franz worked on climate research. And if you didn't work on something that included the two words 'global warming' you wouldn't win any grants in his department. Franz was, however, a bit more pragmatic than his colleague Sophie. He had therefore simply incorporated the word 'global warming' forty-three times in his last application for research grants, even though the study had nothing to do with it. It had given him, and a team of four other scientists, financial support for the next three years. The most important thing was always to get funding to do your job. You could always ask for forgiveness later. Sophie Masson was driven by principles though, and couldn't imagine doing the same. Thus now she had ended up in the unfortunate situation that all the available funding had been appropriated towards String Theory research programs. A theory she didn't agree with. Her last few days, since returning from the physicist conference in Brisbane, had been a dogfight with the research director. She felt that the whole world was against her.

"Do you know what he called me today? He called me an alchemist. I believe it was meant as an insult, but I'll take it as a compliment. Many of the most brilliant scientists of the last centuries were alchemists." Sophie smiled. That's what they had called her old professor as well.

"So what do you do now, Sophie? It's not smart to make everyone who matters an enemy. It doesn't hurt to have a friend now and then."

"I have enough friends," Sophie answered. "I've got more than five hundred friends on Facebook."

Franz laughed. "You are probably right, but you never make it easy for yourself."

"If something is easy then the result will never be any more than average."

"Are you practising your acceptance speech for the Nobel Price, or are you just your usual arrogant you?" Franz asked.

"To believe in what I do is not arrogant, Franz. To believe you know everything though, to bet all your funding and resources on one card, that's arrogant. And that's what our physics department is doing right now. They are directing all funding towards improving the String Theory. What if it turns out that the theory is wrong? It will be like an investigation where all resources are allocated towards one suspect. You try to build a case, and you are totally oblivious of other potential perpetrators. All clues pointing in a different direction than the suspect you want convicted are ignored. In the real world that usually ends up in gross miscarriage of justice. In physics we will end up with a wasted decade." Sophie slammed her palm on the desk again. "I'll show the bastard."

She walked off into her office and sat down next to her laptop. She logged onto the University's database and punched in 'alchemist' while sipping her coffee. She got a couple of hundred thousand hits. She keyed in 'alchemists and physics', and narrowed down the search to a couple of hundred hits. She flipped through the first few ones without finding anything interesting. She wasn't sure what she was looking for, but she had nothing better to do. That arrogant bastard of a research director had called her an alchemist. She owed it to herself to at least find out what an alchemist really was. Most of the hits were about various alchemists trying to transform different types of metal into gold. After having skimmed through a dozen or so articles there was one research paper that caught her attention. 'Nuclear transformation' it was called. It claimed that scientists had actually been successful in transforming the atoms in one element into another element with the help of nuclear power. The procedure was, however, so energy- and cost-consuming that there was little risk someone would ever try to transform lead into gold on a large scale. Sophie printed out the article and packed up her laptop. She smiled. That arrogant pig. Next time she spoke to him she would casually mention that the alchemists were right in the end. It was possible to transform lead to gold.

Sophie jumped when the phone rang. She struggled to place the voice of the person on the other line, a David Dypsvik who had met her on a flight from Brisbane a few days ago. She had definitely not expected a call from this David Dypsvik. He had told her he was on his way to London, so she had found it quite safe to give him her card. Well, that plan was now out the window. He was here in Turkey and wanted to catch up for a drink. She neither had the time nor interest in any relationship, so she started on her well-rehearsed rejection pitch.

Then he said it.

"Excuse me, can you repeat?" Sophie asked.

"I need to get in contact with someone who can teach me about alchemists. Do you know if there is anyone at the university I can speak to?" he repeated.

She agreed to meet him.

Sophie was a physicist. In her world there was no good luck nor bad luck. Your destiny wasn't already mapped out or influenced by the position of the planets on the day you were born. But today. Today she had, for the first time in her life, a strange feeling that it wasn't just a coincidence that David had called her.

It couldn't be a coincidence that he had called her only minutes after she had been called an alchemist.

Could it?

-26-

Sophie stood in front of her bathroom mirror, drying her hair. She had definitely not expected a phone call from David, the nice-enough student she had been seated next to on the plane from Brisbane to Singapore. But the world was full of coincidences. She was a physicist and knew how humans had a tendency to allocate a higher meaning to random events. She could never get herself to understand why humans felt so special. As Carl Sagan had once said, 'our earth was just a pale blue dot in a sea of billions of planets and stars which we called our universe.' And most likely there were billions of universes like ours. No. Humans weren't special. We were a function of random events and time. And right now time was something she had plenty of. The warning from the research director had turned out to be more serious than expected. The university's funds were exhausted. She had a job for the next three months, but then it was over. She had become another victim of the global financial crisis, her boss had said. Probably to make it easier for himself. To make the situation even worse, the university had forced her to take out her accumulated annual leave. She hadn't taken a vacation for years, and the accrued annual leave didn't look good on the university's balance sheet. She had left the meeting without saying much. She had never liked the research director. At least now she didn't have to kiss his ass anymore.

For the first time in years she actually had time to go on a date. Then again it wasn't really a date David had asked her on. He had been quite vague on the phone, only said that he would appreciate if they could meet up. She shook her head. He wasn't her type anyway. She couldn't imagine a worse boyfriend than a business student. If there was one thing she didn't care about in life, it was money. Money was necessary to be able to survive from day to day, but that was also everything it was good for. She had dated a stockbroker a few years back, and she could still, with horror, remember the boring stories he told at the dinner table. Everything was about money. How much money people made. What car they drove. What watch they wore. She assumed that David would be quite similar. She had enjoyed their conversation on the flight. He was a funny man. But he had also dressed up in a suit in order to get upgraded to business class. And he had casually mentioned how much money he made in his last job. Even though it probably wasn't meant as bragging. It had sounded more like whining.

She studied herself in the mirror. Her body naked except for a pair of undies. She needed a new outfit. Maybe not the smartest decision – to buy a new outfit when she had just been told she was out of a job – but it felt right.

Even though she didn't want to admit it, she was kind of looking forward to seeing David again.

David met Sophie at one of the trendy tapas bars in Ankara. He ordered a Stella for himself and a glass of the house champagne for Sophie. She wore a pair of skinny jeans and a black blouse, the outfit she had bought earlier in the day. Her long blond hair was pulled back in a low pony tail, and David was immediately smitten. He remembered she was beautiful. But not this beautiful.

She looked like a supermodel. Although that description probably didn't do her justice. She had beautiful forms and an enchanting smile. David thought most supermodels looked angry and anorexic. He had once read that this was caused by the fashion industry mostly consisting of gay men, who despised the natural shape of a woman. The angry faces were probably caused by the models' constant hunger, he thought. Sophie however was beaming like the sun when she sat down next to David.

"So, what did you want to talk to me about?" Sophie asked after having given David a hug and a kiss on each cheek.

David was pulled back to reality. Not much time for small talk. She was very direct.

"I need a contact at your university. I want to find out whether there is any alchemist society here in Ankara, and I was hoping you knew somebody," David replied as he shot Sophie a smile.

Sophie was glad David hadn't lied on the phone. She didn't really want to admit it, but she had entertained some nasty thoughts. The stockbroker whom she had dated a few years back had experienced some serious problems 'letting go' when they broke up. Maybe it was because he saw it as a defeat to get dumped? Or maybe it was simply because he was a control freak and an asshole? He had, however, stalked her for more than six months after the break-up, and in the end Sophie had seen no other way out than to get a court-ordered restraining order. This MBA student, who was on his way to London, and then suddenly appeared unannounced in Ankara. The phone conversation that casually included the word 'alchemists' only minutes after her boss had called her the same. Could it be a coincidence or had she attracted yet another weird stalker?

"Why do you want to talk to someone in the alchemist society?" she asked.

David wasn't sure how much he should tell Sophie. If he said too little there was a risk she would walk away, and if he told her too much there was an even greater risk for the same. He was unsure. To complicate things he had this strange feeling of being watched all the time. Ever since he landed in London. It was part of the reason he had asked for the meeting to take place at a busy restaurant.

"I'm working on an article, and it would be of great help to talk to somebody with some knowledge about alchemy."

"Don't you have internet in your hotel room?" Sophie laughed.

"You won't find the information I seek on the internet," David replied.

"And what type of information is that?" she asked, leaning closer.

"There is a special type of people uploading information to Wikipedia and web forums. They often have an abundance of knowledge. Knowledge they don't necessarily want to share with everyone else. I want to learn more about the non-mainstream sides of alchemy," David said, leaning back on the soft couch. He wasn't particularly pleased with his phrasing, but he had no idea how to explain to her that he wanted to know why one of Nazi Germany's most highly decorated officers was attending the excavation of what was believed to be King Midas' grave, in the middle of the most intensive fighting of the Second World War.

"Can't help you. Thanks for the drink and goodbye," Sophie said, and rose from her chair. She felt cheated out of a date and now this arrogant business student was sitting there feeding her snippets of an explanation why he needed her help. He was just like her ex-boyfriend.

David was completely taken aback. He hadn't anticipated this reaction at all.

He was, however, able to pull himself together and run after

Sophie before she slipped out of the restaurant. He caught up to her at the exit.

"Ok, you deserve a proper explanation. Give me ten minutes. If you're not pleased after that you can leave and I will never again make contact."

Sophie tilted her head to the side and studied David. The left side of her mouth curled up.

"You've got five minutes. And buy me a glass of nice champagne. Not the house champagne."

David smiled. He did like her.

After having given Sophie a quick explanation David was expecting to be laughed at. He hadn't really reflected on how unlikely the story sounded before he had to formulate it himself to Sophie. Conspiracy theories, missing billionaire, Nazis, King Midas' grave. Sophie was a professor in physics, a ridiculously smart woman. David wondered why she hadn't left already. But to his great surprise she remained seated. And she seemed interested.

"Well, that's some story," she said when David had finally finished.

David smiled. He had a tendency to do that when he was nervous. "I know that the story sounds improbable. To be totally honest I'm not sure what to believe myself anymore. But I do know that there is never smoke without fire. There was a reason one of the most highly decorated SS officers travelled to an excavation in the middle of the hardest battles of the Second World War. Why did he travel there and what did he find? Those are the two simple questions I want answered," David said.

"I know someone you can speak to if you want to learn more about alchemists," Sophie said. She downed the expensive glass of champagne, grabbed David's arm, and they walked out of the restaurant.

-27-

A strong smell of curry was hovering in the warm air. Honking cars and noisy people created a natural sound-blanket over the city of Ankara. This was a different Turkey than the one David had experienced on his boys-trips to Alanya. This was the authentic Turkey. The feeble chatter, from people who spoke every single other language than Norwegian, made David relax. But when he looked out the window of the car he found nothing relaxing about the sight. There were busy people hurtling around in the streets. David had commuted for six months when he lived in Oslo, the capital of Norway. After that experience he had gained even more respect for all the people who commuted to put food on the table. It wasn't that the commute in itself was so bad. David had killed time by reading and listening to audiobooks, doing productive things. It was all the sad people who were the problem. David had hated to look at all the modern slaves being pushed together in a small carriage, only to be transferred to an office where they had to spend the rest of their day working in a rat race they had no opportunity to break out of. That was what had bothered David about commuting. All the sad people. And that's why he wanted a change in his own life. Here, in the middle of Ankara, people seemed as stressed out as in Oslo, as anxiety-ridden as in London and as depressed as in New York. They kept streaming out of large office buildings in big herds, only to be scurried on to some form of public transportation system to make it home for a late dinner with the family.

Sophie grabbed David's arm. "We will be there in half an hour," she said.

David closed his eyes. He hadn't slept properly the last few nights and now this immense tiredness just overwhelmed him. Normally he would have tried to be social with Sophie; chatted about everything and nothing to avoid embarrassing periods of silence. But even though he hardly knew Sophie he felt that he could relax around her. He could be himself around her. They could just sit there, together in a tiny rental car, and just relax without necessarily having to find something to talk about. He realised he really liked Sophie.

He felt comfortable around her.

David woke to Sophie gently poking him in the shoulder. "We need to stop meeting this way," she said. David laughed. He remembered how they had met on the flight from Brisbane. The car had stopped. Outside the car a pale and lanky person stood waiting. Sophie introduced David to her friend Michael Simpson, her old professor. Michael Simpson's face was full of sun-spots, and his back had a slight hunch forward that made him look much older than the sixty-three years he actually was. He was neatly dressed, and had an elegance about him. Many people made the wrong assumption that he was gay the first time they met him, but he was actually a ladies' man with an almost magical ability to seduce the other sex.

Michael Simpson had grown up on a farm in England. Clever at school, he had managed to get through his whole university education on scholarships, culminating in a doctorate in theoretical physics from Cambridge. When he lost most of his money in a failed real estate development deal he had been introduced to the harsh reality of life. He had been utterly shocked by how many of his so-called friends had shunned him as soon as he started to experience financial problems. The episode had left lasting scars on him and after having been declared bankrupt and divorced from his wife of five years, he had simply moved to Turkey to create for himself a new life. The new career had, however, also been fleeting as he had been, unfoundedly he claimed, accused of manipulating the results in one of his experiments in the hunt for a theory of everything – the holy grail for theoretical physicists. A theory that explained matter, space and time, not only on a subatomic level, but in grand scale as well. In the world of everything from bacteria to black holes. A theory that combined Albert Einstein's relativity theory and Max Planck's quantum mechanics. Unfortunately Michael Simpson had to leave his new job in disgrace two years ago, and was now officially unemployed. Not that it seemed to matter much. He supposedly owned a couple of patents that ensured he never had to starve.

"I'm not sure what Sophie has told you," David started. He knew Sophie had called Michael Simpson from the car, but he hadn't been able to listen in on the conversation. He had been halfway to dreamland.

"Not much," Michael Simpson replied. "I understand that you are working on a book. A book about a man who was interested in alchemy."

"I guess you could say that," David answered, glancing over at Sophie. He was glad she hadn't told Michael the whole story. It was just too confusing. And she didn't really know the full story anyway. David hadn't told her about the Oxford University billionaires. How he suspected Professor Grossman of cheating in his study. He would put off telling her about that until he had confronted Professor Grossman about it.

"Well, where do I start?" Michael Simpson asked.

"You can start by explaining what alchemy is and what alchemists are trying to achieve."

"I hope you have plenty of time," Michael Simpson replied before starting on his explanation. "Alchemy is not a traditional field of study. It has never been accepted by the establishment, but it has still managed to fascinate some of history's most famous scientists. Some so much that they spent most of their waking hours conducting alchemic experiments. The amazing scientific breakthroughs history knows them for were merely done to pass time."

"I've read somewhere that Isaac Newton was an alchemist. Is that true?" David asked.

"Sir Isaac Newton," Michael Simpson laughed. "Sir Newton is probably the most famous alchemist who has ever walked the earth. He was an extraordinary man. Many of his scientific experiments weren't even publicised until several decades after he had completed them. He was happy toiling on by himself in his small laboratory. But from his work we got the first laws of physics and some wonderful theoretical considerations. Sir Isaac Newton seemingly gave up his career as a scientist towards the end of his life. Instead he became the head of the Royal Mint in London. Not exactly the most obvious career choice. Unless of course you know what was really the driving force in Sir Isaac Newton's life. As the head of the Royal Mint, Sir Newton got firsthand knowledge about everyone attempting to forge coins, whereas he himself was above suspicion as he immersed himself in advanced alchemy late at night."

Michael Simpson laughed and stroked a hand through his salt and pepper coloured beard.

"What most people don't know, however, is the real reason Sir Isaac Newton applied for the position as head of the London Mint."

"What was that?" David asked.

"To be as close as possible to the world's largest gold reserve. Newton deduced the law of gravity and he proved that objects on earth and the heavenly sky moved according to the same natural laws. But he also had a more revolutionary theory. He believed that gold had a special pulling power, that gold attracted gold."

"What do you mean?" David asked.

"Well, I have a couple of wealthy friends who like to carry around large amounts of cash in their wallets. They hardly need to as nobody really uses cash anymore, at least not in the western world. But they insist that a full wallet brings them luck. That wealth attracts wealth. Sir Isaac Newton had a comparable theory. He was of the opinion that gold attracted gold. The problem he had of course was to measure this force of pull. If you stand by the base of a mountain and drop a ball to the ground, the ball will be pulled slightly towards the mountain simply because of the mountain's large mass. This pull-force, or gravity as we call it, is so weak that it is impossible to observe with the naked eye. With precise instruments, however, we can measure this force for all objects. Newton was of the opinion that there was another force in action when it came to gold, the force of gold attracting gold. I believe he was attempting to develop a method to increase this force. He was trying to find the philosopher's stone."

"The philosopher's stone?" David repeated, mildly confused.

"The philosopher's stone is considered the holy grail for alchemists. Some say it is a formula on how to transform one metal into another, whereas others believe it is a stone with special powers. Newton belonged to the latter camp. He was attempting to create the philosopher's stone, a stone that would attract gold and wealth, an object that would attract luck."

"Did he succeed?" David asked.

"No, not as far as we know," Michael Simpson replied. "But then again Sir Newton didn't develop his theories for the public. Some of his experiments were, as I've already mentioned, not made public until several decades after he had successfully completed them. There is, however, nothing in the known material about Sir Isaac Newton that indicates he was successful with alchemy. And thus we can solemnly agree that alchemy is not possible. If the greatest scientist in the world couldn't make it work – it most likely won't work," Michael Simpson laughed.

"Are you certain he accepted the position at the Royal Mint to work on alchemy? Can't it be that he just wanted to have a more normal relaxing job?" Sophie asked.

"Sir Isaac Newton was anything but normal. One of the more peculiar of his experiments was to take a sharp needle and pick around in his own eye socket to see whether it caused any damage to his vision. Luckily, for science, he didn't end up with any permanent damage. But the action says something about his willingness to take risk in his scientific endeavours. No, Newton took the job at the Royal Mint to experiment with alchemy. There is no doubt about that."

David perused his notes. He wasn't sure what he had expected to learn, but he felt strongly that there was something missing.

"If I say King Midas, does that give you any associations?" Sophie asked.

Michael Simpson peered over at his former student. "Now it's starting to get interesting. Sir Newton was very interested in

Greek mythology. He was of the opinion that the story about King Midas maybe wasn't a myth, but an example of how humans had mastered alchemy in ancient times."

"What do you mean?" David asked.

"Newton was fascinated by the King Midas story. He was of the opinion that it wasn't like the other Greek mythologies. That it might have been based on a true story. He was also of the opinion that humans at some stage in history had mastered alchemy, but that the knowledge had been lost for various reasons."

David was listening intensely. "I have read a little bit about Newton, but I have never heard about this before. Is there a reason for that?" David asked.

"The people who write about Newton have to ensure that all information they print has been crosschecked multiple times. There were many strange rumours about Newton. But most stories are impossible to verify. History is like everything else – coloured by the persons who record it. Newton was a national hero. To tell the true story about him could quite possibly ruin the reputation of one of the most respected scientists in history. Nobody wants that. Thus historians have basically left out many of Newton's peculiarities, in the belief that it would make him a more respected man."

"So what are you saying? Do you believe that humans may have mastered alchemy in the past?"

"Well, there are many indications that the ancient Egyptians, and the Greeks, were working on alchemy. It is, however, unlikely that any of those civilisations were successful. In our time and age we have access to immensely more advanced technology, yet we are still unable to make gold out of lead. So how were they supposed to have been able to do this in ancient times? The argument is that we are influenced by historical research."

Michael Simpson glanced over at Sophie before continuing. "When one commences an education, to become say a physicist or a chemist in today's society, one is automatically loaded up with all the accumulated knowledge of what is wrong and what is right. Many of the scientists thus have a very similar line of attack for new problems. And this colours our scientific progress. We advance, but only in small steps. True progress most often is made when some individual looks at a problem from a totally new angle, and that is hard when everybody has been through the same basic foundations. Take Albert Einstein. The revolutionary ideas he came up with weren't the result of discussions with equal minded academics in the university hall. They were a result of Albert Einstein's relentless pondering and single minded focus on theoretical abstractions, alone in a small crummy patent office in Switzerland, back in 1905. If Einstein at an early stage had discussed his ideas with colleagues at a university, there is a real danger he would have been set forth on a different line of thinking, and quite possibly we wouldn't have the theory of relativity in the form we have it today. The same can be said about Sir Isaac Newton, who came up with most of his theories the year he spent in isolation in his birth town of Woolsthorpe, aged only twenty-three."

David nodded. He had similar experiences with group work at university. It was surprising how much education affected your line of thought. David acknowledged that he mostly had concurring opinions with business-educated colleagues, whereas engineers, philosophers and other students with more exotic educations could have totally different ways of approaching a problem. Education affected your line of thought. There was no doubt about it.

"The last few years of Newton's life he was busy researching ancient civilisations. His last work was called The Chronology of Ancient Kingdoms Amended. In the book he claims that all gods from earlier civilisations were in fact real life kings and heroes from those time eras. It is in this light one has to review his fascination with King Midas. To Newton, the Greek myths weren't only old stories, they were based on true accounts."

"Are you saying that Isaac Newton believed that King Midas had actually been alive, and that he had mastered Alchemy?"

"Based on his written work that is a fair conclusion, yes," Michael Simpson replied.

"What if Isaac Newton was right?" Sophie asked.

"What do you mean?" Michael Simpson asked. He hadn't expected such a response from his old student Sophie.

"Is it so inconceivable that humans mastered alchemy in the ancient world? Most scientific progress is a result of single-minded focus. If what you claim is correct then almost all scientists were heavily invested in alchemy back then. Maybe there were a few who learnt how to master it?"

"If someone had been successful with alchemy, Sophie, then we would have known about it. If someone could turn lead into gold then gold would have been worthless a long time ago."

"But isn't that the point?" David asked. "If you were successful in figuring out the secret of alchemy then you wouldn't share that secret with the rest of the world. The secret only holds a value if nobody else knows about it."

Michael Simpson laughed. "You make a valid point, David. But no, I don't believe anyone would be capable of keeping such a secret. Humans are too vain. We have to tell the world what we have achieved."

"Not if you were built like Isaac Newton," Sophie remarked. "Didn't you just say he waited decades before publishing some of his theories? It doesn't sound like he had any problems keeping a secret."

Michael Simpson stared out into the air. It didn't seem like he had an answer.

"And just to have mentioned it. I did a search in the university's database. Scientists have actually been successful in transforming the atoms of one element into another element. Alchemy is very much possible, it is just incredibly expensive," Sophie said.

"Come, there is something I have to show you," Michael Simpson said suddenly before rising from the couch. He led them down to his basement, where books covered the room from floor to ceiling. He traced his finger over the dust jackets of the books, skimming the titles. Suddenly he stopped and pulled out a brown, leathery book.

"Some of my friends involved in history studies have always wondered why so many of the ancient civilisations seemed to vanish overnight. Often this occurred when they were at the peak of their greatness, as the Mayan empire with their gold-lined streets, or the Egyptians with their impressive pyramids. There are many theories. One of them is that these civilisations were heavily involved in alchemy, and that this may have had unintended consequences.

Michael Simpson placed the dusty, brown book on a large wooden table, and opened it. The pages were yellowish and seemed fragile.

"How old is this book?" David asked.

"Old," Michael Simpson replied, turning the pages until he found what he was looking for. "Here. What do you see?" he asked David, pointing at the drawing of a pyramid.

"I see a pyramid," David replied. "It looks like the Giza pyramid in Egypt."

"That's correct," Michael Simpson answered. "But what is it really? What was the purpose of the pyramids?"

"I thought they were burial places for kings and queens in the ancient Egypt," David replied.

"That's one theory. But if they were only graves for kings and queens, why did the Egyptians bother making the constructions mathematically perfect?"

"I don't know," David replied. "I must admit that I should probably know more about the pyramids. My dad was an historian. He took me to the Giza pyramid when I was ten years old. We were on a vacation to Egypt, and as usual when we were on vacations, he wanted to give me a lecture about history. I would rather be at the beach so I bothered him enough to cut the visit short. Maybe I should have listened?"

"Well, that would have helped. But it is not that important because there are a multitude of theories. Most people are of the opinion that the pyramids were burial places for important people. Monuments over great kings and their inflated egos. But there are also those who believe that the pyramids are everything from remnants of intergalactic weapons, to monuments created to honour visitors from alien planets. All these theories are of course impossible to verify. And also totally improbable, I might add. If ancient worlds had knowledge to make intergalactic weapons then it would be fair to assume that there would be other advanced items from this period lying around as well. But all we can find is arrowheads and old pots. The argument of alternative historians who believe in these theories is that the pyramids are much older than one has thought. That they are the leftovers from an ancient advanced civilisation, and that the reason for the absence of other advanced items is that they have basically disintegrated over time."

David looked at Michael Simpson with astonishment. He didn't believe his own ears. Was Michael Simpson serious when he talked about the pyramids being intergalactic weapons and Earth having been visited by aliens from other worlds?

"I don't believe any of those theories. Carbon dating of the pyramids proves, beyond the shadow of a doubt, that they can't be any older than four to seven thousand years old. I will admit that there are some controversies surrounding the exact age of the pyramids. But regardless, they are too young to represent an advanced ancient civilization," Michael Simpson said. David was immediately comforted. "But I'm not so arrogant that I believe everything that is being presented as facts, either. When you review how historians use pieces of information to create a vivid picture of how a civilisation looked more than 3000 years ago, you have to ask how much we really know about what happened on Earth back then. I don't think you can create a perfect picture of a civilization based on the finding of a cracked pot and a broken arrow head. Thus I am open to the possibility that the pyramids were built for something other than burial chambers if the arguments are strong enough. And one theory is that the pyramids were large factories for alchemy. They were built according to strict mathematical rules and laws because this was necessary in order to perform alchemy. And when I talk about alchemy I don't necessarily talk about transforming lead to gold, but about changing the values of an object."

"By transporting them to another dimension, the fourth dimension," Sophie finished Michael Simpson's reasoning.

"The fourth dimension?" David asked.

"I should probably give you a proper explanation," Sophie said. "We live in what we call a three-dimensional world. By that we mean that everything we observe in our world can be measured in three points – height, length and depth. Albert Einstein introduced the fourth dimension – space-time. But the essential thing here is that we can only observe three dimensions. In 1884 Edwin A. Abbot wrote a novella called Flatland. It describes a world full of circles and squares which live in a two-dimensional world. For the inhabitants of Flatland reality is what they observe in two dimensions, and to speculate about a third dimension is unimaginable. When one of the inhabitants claims that he has seen a person from the third dimension it is as inconceivable for them as if you were to claim that you had seen a person from the fourth dimension. Understandably enough, the main character is jailed for his claims. But is the idea of multiple dimensions unthinkable?" Sophie asked. "Is the thought of multiple universes inconceivable? Most people in the world are religious and their worldview is, to a large extent, coloured by what a so-called prophet scribbled down a couple of thousand years ago. Most of the claims in all religions are inconsistent with simple logic and evolutionary evidence, yet many incredibly smart people blindly believe in an almighty creator and life after death. None of the so-called prophets ever delivered any revolutionary insights like 'the Earth is round', none of them revealed any of the mysteries of the universe or bothered to explain some basic laws of physics. Instead we had to wait a couple of thousand years before Sir Isaac Newton developed the law of gravity. To me it is therefore obvious that we still know nothing. The universe around us is probably magnitudes more complex than we assume. We are the real inhabitants of Flatland. We live in blissful ignorance about all the worlds surrounding us simply because we can't observe them with our own eyes. When we, at one point in the distant future, stick our head up from our Flatland and peer into other dimensions, our world view will change forever."

"So you believe alchemy is about sending objects to the fourth dimension, and that they could return with amended properties?" David asked.

"I guess that's the essence of the question," Michael Simpson replied. "To make gold out of lead is just one of the possibilities such a gate to another dimension could create. But if you really found a method to send objects to the fourth dimension you would in theory be able to send humans there too."

Michael Simpson took a deliberate pause. "History has lots of gaps. We still don't know why or how so many of the ancient civilizations disappeared. Maybe they were wiped out by natural catastrophes or plagues? Maybe they were eradicated by other more primitive and aggressive civilizations? Or maybe, just maybe, something totally different happened. Everything is speculations. What we do know is that these civilizations, which almost disappeared overnight, had one thing in common. They were all obsessed with gold. And it just so happens that they had accumulated massive amounts of it."

"The reason I lost my job was that I wanted to develop an alternative theory to String Theory," Sophie said. "String Theory rests on the foundation that there exist at least ten dimensions. That is about the only thing I agree with. I believe we live in a world with multiple dimensions. Dimensions we can't see. Our brains are so well rehearsed in thinking in three dimensions only that we will probably never be able to comprehend these higher dimensions. These dimensions would, however, have to be smaller than an atom in size. To claim that these civilisations disappeared into the fourth dimension is the most ridiculous thing I've ever heard," Sophie said.

"The old mystics thought that the spirits lived in these dimensions, as they were not bound by the physical laws of earth.

I don't know whether it is right or not, but is it so inconceivable to believe that we can send physical objects into these dimensions? All you need is a medium, and I believe that medium is gold," Michael Simpson said. "Throughout all of history there has only been exhumed about 165 thousand tons of gold. That's barely enough to fill up a supertanker. Or to provide you with a more telling picture, if you gathered all the gold that has ever been unearthed and melted it into two cubes, those two cubes would fit nicely into two Olympic pools," Michael Simpson continued. "Gold is more powerful than you can ever imagine."

He glanced over at David before continuing. "Who controls more and more of the world's gold resources?" he asked.

David thought back over the last week's news broadcasts. "China?" he replied.

"Correct. But not only China. The whole of Asia." Michael Simpson scratched his chin. "The western world has gradually made itself independent of gold. A few decades ago the value of a country's currency was intertwined with its gold reserves. But that's not the case anymore. Is it a coincidence that the western world is in decline while the Asian economies, which all share a strong fondness for gold, are thriving? I am not superstitious, but I believe that gold has properties we still don't fully understand. And I'm afraid that what we are now seeing is a shifting of the world power from the West to Asia, not only because of the West's recent borrowing craze, but because Asia controls more and more of the world's gold reserves. And I am truly afraid of what they are going to do when they understand what sort of power this may give them."

"So you believe, like Isaac Newton, that gold attracts gold?" David asked, dumbfounded.

"I believe that gold attracts wealth. Gold attracts luck. And if you gather a large enough amount of it in one place then it could have unforeseen consequences," Michael Simpson replied.

David let the information sink in. He had never considered that something could attract luck. His simple world view was that the world was ruled by randomness and probabilities. You could influence your own future by making sure that you were in the right place at the right time, but you couldn't influence your own luck. It was roughly the same probability that he would be struck in the head by a meteorite as he was going to pick next week's lotto numbers, and there was frustratingly little he could do to influence any of the outcomes.

Sophie shook her head.

"I disagree with you, Michael. I'm not so arrogant that I believe we know everything, but the world is still controlled by random events. That's just the way it is."

"That's just the way it is. Is that your argument, Sophie? You were one of my best students, you can do better than that."

"I think you are a wonderful physicist and I have always supported you, Michael. But you ruined your career by making claims you couldn't back up with evidence. Science relies on evidence, you know that."

"I know that, Sophie, but sometimes you have to have the courage to have faith. Faith that there are grander things than what we can observe with our own eyes. It is easy to be a physicist today. Almost everything can be tested. There is no room for great thoughts anymore. Philosophy is dead and buried a long time ago."

"I've just lost my job because I didn't want to play by the rules of their ridiculous game. So don't try to teach me about life. I have kept my integrity," Sophie said, her voice almost breaking.

"It's not an accident that you are here today, Sophie. It's not an accident that you met David. These events are a consequence of your choices. If you want to continue then you have to be open to the possibility that the world is not all what it seems. Are you willing to do that?" Michael Simpson asked.

Sophie didn't reply. She wasn't prepared to put aside everything she had been taught to believe. All the years at school and university had convinced her that humans didn't have any greater purpose in life than to reproduce, to simply ensure the survival of our genes. To believe that things happened for a reason was naïve, just plain and simple naïve.

When he didn't immediately get a response from Sophie, Michael Simpson glanced over at David instead. "Looks like she has made up her mind. What about you, David? Are you ready to broaden your horizon?"

David felt a bit overwhelmed by the discussion, and his yes was barely audible. "Yes," he repeated with a clear voice.

"Well, if you are open to new knowledge, to new insights, then I propose that you go on a small trip," Michael Simpson said.

"A trip? Where to?" David asked.

"You don't have to travel far. You need to go on a trip in history. You can learn a lot from books. But sometimes you need to experience things yourself. If you truly want to understand people's fascination for gold you need to see how it is processed."

Sophie looked at David. David didn't know what to say.

"Gold is the key," Michael Simpson said. "Gold has always been the key," he repeated softly, peering at the gold watch he had just pulled out from his breast pocket.

-28-

Police Officer Mike Ware surveyed the room as he pushed the door to the Hyde One penthouse wide open. He had just picked the lock. The living room reminded him more of a hotel lobby than a place a single woman would choose to call home. It was one of those apartments where everything had its place. If you placed a book on the table it would look messy. The furniture was either kitsch or regal. Police Officer Mike Ware was unsure which it was. The furniture looked expensive though. There was no doubt about that. White and gold was the overarching theme.

The insane cold pulled Officer Mike Ware back to reality.

"We constantly monitor the systems of all our apartments. Last night the temperature in Ms Sampa's apartment was set to a very low temperature. I've tried contacting her but she doesn't pick up the phone. Unfortunately this is one of the few apartments we do not have a key to."

"You did the right thing when you called us," Mike Ware said. He had pulled out his service gun.

Mike Ware had seen a lot of crime scenes in his twenty-five years as a police officer in London. He knew this would be another one.

"Please wait outside," he told the concierge.

"But I can't let you enter the apartment by yourself. It would be against protocol," the concierge replied.

"I don't think the owner will make any fuss about it. This is now a crime scene. Please wait outside," Mike Ware said with a clear and authoritative voice.

The insanely cold air, the air-conditioning system running on full machine, the closed drapes. Mike Ware had immediately understood that this was a crime scene.

Now all that remained was to find out how many dead there were.

-29-

All the noise from honking cars and whirring engines made it hard for David Dypsvik to concentrate. Sophie was driving like a native. There was no room for hesitant drivers in Turkey, the system only worked when everybody acted aggressive. Sophie waved her fist out the window. David smiled. She blushed. Not much, but enough for David to notice.

"It's ok," Sophie said. "I think I know where we are now."

With relief David put away the map. It was scary enough to look out the window when Sophie drove. Having your eyes fixated on a map was even scarier.

After five minutes of looking at the scenery he changed his mind though. He came to the conclusion that it was simply impossible to relax. All Turks drove like they had stolen the cars. David was certain that they had narrowly avoided death three times in the last two minutes. He needed a distraction from his thoughts. He pulled out the Kindle reader and started to read the next principle.

Principle 7: Persistence

It's good if you have decided to become an entrepreneur. But the decision in itself is by no means a guarantee for success, far from. It is now the real work begins. It is now that life will test you. And the most important test will be your persistence, your willpower.

You will constantly be surrounded by little people who secretly want you to fail. Who wish you will give up so that they, with malicious pleasure can say: Told you so. The challenge is to not listen to any of these people. But you will also have yourself to fight against. Your inner voice which will beg you to come to your senses and do what everybody else does. To use your common sense. To get a good education, and a safe and secure job. It is harder to fight yourself than it is to fight others. And that's where true persistence comes into the picture.

A lot of people are quick to point out that someone was born with good genes or came from a wealthy family when that someone succeeds. But if you study history more closely you will notice that it is not always the ones with the best starting point who succeed. When you read about successful people you often forget that there is always a back-story.

I was ready to give up many times in my career. Life felt hard, difficult and unfair. But what doesn't kill you makes you stronger, they say. And life has a tendency to test us humans. The person who is persistent will over time become successful. But it can be testing while it's ongoing.

The first time I went out fishing with my own vessel we ended up in a terrible storm. We were close to sinking several times, and three weeks after leaving shore we still had no catch. We hardly had any food left, and as captain I soon had to make the tough decision to return empty-handed. It was my first trip as owner and skipper. I had chosen both route and area to fish. The mood of the crew was strained. Even though nobody told me directly, it was clear that I was about to lose their respect. And there was a real danger that I wouldn't have a crew for my next trip. The easy solution would have been to sail to another area. To give up my plan of fishing in this particular area, to at least salvage a small catch that could give some contribution towards the cost of crew and boat. But there was a reason we were where we were. I had used my knowledge and experience to pinpoint the area. This had been my plan when I bought the boat, to fish in this area where no one else did. And I had been certain that it would be a success. Now, as I stood on the bridge, I realised that my dream was disappearing fast. I grabbed the radio and readied myself to give the order to turn back. Then suddenly, from out of nowhere, the ocean started to boil. Less than a couple of hundred meters from where we had put out our nets, fish were splashing on the surface. I turned the boat and we were able to surround the shoal of fish. We caught more fish in the space of a couple of hours than we had done for weeks on other vessels. My reputation was cemented. Nobody would ever again question my decisions. I had been seconds away from making a decision which would have resulted in me giving up only a few hundred meters from riches.

That day I learnt to never give up. When you are faced with obstacles you just fight a bit harder, because it is only life testing you. Life rewards those who are tough enough to not give up, but stand by their principles and follow their intuition.

David pondered the statement. He had been close to giving up several times already. It would be very easy to return to Bond University. All he needed to do was to buy a plane ticket, and he would be back to his normal life in a day. But wasn't that the point? It was when you were close to giving up that you had to bite your teeth together and continue.

He knew what he had to do, even before he had finished the

seventh principle.

There was only one solution.

But he couldn't do this on his own.

He needed help.

-30-

David wasn't sure how he had managed to persuade Sophie to join him. It was true that she had just lost her job and therefore had ample time to come along. It had also helped that David paid for all expenses, and that Michael Simpson had made it sound exciting to learn more about gold. But what were they hoping to learn by visiting a gold mine? David had been sent to London to figure out the real identity of a billionaire who disappeared more than thirty years ago. The search had taken him to Turkey, and an excavation site that the locals claimed had contained the ancient burial chamber of King Midas. There David had managed to get a confirmation of Yossar Devan's real identity in record time. His job was in essence over. He should be on a plane back to Australia, delivering the good news to Professor Grossman. Instead he found himself trying to find out more about what had really happened back in 1944. David knew there was more to the story than he was being led to believe. Yossar Devan had been a poor Turkish peasant working on the excavation site with his dad. He had been the only survivor when the excavation collapsed. Was it possible that he had seen something inside the grave before it collapsed? The grave the locals claimed had belonged to King Midas? Was that the real reason for Yossar Devan's wealth? Had he found King Midas' secret?

It just sounded too far-fetched. The ancient myth about King Midas having the power to turn everything he touched into gold was just that, a myth. There had to be another explanation. But what was it? In the absence of any better leads David had accepted Michael Simpson's offer to visit a gold mine. It couldn't hurt to learn more about gold. After all Yossar Devan had been known under the name 'the Alchemist' when he grew up, and he had continued to invest in gold during his business career. A substantial part of his assets, when he disappeared, had been gold.

Michael Simpson had initially suggested that they visit a mine in Africa. So that they could better comprehend what gruelling toil was required to extract a few grams of gold. David had of course refused. He was on a tight budget. Instead Michael Simpson had organised for them to visit one of the largest gold mines in Turkey. Michael Simpson was a close friend of the MD there, Caroline Summerfield. A few years back they had both signed up for a Salsa course. Michael Simpson had initially been searching for a female companion, but it hadn't taken him long to understand that Caroline Summerfield was actually after the same. She was playing for the other team. They had hit it off though, and stayed in touch. They both appreciated the friendship they had developed – friends without benefits.

Caroline Summerfield was a good looking woman. David found it hard to guess her age as her face was still youthful and almost wrinkle-free. The aging skin in her neck area gave her off though. She had either passed fifty or spent a lot of time outdoors in her youth. David didn't know which it was. The only thing he knew for sure was that Caroline Summerfield looked stunning for her age, whatever it was. She also dressed nicely. Sophie had admired her suit for the last five minutes. It looked expensive.

"I thought we could start off with a drive before we enter the mine. It always helps to put things in perspective," Caroline Summerfield said.

"Sounds good," David replied.

"How long have you worked here?" Sophie asked as they left Caroline's office.

"About seven years. But I've basically grown up around gold mines. My dad worked for various mining companies in South America, Asia and America throughout my childhood. And I learnt my trade in South Africa, where I lived for three decades. So you can say it is in my blood." Caroline Summerfield laughed.

"Did you always want to work with gold?" David asked.

"Always," Caroline replied. "I've always been incredibly fascinated by gold. So my choice of profession was quite easy."

"What do you find so fascinating about gold?" David asked.

"Take a look at these photos," she said, pointing to a couple of large black-and-white photos hanging in the hallway of the office barracks. They appeared to be of old mines. "What is the first thing that comes to mind?"

"I don't know. They all look alike to me," David said.

"Exactly. Those pictures are from different mines, different continents and different decades. Yet they all look alike. Humans have always been attracted to gold. Even isolated civilisations without contact with the outside world have intuitively understood that there is something special about gold."

"But gold is only special because we have decided it is special," Sophie said.

"People have been searching for gold long before there was a market for gold. I believe that humans intuitively understand when something has a value. And gold has a value. Gold is not a piece of paper we have printed a number on. It is a metal. A metal that only exists in a limited supply. And somehow we can feel it. It doesn't matter whether we live here in modern Turkey or in a desolate jungle in South East Asia," Caroline Summerfield said enthusiastically.

David noticed that Caroline was wearing some gold jewellery. It was relatively discreet, but it was obvious that her enthusiasm for gold also extended to her dressing habits.

"Jump in," Caroline said. They had just left her sparsely furnished office barracks and walked out to the parking lot. In front of them a black Range Rover stood parked. David got into the front passenger seat. Sophie jumped into the back.

As the Range Rover bumped down the dirt road, Caroline Summerfield steadily continued to talk about gold and all the good things it represented. She is really brainwashed, David thought. But he also secretly wondered whether she could be onto something. Michael Simpson was a bright guy; he had a bloody doctorate in physics for Christ's sake. Still it sounded as if he believed in the crazy theory that gold was an antenna for riches, that gold attracted gold. He had even given David and Sophie a gold coin each when they had left the other night. Initially David had refused to accept the coin. Michael Simpson didn't really seem to be in a position to give away anything, jobless and all, but he had insisted. You will thank me later, he had said. David didn't know what he meant.

David pressed his fingers around the gold coin in his right front pocket. 'Always carry some gold,' Michael Simpson had said. 'It will bring you good luck.' David wondered why Michael Simpson had lost his job at the university, and evidently was in a bit of a financial slump. Didn't he keep a gold coin for himself? David smiled thinking about it. This fascination with gold and belief in its secret powers was probably some bullshit.

Caroline Summerfield on the other hand seemed to be convinced otherwise. She continued talking about the history of gold. "Gold is imperishable. You can do anything to gold, but it will never disappear. Other metals or minerals can be transformed until they are almost unrecognisable. But not gold, gold always retains its properties," Caroline said.

"She has obviously not heard about nuclear transformation," Sophie whispered to David, with a smile. It was evident that Sophie, like David, had her doubts about the power of gold that Michael Simpson had spoken so vividly about the day before.

"Gold is so malleable that it can be shaped into anything you want. One gram of gold can be stretched three and a half kilometres, but it will always remain gold. When you look at what we have extracted of gold throughout history then most of this gold remains in circulation today."

"One hundred and sixty-five thousand tons," David said. He remembered Michael Simpson's estimate.

"Sounds like a good guess," Caroline Summerfield replied. She was in a good mood. She obviously enjoyed that he took interest in her lecture. "Some of this gold is found on the bottom of the ocean, in old shipwrecks. Some of it is located in museums around the world. But most of it is actually on us. It is located in our teeth, on our fingers and in our ears. We carry around most of the gold ever extracted through time," she continued.

"I think that this fascination with gold is a bit strange," Sophie said. "With steel you can build skyscrapers, cars and airplanes. You can't build anything out of gold. Still it is gold we crave. Still it is gold that we deem valuable."

"That's correct, Sophie. But long after the steel in your car has rusted and lost its original shape, your gold ring will still exist just as it does today. Gold is immortal, and we all long for immortality."

David squeezed the gold coin Michael Simpson had given him harder. He didn't really long for immortality, but he wouldn't mind surviving the car trip. Based on Caroline's driving, his odds weren't good though. He held on to the doorhandle as they skidded around a corner on the dirt road down to the mine. Through the window he could now see the hole in the ground they were about to descend into. Gigantic wheeled loaders, painted in yellow and black, kept passing them.

"To extract gold requires enormous resources," Caroline Summerfield continued. "To extract enough gold for a simple gold ring we need to go through twenty tons of dirt. This is one of the most efficient mines in the world, but we can't afford to rest on our laurels. We have to improve every single day. More output with less waste. More efficiency with less labour."

"Why is the industry so resource-intense?" David asked.

"The problem is that gold is thinly spread over great distances. Even though gold is a rare metal you can find it in small quantities, almost everywhere in the world. The trick is to locate those places where the concentration is large enough to justify mining operations. To have a profitable open mine operation like ours you need at least a couple of milligrams of gold per kilo of dirt. Think about it. None of the gold extracted here is visible. We are extracting gold we can't see."

"That's a shame," Sophie said. "So I won't be able to stumble upon a gold nugget when we get out of the car?"

Carline Summerfield laughed. "Those times have passed. At least in this mine."

"So where does gold originate from? Is it, like diamonds, created by pressure?" David asked.

"No, not quite. It has been claimed that all gold ever extracted by humans originates from meteorites that through time have crashed into Earth. Due to the high density of gold, all Earth's own gold would have sunk close to earth's core millions of years ago."

"So none of the gold being extracted is actually from Earth?" David asked.

"That's correct. Nobody has ever seen Earth's own gold. And of course that has led to stories about gold with magical powers."

"Magical powers? Are you serious?" David asked, a bit dumbfounded.

Caroline laughed. "Well, there are those who claim Earth's own gold attracts luck and immortality. Gold has always attracted fortune hunters though. There have been many gold rushes around the world. It is almost as though humans are predisposed to lose their rationality in the face of the possibility of a big reward. Three hundred thousand people moved to California during its gold rush at the end of the 1800s. The sad reality is that most of them never found any gold."

"While the ones selling pickaxes and shovels got rich," David said.

"Exactly," Caroline continued. "Those who viewed the gold rush as a business opportunity made money. It may not be so sexy to run a gold mine the way we do here, but it is pretty predictable. We know how many tons of dirt we need to go through to make our daily quota. We don't gamble on making a lucky find. This is industry. Pure calculation."

David sat idle, staring out the window. He stared at the massive hole in the ground. This was the result of humans' hunger for gold. The area was cleared of trees, and gigantic wheeled loaders, some of them larger than houses, passed them as they descended down the hole. The mine reminded David of a volcano. But this wasn't a volcano created by Mother Earth. This was a wound in Mother Earth's skin created by humans.

"I didn't take you on this excursion to give you a fairy tale story about gold," Caroline Summerfield said. She had obviously noted Sophie's reaction and David's absentmindedness. "Michael is a good friend of mine, and he asked me to give you a proper tour of a gold mine, warts and all."

"Thanks," Sophie replied. "I really appreciate that."

"I'm not going try to hide the fact that gold mining has a range of negative consequences. But it is a fact that if there is a demand for something then somebody will always try to satisfy that demand. My contribution can be to run this mine as environmentally friendly as possible, but it is unrealistic to believe that the industry will ever disappear."

"You can relax. We're not from Greenpeace," David said.

Caroline Summerfield wrestled the wheel to avoid a big hole in the road. Sophie was thrown against the window, but was stopped by the safety belt.

"Good, I have got enough of those," she said.

Sophie and David sat in silence, while Caroline drove the last few hundred meters down to the heart of the mine.

All the dust made it hard to breathe when they exited the car, and it was hard to talk through the noise of the wheeled loaders and other machinery.

"You will never look at gold again the same way after this excursion," Caroline Summerfield said as they observed the work. Only seconds later they heard a massive explosion. The ground shook under their feet and it felt like a small earthquake. Caroline Summerfield held on to the car door with a clenched face. She peered up at the office barracks they had left ten minutes earlier. Parts came flying through the air, and a column of smoke rose up towards the sky.

"What the hell was that?" David exclaimed.

"It was a message to me," Caroline Summerfield said.

"A message? Who the hell blows up a building to send a message?" he yelled.

"We were inside that building ten minutes ago," Sophie said, her voice trembling.

"They wouldn't have blown it up with people inside. But they are getting bolder. One day they will make a mistake and human lives may be lost."

"Do you know who did it?" Sophie cried. "Is it an everyday occurrence that somebody blows up your office?"

"Nahh. We have some problems with the locals. There are a few people who have fallen sick in the surrounding villages. Of course they claim we are responsible."

"Are you?"

"Most certainly not," Caroline Summerfield snapped. "People always need a scapegoat. And in us they have found one with deep pockets. We are due in court in six months' time. A pack of sixteen lawyers represents the plaintiffs, but they have no case. We have used cyanide for years and it has never been proven to cause any toxicity in the ground water or the environment. I'm one hundred and ten percent certain that we will win this case. And the more desperate things they do – like blowing up my office today – the stronger our case will be." She brushed some dust off Sophie's shoulder. "Now, should we get started on this excursion?" she asked.

-31-

Sophie stretched out on the hotel room couch. "I'm surprised," she said. "I had no idea I knew so little about gold."

"I'm more surprised to learn about how much unhappiness gold creates," David said. "I can't understand that gold is supposed to attract luck when it leaves behind so much unhappiness." Caroline Summerfield had told him some horrific stories about how humanity's greed for gold had obliterated whole civilisations throughout history. She had also thrown in some sad stories about child labour, from her own experience in South Africa, to make it more real. The stories had hit home with David.

"Maybe that's how nature balances it out. The luck replaces all the bad stuff gold brings along," Sophie said sarcastically. "Honestly, you don't really believe that gold attracts gold? That gold attracts luck?" she sat up on the couch.

"I don't know," David replied. "I just think it is tragic that we exploit people and the planet this way."

Sophie nodded. She leant into David's chest. He wasn't the person she initially had thought he would be. He wasn't like her ex-boyfriend, the stockbroker. David planted a kiss on her forehead. She looked up at him with surprise in her eyes. He brushed the hair away from her face and kissed her again. This time on the cheek, then on the mouth. She didn't resist. She didn't want to resist. He pulled her sweater over her head.

She took his hand and led him to the bed.

It was nine o'clock in the morning when Sophie woke up. A solitary sunray snuck its way through the curtain gaps, gently caressing her face. She turned to face David. He was still asleep, his chest heaving up and down. But he hardly made a sound. She smiled. He really did sleep quietly. Gently she lifted his arm to the side and got out of bed. She walked naked the few steps into the bathroom and turned on the shower.

When she was finished in the bathroom David was sitting upright in the bed, working on his laptop.

"What are you doing?" she asked.

"I haven't had time to find out what really happened to Dr Hans Kammler. The Wikipedia article was a bit vague on the details. Thought I would check it out now," he replied.

"Do you need any help?"

"Yeah, I wouldn't mind some help."

"Why don't you go and pick up a couple of coffees and I'll see what I can find out," Sophie said.

"Already on my way." David jumped out of bed. He was dying for a coffee.

Sophie sat cross-legged in the bed, laptop by her side, when David returned. He put the coffees and some croissants on the TV table.

"What is it?" he asked when he noticed Sophie's expression. She looked scared.

"I think you should have a look at this," Sophie said, handing David the laptop. The internet browser was logged on to a web forum focusing on the Second World War. A grainy black-and-white picture covered most of the laptop screen. It was a picture of an airplane. It looked like an old transport plane from the war.

"What is that?" David asked.

"How did Dr Hans Kammler die?" Sophie asked, disregarding his question.

"He committed suicide," David replied. Dr Hans Kammler's official death was surrounded by controversy. There were actually four different accounts of his death. In one account he committed suicide by swallowing a capsule of cyanide on the seventh of May 1945. In another he committed suicide in a forest between Pilsen and Prague on the ninth of May, two days after the surrender of Germany. There were also accounts of him being killed in a rain of bullets from Czechoslovakian partisans, and claims he had been executed by Russian soldiers along with two hundred other SS officers. The problem with all the various accounts of his death was that there existed no firm evidence. Nobody had actually seen Dr Hans Kammler die. And it was quite impossible to die four times anyway.

"What if he didn't commit suicide? What if he didn't die?" Sophie asked.

David peered over at her, unsure of what she was getting at. "I agree that the various accounts of his death have a few holes. But you have to remember the chaos the Germans and the Allied Forces were operating under during the final days of the war. There are four separate accounts of his death. It's fair to assume that at least one of them is correct."

"The Germans were bureaucrats. If Dr Hans Kammler really died between the seventh and ninth of May 1945 then there would be records. There are none," Sophie said.

"Where are you going with this?" David asked.

"Look at the picture again," She pushed the laptop closer to David.

David was confused. The screen only showed a grainy black-and-white picture of an old German transport plane.

"I tried to dig a bit deeper into Dr Hans Kammler's last days," Sophie said. "The last sign of life the world ever received was a telex he sent to Himmler on the 17th of April 1945."

"The leader of Gestapo, Heinrich Himmler?" David asked.

Sophie nodded. She clicked the mouse and a barely readable copy of the telex filled the laptop screen. "In the telex, Dr Hans Kammler declines Heinrich Himmler's request for the use of a heavy truck from the Junkers pool. He can't spare any trucks, he writes in the very formal reply."

"Why would the leader of the Gestapo ask Dr Kammler for the use of a truck? It doesn't make any sense," David said.

"Correct. It doesn't make any sense. So I did a couple of searches on truck and the German army. It turns out that the Luftwaffe used the description 'trucks' for their largest transport planes, the Ju 290 and the Ju 390."

"So Heinrich Himmler wanted a transport plane. Could have been handy if he was planning to flee," David said.

Sophie nodded. "But he didn't just request any transport plane," Sophie started. "Ju 290 was the workhorse in the German air force. With its four engines and long reach it was an extraordinarily effective transport and bomber airplane. The Ju 390 was, however, even more impressive. A six-engine long-distance airplane the Germans only had time to build two of before the war ended."

"I suspect Dr Kammler had one of them," David said.

Sophie nodded. "But that's not all." She pointed to the telex at the laptop screen. "The SS had established their own evacuation plan. That's probably why Heinrich Himmler didn't bother arguing with Dr Hans Kammler when he declined Himmler's request for a transport airplane. Dr Kammler's evacuation plan superseded everything else."

David pondered what this could mean. He had no idea.

"One of the Nazis responsible for executing the evacuation plan, SS Sturmbannfuhrer Rudolf Schuster, was captured by the Allied forces after the war. During interrogations he claimed that a Ju 390 had flown from Germany to Bodø in Norway, with materials and blueprints from the Chronos and Lanterntrager projects, towards the end of April 1945."

"The Chronos and Lanterntrager projects? I haven't heard about them before. What were they?" David asked.

"I will return to that," Sophie replied before continuing. "In Bodø a Nazi that just went under the nickname, 'the Norwegian' had taken responsibility for the cargo and the airplane."

David coughed. Sophie looked up at him before continuing. "This Ju 390 plane was a very important airplane." David nodded to make her continue. "Even though there were only ever two prototypes built, the Ju 390 had the potential to change the course of the air war between Germany and the Allied forces. One of the planes took off from France in the final days of the war and didn't turn around until it was twelve miles away from New York, a roundtrip flight of 32 hours. Nobody knows for sure what the purpose of the dangerous flight was. But the Allied Forces long speculated whether it had been to check whether the Germans could reach American targets. Something they clearly had showed beyond a shadow of a doubt."

"So the Germans had the opportunity to reach American targets in the final days of the war. Far out. We should be glad they never managed to make a nuclear bomb," David said.

"It gets worse," Sophie said. "The Chronos and Lanterntrager projects were codenames for an overarching project that went under the name 'Die Glocke' or 'The Bell'."

"Dr Kammler's secret weapons project," David exclaimed.

Sophie nodded. "The project that made him travel to Turkey. The Germans' Wunderwaffe."

David brushed his left hand through his hair. "So there is a connection between King Midas' treasure and this secret weapon called Die Glocke that the Nazis were developing. But what was this weapon? The Germans never succeeded in building an atomic bomb. The Allied Forces won the weapons race," David said.

"I'm not so sure about that," Sophie remarked. "This person who only went by the name, the Norwegian, he was a physicist. Apparently a brilliant one."

"What did you just say?"

"The Norwegian was a brilliant physicist," Sophie repeated.

It was as if David's blood immediately turned to ice. It couldn't be.

No, it was impossible.

It couldn't be.

It was just unthinkable.

-32-

"It will work. It must work." Wen Ning was utilising all his energy to keep up the façade, to give them the respect they expected, but did not necessarily deserve. What he really felt like doing was to jump across the table and cut the ambassador's throat. But that action would hardly benefit his case. Wen Ning was having lunch with the Chinese ambassador at an upmarket Chinese restaurant in Ankara. The quiet lunch had turned somewhat hostile during the last few minutes. "They are worried about the risks," the ambassador said with a soft, almost apologetic voice. Wen Ning had troubles hearing him properly, and gently leant across the table to avoid the ambassador becoming aware of the problem. Wen Ning was unsure whether the ambassador was shy or just had grown so accustomed to people listening when he spoke that he didn't even bother raising his voice anymore. He assumed the latter alternative was the correct one.

"I can appreciate that," Wen Ning replied. "But we have initiated a process, and we have crossed the point of no return a long time ago. We need to finish it. I can't even fathom the consequences of stopping now."

"We want you to come up with alternatives. We have no guarantees it really exists, and we can't risk being linked to this."

"Have I ever failed you? For more than twenty years I have

done everything the country has ever asked of me. I have obeyed every order. I have given up my own life to serve the cause."

"Nobody doubts your loyalty, Wen. And you will be richly rewarded when the time comes, but there is too much publicity around your actions. We can't risk our relationship with the West. We have sacrificed a lot to get where we are today."

Wen Ning studied the ambassador's fat face. Too many fancy dinners had clouded his ability to assess situations and decide on the appropriate action. His appearance had always reminded Wen Ning of Kim Jong-un, the new dictator of North Korea. Even though the online version of China's communist party paper, The People's Daily, incorrectly had reported that Kim Jong-un had been voted the sexiest man of 2012, after a satirical announcement in an American paper, Wen Ning had realised that it was a joke almost immediately. Like Kim Jong-un the ambassador was not a handsome-looking man. Wen Ning despised him. "Please tell our great leader that I will do what is best for our country. He can be certain of that," Wen Ning said before rising from his seat. He threw his napkin on the plate in front of him. It landed on the half-eaten Peking duck. The ambassador stared at him with an open mouth, struggling to believe Wen Ning's audacity.

While he was standing outside the restaurant, waiting for a taxi, Wen Ning thought about Kim Jong-un. The great leader of North Korea couldn't care less what the West thought of him. He did what was required. Wen Ning was glad he had lost his ability to smell and taste. He wasn't distracted by all the things that compromised his Party comrades. He didn't care whether he was served Peking Duck and expensive French wines or rice and water. What mattered for Wen Ning was that his country flourished. Truly flourished.

He had recently read an article in the Wall Street Journal

that claimed that seventy-five of the richest one thousand people in China held a seat in the three thousand large People's Congress. The average net worth of those seventy-five members was 1.1 billion dollars. In comparison all the 535 members of the legislative senate in the US had a combined net worth of less than 6.5 billion dollars. It was hard to know who the capitalists in today's world were.

Nothing was black and white anymore.

Everything was grey.

-33-

hen Sophie had gone for a run, David snuck out of the hotel. He hadn't done it with a light heart, but it had been necessary. Even though he had only known Sophie for a few days he had started to develop strong feelings for her, and he didn't want to expose her to any more danger. And that was what he was afraid of. That he was involving her in something dangerous.

There was a reason for David being involved in this case. He had been gullible when he had listened to Professor Grossman's flattery. What an idiot he had been. Professor Grossman could have employed anyone he wanted. Why would he even consider David? There had to be a hidden agenda for his actions. And Sophie had come up with the first clue earlier in the morning. The German transport airplane that had landed in Bodø in April 1945 had carried parts of a secret German weapons project. Chronos, Lanterntrager, Die Glocke, the Bell. They were all codenames for the same secret project. A project Adolf Hitler had believed could hold the potential to win the war for Germany. A project so important that the Allied Forces had taken the detour through Pilsen and Prague instead of heading straight towards Berlin. What was Die Glocke? And who was the Norwegian who had welcomed the transport plane in Bodø? The mysterious SS officer who had only gone by the name 'The Norwegian'? Could it be the person David suspected?

David had tried to get in contact with Professor Grossman the whole morning, and he had left numerous messages the previous night. Where was he and why had he hired David? David was frustrated, but he couldn't just sit still and hope that the professor would call him back. He needed to do something. He needed to set things in motion.

He decided to investigate the 1944-accident more thoroughly. He drove to the local library, where he was hoping he could get hold of some copies of the original newspaper articles. The grey building didn't give off an inviting vibe, and the elderly lady behind the counter was even less inviting.

David asked politely if he could review the local newspapers in the period starting two weeks before the accident at the Tumuli Heights in 1944. The older lady replied that they didn't keep copies of old newspapers. Who was interested in reading old news?

David was in the process of leaving when she called out that he should check with Ahmed Hasim. Ahmed had worked as the official newspaper photographer at the time, and there was a remote possibility that he would remember something from the accident. David got the address, and after a few detours he arrived at Ahmed Hasim's house. Ahmed was ninety-three years old and one of those old people who just longed for human contact. He was therefore quite quick to invite David inside. They sat down at a table in Ahmed's garden, and David was served Turkish tea. Ahmed asked David if he wanted to play a game of chess, but David excused himself, saying he didn't know the rules.

"I was wondering whether you still have some copies of

the pictures you took of the excavation in 1944. The one that collapsed." David started.

"In 1944. Hmm. That is a long time ago. Why are you interested in those pictures now?" Ahmed Hasim asked.

"I'm working on an article, an article which hopefully will shed some light on the terrible things that happened here after the accident. But I need information."

"What good can come of digging in this old case?"

"I honestly don't know. But I do know that we owe it to the people who were massacred here to tell the world what really happened. We owe it to them to tell the truth."

"Telling the truth is not always the wisest thing to do. Sometimes it is best to leave things as they are." Ahmed Hasim rose from his chair and walked out of the dining room.

David sighed. It looked like this was going to be another dead end.

Ahmed Hasim returned to the living room a few minutes later. In his hands he carried an old shoebox. "I wasn't a very skilled photographer," he said. "I was only a young kid when I took those pictures. I was actually working as an errand boy at the time, but the regular photographer was ill so the paper sent me instead. It was my first job. What a job it turned out to be," he laughed bitterly. "I've kept most of the pictures I took the first six months on the job. I thought they might bring some luck in life, a little bit like the first dollar you make. They didn't. But I did get employed as the paper's permanent photographer after the accident."

David lifted the lid of the shoebox to the side and started to flip through the stacks of negatives. After about twenty-five minutes he found a series of negatives from the excavation. And there on the third strip of pictures he found what he was looking for. "Can we enlarge this?" he asked.

Ahmed Hasim got up and walked over to his writing desk. He pulled out a magnifying glass from one of the drawers. "What are you looking for?" he asked when he sat down again.

"Nothing special. Only a good picture for my article," David lied. He raised the magnifying glass to his right eye and studied the negative.

There was no doubt.

It was a picture of Dr Kammler and another man dressed in an SS uniform, a person David had seen before.

"Do you know who this is?" he asked, handing the negative and the magnifying glass to Ahmed Hasim.

"A monster," Ahmed Hasim spat out. "They were all monsters. He came here with the general and was one of those who survived the explosion."

"Explosion?" David asked.

"Yes. The grave collapsing was never an accident. I can tell the difference between a grave collapsing and a grave being blown up. Whatever they found in that grave they didn't want anybody else to find it. They blew the whole thing to pieces with so much explosives that there was hardly anything left. How the Alchemist survived I have no idea," Ahmed Hasim said.

"Did you speak to him?" David asked, and pointed to the man next to Dr Kammler.

"You didn't speak to the Nazis. They didn't consider us human beings. We were 'Untermenschen' to them – we didn't exist."

David asked if he could borrow the negatives for a few days so that he could make some copies and develop the pictures. Ahmed Hasim nodded. "It's about time the story is told," he said.

David said thank you, and left the old man's house. Outside

he stopped on the pavement for a second and took a deep breath. The unknown person in the picture was David's granddad, he had seen pictures of him at home in his parents' house.

The Norwegian.

Dr Kammler's partner in crime.

The physicist.

There was no doubt. David's granddad had been at the excavation.

His granddad had been an SS officer.

David had decided not to tell Ahmed Hasim. Turkey was a country where blood revenge could still be exercised for all he knew.

An eye for an eye.

If somebody discovered that David's granddad had been involved in the massacre, then his life could be in danger.

Priority one was now to find out why Professor Grossman had hired him for this assignment. It wasn't accidental. That was pretty obvious. But why had David been involved? What was the motivation? And who was pulling the strings? It had to have something to do with his granddad, but what?

David hardly knew anything about his granddad. They hadn't spoken much about him when David grew up. He was the family's dark secret. The one they never mentioned. At age twenty-five he had enlisted for the German front. He had wanted to fight the Red Threat, his father had said. He was one of many Norwegians who had thought they did the motherland a favour by fighting communism before it hit the Norwegian borders. But he had made a terrible choice. The Nazis had taken over Germany and suddenly he had ended up fighting for the wrong side. David's granddad had been one of the youngest postgraduate students in physics at Oslo University when he enlisted. He had basically shocked everyone when he packed his things and left for the East German front. But that was the way he apparently had been, impulsive and idealistic. David's dad had once told him that the granddad had died in a bombing raid on Germany, in the final days of the war.

David had never experienced any negative consequences from his grandad's involvement with the Germans during the war. It was different for David's dad though. He had never escaped the granddad's shadow. Perhaps that was why he had become an historian? He always did say that history was written by the winners, but that he tried to delve deeper than that. He wanted to portray history as it had really unfolded. Without makeup. With all its gore and dark secrets exposed. Well. Congratulations. Now one of those secrets had surfaced. David's granddad had been involved with Nazis who had executed twenty-two innocent kids in Turkey. What else had he been involved in during the war? Had he been Dr Kammler's partner in crime?

David felt sick and dry retched on the street.

He had to find out what his granddad had been involved in.

But first he needed to get hold of Professor Grossman. He needed to get an explanation of why he had been engaged in finding Yossar Devan's real identity. Not a constructed story about how he was skilled in finding people hiding from the press. But the true reason. He deserved that much.

After several unanswered calls to Professor Grossman's office, David gave up. Instead, he called one of his friends from the MBA class.

"Where are you?" his friend JC asked.

"I'm in Europe, but that's not important. Could you do me a favour?"

"The police have been here asking for you," JC said, disregarding David's question.

"What?"

"The police. They came to the door this morning. Something about whether you had been in contact with Professor Grossman last week."

"Why did they want to know about that?"

"Haven't you heard the news? Professor Grossman has disappeared. When they searched his apartment they discovered it was covered with blood. They speculate that he may have been murdered. It's been on the news."

David had problems breathing. It felt like someone was sitting on his ribcage. He considered himself as a person who seldom panicked. But right now that was exactly what he was about to do. He struggled to breathe properly. Was he about to have a heart attack? No, he was too young for that.

"I have to go," he told JC before hanging up. He clenched the phone in one hand. With the other he attempted to support himself against the wall. What the hell was happening? What had he managed to get involved in? Professor Grossman was the only person able to shed light on why David had been involved in this case. And now he had disappeared. There was a possibility he had been murdered. David should head off to the nearest police station and tell them everything he knew. He hadn't done anything illegal.

But if he did that the truth about his granddad's war crimes would be revealed. Did he want that to happen? David's dad had always claimed that David's granddad had never been a Nazi, just a naïve soldier who due to unforeseen circumstances had ended up fighting for the wrong side in the war. 'The history is always written by the winners,' his dad had said, 'but on judgement day we all have to face what we have done, for good or for worse.' David had never understood what he had meant. And they had never discussed it any further. David had been an atheist for as long as he could remember, and he certainly didn't believe in a life after death where you had to be held accountable for your sins. You had to live your life as best you could, but when it was over, it was truly over. He found it surprising that his dad, who had been an exceptionally smart man, could believe in God. David's dad had been an historian with a natural scepticism of historical events. He had believed that you should approach all information with caution because everything was coloured by the people who recorded it. Still his dad had believed in the Bible, something that David thought was nothing more than a bunch of fairy tales, written without evidence of any sort. This conflict of blind faith versus logic David didn't understand much of. But right now there was nothing else he wanted more than for his father to be alive. He was always so wise, and David needed some of his wisdom right now. Someone who could look at the situation without emotions, pick it apart, piece by piece, and make sense out of everything.

He realised he missed his dad immensely. David had left for Australia less than a year after his dad had died. He had often wondered if that had been a selfish decision. If maybe he should have been there for his mother instead. But she was a tough lady, and had told him that there was no need to postpone the MBA degree. They could speak on the phone if there was something. And they did. David called his mum at least once a week.

David started to walk down the street. If he truly was in any danger he should attempt to move as much as possible. He kept looking over his shoulder, to check if someone was following. No one was.

It reminded David of the time he had taken a high school math exam for a friend. It had started out as a silly bet. His friend had told him that he would buy him a bottle of wine if he took his exam. The friend was a smart guy and didn't need to cheat. But David had liked the idea. He had borrowed the friend's driver's licence and attended the friend's exam. David hadn't been nervous, but something unexpected had happened. He had made an effort to make himself look like his friend, or at least not like himself. A pair of glasses without strength, a white cap pulled as far down on his face as possible, and some bland clothing had done the trick. He felt invisible. The exam guards were all unknowns and had all hit their late sixties so he had assumed the risk of getting caught was minimal. Still, after an hour or so he had started getting this feeling that they had figured him out. Every time a couple of the exam guards either talked together or wandered down the aisle he thought he was busted. He expected them to walk over to him and tell him to pack his stuff. It had of course never happened, but he had learnt first-hand how paranoia worked. And he had, there and then, decided to never become a criminal. It had been so exhausting, so incredibly exhausting. He tried to convince himself that what he now felt was the same. There was no one chasing him. It was just the paranoia playing games with his brain.

He still had to come up with a plan though. He had to figure out who it was who had involved him in this case. Out of nowhere he had been asked to participate in the search for Yossar Devan's real identity. Yossar Devan, who it turned out, was involved in everything from Nazi conspiracies to the myth about King Midas.

Professor Grossman, the man who had hired David, had

disappeared, and was possibly murdered. David's granddad had been involved in the slaughtering of twenty-two Turkish kids during the war. It was all a big mess. What was it that didn't add up? What was it he failed to see? The granddad was the link. It was he who connected David to the mystery. But how and why?

David was riddled with uncertainty about what to do. He felt afraid and alone.

He tried calling Peter Swarkowski, but only got a message that the number was no longer in use.

Professor Grossman had disappeared. Swarkowski had gone underground. Whom could he contact? Who could help him?

He decided to call his mum. She was staying at their vacation house in Turkey. He needed to escape all the chaos he felt surrounded him. Maybe he could stay with his mum for a few days? Get his sanity back?

He pulled out his phone and dialled her number. "Hi mum. It's David."

"David. How are you? Is the weather nice in Australia?" his mother asked.

"I'm not in Australia, mum. I'm in Turkey. Long story, but could I come and stay with you for a few days?"

"Of course, David. Are you sure everything is ok?"

"Yes, everything is ok. I'm here as part of my studies. Thought it could be a surprise for you, but I just wanted to make sure you were home. I will leave Ankara tonight, so I should be at your place tomorrow morning."

"Look forward to it," his mum said with true happiness in her voice.

There was a pause before David continued.

"Mum, did dad ever talk about granddad?"

"Why do you ask me that? Are you sure you're ok, David?"

"Yes, yes. I'm fine. We can talk when I see you tomorrow," David said. He didn't want to worry his mum for no reason.

He hung up. He realised that he wasn't going to be able to sleep so he decided to read another of the principles. He pulled out the Kindle reader and turned it on.

Principle 8: Giving back.

The first few years of my working life I spent every single pound I made on myself. I did, as mentioned in the second principle, understand that I had to let my money work harder for me if I was serious about changing my life. So I started to invest. And after a few years my money started to grow. But my money only made me richer. I never shared with anyone. I viewed the business world as a big competition. It was me against everybody else.

Me against the world.

Several years passed before I learnt the importance of giving back. Accumulation of riches is not different from most other things in this wonderful world we live in. Think about it. What is the easiest way to get a smile? To smile at the person you want the smile from! In the same way the easiest way to get money, love, friendship and everything else important in life is by first giving it to others.

Ever since I understood this principle I have tried to give back as much as I can. It hasn't always been easy. It is difficult to give away money when there are things you want yourself, or to smile at a person when all you want to do is be alone. But it is at these moments the principle really works.

I didn't realise this until late in my life. I always thought I would give back after I had made a little bit more. Let my money work a little bit harder before I shared it with others. Of course I ended up never giving away anything. I always came up with an excuse.

But life is short. And when it gives you an opportunity, you have to seize it. My life gave me an opportunity to learn how to give. And I am eternally grateful for that opportunity. It has been instrumental in the building of my business empire.

One of my oil tankers had an accident in the Middle East, in the mid-1960s. We were sailing in an area with several conflicts, and there was always the risk that something could go wrong. I did what I could to ensure that safety was taken care of, but we were unlucky and sailed into a situation. To make a long story short: Two of my Filipino crew were shot and killed by modern-day pirates. They were the breadwinners of their respective families, and they left behind wives and children. We did have standard insurance policies in place that covered instances like this, but I wanted to do something special. I knew both men personally. They knew what they had signed up for and the risks that were involved. Still they had chosen to take the jobs because we were performing a necessary service by bringing oil to areas that were isolated due to violent conflicts. And of course, they needed to feed their families.

I chose to personally fly down to inform the wives of their losses. I also gave them my personal word that their futures would be taken care of. I set up a trust for each family, which in addition to providing them with adequate funds to cover living costs, also paid for their children's educational needs. The children could choose to study whatever they wanted to – it was all covered. It cost me a lot of money, but for the first time in my life I felt that I had done something important. I had made a difference.

It didn't take long though before I was back in my normal mode of thinking about profit margins and what my competitors were doing. I simply forgot about the whole incident.

And then six months later I was arrested in the Middle East. I was accused of breaking trade embargoes and using oil from the tankers to fuel the ships. The claims were ridiculous and without any merit in reality. But nobody cares about what is true or not. The important thing was to find a scapegoat. An example for the rest of the industry that war profiteering wasn't accepted. I was put in a dark prison cell for three months. The world's most expensive lawyers and a well full of money didn't seem to help. Instead, the help came from somewhere totally unexpected. The wives of the two Filipinos, who had died working for me, came to my rescue. They pooled the money I had given them and started fighting for my release. They did something my lawyers never could have done. They gave the so-called war-profiteer a human face. And they changed everybody's perception of me. They got me released.

The story would have been great if it ended there. I discovered, however, that this wasn't an isolated incidence. It was part of a wider phenomenon. It turned out that every time I did something unselfish, it could be something as simple as helping somebody get a job or providing some financial aid, I eventually ended up getting back more than I gave. And finally, after so many years, I understood the wisdom in the phrase 'give and you shall receive' because there is more between heaven and earth than we can see with our own eyes. I don't believe in a God. But I do believe that the universe rewards those who act altruistically.

Recording these principles is my way of giving back – to share something I believe is valuable to others.

David turned off his Kindle reader. He hadn't expected generosity to be one of the principles for riches. His experience was different. It was always the most selfish and stingy people who managed to get rich. Only after they had amassed their enormous fortunes had they started to give back. When they were building their businesses there was never any room to give away money. It was necessary to pay yourself first, to always pay yourself first. How else could you put your money to work? But maybe Professor Grossman was right? It didn't necessarily have to be money you gave away. You could help in many ways. David pondered whether there was a way he could implement the principle in his own life. He wasn't very keen to give away any money when he was still living on a student loan, which he at some stage had to pay back. With interest.

Was that selfish of him? He still very much lived a life of privilege, even though he couldn't afford to eat at restaurants every week. David decided to become more generous in his own life. To not expect something back every time he did a good deed. Maybe this search for Yossar Devan could be something he could share with others at some stage. If the principles really worked then they could possibly help others to gain a better life.

But all these things lay far ahead in time. Right now he had bigger problems than to feel sorry for himself because he didn't have a bank account with seven digits. What did money and material goods count for in the real world anyway? He had enough to get by. He could only eat dinner one time each day. It wasn't necessary, it probably wasn't healthy, that life was both a game and a dance on red roses. It was situations like the one he now found himself in that defined people, that created character. David needed to find out why he had been involved in the search for Yossar Devan's real identity. It didn't matter so much whether he found a secret formula for wealth.

But he had to find out why Professor Grossman had involved him.

-34-

The phone's thermometer app read twenty-five degrees Celsius, but it felt substantially warmer. David was sitting in the hotel lobby, observing daily life. A mother kissed her ten-year-old kid on the head before she tied his shoelaces. He seemed embarrassed and pushed her away. He probably felt he was old enough to tie his own shoelaces.

David picked at the Heineken label of his beer bottle. A circle of moisture surrounded the base of the bottle. He glanced over at the TV in the corner of the room. There had been something familiar with the face flashing on the Sky News broadcast only seconds earlier.

He rose from his chair, walked over to the TV, and turned up the volume.

"It is with great loss that Mitchell Properties Ltd this morning announced the passing of their founder, the billionaire John Mitchell. John Mitchell is the last fatality after the workplace accident at one of Mitchell Properties' developments four days ago. Two other executives from the company also perished when one of the construction lifts malfunctioned and dropped eighty metres before hitting the ground. John Mitchell was admitted to Saratona Hospital with life-threatening injuries. Unfortunately, the hospital today confirmed that John Mitchell died last night due to a massive cardiac arrest. Mitchell Properties has yet to publicly comment on the cause of the accident, but no foul play is suspected. The police have, as a matter of normal procedure, initiated an investigation. The results are expected within three weeks. John Mitchell is survived by his wife Miranda and two teenage sons. In other news we will today review the rapidly climbing price of gold. Our finance expert, Marcus Fielding, asks if we are witnessing a new bubble in the making."

David stared at the TV screen. A few days ago John Mitchell had almost thrown him out of his office. Now he was dead. David didn't really know John Mitchell. But he had this uncanny feeling that just didn't go away, a feeling that John Mitchell had been afraid of him. What could he possibly have been afraid of? And was it a coincidence that John Mitchell had died just days after meeting David? Professor Grossman was also possibly dead. There had to be a connection.

David placed his half-drunk Heineken onto the first available table and walked briskly over to the elevator. He took the lift up to the fourth floor and walked over to his room. Then he stopped. The door. Was it open? He gently pushed the door, but it didn't move. It was closed. It was just his mind playing tricks again. He pulled out his key card and unlocked the door. His laptop lay in the middle of the bed, just as he had left it two hours ago. He unfolded it, opened the Firefox internet browser and logged onto his Hotmail account. Jon Berthelsen's email had contained a number of names with the description 'deceased' next to them. David keyed in the first name in the Google search engine.

'Mary-Rose Whitton.'

A number of articles filled the screen. David clicked on an article from News.com.

'30. June 2012. Mary-Rose Whitton perished in a light

airplane accident outside Nevada yesterday afternoon. The avid pilot, billionaire, real estate investor and founder of the fast-food chain Maro had just left Montana airfield for a morning joy ride when her plane experienced some technical problems.'

She had lost radio contact with air control soon after reporting some minor navigational problems. The plane had crashed shortly after. The wreckage was located within an hour, but Mary-Rose Whitton was declared dead at the scene. She had died on impact.

David conducted searches on the other names: Cameron Milner, Chris Walsh, Ralph Ferguson. They had all been killed in accidents over the last six months. Ryan Mortimer, the billionaire Jon Berthelsen had noted 'missing' next to, was also presumed dead. He had been reported missing after falling overboard from his hundred and ten-meter-long sailboat 'Phoenix Rising' in Thailand last spring. Relatives were still searching for him, but so far they hadn't found a trace of his body.

David folded his laptop together. Was it a coincidence that so many of these billionaires had perished over the last few months? He pushed the thought away. The newspaper reports had been quite clear when labelling all the deaths tragic accidents. None of them had been ruled suspicious. That was how the world worked. You never knew when your hourglass had reached the precious last few grains of sand. It was the same with David's dad: After having worked hard his whole life he had looked forward to retiring in Turkey. But then he had happened to be in the wrong spot at the wrong time. And just like that, his life was over. That's how quickly it could happen. David knew from his own experience. There was no reason, no fairness. Death didn't care whether you were a billionaire or lived on food stamps. Death didn't care whether you had worked your butt off your whole life or if everything had just fallen into your hands. It simply didn't matter. Accidents happened. Randomness ruled life. He took a deep breath, and sighed. He had to learn to relax. To not fear the worst every time something unexpected happened. David lay down on the bed and stared at the ceiling. The Kindle reader was lying on the table. It was a new day. That meant a new principle. He rolled over to the nightstand and turned on the Kindle reader.

Principle 9: Decision

Nobody has ever achieved anything truly exceptional without making a decision. Making decisions is essential for succeeding. That goes for riches as for most other things in life. I used to tell my employees that it was better that they made some wrong decisions than none at all. All progress in our world is created by men and women making decisions. If you don't make decisions then nothing happens. If you make a wrong decision then at least something happens. In the worst case scenario you can at least learn something from that wrong decision.

I was always quick to make decisions, and slow to change them. You can't afford to be indecisive. You have to stand by your choices in good and bad times.

I am of the opinion that the two most important decisions in a person's life are the choice of partner and choice of job. If you make the right choices in those two decisions then you will have a good life. A job you enjoy, that has a meaning and gives you the feeling that you are making a difference. And a life partner who supports you in your decisions, and makes you a better person. In my world that is a recipe for happiness.

It is therefore rather strange that the decision-making process for those two choices often is so fundamentally different. When you choose your life partner you most often listen to your heart. You find the person you want to share the rest of your life with, and suddenly everything else becomes irrelevant. You find the one who makes you happy and you go for it. You choose with your heart and focus on the upside.

When you choose a job you often don't choose with your heart. You embark on an education that you know will provide a good probability of employment. You choose an occupation with stability and low risk. You choose with your brain and very often you only focus on the downside.

I'm not qualified to give relationship advice. I never found my life partner. I was tough in business, but soft in my personal life. A dark day, many years ago, I lost everyone who was close to me, and it did something to me. The result was that I never took chances in my personal life, and I never found someone to share my life with. But I am qualified to talk about business and jobs. And I believe that if more people did as I, and chose their job with their heart instead of their brain, then we would have more successful people. Because the world's resources are not a zero-sum game where somebody has to lose what others gain. The world has an abundance of riches. We are the ones who limit ourselves.

If I were to analyse my own career, I would realise that my success and my wealth are a result not of working harder than everybody else, but of a few important decisions I made. If I hadn't made those decisions, then my life would have turned out very different.

I decided that I had to work with something I was passionate about, and after buying a colleague a beer I realised that I had to let my money work for me instead of working for my money. Those decisions were instrumental in changing my life and setting me on the path to riches. But the most important decision

I ever made was to put aside my fear. To put aside the fear of going back to the place where darkness first appeared in my life, the place where my life was turned upside down. It was in this place, the place responsible for all my nightmares, that I also found the secret. The secret that has created all my wealth.

A secret that is available for everyone.

A secret so simple that you won't understand how you have been able to miss it for all these years – the tenth principle of wealth.

David put away the Kindle reader. What was it Professor Grossman was referring to? Why had he built up the expectation to the next principle? Had he figured out what Yossar Devan's secret was? There could be no other reason. One thing was for sure though. David wouldn't get to know what it was. Professor Grossman had disappeared, possibly been murdered. And there was thus no one to upload the last principle to David's Kindle reader.

David swore silently.

He was frustrated. It wasn't just the fact that he wouldn't be able to read the last principle. He also thought that the professor's principles were hard to implement. It was too easy to say that you had to live your life as if every day was your last. Most people, David included, had bills to pay. He shook his head and brushed his hand through his hair. Or was he just coming up with excuses?

He knew one thing for sure though. If he was going to die tomorrow, he would regret not spending the rest of the day with Sophie. He missed her already.

David pondered the ninth principle. Was it true that all the events and job choices in his life had contained an underlying meaning? He couldn't see how that was possible. The only thing he knew for sure was that he didn't want his life to continue in the direction it was going. Which important skills had his jobs in banking and media helped him acquire? Precious few that could help him establish himself as an entrepreneur. But those jobs had provided him with invaluable skills in the search for Yossar Devan's true identity. They had led him the whole way.

Maybe this was his mission in life? To figure out the mysteries of history like his dad? Maybe he wasn't meant to be an entrepreneur. Maybe he was meant to write about them?

The search for Yossar Devan's true identity had been like an onion. Every time he had felt closer to finding the solution, a new layer of truths had appeared. Would he ever be able to reach the core? And would he like what he eventually found there?

-35-

Anna Dypsvik was a good-looking woman. David's mother had been lucky with the genes. But her best quality was her willpower. Every single morning she went for a long walk. The weather was never an excuse. It almost had to be like that when you lived in Bergen, the wettest city in Norway. Anna had grown up in Denmark, as the youngest of four sisters. Her family had moved to Norway when she was seventeen years old. She had met David's dad, Jan-Olav, at a barbeque the following year and it had been love at first sight. So grand had their love been that Anna had accepted to live in Bergen even though she couldn't stand the weather.

Just prior to their thirty-fifth wedding anniversary, David's dad had bought a holiday home in Turkey. It was supposed to be their personal sanctuary. A place where they could spend their retirement together. David's dad had just celebrated his sixty-seventh birthday and was ready to retire from his position as an historian at the University of Bergen. His wife still had another year left before she would be able to retire so the plan had been that Jan-Olav should spend a year by himself in Turkey, writing and reflecting on life. But life had had its own plan: Jan-Olav had perished in a car accident only six months into his retirement. After the death of Jan-Olav nothing was ever the same in the

Dypsvik family. David moved to Australia and his mum moved to Turkey. She loved sunbathing. Just as David felt alive when the rain splashed down on his face, his mum felt most alive when the rays of the sun prickled her skin.

"Hi mum," David called out as he entered the rose-covered garden.

"David, why didn't you call? I could have picked you up." Anna Dypsvik sounded a bit hurt as she rushed towards the gate to greet him.

David did, however, still have this uncanny feeling of being watched. He had therefore chosen to drive. After attempting numerous diversion manoeuvres on the way to his mum he had almost felt like he was in a James Bond movie. He had no idea whether somebody had really followed him though.

David's mother smiled from ear to ear when he gave her a big hug. "Do I look old?" she asked, as they wandered up toward the house.

"No mum, you don't look old. You look good."

David's mum had evidently spent a few more hours at the beach than the Cancer Council recommended, and had acquired the bluish tan older Norwegians often got after decades in the sun without protection.

"Take off your T-shirt and get some sun on your body," she said to David. "You look like an Englishman. I thought you lived in Australia. Are you allergic to sun?" she asked.

David laughed, but didn't stop walking. His mum hadn't changed. She always complained about him being pale and not eating enough. She said it in a humoristic way though.

"No, mum. I'm not allergic to sun. I am just a bit careful. And I eat well. How are you?"

"I'm well, thank you. Got lots to do. The days are flying by.

Just started on a chef course."

"Are you doing a chef course? You don't even like to cook."

"Never too late to try something new," David's mother said, opening the door to the house.

The house was warm and cosy. If David's mother didn't like to spend much time in the kitchen, she made up for it by being a master interior decorator. The house was white and summerish. It basically screamed welcome.

An hour later David and his mum were sitting in the garden, eating pasta. David's mum sipped from a glass of Sauvignon Blanc. David enjoyed a cold beer.

"You were very brief on the phone. Tell me why you are here," his mum said.

"What did dad tell you about granddad?" David asked, disregarding his mum's question.

"What do you mean?"

"We never talked about him. How was he? Who was he?"

"What's going on, David? You are coming to Turkey in the middle of your semester, wanting to talk about granddad. It doesn't make sense," she said waving her arms. David thought the whole scene was a bit theatrical, but he acknowledged that he did owe her a proper explanation. He didn't mention anything about the missing professor, the dead billionaires or the fact that he suspected that he might be followed. He only told her that he had come across some pictures involving his granddad in a massacre during the Second World War.

Anna Dypsvik looked terrified. "I never asked Jan-Olav about his dad. And he never spoke about him. Your dad never got to meet his own dad. That's all I know. Jan-Olav was conceived when his dad, unannounced, arrived home from the German front towards the end of the war. Jan-Olav's dad was in Norway one night. One night, and that was enough for Jan-Olav to be conceived. One single night in 1945, after having been gone for more than seven years. Can you imagine that? Your grandmother told Jan-Olav his dad had left the very next morning. And that was the last time anybody ever saw or heard from him. Jan-Olav was born nine months later. But he never got to meet his dad. The rumour was that he had died during a bombing raid in Germany shortly after."

David's mum started crying. "Whatever your granddad did is irrelevant. Your dad was a great man. The kindest soul I have ever met."

David wrapped his arms around his mother.

"I'm sorry if I upset you, mum. I didn't mean to criticize dad. I just wonder why I've never heard anything about this. Dad was an historian. He specialised in the Second World War. He would have known if granddad was involved in a massacre, wouldn't he?"

"Your dad always wanted the best for you, David. If he knew, and kept it a secret, he would have done it for a reason. He was always watching out for you."

"I know, mum, and I miss him immensely. But I've got this feeling that it is important that I figure out what dad knew about granddad. There is something that doesn't add up here."

David's mum turned on the light in Jan-Olav Dypsvik's office. It had remained untouched since his passing. David's mum had thought about cleaning it out a few times, but she hadn't been able to. The grief was still too strong. She took pleasure in walking past his office and casually noticing his messy desk. The bookshelves were a disorganised chaos. No books were in alphabetical order, but Jan-Olav had known exactly where every bit of information he needed would be found.

Jan-Olav's office was like his personality had always been. Complicated, but warm.

David started to go through his dad's desk. There was nothing out of the ordinary. Why did David think he was going to find something in the office? Something that could provide him with an answer to why he had travelled across half the globe to search for the identity of a man who had never existed. Only to end up discovering that his granddad had been a coldblooded killer, an SS officer involved in the execution of a number of innocent Turkish kids.

David and his mum had travelled to Turkey to attend to all the formalities after the freak car accident that killed his dad. David couldn't count all the days he had spent on top of that cliff where his dad's car had lost its grip on the road and careered off. He had just stood there for hours, peering out over the vast ocean. He had never told anybody, but what he had really done was to wait for his dad to come climbing up the edge of the cliff, brush some dust off his shoulders and ask David how he was. Every time he heard a sound from the door of their holiday house he was anticipating his dad to walk through the door. The first weeks he recognised his dad's face several times a day. In the shop, driving a car, everywhere he went. During the last twelve months it had happened less frequently, but he could still not fathom that he had lost his dad. The dad he never really had realised how much he looked up to and loved.

He had spent most of the time in the holiday house looking for his dad's laptop. Unfortunately he had never found it. David had even contacted the local police to check whether they had located it in the car wreck, when it was hoisted out of the ocean. But they weren't very helpful, and no personal items were apparently ever recovered from the wreck. His dad's laptop was gone.

It had angered David. For a long time he had hoped to find his dad's unfinished novel. A last memory of his beloved dad. Maybe he could even have it published? Maybe the novel was almost finished, and David could honour his dad's memory by publishing it post-mortem? Distressed, he walked back into the living room. His mother was head-down in a book. She put the book away and smiled at him. "David, can you do me a favour?" she asked.

"Of course, mum."

"I've heard that everybody is on Facebook these days. Could you set up an account for me?"

David smiled. What was going on with his mum? Cooking school and a Facebook account. She was having a new youth.

"Of course. Where is the computer?"

"It's still in the bedroom."

David turned around and walked back, past the office, to his mum's bedroom. He found the power button and started up the old desktop computer. The hard drive kept making a screeching sound and David figured it was singing its last verse. His mother wasn't very good with computers so he decided he would make a backup of her files. If her computer broke down some dodgy Turkish IT guy would probably otherwise charge her an arm and a leg to restore the files. He pulled out the drawer of his mum's desk to look for the external hard drive.

And there, sitting on top of a stack of paper, was his dad's laptop.

David picked it up and walked briskly into the living room. "Did you find dad's laptop?" he asked, excitedly.

"Oh yes, forgot to tell you. Found it in the garage a few months back. Jan-Olav must have put it there while going back into the house to look for something. It had fallen behind the lawn mower."

"Does it work?"

"No," his mother replied. "I tried turning it on, but it kept asking for a password."

David smiled. It meant the laptop worked.

"I'm just gonna be in dad's office for a while," David said.

"No problem. Relax, take it easy David. You need some rest. You look really skinny."

David turned on the laptop. As expected, the computer asked for a password. David had no idea what his dad would have used as a password. But he knew the system. David's dad changed his passwords every month. David couldn't really understand who would be interested in hacking an historian's computer, but that was how his dad had rolled. The system was pretty simple. It was the numbers 925 followed by something he could see from his desk. This system helped him if he at some stage would forget his password.

David punched in '925coffecup'. The laptop beeped. He keyed in '925sunglasses'. It beeped again.

He searched through the mess on the desk. There were a number of notepads lying there, but they were all brand new and by the looks of it unused apart from some pages having been ripped out. There was nothing that stood out. Or was there? In the left corner of his eye he noticed something that didn't belong, a lotto ticket. David's dad never played lotto. It was against his beliefs.

David remembered the one time he had asked his dad to buy a ticket for him. His dad had bought a ticket, but he had chosen the numbers 1,2,3,4,5,6,7 – ten times, out of pure spite. It had annoyed David. It had been one of those jackpot drawings where the whole country bought tickets, and although David didn't expect to win he would have liked to have a chance.

His dad simply explained that the chance for the numbers one to seven to be drawn was exactly the same as for any other combination of numbers. There was no point arguing of course, his dad was correct. But it didn't feel right.

What were the numbers on the lotto ticket? 12, 21, 32, 15, 31, 10. He tried seven different combinations with numbers and words related to lotto, but nothing worked. The laptop kept beeping. The screen showed he had used forty-seven of fifty tries for the code. He only had three tries left.

Frustrated, he leant back in the office chair and covered his face with his hands. There were millions of different number and word combinations. He could be sitting there a whole lifetime without hitting the right one. How was he supposed to know what had occupied his dad's last thoughts? He had hoped it would be something easy as his mum's or his own name. But it had of course not been that easy. David's dad had had other things than David to worry about in his retirement.

David crumpled the lotto ticket together and threw it in the direction of the dustbin. It hit the edge and dropped down on the tiles.

David got up and picked up the wrinkly lotto ticket. He was about to place it in the dustbin when he noticed something strange.

There was a piece of folded paper in the dustbin. There was something familiar about it.

He picked it up and placed it on the desk. It was a yellow piece of lined paper, just like the notepads his dad used for work.

There was no text on the piece of paper, but in the right upper corner there was a drawing of a shape David recognised.

A bell shaped form.

A forgotten item from the Second World War.

Die Glocke.

He punched in '925dieglocke' on the keyboard.

The laptop started up.

-36-

Wen Ning wiped the mirror with his elbow. His eyes were bloodshot and big bags were fighting gravity underneath his eyes. He immersed his face in the ice-cold water in the sink. It burned his forehead and a tiny ribbon of blood floated off into the water. After thirty seconds he pulled his head out, and exhaled.

He squinted at his own reflection, while he put away the bloodstained knife.

Wen Ning had been born with an extraordinary gift; the ability to recognise people. Even though today's facial recognition technology made it possible to create algorithms which could predict how you would look like thirty years from now, they would never be able to replace people like Wen Ning; people with the unique ability to recognise other people. It didn't matter if the person had been through a hundred plastic surgery operations. Wen Ning always recognised them. But staring at his own reflection in the mirror Wen Ning realised he could hardly recognise himself.

-37-

David sat dumbfounded and observed the laptop starting up. His dad's password had been 'Die Glocke', the secret project the German SS general Dr Hans Kammler and his own granddad had been working on.

A small doodle. One of those his father had a habit of drawing when he was bored, or when his mind was preoccupied with something else, had been the answer. David's dad had known about Die Glocke.

David leant forward in the chair and opened the folder containing personal files.

He sorted the Microsoft Word files by dates and opened the last document. It looked like a diary, and the last entry had been done on the same day his dad, Jan-Olav, had perished in a car accident. David started reading.

"Finally breakthrough. Identified site. Will check more tomorrow."

A cold shiver went through David's body. His dad had made an important discovery the very same day he died. Professor Grossman had disappeared. In Australia there were rumours he could have been murdered. Had David's dad been murdered because he discovered something he wasn't meant to? Had the car accident just been a cover up? And who was his family? He had just learnt that his granddad had been a Nazi, involved in the execution of a number of innocent Turkish kids during the Second World War. And his dad had lived a secret life where he had been investigating some case without telling anyone what he was doing.

David was struggling with mixed emotions. He felt betrayed by his dad, who hadn't been honest with him. He felt betrayed by his dad, who had kept secrets from him.

David had always thought his dad was working on a novel in Turkey. But he had evidently been involved in some kind of investigation. An investigation to find out what David's granddad had been involved in during the Second World War, he presumed. Was this what Jan-Olav Dypsvik had been afraid of when he always said that you had to face your sins at life's end? Had his dad figured out what the granddad had been responsible for doing?

David started to go through the other entries in his dad's diary. They weren't very structured. Sometimes his dad wrote about what he had been eating for dinner, whereas other entries were of a more academic nature, about matters of which David had limited knowledge. David also found a few entries where his dad wrote about how much he missed David. David was close to crying several times while he was reading the diary, and he was sad that his dad never had been able to express those emotions to him, face to face. An hour passed before David's mum called out for him. David was yanked out of the trance he had found himself in. He had forgotten both time and place. If his dad had been murdered because he discovered something he wasn't supposed to, his dad who as far as David knew hadn't told a living soul about whatever it was he was working on, then David had just put his mum's life in danger. He had to assume he was being monitored. Why had he been involved in the search for Yossar Devan's identity? It had to be related to what his dad had discovered; it had to be related to what his granddad had done during the war. There simply were no other possibilities.

David glanced at his watch. Seven. It was too late to travel now. But he had to leave as soon as possible, he thought as he could feel small pearls of sweat form on his upper lip.

He folded the yellow piece of paper with the bell-shaped doodle, and put it into his shoulder bag together with the laptop. He glanced at the crumpled lotto ticket. He picked it up to throw it in the dustbin, but hesitated. He reviewed the numbers again. And suddenly he had an idea. What if the numbers were important? He opened up Google Earth and punched in the numbers in the search field. A position in the middle of an ocean popped up. Not exactly what he had expected. Instead he keyed in the numbers directly in his web browser. It didn't reveal any useful answer either. Just an informational website about Egypt. Frustrated, he straightened out the lotto ticket, folded it four times and slid it inside his wallet. A last memory of his dad. He turned off the lights and walked into the living room. His mum was still reading a book.

"What are you reading?" he asked.

"I'm reading one of dad's favourite books. The Old Man and the Sea, by Ernest Hemingway."

"Is it any good?"

"No," his mum laughed. "But it was the skinniest book I could find. Your dad always bugged me about not reading books, and I always promised that I would read more when I had time. But you never know how much time you have, David. I always envisioned your dad and me, sitting here in Turkey, reading all these books he enjoyed so much, sharing a good bottle of wine. But it didn't turn out that way. I think I disappointed him by never reading. So now I try to go through them one by one."

"Dad loved you, mum. He just didn't know how to express it," David said, and walked over to her. To his own surprise he gave her a kiss on the head. It had to be more than ten years since he had last given her a kiss, maybe even longer, probably not since kindergarten.

He considered showing her the diary, but decided against it. It could be dangerous. It was better if she knew nothing.

"I'll have to leave in the morning," he said, trying to sound joyful. "I'll have to follow up some leads in London."

"Are you leaving again so soon? You have only just arrived. Why don't you stay a few days?"

"I can't, mum."

"Then at least let me take you out for dinner tonight. Let's at least have one nice night together."

David felt a sting of remorse. Nobody ever worried about Anna Dypsvik. She always looked fit, suntanned and happy. But David knew that she was extremely good at keeping up a façade. She had even been diagnosed with cancer without telling a living soul about it. No, it's just a cold, she had explained, but the truth had been revealed when the family doctor had been attending a fundraising function with Jan-Olav, David's dad. The family doctor had asked if the treatment was going well and just like that the cat had been let out of the bag. David's dad had been quite angry and had felt betrayed. David's mum had excused herself by saying she didn't want to worry anyone. But the result had of course been the opposite. After that incident everyone had been worried all the time, because they all knew that she never told them the truth.

They had both had secrets, David's mum and dad. Things they didn't talk about. Things they hid from David. Had they done it to protect him? Hadn't they trusted him to be able to handle the truth?

"We don't need to go out," David said. "I can make your favourite dish, chicken Parmigiana."

David's mother smiled. David attempted to smile back, but it only came out fake.

The morning after, when David was still in the shower, his mobile rang. He let it go to message bank. While he was eating breakfast he called up to check his messages.

"Hi, this is Neill Flynn," the message started. "You came by a few days ago to talk about Yossar Devan. I know what is about to happen. Nothing is as it seems. Call me back at 20 7621 1111."

David's hand was shaking as he keyed in the number. He was so excited. Did Neill Flynn have information that could help him?

Neill Flynn's wife, Mary-Rose, answered the phone.

"Hi David, I'm sorry, but the moment has passed. Neill was so clear earlier today and he really wanted to speak to you. He kept raving that something terrible was about to happen. That they would all die."

"Did he say something more?"

"No, that was all."

"Do you know what he was doing when he had his clear moment?"

"Nothing. He was just watching the news."

"Can you remember what was on the news? Was there a special report that triggered his memory?"

"No, it was just the usual stuff. War and misery. I think there was something about the rising price of gold and China. No, I'm not really sure."

"It doesn't matter. Thanks for the help anyway," David said, and hung up. He swore silently. He wished he knew what Neill Flynn had wanted to tell him. Neill Flynn had developed a theory about what had happened to Yossar Devan, a theory that people higher up in the system had disapproved of, a theory that had ruined his career.

What was this theory and what had Neill Flynn meant by saying they would all die?

PART 3

–38–

David didn't know what to believe on his way back to Ankara. He had utilized most of the night to go through documents on his dad's laptop. And David had been wrong. He had been terribly wrong. His dad hadn't moved to Turkey to write a novel. He had moved there to put together the last pieces of a puzzle he had spent most of his life trying to solve. David's dad had lived a secret life where he had spent most of his waking hours trying to figure out what had been his own dad's role during the Second World War. All those trips to foreign countries – Germany, Poland, the US and England. David and his mum had always been told that they were necessary work trips. That he was invited to hold a lecture. That he had to check some sources. He had probably done those things as well. But it appeared he always had had his own agenda. Jan-Olav Dypsvik had managed to get Bergen University to fly him around the world. He had done his job, but he had also been very busy with his own pet project: Trying to unravel the threads in his own father's life. The search for the truth about his own dad had taken him around the world before he had ended up in Turkey. The discovery that David's granddad had been present at the disastrous excavation in Turkey had been an important breakthrough. So important that David's dad had decided to move to Turkey when he retired. To wholeheartedly focus on fitting the last pieces of the puzzle together.

What was it with the alleged King Midas' grave and Yossar Devan that was so important? And why had his dad never confided in David or his own wife? There was only one way to find the answers to those questions. David had to find out what his father had discovered.

David had to follow in his father's footsteps.

It would be hard, but it was the only way he could find out why he had been involved in the search for Yossar Devan's real identity.

There had to be a connection between David's dad's investigation into Die Glocke and David's granddad, and the fact that Professor Grossman had chosen David to help search for Yossar Devan's real identity.

Why did he choose David? An average MBA student. An average banker. An average journalist. Average everything. Professor Grossman could have chosen whomever he wanted. Why did he choose David? Why did he choose average?

There was only one thing David was certain of. He couldn't do this alone. He needed help.

He had skimmed through the information in some of the folders on his dad's laptop. Most of it was totally Greek to him. David's grandfather had been a physicist. David had chosen to study business in order to avoid the hard math. So even though he didn't want to, he had to ask Sophie for help again.

But this time he would be honest. This time she needed to know what she was risking.

–39–

The chancellor of Germany, Angela Merkel, stood at the podium at the United Nations' premises in New York City, ready for her improvised speech. She had just finished a meeting with the American president Barack Obama and looked worn and tired. No wonder. The last years had been tough for the East German iron woman. She had led a strong Germany through the global financial crisis, but it hadn't only been smooth sailing. Germany, which had favoured moderation and frugality over growth and prosperity for the last decade, had been forced to bail out country after country in the European Union. Angela Merkel had, however, drawn a firm line in the sand with Cyprus. There was a limit to how many countries she was willing to let her fellow German citizens foot the bill for. Especially if they weren't big enough to matter.

Germany had never fallen into the borrowing craze and financial irresponsibility that threatened to ruin their fellow members of the European Union. But with the never-ending stream of bad news – news about country after country struggling to honour their debt commitments, news about increases in unemployment to levels not seen since the 1940s – there was a risk that even Germany could end up in trouble, and she had to take her precautions.

She had just made the dramatic decision to recall all the German gold held in New York over the next few years. She had already two months ago reclaimed several hundred tons of gold from France. It had represented all the gold Germany had ever held in Paris.

"Why do you reclaim the gold now?" One of the reporters asked. "Are there doubts that the gold exists?"

Angela Merkel squinted at the audience before she leant forward to the microphone. "We all know there have been some conspiracy theories circulating on the internet. Our internal auditing division raised some questions about the treatment of our gold reserves simply because we hadn't physically inspected them for some time. This is, however, quite normal. The storage of gold, between allied countries, has always been based on trust. Trust built up over decades. We have never been in doubt that our gold is being taken good care of here in New York, by our dear and trusted friend and ally, the United States of America. But the cold war is over. There is no longer a need for Germany to store the gold in the US. That is the reason, and the only reason, we take our gold back."

"How are you going to transport six hundred tons of gold from the US to Germany? With today's price of gold that is almost thirty-seven billion dollars. How are you going to transport this in a safe and appropriate way?"

"That I can't tell you," Angela Merkel said with a crooked smile on her lips. "Everyone listening may not have good intentions." The reporter laughed. It wasn't exactly a regular occurrence when the Chancellor joked. Maybe she really was tired and had lowered her guard for a moment.

"There will be time for additional questions after the meeting with Francois Hollande tomorrow morning," interrupted Angela

Merkel's press attaché. "The chancellor has had a long flight and a long day."

Twenty-some reporters, some of them with their arms still raised in the air, regrettably had to accept that the session was over. Basically without learning anything they didn't already know. Germany retracted their gold. Yes. But what was the real motivation? Had the Germans lost faith in the US? Or was it as simple as the conspiracy theorists speculated on the internet; that countries storing gold in the US had very little control over where it was actually stored? Several countries hadn't been allowed to inspect their gold reserves for several decades. It was supposedly stored at several secret locations scattered across the US.

Nobody had a clue how each individual country's gold was labelled, or what routines were in place to prevent it from being stolen or sold. At least Germany had felt the controls weren't up to scratch. They wanted their gold back.

Every single ounce.

Which country would be the next one to request their gold back?

That was the real question the reporters were asking themselves.

-40-

Sophie Masson was sitting in a lotus position on the couch, sipping a cup of green tea. She had just arrived home from Yoga practise and was still sweaty. The shower would have to wait a few more minutes, she thought as she heard the doorbell ring. She wandered over to the front door and pushed the button that turned on the intercom. "Who is it?" she asked, sounding slightly annoyed.

By the tone of her voice, David immediately knew she wasn't in a good mood. He hoped the reason for her grumpiness wasn't him and his recent actions, but he assumed they were. And it would only be fair. She was the one who had discovered the clue about the Norwegian in Bodø. She was the one who had spent several days of her own time helping David. And still he had just dismissed her. Left her and gone to check out the Bodø lead by himself.

She had no income and should probably be looking for a new job instead of helping David figure out what had happened to a billionaire in London more than thirty years ago. But still she had offered to help him. Introduced him to her old university professor, Michael Simpson, the guy who believed in gold with magical powers. She had spent a day with him in a gold mine, a gold mine that had almost killed them. They had left those office barracks only minutes before they blew up.

And still he hadn't trusted her.

And to make it even worse.

They had just slept together.

They had just had sex and he had bounced without even saying goodbye. What a coward he had been.

"Why are you here?" Sophie asked when David was standing outside the door.

David felt uncomfortable and stared at the floor. "I'm sorry that I left. It wasn't very adult of me. I'm very sorry, Sophie."

He was expecting to have to explain his actions. Instead she asked him: "What did you find out?"

David looked her straight in the eyes. He still needed to explain himself. "I didn't want you to get mixed up in my problems, Sophie. There is obviously a reason that I was involved in this case. My professor at the university, the one who hired me, has disappeared. Rumour is that he may have been murdered. It's impossible to get hold of Peter Swarkowski, the man who supposedly by accident discovered that Yossar Devan was the same person as the boy in the picture with Dr Kammler. And now it turns out my grandfather was part of Dr Kammler's SS group. My own grandfather was a Nazi officer."

"Your grandfather? The Norwegian, the physicist. Was he your grandfather?"

David nodded. He told Sophie what he had found out at the old photographer's house. And he told her that he had found his father's laptop, a laptop where the last diary entry had been that he had discovered something important. What had he discovered? And had it really been an accident or had his dad been killed? Murdered because he had started asking questions?

"I can't guarantee your safety, Sophie. I simply don't know

what is going on. Maybe we are already in danger?" David said.

Sophie Masson put down her cup of tea. Her life had taken a new turn when she met David. She had lost her job and she had learnt about strange theories about alchemy and Earth's own gold. Only a week ago she would have rejected it all as pure horse manure. But she couldn't help herself. What if there was something there? What if there was something we didn't know about?

"Why do you need my help?" she asked.

"My granddad was a physicist," David replied. "I believe he was helping the Germans build a new weapon called Die Glocke. I'm not sure what kind of weapon this was, but I believe that's what my dad tried to figure out before he was killed."

"And you need my help to figure out what your grandfather was helping the Germans build?"

"Don't you see? It's all connected. Yossar Devan. Dr Kammler. My granddad. King Midas' treasure and Die Glocke. They are all connected. I just need to figure out how," David said. "And to do that I need your help."

"The help of a physicist?" she asked.

David nodded. "Somebody who can figure out how these things are connected. Somebody smart enough to understand what Die Glocke was meant to do."

Sophie Masson wasn't quite ready to forgive David. He had both hurt and angered her. She wasn't totally unfamiliar with one night stands. But David had made her feel cheap when he had left without saying goodbye. Not even leaving a note. She was used to being in control. She was used to being the one who left. And she didn't like to be in the position David had put her, to not be in control.

"Ok, give me the laptop. Let's have a look at what your father found out," she said after considering the proposal. She would give David another chance. She had after all missed him.

For the next few hours David and Sophie worked in intense concentration. They were going through the information on David's dad's laptop with a fine-toothed comb. David was responsible for everything dealing with history and personal notes, whereas Sophie was responsible for everything dealing with technology, maths or physics.

"Do you know what we are looking for?" Sophie asked after a period of silence.

David shook his head. "The day my dad died he wrote that he had cracked the code. There has to be something in his notes that can give us an indication of what he was looking for, of what he found."

"This is going to be like looking for the needle in the haystack," Sophie said. She was smiling. She enjoyed looking for needles in haystacks.

-41-

" I don't understand how it is possible to lose the target." The CIA director, Mark Green, brought down the palm of his hand so hard that the table shook. "Where was the last observation?" he asked.

"Ankara," the agent on the screen replied.

"Has he engaged in contact with any locals?" the CIA director asked, shaking his head in frustration.

"We have a list of names. A couple of locals near the excavation. We have them under surveillance. He is accompanied by a young woman, but we haven't been able to identify her yet."

"Any ideas how we can find out who she is?" the CIA director asked.

"They visited a gold mine and got something that appeared like a private excursion by one of the executives a few days ago. We have the executive's name. She may be able to shed some light on who the other woman is," the CIA agent said.

"Ok. Start with the gold mine. I want to have control on David Dypsvik's whereabouts within twenty-four hours. There is too much at stake here," the CIA director said, and hung up. The screen turned black, as he swung around to face the two others in the room.

"I leave before the weekend. We can't risk that these

incompetent idiots ruin the whole operation."

The two agents in the room nodded and rose from their chairs. One of them pushed a brown envelope towards the CIA director. "The last inventory update," he said before leaving the room.

The CIA director sat down in the chair and pulled the envelope toward himself. He didn't want to open it. He didn't want to know the numbers. He knew they weren't good.

If he wasn't able to contain this situation soon, he would be out of a job.

But that was probably the least of his worries. The question was whether he would have somewhere to go home to. Whether the world he knew would ever be the same.

-42-

"What do you think?" Sophie asked.

Michael Simpson, Sophie's old physics professor, was seated in a worn recliner in front of them. He looked exhausted. He was nicely dressed and clean shaven, but the dark circles around his eyes gave him away. He held his hands up, in front of his closed eyes, and formed the shape of a pyramid with his scrawny fingers. He was clearly struggling to come up with a clever and intelligent answer.

"I think I would have walked away," he finally said.

"Why?" David asked. "Somebody has clearly made an effort to get me involved in this case. There has to be a reason for it."

"Exactly," Michael Simpson replied. "Someone has gone to great lengths to involve you, someone with an agenda. And you have no idea who they are or what their agenda is. But I'm pretty certain that it is not good news for you. If they had good intentions they would have let them be known by now. But that hasn't happened. So ergo you are a pawn in a larger game, and we all know what happens with pawns in a game of chess."

Sophie nodded. "David, maybe Michael is right. Is it worth risking your life for something when you don't even know what that something is?"

David got up from his chair. "The people behind all this may also be responsible for my father's death. I can't stop now. I need to figure out what has happened. Don't you understand that?" he asked.

Sophie nodded, but didn't reply.

Michael Simpson got up from his chair and extended his hand.

"I'm an old man, David. I don't have much to lose," he said. "To be honest I'm quite bored. It's not every day I get the opportunity to help solve a mystery. So if you want my help I'm in. But I suggest we keep Sophie out of this. She shouldn't get more involved than she already is."

Sophie almost jumped out of her chair. "What the hell do you think you are doing? Making decisions for me? I'm old enough to make my own decisions, thank you very much," she said with a voice on the verge of breaking. "And I don't have much to lose either. I have no job. I've worked day and night the last five years for what? Just to be fired because I have a slightly different opinion than the rest of my colleagues in the physics department. Fired because I have an opinion."

She stretched her hand out. "To hell with it. I'm in too."

Michael Simpson led them down to the basement. Sophie had been through most of the information on David's dad's laptop that dealt with Die Glocke, but she still hadn't been able to make up her mind what Die Glocke really had been. It didn't appear that David's dad had been able to, either. They needed Michael Simpson's help.

"Could you go through the main points of Die Glocke one more time?" Michael Simpson asked, facing David. They were all seated on a large couch in his basement.

David cleared his throat. "Die Glocke was a project, which

according to a Polish war investigator, Igor Witkowski, was established in January 1942, under the codename 'Tor'.

"Gate?" Michael Simpson asked.

David nodded. 'Tor' was the German word for gate. In August 1943 the project was split into two. The codename Tor was replaced with Chronos and Lanterntrager. But both projects were still ultimately about the development of Die Glocke."

"Chronos is the Greek word for time, Tor is the German word for gate, and Glocke is the German word for bell. Based on the codenames it appears that they were building some kind of a weapon, and that time was a crucial element." Michael Simpson said.

"Codenames are meant to be codenames," Sophie said. "If a codename is too descriptive it would defeat its purpose. Regardless there is nothing in those codenames that indicates it was a weapon they were building."

"What does Lanterntrager mean?" Michael Simpson asked.

"Lantern carrier," David replied before Sophie had a chance to open her mouth.

"I don't understand what that has to do with it," Sophie said.

"The lantern carrier can also mean he who carries the light."

"Lucifer?" Sophie asked.

Michael Simpson nodded. "The Germans were extremely interested in the occult, and if the codename for the project was Lucifer, the name of the devil, then we can safely assume that what they were working on was a weapon. Maybe time was chosen because it was important that they completed the weapon before they lost the war."

David wasn't convinced, but continued.

"The Glocke project was one of many different projects SS officer Dr Hans Kammler was responsible for during the Second

World War. But we believe it may have been the most important one by far."

"Why?" asked Michael Simpson.

"Because it was the only project airlifted out of Germany in the final days of the war," Sophie said. Sophie told about the discovery she had made, about the German transport airplane that had flown to Bodø in April 1945, loaded to the hilt with blueprints from the Glocke project, maybe even with Die Glocke itself. She told about David's grandfather who had been a physicist in Norway before the war broke out, and how he had been present at the excavation in Turkey just months before the end of the war. She told about how David's grandfather had been the last person alive to handle all the information related to Die Glocke project. After Bodø there was nothing. The plane, Die Glocke and David's grandfather, they had all vanished from the face of the earth.

"So you believe that if we find out what Die Glocke was, then the answer could lead us to find out what happened to David's grandfather?" Michael Simpson asked.

"I believe that by following the same clues my dad did we can find out what happened to my grandfather, and at the same time find out why I was involved in this case," David said. "I don't know what is relevant or not, I don't know whether King Midas' grave existed or not, whether the Germans were successful in making a terrible weapon or not. All I know is that I was lured into this investigation. I was deceived into searching for a man who had never lived, tricked into looking for a secret formula for riches. Everything, all this crap, has only been a game to make me retrace my dad's footsteps. I want to know why. Why has somebody gone through such extreme measures? Why has someone made me travel across the globe? What's the motive?"

Michael Simpson gazed at him with sorrowful eyes. "I don't

know David," he said. "But you're not going to find what you're looking for here in Turkey."

-43-

W en Ning looked over his shoulder before crossing the street. Things hadn't worked out as planned, nothing had worked out as planned. He had believed that David would be the solution, that David would lure him out of his hiding place. But nothing had happened.

And now he had made a mistake. He had become too bold, too careless. There was actually a real danger that the police would be able to connect the dots. Wen Ning had just watched the last news broadcast and it was now confirmed that the English police no longer treated the death of billionaire real estate developer John Mitchell as accidental. There were strong suspicions that the work lift had been tampered with. Well, at one stage something had to go wrong. It was just a shame that it had happened now. Now that he was so close.

Wen Ning glanced around before he continued up towards the embassy street. The ambassador was a creature of habit. It was soon time for his nightly exercise.

-44-

D avid stared at the traffic coiling itself in front of the rental car. Michael Simpson had said that they wouldn't find any answers in Turkey. If David was serious about finding out what his dad had discovered, then they would have to retrace his footsteps. That was the reason they right now found themselves in Poland. Dr Hans Kammler had run his operations from the headquarters in Berlin until March 1945, when he transferred it to Munich. But it would be a waste of time to search for physical clues in Berlin or Munich. It was more than sixty-eight years since the Second World War. If they were to have any hope at all of finding out what had happened to David's granddad, and Dr Hans Kammler, they would have to rely on historical documents. And it just happened to be that tens of thousands of documents had only been declassified after the fall of the Berlin Wall in 1998. Most of this material was still not fully reviewed or understood. Maybe David's grandfather's fate was hidden in one of those documents? It was a big risk to take – to travel all the way to another country to search documents that no one had bothered going through in detail. But there wasn't much more they could hope to achieve in Turkey. If they wanted to keep up the momentum they had to go where the leads took them.

They had arrived at Warsaw airport early in the morning.

David had withdrawn as much cash as he could from an ATM in the city the night before. It was a good thing his student loan for the next semester had already arrived in his bank account. He needed the cash, and if someone was keeping tabs on him he would at least make it as hard as possible for them to track him. There was however little he could do to hide the fact he was getting on a plane. David would have preferred going by car, but he had been voted down.

After the establishment of the European Union you could relatively easily cross the borders from Turkey to Germany without getting registered in any official records, but that drive would have taken them more than twenty-four hours. Michael Simpson hadn't been too enthusiastic about the suggestion. Instead they had bought a flight-and-rental car deal from Ankara to Warsaw.

"I'll see you later tonight," David said as he dropped Sophie and Michael Simpson off outside the Warsaw War Museum. After mutual agreement they had been assigned tasks according to their respective skill sets. Michael and Sophie were scientists by heart. They were trained in locating the information they were searching for in books and documents. David, on the other hand, was better at extracting information from people. Good at making people feel comfortable and open up. Good at letting them spill their secrets without even realising. He had been a good journalist and at first he had loved it. It was just a shame that it was such a dying occupation. You couldn't avoid reality. There was no point in opening a video store or a bookstore. And there was no point starting a degree in journalism. The best years were gone a long time ago. You had to think forward. David had thought forward and decided to become a banker. People always had to borrow money, didn't they? He had entered at the worst possible time though. The global financial crisis had stalled lending growth, and the banks desperately needed to make more money with fewer people. Cost cutting, outsourcing, synergies. All the fancy words he had learnt at business school had suddenly been used against him. It had been so easy solving a case at university. To crunch the numbers and make recommendations. Shut down two factories, outsource the IT department, cut 20% of the workforce. After having worked in the frontline of this environment for two years he knew, however, that most of the things he had learnt at school were plain wrong. They were short-term solutions that suited public companies that needed constant assurance that management was on the ball. If you had a long-term perspective most decisions would be different. If you had a long-term perspective you didn't make up the numbers in reports so that it appeared that all the strategies you undertook worked.

Disillusioned with how work life really was, he had quit his bank job and gone back to university. Not to learn more about business. But to have time to come up with a brilliant business idea. An idea that would provide him an opportunity to change his life. He smiled at his own naiveté. His fascination with money had been the reason he so quickly had accepted Professor Grossman's offer to investigate Yossar Devan's background. A mystery, a missing billionaire and a secret formula to riches. David hadn't even questioned it. He had been blinded by the possibility of learning about the secret to riches. He had happily accepted everything he had been told.

The purpose of the trip to Poland was quite simple. After dropping Sophie Masson and Michael Simpson off outside the Warsaw War Museum, David was supposed to travel alone to Ludokowice, to investigate one of Dr Hans Kammler's old bases. David had checked the distance on Google Earth before departing.

It should only take him about three hours. Add a couple of hours for scouting the area and he would be back for dinner at the hotel later in the evening. David put his foot to the gas pedal and sped out into the traffic.

It was relatively cold in the grand reading room of the Warsaw War Museum. Michael Simpson and Sophie were seated in deep concentration, skimming through the mountain of documents that had only been released to the public more than forty years after the Second World War. There was so much information, thousands and thousands of documents, that nobody had managed to go through most of it, even twenty years after the fall of the Berlin Wall.

But Michael and Sophie had an advantage. Michael knew people all around the world. In Ludokowice he knew a washed-up Polish war investigator, and in Warsaw he had a friend who was a professor of history at the local university. David was supposed to catch up with the war investigator in Ludokowice, and Michael Simpson's professor friend had provided them unlimited access to all the war-related documents in the library of the Warsaw War Museum. It also helped that they had a very narrow area of interest – they wanted to find out as much as possible about Dr Hans Kammler, the coldblooded mass murderer Dr Hans Kammler.

Sophie pulled her grey sweater up under her chin and looked around. It was as if the temperature in the room had suddenly dropped several degrees. The air had a scent of metal and it felt harder to breathe. Michael Simpson's friend had organised for them to have a private room for the day. No one else was allowed to enter. But she could swear she had just heard something, heard someone open the door.

David checked his watch. The trip that was supposed to have taken three hours had taken more than four. But at least he had finally found the exit to Ludokowice. He had now parked the car and was stretching his legs.

In the early morning hours of the sixth of May 1945, a group of American soldiers, the 16th Armored Division, had rolled into Pilsen. Everyone in Europe knew that it was just a matter of days before the war would be over. Hitler had committed suicide five days earlier, and among locals and soldiers stories were shared about how German battalions were surrendering everywhere.

The most important matter for the American soldiers of the 16th Armored Division was to survive. Nobody wanted to become a statistic now that the victory was within reach. They all just wanted to be as careful as humanly possible.

But General Patton hadn't shared their attitude. He kept advancing his troops as if there was nothing more important than to make as much ground as possible. Why this rush? Why had it been so important for General Patton to conquer Pilsen and Prague? Why not head straight for Hitler and Berlin?

Sophie had found a possible solution before they had left Turkey. Dr Hans Kammler's Skoda Works was located on the wrong side of the partition line. The Allied Forces and the Soviet Union had, already before Germany capitulated, split the land areas between themselves. It was the privilege of the victors to draw up new borders, to share the spoils of victory.

But this tradition also meant that the Skoda Works, Dr Hans Kammler's secret laboratory in Pilsen, would end up in Russian possession when Germany fell.

There had, however, been a way out for the Americans. If they arrived at the Skoda Works factory first, then they could take whatever they wanted before the Russians arrived. And that was exactly what they had done. The Americans had broken all agreements and normal conventions of war. They had entered the Russian zone, and they had held it for six full days before handing it over to the Russians. Plenty of time to locate and take whatever they wanted. The Russians were of course very displeased with the Americans' breach of the rules. But what could they do? The reality was that they could do nothing.

"Are you lost?"

David turned around. In front of him a broad-shouldered man wearing a camouflage outfit stood with a rifle in his hands. The barrel was pointing straight at David's chest.

A scream echoed through the walls of the Warsaw War Museum.

"So much for privacy," Michael Simpson said in a grumpy voice. A school class entered the room and ran down the aisle. A stressed-out teacher kept hushing them and looked at Michael with apologetic eyes. "I thought we had the room to ourselves," Michael Simpson whispered to Sophie.

Sophie smiled. Michael Simpson had once told her that he never had wanted children. He simply couldn't handle noise, didn't have any patience for it. Maybe it would have been different if it had been his own children? But it could also be the fact that he had been living alone for way too long. Had acquired too many peculiarities and routines. Simply become too self-centred to ever want to share life and the attention of others with a child. She felt the same way herself sometimes. She had been alone since the break-up with the stockbroker and she had never missed a man. Certainly not a kid. Would she turn into Michael Simpson at one stage, she wondered? "I think I've found something, Michael," she said, and took her hand off the microfilm machine.

"Wilhelm?" David asked.

The broad-shouldered figure nodded and David noticed a smile behind the full-bodied red beard.

David reached out a hand and introduced himself. Wilhelm Vogts was Michael Simpson's contact in Poland. A retired war reporter who spent his days and weeks combing through declassified war documents. He was supposedly working on a book. But according to Michael Simpson the project was now going on its tenth year. It was thus unlikely that a book would ever be published.

"You're late," Wilhelm said.

"Sorry, bad traffic," David explained.

"Well, we might as well get going straight away then," Wilhelm said, and started wandering into the forest. David threw the backpack onto his back and followed.

They had walked for about twenty minutes when they arrived at a clearing in the woods. David had already tried to start a conversation a few times, but the big Pole wasn't the most talkative person he had ever met.

"This is the place the so-called Die Glocke was tested," Wilhelm finally said, pointing at something that reminded David of the Stonehenge monument in England.

"What is it?" David asked.

"It's the flytrap," Wilhelm replied.

"And what is the flytrap?"

"There are many theories. Some claim it was a test rig for Die Glocke. But most likely it is just the remaining skeleton of a cooling tower."

"A cooling tower for the Glocke experiment?"

Wilhelm shrugged his shoulders. "Maybe, maybe not."

"You don't sound very convinced," David said. "Don't you believe any of the stories?"

Wilhelm sniffled. "I've almost worked a lifetime as a defence force journalist. I'm used to gathering evidence before making any claims. And that's what's missing with Die Glocke. There are many stories, but far between the hard evidence."

"What's your theory? What do you think Die Glocke was?" David asked as they approached the concrete skeleton. It was a circular concrete construction, about thirty metres wide and ten metres tall. The twelve free standing concrete pillars, each stretching ten meters up into the sky, made an impression on David. As with everything else in the area it appeared that the Germans had gone to great lengths to camouflage the construction. Residue of green paint could be spotted everywhere on the surface of the old cement.

Suddenly Wilhelm stopped in his tracks. It appeared that he had been pondering something.

"I simply don't know. Every time I hear a new testimony or locate a document that relates to Die Glocke I change my mind. There is always something new, but never an answer. I don't know what Die Glocke was. I don't think we will ever know what it was."

David reviewed the pictures he had printed out before the trip. He had purchased Igor Witkowski's book, The Truth About The Wunderwaffe, and it contained a couple of black-and-white pictures of the area. "The area looks different," he said.

Wilhelm nodded. "There used to be a power station here. It was pulled down a few years ago."

"What was the purpose of the power station?"

Wilhelm shrugged his shoulders. "Hard to say."

David sighed. This was going to be a long day. It was easier to pull teeth, wisdom teeth, than to get a sensible word out of this guy.

David asked whether they could take a closer look at the area where the power station had once stood. Wilhelm nodded and led the way.

"You know, whatever Die Glocke was, it wasn't the result of brilliant scientists. All these theories about the Germans developing a super weapon here in Ludokowice can't be right."

"Why do you say that?" David asked.

"Because the Glocke project wasn't defined as important until after the accident."

"Which accident? The accident where some of the scientists died?" David asked. He had read that almost the entire first team of scientists were killed during an experiment. It was supposedly before they managed to control the radioactive emissions of Die Glocke."

Wilhelm nodded. "That day everything changed here in Ludokowice. The SS general Dr Hans Kammler arrived with his men and took control over the project. He shut down the whole area, and clouded the project in secrecy. But the rumour is that he never managed to replicate the experiment that killed the first team of scientists."

"Do you know what that experiment was?" David asked.

Wilhelm shrugged his shoulders. "Who knows? The scientists supposedly died from inhaling toxic fumes, not radioactivity like most people believe. But there were rumours that the laws of the universe, for a brief moment, ceased to exist here in Ludokowice. That the sky opened and a new world appeared. And all just because they had run out of materials." Wilhelm Vogts laughed.

"Run out of materials?"

"Yes. This was during the worst fighting of the war. There was a shortage of almost everything. Die Glocke's original team of scientists ran out of some of the raw materials required for the experiment. Instead they used substitutes. It was most likely a coincidence that caused them to stumble across a solution that made all these SS people so excited. But as I told you, they never managed to recreate the experiment, not even with access to the unlimited resources of Dr Kammler. And as all the scientists of the original experiment unfortunately had died, no one knew what they had used as substitutes."

"How was Dr Kammler able to procure raw materials if there were shortages of everything during the war?" David asked.

"The world was different for Dr Kammler. All he needed to do was to issue an order that he required copper, and hundreds of concentration camp prisoners were sent out to disassemble copper tubes from factories and people's private homes. In Dr Kammler's world, the word impossible didn't exist. If you were given an order by Dr Kammler you found a way to comply with that order. The alternative was death."

"What have you found?" Michael Simpson asked.

"This is a report from Dr Kammler to Heinrich Himmler." Sophie pointed to the microfilm on her screen. "The Germans have increased the efficiency of the gas chambers in Auschwitz by six hundred percent, from ten thousand men to sixty thousand men per day."

Michael Simpson nodded. "Yes, it was one of Dr Kammler's tasks to increase the efficiency of the gas chambers. We already knew that."

"Yes, but there is something strange with the numbers."

"What do you mean?"

"If they increased the efficiency of the gas chambers by six hundred percent, then you would assume that other things would have increased proportionately."

"Yes?"

"But it turns out the amount of confiscated gold fell in the same period," Sophie continued.

"Maybe the Jews arriving at Auschwitz, later in the war, had less gold in their possession? Or maybe they were simply better at hiding it?"

"The gold came from their teeth," Sophie said.

"Ohh..." Michael Simpson had just gotten an image in his head he didn't want there.

"And confiscations of other valuables, did they also drop?"

"No, only the gold confiscations. That's why it's so weird," Sophie said.

"Maybe there was somebody embezzling gold, maybe the gold was stolen by corrupt soldiers?"

"No, higher ups in the camp administration would have noticed the same as we did. This must have been an accepted and conscious underreporting of gold."

"But why?" Michael Simpson asked.

"That's what we have to find out," Sophie Masson replied.

–45–

"When did this occur?" the CIA director yelled into the phone.

"This morning," the agent on the other line answered.

The CIA director swore silently. Nothing was going according to plan. "Who knows?" he asked.

"The Turkish police, the ambulance personnel. As far as we know relatives haven't been contacted yet, but the information will come out sooner than later. She was a high ranking executive. It won't be possible to keep a lid on the information."

"So, what's our alternatives?"

Another voice came on the line. "The company had problems with environmental groups. The business had been sued several times over the last few years, mainly for escalated values of cyanide in the ground water. One of their office barracks was blown to pieces only a few days ago. It will be an easy job to direct the attention of the investigation towards the greenies."

"Ok. It's settled. Make sure the case disappears. And make sure you locate David Dypsvik before this whole operation spirals out of control."

The CIA director hung up. This case could ruin his career.

He was the one who had authorised Operation Aurum. It had appeared an acceptable plan for a complicated problem. And if he was to be honest, they hadn't really had that many alternatives. Sometimes you had to throw in a bait to get the big fish. But things hadn't turned out as planned. People had started dying, a lot of people, and all of them had had some sort of contact with David Dypsvik, the Norwegian student who was supposed to lure him out from his hiding place.

On the other side of the phone line, in Turkey, agent Wen Ning was seated next to one of his colleagues from the local CIA office. They had just been ordered by the boss to put in place a cover-up operation regarding the death of Caroline Summerfield. Agent Wen Ning and his colleague had driven out to Minuza Mining earlier in the morning to have a chat with Caroline Summerfield. They had hoped that she knew the location of David Dypsvik, or at least knew the identity of this woman he had been spending time with. The trip hadn't been successful. They had found Caroline Summerfield in a pool of blood.

Someone had cut her throat during the night.

Wen Ning knew exactly who had done the deed.

He put his left hand in his left front pocket. He fondled the gold necklace she had been wearing the night before. He found it strangely calming.

-46-

I t was dead quiet in the car. The previous night the chatter had been lively and the jokes had been flowing. Sophie, Michael and David had all been in a good mood. They still had no good idea of what Die Glocke really was. But they had at last found a connection. Something that tied King Midas' grave and Yossar Devan together with Die Glocke and Dr Hans Kammler.

Gold.

The Germans had been under-reporting the confiscation of gold in the Auschwitz death camp.

Yossar Devan had been one of the richest people in the world, with massive gold holdings.

And according to the ancient tale, everything King Midas touched turned into gold.

Gold.

David thought back on his first meeting with Michael Simpson. Michael had told David and Sophie that gold was the key and he had introduced them to his friend Caroline Summerfield. Caroline had spent a whole day with them, lecturing about gold.

Michael Simpson couldn't have known how right he would be.

But gold was the key.

Gold was the common denominator. The thing that connected it all.

The polish war investigator, Wilhelm Vogts, had given David a thorough tour of Ludokowice. After inspecting the ruins of the flytrap and the power plant, they had spent the remainder of the afternoon going through the many mines in the area. The problem was that the Germans had flooded most of the mines before evacuating Ludokowice towards the end of the war. Some of the mines, like the Walter mine, were still quite radioactive. It prevented David from looking for clues about the Glocke experiment. The area was also way too big. Due to the Allied Forces' continuous bombing of the German ammunitions facilities, it had been decided to move most of the war production underground. In an impressive effort the Germans had succeeded in transforming old mines to factories for the assembly of everything from V2 rockets to ammunition. And their network of tunnels and underground halls covered large areas.

The Wenceslaus mine in Ludokowice had already before the war started consisted of more than thirty million square metres of tunnels and underground halls. It had in fact been one of Europe's biggest coal mines. Now it was just an old memory of a war that had cut so many lives short.

But when Wilhelm Vogts gave David a private tour around the part of the Wenceslaus mine that hadn't been flooded, David got a surprise. It was almost as if he had been there before. He didn't know why, but the place had looked strangely familiar.

"Turn left at the next intersection," Sophie said with a sombre voice. She had been in a depressed mood since breakfast. David, Michael and Sophie were on their way to Auschwitz, and the realities of Dr Kammler and his accomplices' crimes had started to sink in. It had affected David the most. He still didn't have any good idea of what his granddad had been involved in during the Second World War. He was simply non-existing in official documents. Sophie and Michael had at least found Dr Kammler's name on some documents. But Dr Hans Kammler had been an oberstgruppenfuhrer, a four-star general, who towards the end of the war reported directly to Adolf Hitler. It would have been outright impossible to remove his name from all documents. David's granddad's name, however, wasn't mentioned anywhere.

He was a ghost.

The only place they had found traces of him was on the black-and-white picture, from an obscure excavation of what was believed to be King Midas' grave in Turkey 1944. His name had also been briefly mentioned in a passing sentence during the interrogation of a Nazi officer in Bodø. The Nazi officer had, however, never mentioned him by name. Just called him the Norwegian. Just called him the physicist.

There could only be one reason for the absence of David's grandfather's name in any official documents. It meant that he had been important.

Sophie had discovered something else as well at the Warsaw War Museum Library. There had been several high-ranking SS officers who couldn't be charged at the war tribunal in Nuremberg after the war. They had either been successful in disappearing, or one had uncertain accounts of their deaths. Most of these war criminals were charged and convicted in absentia for their crimes. Not even in death should they be able to escape their horrific crimes.

Dr Kammler, however, had never been convicted in absentia. The Allied Forces had never even bothered looking for him. Why not? Why not look for the mastermind behind the concentration camps? Why not search for the man responsible for the extermination of millions of Jews? Why not look for the man in charge of all of the most important weapons programs in Germany? A man who had randomly executed Germans and prisoners just so that he could keep his projects a secret. A man so devoid of human compassion that tens of thousands of prisoners had simply died of exhaustion adhering to his unrealistic construction deadlines.

The very definition of a war criminal.

The very definition of evil.

"It could mean that Dr Kammler got away," Michael Simpson remarked.

Sophie stared at him like a big question mark, and Michael realised that he had spoken without providing any context. "My apologies. I was thinking about the lack of evidence surrounding Dr Kammler's death. And the fact that his name is hardly mentioned in official war history. It is almost as if someone has made a deliberate attempt to remove him."

"Why would that mean he got away?" Sophie asked.

"Think about everything Dr Kammler had access to. Think about all the knowledge he could have offered the Allied Forces. If Die Glocke, or any of the other secret weapons projects he was working on had any practical application, then Dr Kammler would have been the most valuable man of the Third Reich towards the end of the war. The acquisition of German technology was probably the most important goal for the Allied Forces the second they realised that they would win the war. Any revolutionary technology from a secret German weapons lab would have been a great negotiation card for Dr Kammler."

"But the Allied Forces already had a technological advance on the Germans. The Germans never managed to develop the atomic bomb," David said.

Sophie and Michael Simpson looked at each other. Like they

knew something David didn't.

"That may be right. But the Germans may have been able to develop something else. Or may have been close to developing something else. Even though Die Glocke, whatever it was, wasn't an operational weapon, it could have had value for the Allied Forces. Adolf Hitler did after all believe that Dr Hans Kammler was going to build him a doomsday weapon, a weapon that would change the course of the war. Dr Kammler must have been working on something exciting," Michael Simpson said.

David nodded.

"But if we assume that Die Glocke was a weapon, and that Dr Kammler defected to the Americans, how can we get any of this confirmed?"

"We will have to figure out what was so special about the Glocke experiments. Maybe we can check whether the Americans were doing research on something similar after the war?"

David nodded. But he felt he had missed something, something important.

Wen Ning glanced at the GPS tracker. David and his friends had rented a car at AVIS Car Rentals in Warsaw. The car had a built-in GPS tracker in its navigation system. Wen Ning therefore knew the exact position of the car. But he didn't understand why it was where it was. David had told the office manager at AVIS that he was planning to stay in the Warsaw area. But when Wen Ning looked at his screen it showed that the car was somewhere totally different.

Auschwitz.

What the hell were they doing at Auschwitz?

-47-

The sun was warming the brick building in front of David. It looked like any other old brick building. An English boarding school where kids could have a play at the green lawns at recess? An old bottle factory? It was hard to tell by just observing the buildings. But these buildings had a very different story, a terrible story. And it wasn't only the leftover barbed wire in the streets that hinted that something bad had happened there. You could see it in the eyes of the tourists wandering around. The sad eyes. The small steps. The almost apologetic whispering.

It was as if they couldn't allow themselves to be happy at such a place. A place where horrendous crimes had been committed during the Second World War. A place where hundreds of thousands of people's lives had ended.

The building right in front of David was part of the administration buildings of Auschwitz. Maybe it was there Dr Kammler had been sitting, pondering on how he could increase the effectiveness of the gassing of Jews? The thought made David nauseated. The possibility that his grandfather had been involved made him almost sick.

He turned away and squinted at the sky. As he took a deep breath a warm hand encircled him from behind. Sophie had understood that he was struggling with the experience, and offered him some human compassion. Something this place had experienced very little of during the war.

"I can't understand how people can commit such atrocities. How people can go from being normal to animals. Why didn't anyone say stop?" David asked.

"Humans can get used to everything. We are more adaptable than cockroaches. My sister once had a job at a chicken processing plant in France. The first few days she couldn't stop crying. She just couldn't handle watching all the chickens getting killed. She was ready to quit. But she stayed on. And after a couple of weeks she realised that she hardly cared anymore. She had stopped viewing the chickens as animals. Then she quit, when she realised that she had lost her ability to feel compassion for the chickens. I believe many Germans must have felt the same way. They were extraordinary times. There was war and misery wherever you looked. Germans were told to not view Jews as humans."

"That's no excuse," David said.

Sophie shook her head. "It wasn't meant as an excuse. It was meant as a possible explanation. We simply know too little. Some of the soldiers may have committed horrible acts because they deep down were monsters and got off on the cruelty. Others may have participated just to keep themselves and their families alive. It is impossible to know how people will react when faced with extraordinary circumstances. Let's just hope it will never happen again."

They both knew the last sentence was pointless. Horrible crimes against humanity were committed every single day. They were just a bit farther away from David and Sophie's homes now. In Africa, the Middle East, and other war-torn places. It was said that the more you could identify with a crime or accident, the bigger impression it would make. Reading about someone killing a cat in the street you grew up on would most likely make a bigger impact than reading about someone killing ten people in Namibia. And that was the reason why David felt so nauseated. He could really identify with the victims here. His grandad might even have been one of the people responsible for the atrocities committed.

It wasn't just the number of dead that was horrific, though. It was how the Nazis had turned killing into an industrial process. David and Sophie had just been inside a room. It had been filled from floor to ceiling with empty Zyklon B cans. One can had contained enough gas to kill one hundred prisoners. Auschwitz had been going through thousands of those boxes during the war.

"Where at the map was IG Farben's Buna Factory located?" Michael Simpson asked. He was the only visitor who didn't seem affected by the experience. He had just removed his earphones and David could hear Wagner's symphony C stream, at full volume, from the white Q-tips curling over his shoulders.

"The Buna Factory wasn't located in the camp itself. It was built about ten kilometres south of here," David replied.

"Close enough that the Allies wouldn't risk bombing it. Close to an unlimited supply of manual labour, labour that would never be able to speak about what they witnessed. And still far enough away to be kept a secret."

Sophie nodded. "In addition it was close to water and infrastructure."

"The resemblance to the Manhattan Project in the US is remarkable," Michael Simpson said.

"The Manhattan Project?" David repeated.

"The Americans' secret project for developing the nuclear bomb," Michael Simpson replied.

"I know what the Manhattan Project was. I just don't

understand the connection," David said.

"The Buna factory of Auschwitz was the world's largest factory for production of synthetic rubber. A factory constructed by more than three hundred thousand slave workers, whereof twenty-five thousand simply were worked to death. The factory used more electricity than the city of Berlin during the war. Yet not one single gram of synthetic rubber was ever produced there. What's wrong with that story?" Michael Simpson asked.

"It wasn't built to produce rubber?" David asked.

Michael Simpson nodded. "Bingo."

"But what were they going to produce if it wasn't rubber?" David asked.

Michael Simpson shrugged his shoulders. "The Germans may have built the factory just to exhaust the prisoners. They already had capacity problems in Auschwitz. They weren't able to get rid of the corpses fast enough." He turned around to face David. "Or maybe the story we've been told at school wasn't entirely correct."

"The Germans were building an atomic bomb," Sophie exclaimed ecstatically.

"All the signs are there," Michael Simpson said. "The Nazis had secret projects in the Hartz Mountains and here at Auschwitz. They had access to large quantities of uranium from the Sudetenland in addition to confiscated land areas in Belgium. What if Heisenberg and Germany's official atomic bomb program was only a front? What if the real atomic bomb program was under Dr Kammler's supervision? He did have the responsibility for almost all other weapons programs, you know."

"It could explain why the Germans' work on the atomic bomb doesn't parallel their work on other weapon systems. The Germans had a technological advance in almost all other areas. But their attempts to enrich uranium seem almost amateurish.

As if they were sabotaged from the inside."

"The gold. They used the gold to finance a black operation," David said.

Michael Simpson nodded.

David stopped. "But there is a big hole in your theory. If the Nazis had a black atomic bomb project here at Auschwitz, financed directly by the SS and their under-reporting of confiscated gold from the concentration camps, why haven't we heard anything about it before? Why didn't the Germans drop an atomic bomb on London?" David asked.

"Maybe we will never know? Maybe Dr Kammler still had a touch of humanity left inside him. Maybe he didn't want to win the war that way? To drop an atomic bomb on London would be like breaking all the rules of warfare. It would be like using chemical weapons."

"Chemical weapons? The Germans gassed six million Jews. I don't think they cared about the rules of warfare."

"The gassing of Jews was probably not seen as part of the war efforts. On the battlefield the Germans mostly stuck to the rules. As a soldier Dr Kammler may have considered the two scenarios differently. The Jews were an internal problem they could use all means to solve. The war was an arena where they had to follow the rules of warfare."

"They may actually have dropped an atomic bomb during the war," Sophie said.

Michael and David both turned around. Astonished by the claim.

"What are you saying?" David asked.

"Think about how the Nazis' thought processes were. The Second World War was to a large extent a racial war. If the Germans were about to test a nuclear bomb then the Allied

Forces wouldn't be their first choice to test it on. The Germans would have tested it on the Russians. The Russians, whom they considered genetically inferior to themselves. When Michael and I were going through the documents in the Warsaw War Museum I found two articles mentioning the use of a new weapon on the east front near Kursk in 1943. It was described as a weapon from hell. A weapon that eradicated entire regiments."

"Don't you think we would have heard about it if the Germans used nuclear weapons during the war? Especially if they used them as early as 1943?" David said.

"I'm not so sure," Michael Simpson replied. "The morale in the Russian army would have been extremely low by that time. They had been fighting under inhumane conditions for a long time. If news about a new German superweapon had erupted – a weapon they had no means to defend themselves against – then this news could potentially have led to mass mutiny in the Russian army," he said, while picking a rock from the sole of his shoe. "But I don't believe Dr Kammler was working on an atomic bomb here."

"What was it if it wasn't an atomic bomb?" Sophie asked.

"Think about all the coincidences. In a speech close to the end of the war, Dr Joseph Goebbels claimed that he had witnessed a weapon so terrible that it would make your heart stop. Adolf Hitler claimed that Germany would soon have weapons that would ensure victory. The Germans just had to hold on a bit longer. And they had to defend Prague and Silesia by all means necessary.

Then on the on the 11th of April 1945 President Eisenhower decides to send his trusted General Patton south towards Thuringia instead of towards Berlin. Germany only had one weapons program classified as vital for the outcome of the war. It wasn't Heisenberg's atomic bomb project. It was Die Glocke. Dr Kammler's blackest of the black projects."

-48-

"It defies all logic," Sophie said.

Michael Simpson straightened the collar on his jacket. "Au contraire. It's completely logical. The Germans may have had an enrichment program for uranium here at Auschwitz and in the Hartz Mountains, but still the Allied Forces never found traces of any nuclear bombs. There is only one solution – they were building something else."

"And what was that?" David asked.

"To be able to answer that question we first have to find out what happened to your grandfather and Dr Kammler."

"My granddad?" David repeated.

"If your grandfather was a physicist who purposely was omitted from all official documents, then we have to assume that he was essential for whatever it was Dr Kammler and his band of Nazi scientists were trying to create here."

David wasn't nauseated anymore. He was fuming with anger.

His grandfather had been a traitor, a Nazi officer, a monster. He may even have been the single person who could have turned the war for the Germans. Luckily that had never happened.

David's dad had told him that the grandfather had left for Germany to fight the Red Threat from the East, the communists. And that he almost by accident had found himself on the wrong side when Germany declared war against the rest of the world.

It had all been a lie.

The grandfather hadn't been a naïve Norwegian who volunteered to fight at the German front to defend the West against the threat of communism. He had been one of the architects behind the Germans' secret weapons programs, a Nazi officer who had been just as responsible for the millions of casualties in the concentration camps as the executioners who had closed the doors to the gas chambers.

"So, where do we go from here?" David asked.

"We will have to figure out why the Nazis embezzled all this gold from the concentration camps, and what the money was used for. What did they buy? If we can figure out what materials they used to develop Die Glocke then we will have a much greater chance of understanding what it is they were trying to build," Michael Simpson said.

'Follow the money.' David's own mantra when he worked as a journalist. It was this mantra that had brought him to Turkey and King Midas' grave. There was always money involved. And money always left traces.

They wandered back to the rental car in silence. David because he was still shocked by the realisation that his own grandfather might have taken part in all the terrible things that occurred in Auschwitz during the war.

Sophie and Michael because they were thinking.

It was Sophie who finally broke the silence when she opened the car door.

"What if we are thinking about this the wrong way?" she said.

"What do you mean?" Michael Simpson replied.

"We know that the Nazis under-reported gold confiscation

from the Auschwitz camp," she started.

David and Michael nodded.

"But we don't know where the gold ended up. We don't know if it was sold to the highest bidder, whether the profits were used to fund the development of Die Glocke or a secret atomic bomb project. We don't even know if the gold was stolen by corrupt soldiers or if the embezzlement was sanctioned by top Nazi party officials. For all we know the gold could have been stashed away, as a security net if the Third Reich failed and someone had to start again at some stage."

"I don't understand where you are going with this," Michael Simpson said.

"What if the gold was under-reported because it was used as an input factor in the development of Die Glocke?"

Michael Simpson studied his old student. She seemed totally convinced about her own hypothesis. It reminded him of the time she had defended her own doctoral thesis. She had seemed so convinced, like she had just seen the light.

"Gold as an input factor? What would be the point of that? The only purpose gold could have in such a project would be to protect against radiation. Lead is a lot cheaper than gold, and it does the same job," Michael said.

"Exactly. Lead is cheaper than gold. But think back on what that Polish war investigator told David in Ludokowice; the first team of scientists in the Glocke project ran out of some raw materials, and they had to use substitutes. Only then something unexpected happened. What if this unexpected reaction was brought about by gold?" Sophie asked.

Michael Simpson scratched his chin. "It could explain why Dr Hans Kammler travelled to Turkey in the middle of the most important period of the war. He could have gone there to secure

King Midas' treasure."

"I didn't know that King Midas' burial chamber was supposed to contain any gold," David said.

"It doesn't really matter what it was thought to contain. Nazi Germany was obsessed with the occult. They may have believed that King Midas' burial chamber contained a gold treasure. Gold they would have been dependent on to complete the development of Die Glocke."

"But what other materials were used in the Glocke experiment? If lead was replaced by gold, what was the original purpose of lead?" David asked.

Sophie glanced over at Michael Simpson, who nodded. "Probably to protect against exposure to radiation. But we don't know what sort of ingredients caused that radiation. The only toxic material we know for sure was used in the Glocke experiment was mercury. And mercury is not radioactive," she said.

"But it is poisonous. And lead containers would be an efficient way of handling mercury," Michael Simpson said.

"The same would iron containers," Sophie remarked. "The only thing that wouldn't be efficient is gold. It is elementary chemistry that gold and mercury react and amalgamate."

"Exactly. The elements react to each other. There is a chemical reaction when you mix gold with mercury."

"But surely no one in their right mind would have considered using gold containers to store mercury. Everybody knows that gold and mercury amalgamate. That gold dissolves in mercury."

"It's not entirely certain that common soldiers in the German army knew this."

"This reminds me more and more of alchemy," Sophie said. She knew that alchemists throughout history had considered mercury as the 'prima materia', the basis of all materials. The noblest material was gold, and with the help of mercury the alchemists were trying to transform impure materials such as lead and iron to gold. Mercury poisoning had been such a regular occurrence for alchemists throughout history that historians even had found traces of mercury poisoning in a strand of hair belonging to Sir Isaac Newton.

"It could also explain a few other events that happened towards the end of the war," David said.

"What do you mean?" Sophie asked.

"After the end of the war large quantities of mercury were found in captured German submarines." David had studied Igor Witkowski's book about Die Glocke, and he had found a couple of innocent paragraphs about mercury. There existed no proper explanations why the Germans needed large quantities of mercury in their war production. But in April 1944 a submarine sank outside the Malacca Strait close to Indonesia. The submarine had been on its way to Japan. The cargo wasn't retrieved until 1972. When the rescue team opened the sub they got the surprise of a lifetime. The sub had carried almost thirty-three tons of mercury. In addition, a Japanese I-52 submarine had been sunk by the Allied Forces near Gibraltar in 1944. Its cargo had also mainly been mercury.

The most credible evidence that mercury had played some sort of important role in the Germans' plans towards the end of the war was, however, the capture of a German submarine in May 1945. The submarine, the type XB U-234, had sailed out from Norway in April with intended destination Japan. Of a total cargo of ninety-five tons, more than twenty-four tons was mercury. Historians, like David's own dad, had never been able to properly explain why the Germans needed all this mercury. There had been nothing that indicated that they needed such large quantities. Some historians had even speculated that the Germans were working on a new weapon, a new weapon for which mercury played a significant role.

David now understood that they could be onto something.

Great quantities of mercury being shipped towards Japan in the final days of the war.

Great quantities of gold simply disappearing from the concentration camps.

There could be a connection.

There had to be a connection.

-49-

Wen Ning studied the small red dot on the screen. They were on the move again. It appeared as if they were leaving the parking lot outside the Auschwitz concentration camp. Wen Ning swore. He had expected David to bring the Kindle reader wherever he went. The Kindle reader Wen Ning had equipped with an expensive tracking chip. But David had obviously grown tired of the Kindle reader. Maybe it was because he had already been through Professor Grossman's nine principles of riches? Maybe it was because he had become suspicious? It didn't really matter what the reason was.

Wen Ning's plan had failed.

There was still no sign that he would ever show up. If he had been alive, he would surely have made contact by now. Wen Ning had to admit the defeat. He was most likely dead.

It was time to tie up the loose ends.

"Ok, so we have the framework of a possible theory. Dr Kammler and David's grandfather worked together on a black project in Nazi Germany during the Second World War. The project was called Die Glocke. We don't know what Die Glocke was meant to do, but the codename Lanterntrager indicates that it was something bad. Something very bad. Out of all the secrets

Dr Kammler could have chosen to save from the collapsing Third Reich he only chose to salvage the Glocke project. This points to the fact that the Glocke project was important. Official statements from Joseph Goebbels, and Adolf Hitler himself, indicate that the leaders of Germany thought that Die Glocke had the power to change the direction of the war. Die Glocke is flown out of a war-torn Germany and lands in Bodø, a small town far north in German-occupied Norway. And that's where all leads end. Gold and mercury were quite possibly important ingredients in the Glocke experiment. But the question remains: What was Die Glocke? And where did the plane with Die Glocke and David's grandfather go?" Sophie asked.

"Don't forget Dr Kammler," David challenged. "The reports of his death have so little credibility that we must presume that he survived."

"Ok," Sophie remarked. "So we have two Nazis and a super-secret project called Die Glocke, most likely a weapon of mass destruction. Where would your grandfather and Dr Kammler have gone from Bodø?"

"They had a Ju 390 at their disposal. That means that they could have flown almost anywhere. They could have gone to Argentina, as so many other Nazis. There they would have had access to money and protection," David said.

"Or they could have gone to the US," Michael Simpson said.

"What are you saying?" Sophie asked.

"It's not that improbable," Michael Simpson started. "Hundreds of German scientists were brought to the US after the war, it was called Operation Paperclip."

"That's correct. But none of those scientists were responsible for the atrocities Dr Kammler committed. The West would simply never have allowed a war criminal being given amnesty for his crimes. It wouldn't have mattered if he offered the military some secret technology."

"Correct. It goes against everything we believe in. Our sense of right and wrong. A war criminal like Dr Kammler could never have been part of a half-official project like Operation Paperclip. At some point in time that operation would be declassified and the truth would be revealed to the public. If Dr Kammler was brought to the US he would have been brought there under the cover of a black operation."

"So you believe Dr Kammler and David's grandfather gave the Glocke blueprints to the Americans. That they traded their freedom for technology?"

"It's a theory," Michael Simpson replied.

"I've got a problem with that theory," David said. "Humans aren't built to keep secrets. Just look at Wikileaks, Julian Assange and Edward Snowden. You will always find people with qualms of conscience or someone who can't resist the temptation of fame. There is always someone who will talk."

"You're right, David. Why continue to hide the fact that Germany may have had a successful weapons project, maybe even more destructive than the atomic bomb, several decades after the Second World War ended? There can only be one reason. The secret weapons project had unintended consequences. Maybe it led to a paradigm shift within physics? Technological advancement is important for progress. But if the Germans stumbled across a terrible invention, a revolutionary technology that could result in the development of weapons that would make your heart stop, as Goebbels so appropriately coined it in his speech, a possible doomsday weapon; then that may very well be the reason Die Glocke has remained a secret all these years."

"But if the Germans managed to develop something

revolutionary during the war, why haven't any other countries managed to do the same? It is almost seventy years since the Second World War. The world has surely advanced since then."

"Indoctrination," Michael Simpson replied. "We still base our science on the Theory of Relativity. Not because it is one hundred percent correct, but because it provides us with the most accurate picture of the universe per today. The Nazis considered the Theory of Relativity as a predominantly Jewish theory. The Germans developed Quantum Theory, a theory which in many cases has solutions that contradict our common sense. But the solutions are only illogical because we compare them to what we can observe here in our little corner of the universe. We assume that our world is normal, but it isn't. Our little world is an abnormality in the universe. With this perspective everything becomes much clearer. A team of scientists, relieved of all historical doctrine, open to the occult and totally devoid of any morals and human worth. Such a team of scientists may have come up with totally new concepts and ways of approaching problems. Maybe they came up with a new theory. An alternative to the Theory of Relativity. A theory that doesn't have the limitations the Theory of Relativity has."

"I know you, Michael. There is something you're not telling us. What are you thinking about?" Sophie asked.

"I'm thinking about these codenames for the Glocke project. Tor and Chronos. Portal and time. I'm not sure if Die Glocke was just a weapon. What if Dr Kammler was attempting to develop a way to influence space and time?"

"A time machine?" David asked, sceptically.

"I know this may sound a bit far-fetched," Michael Simpson replied.

"Far-fetched? It sounds insane. The Second World War was

at its worst. The Germans knew they were about to lose within months. The only thing that could have saved them was an atomic bomb. Yet you are proposing they were prioritising working on a time machine?"

"Dr Kammler's task was to think outside the box. To, at any cost, come up with something that would ensure victory over the Allied Forces. A machine that could influence space and time could also have been a dangerous weapon if it was successful."

"But why a time machine? If they really had come up with revolutionary scientific and technological breakthroughs, why not use this knowledge to create something they could utilise against the Allied Forces? Why didn't the Germans drop nuclear bombs on London and New York?"

Michael Simpson shrugged his shoulders. "That's what we have to find out," he answered.

"Gold is the common denominator," Sophie said to herself. "What in hell could gold have done to the Glocke experiment? What could have happened? And why wasn't Dr Kammler able to recreate the successful experiment that killed the first team of Die Glocke scientists? Is it possible that gold and mercury could have a chemical reaction we don't know about?"

David had felt a little bit left out of the conversation. It wasn't as easy to talk to backs as it was to talk to faces. He leant over the mid-console of the rental car.

"Michael, your friend Caroline Summerfield said that the Earth's own gold was believed to possess magical powers. That it could lead to immortality and infinite riches. Is there a reason some people would believe this?"

Michael Simpson laughed. "Yes, that sounds like Caroline. She probably said that almost all gold on Earth originates from meteorites. That all the Earth's own gold had sunk into the core of the Earth."

David nodded.

"I'm sorry to have to disappoint you David. The myth about Earth's own gold is just that, a myth. We are all products of the universe. Nothing really originates from Earth. We humans are a product of stardust, light elements which at some stage in the early days of the universe clustered together to form the Earth we know. Gold on the other hand...we, for a long time, struggled to understand how gold was formed. We simply didn't have a good explanation for how the heavy elements like gold and platinum were created. But it turned out the answer was quite simple. Gold is created when two stars collide. Humans are made out of stardust and gold is the leftovers after stars colliding."

"So this theory about Earth's own gold, a magical gold, they aren't true?" David asked.

Michael Simpson shook his head. Then suddenly he stopped.

"Of course, why haven't I thought about that?"

"Thought about what?" David asked.

"We need to find a library. I think I know what Dr Kammler and the Nazis were looking for in King Midas' grave."

-50-

They were seated around a wooden table in the grand reading hall of the Warsaw Public Library. In front of them lay a stack of books. Sophie had just logged onto the Library's WIFI network and was waiting for Wikipedia's homepage to load on her screen.

Michael Simpson flipped through the pages of the large encyclopaedia in front of him.

"What are you looking for?" David asked.

"I'm not sure," Michael replied. "But I'm certain that I've seen those measurements before."

"Which measurements?"

Michael Simpson looked up from the reference book.

"Do you remember the first time you came to see me? You asked me what an alchemist was," Michael Simpson started.

David nodded, he remembered the incident well. Michael Simpson had talked about Sir Isaac Newton and Albert Einstein for a good two hours.

"I asked you to have a look at a picture that night."

David nodded again. Michael Simpson had shown him a picture of the Giza pyramid in Egypt.

"The Nazis were extremely interested, verging on obsessively fixated on the occult. Especially Heinrich Himmler," Michael

Simpson continued. "On the first of July 1935 Heinrich Himmler and a group of loyal Nazis established the Ahnenerbe, a pseudo-scientific institute which was supposed to conduct research on the alleged archaeological and cultural history of the Aryan race."

"They weren't only focused on archaeology. They also conducted a range of horrible experiments on Jewish prisoners," Sophie said.

Michael Simpson nodded. It was well known that the Ahnenerbe was responsible for inhumane experiments in their quest for knowledge. When you wanted to know how much pain, suffering and physical strain the human body could withstand before collapsing – you had to do cruel things.

"If Dr Kammler and his Kammlerstab were behind the blackest of the black projects in Germany, those which could never withstand the light of day...." Michael Simpson started.

The sentence made David shiver with disgust. The gassing of women and children, amputations of human limbs to see how long a person could live before succumbing to the blood loss, submersion of prisoners in freezing water to test how long it took them to die from the cold. All these experiments had been accepted as important for the war, and were almost being conducted in the open. Dr Kammler's projects were black. They would never withstand the light of the public eye. What was it that the Nazis had been doing that was so terrible that it had to be kept secret at all costs? So secret that all sixty-two scientists working on the Glocke experiment had been taken out into the woods and shot in the last days of the war. So secret that they had resorted to utilising concentration camp prisoners to build the premises they were conducting their experiments in. Prisoners who would never live long enough to tell anybody about what they had seen.

"......then it is possible that projects that didn't fit into Ahnenerbe would have been included in Kammlerstab," Michael Simpson concluded.

"And what does that mean?" Sophie asked.

"Think about what Ahnenerbe's mission was. It was to find evidence of the racial heritage of the Germanic people. The Germans sent expeditions as far as Tibet to look for traces of the Aryan race. But Himmler had an even more farfetched theory. He believed that the Aryan race descended from extra-terrestrial beings."

Sophie rolled her eyes. It was a wonder that Michael Simpson had been allowed to teach as long as he had at the university. He was an extremely smart and clever physicist. There was no doubt about that. But his imagination was too vivid for most academic institutions. It didn't help that he also was quite naïve. That he always saw what he wanted to see. It had been his doom at the university. Michael Simpson believed so strongly in his theories that he almost decided in advance that they were correct. "If you're going to start talking about extra-terrestrial beings again, you can count me out," Sophie said.

Michael Simpson shook his head frantically.

"No, no. We've been through this before, Sophie. I may believe that there is intelligent life elsewhere in the universe, but that doesn't mean that I believe that they have ever visited Earth."

David let out a big breath. He wasn't totally convinced that Michael Simpson was sane. After all, he had claimed that some people believed that the ancient pyramids in Egypt were remnants from an intergalactic war the first time David met him.

"My thought was that there had to be a reason for Dr Kammler to travel to that excavation in Turkey. If it was only gold they were after, then they could have sent someone else. And if it was part of their occult beliefs, then it would have fallen in under The Ahnenerbe's responsibility. Heinrich Himmler was after all in charge of the SS, and Dr Kammler's direct superior at the time. He must have had a reason for sending Dr Kammler to Turkey."

"And that was?" Sophie asked.

"I'll first have to talk to Caroline, but I don't think it was any normal gold they were looking for in King Midas' burial chamber," Michael Simpson said.

-51-

"Have you located him?" the CIA director asked.

"Negative," agent Wen Ning replied. "Last known observation was in Ankara two days ago. But we have an experienced team on the case. Eventually he will surface. And then we'll get him."

"Time is a luxury we don't have," the CIA director said. "Find him before this day is over. Or start looking for a new job."

Wen Ning studied his mobile phone and laughed. The asshole had hung up. Find a new job. Hah. Wen Ning didn't need the job. He didn't need to work another day in his life. The position in the CIA was simply something he had taken to be able to fulfil his mission. A simple means to an end. He turned the phone on silent, and placed it in his pocket. He checked his gun. Not his service gun, but the untraceable SIG-Sauer P230 he had stolen from a drug dealer more than a year ago. He adjusted his sunglasses and squinted at the big building in front of him. The Warsaw Public Library.

"What do you mean it wasn't any ordinary gold the Germans were looking for?" Sophie asked.

Michael Simpson lowered his mobile phone and placed it on the table. Caroline Summerfield hadn't picked up.

"Earth's own gold. Gold with magic powers. It is a myth that has been with us since the birth of the civilised man. Without exceptions wealthy civilisations have been fascinated by gold and its power."

"If you call it civilised to butcher whole populations, to start wars and commit genocide, all for the sake of some nuggets with a yellow colour, yes then you are right."

Michael Simpson didn't seem to care about Sophie's outburst and continued relatively unfazed.

"It got me thinking. These measurements of the Buna factory in Auschwitz. There was something familiar with them. A floor area of fifty-three thousand square metres. That is a massive building. A massive size for a factory that never produced a single gram of synthetic rubber. But still consumed more electricity than the city of Berlin."

Michael Simpson pointed to a picture of the Giza pyramid. "Look at the measurements," he said.

Sophie read the text underneath the picture.

'The Giza pyramid had a ground floor of fifty-three thousand square metres.'

"A coincidence? Or have we stumbled across something important?" Michael Simpson asked.

Sophie started reading. The great pyramid of Giza was one of the largest ancient constructions in the world. It was an established truth in modern archaeological theory that the three pyramids situated on the Giza plateau were burial chambers for three great kings, namely Khufu, Khafra and Menkaura. These three kings were the regents in the fourth Egyptian dynasty, which had its days of glory between year 2575 and 2465 before Christ. There was, however, no documentation proving this.

There had been no inscriptions on the pyramids about who

the builders had been. In all later dynasties the pharaohs had been very attentive in assuring that their names were engraved several hundred different places on the pyramids. When the Arabic Abdullah Al Ma'mun broke into Khufu's burial chamber in year 830 after Christ, the first time the burial chamber had ever been opened since being sealed in ancient times, they only found an empty coffin.

Not one single trace had ever been found inside the Giza pyramid proving that someone had ever been buried there. Even the coffin itself was too big to be moved from the gallery to the main chamber. Ergo the coffin had to have been placed there before the construction of the pyramid itself.

"Listen to this," Sophie said. "The Giza pyramid was originally 146.7 metres tall and covered an area of fifty-three thousand square metres. It consisted of two and a half million blocks of limestone, with an average weight of 2.6 tons. That's more building material than what has been used in all the churches and cathedrals in England."

"It is a unique construction," David said. "My father could never understand how the Egyptians had managed to build the pyramid several thousand years ago. He found so many holes in the universally accepted theories. How had the Egyptians been able to lift all those heavy rocks 150 metres up in the air? Even with today's technology that would have been an achievement. There was this Danish civil engineer, P. Garde-Hanson I think his name was, who calculated that a ramp all the way to the top of the pyramid would have required seventeen and a half million cubic metres of building material, almost seven times the amount used to build the pyramid itself. Where did all this building material go?"

"I thought you said you didn't know much about the Giza

pyramid," Michael Simpson remarked.

"I just haven't thought about it," David said dismissively. "Personally I haven't been that interested in pyramids, but I must admit I have heard my father talk about them. The information must have seeped into my subconscious memory."

Michael Simpson didn't pursue the argument any further. Instead it was Sophie who broke the uncomfortable silence.

"If you think that is strange listen to this. The main chamber was built of solid blocks of red granite, some as heavy as fifty tons. How did the Egyptians manage to transport them from the quarry in Aswan, more than 600 miles south of the Giza plateau? How did they manage to place the granite blocks inside an area of the pyramid where only four to six workers were able to stand shoulder to shoulder? The weight of these rocks would have required the strength of a thousand workers," Sophie said.

David shook his head. "I don't know what is true or untrue about the pyramids, but I do agree with my dad. I think there are many unanswered questions surrounding the construction of the Giza pyramid."

"We can all agree on that," Michael Simpson said. "But my point wasn't to direct attention towards the finer technicalities of the various building techniques the Egyptians utilised. My point was that no one knows how old the pyramids are."

"Didn't you listen to what Sophie read out earlier?" David said. "The pyramids were constructed during the fourth Egyptian dynasty, two and a half thousand years before Christ. Ergo the pyramids must be around four and a half thousand years old."

Michael Simpson smiled. "This has always been my problem with the pyramids on the Giza plateau. First of all, carbon dating of the pyramids has returned a range of different answers. Everything from two to five thousand years before Christ."

"So the pyramids may be up to seven thousand years old. What does that mean?" Sophie asked. She was afraid Michael was going to start theorising about the pyramids being ancient ruins of intergalactic weapons again. It was embarrassing when he started on his wild theories.

"The problem is that carbon dating of the mortar used on the Giza pyramid returns answers all over the place. The mortar used on top of the pyramid is on average a thousand years older than the mortar used on the bottom," Michael Simpson said.

"So you mean to say that Khufu started to build the pyramid in thin air?" Sophie asked.

Michael Simpson laughed. "Well that's what the evidence tells us."

"We can only carbon date organic material. The archaeologists would therefore have had to date the mortar and not the granite blocks. That also means that if the Egyptians had to do repairs on the bottom of the pyramid, then they may have used newer mortar. That could easily explain the age difference," David said.

"That's correct, David, but could there be other reasons?" Michael Simpson asked.

It was as if a spark of electricity flew through Sophie's brain. Suddenly some of the pieces of the puzzle fell into place.

"Radiation. The pyramids could have been exposed to strong radiation. A so-strong radiation that carbon dating would never provide us with the correct answer."

David raised his head. "What have you guys been smoking? The pyramids were built four and a half thousand years ago. How can they have been exposed to radiation?"

"Alchemy," Sophie said.

Michael Simpson nodded.

"Alchemy? Can somebody please tell me what you guys think

you've realised?"

"Why did the Egyptians build the pyramids with mathematical perfection? Why did the airshafts all point towards the star constellation Orion?"

David shrugged his shoulders. He had no idea.

"Excuse me a second. I just have to make a call," Michael Simpson said, and left the table.

He arrived back a few seconds later with a worried facial expression. "That was strange," he said. "I can't get hold of Caroline. She is almost always available."

"Everybody is allowed to be offline. You should try it yourself sometime," Sophie said. Michael Simpson understood the not-so-subtle comment. He had become an information junkie in his old days. Always with a tablet, a mobile or a laptop within reach.

"Do you have to talk to Caroline before you tell us what it is you think you have figured out?" David asked.

Michael smiled. "Today's youth. Always so impatient," he said, lifting the book about Egypt to the table in front of them. "But I guess you're right. No reason to wait."

"Tell us, Michael," Sophie said. She was getting impatient as well.

"I believe the Nazis were searching for Sirius gold," Michael Simpson said.

"Serious gold?" David asked.

Sophie smiled. "Sirius Gold, Sirius like the star system. It's just a different word for what Caroline called Earth's own gold."

Michael Simpson shook his head. "No, no, no. The Earth's own gold doesn't exist. It is a theoretical impossibility as all gold on Earth originates from stars colliding millions of years ago. Sirius gold is the result of such a collision. Or rather, the legend of Sirius gold is that a special kind of gold landed on Earth after the collision of two stars in what we today call the Sirius constellation."

"Gold with magical powers?" David asked.

Michael Simpson nodded. "It's all just horseshit of course. There is no such thing as magical gold. But the Nazis were obsessed with the occult. And if Heinrich Himmler ordered Dr Kammler's trip to Turkey, then it might just have been Sirius gold he was looking for."

"I still don't understand what this has to do with the Giza pyramids," David said.

"As I said the first time we met, David, there are many different theories about why the Giza pyramids were built. Most people, like you, believe that they are burial chambers for great and powerful kings. I belong to the group who believe they were large factories for alchemy and observational posts for astronomy. And it is a fact that the Egyptians had a special relationship to the star constellation Sirius."

"There is a perfectly good reason for that," Sophie started. "Sirius is the brightest star in the night sky. Almost twice as bright as Canopus, the second brightest. To the Egyptians the river Nile was the source of life. The heliacal rise of the star Sirius marked the annual flooding of the Nile in ancient Egypt. Ergo it had a direct impact on the locals' lives. It's therefore no surprise that the Egyptians worshipped the star. They were simple people who saw miracles wherever they wanted."

Michael Simpson glanced over at Sophie. There was tension in the air. He obviously wanted to offer a counterargument, but he restrained himself. There was no point in trying to convince Sophie, she had to arrive at her own conclusions.

"Look at the dimensions of the Giza pyramid and tell me

that it is a coincidence that both the Buna factory and the Giza pyramid had the exact same ground measurements. Tell me that it is a coincidence that archaeologists have found traces of mercury in both the ancient Egypt and the Mayan culture, that they all worshipped gold and believed in gold's magical power," he said, and pushed the book over to Sophie.

Sophie remained silent.

David was seated by himself. Lost in deep thoughts. He knew there was something he had missed. Something right in front of their noses.

The gold that was embezzled at Auschwitz.

They had tried to follow the money, but there were no cash flows to follow.

The gold had been used in the Glocke experiments. Gold from the star constellation of Sirius.

Magical gold.

Had the Nazis really believed in all this?

Sirius. Follow the money. Suddenly it was clear to him. It had been there the whole time. It had been the reason he had travelled to Turkey.

David opened his laptop and located the folder with the scanned copies of the documents Neill Flynn's wife had given him.

The retired chief investigator of the missing person case of Yossar Devan had developed his own theory. A theory his superiors had disliked.

A theory that had meant the end of his career.

David quickly found what he was looking for. The overview that Neill Flynn had prepared outlining the main cash flows of Yossar Devan's conglomerate of companies. Flynn had made some notes in the margins of the document. Why the large transfers to Turkey? Suiris Export and Import. A company that had received tens of millions of dollars in support, but never had contributed with any revenue.

A massive black hole.

The only loss-making business Yossar Devan ever had owned. Suiris.

Sirius spelt backwards.

"I think I've got something," David said.

"What is it?" Sophie asked.

"I don't think King Midas' burial chamber is located where we thought it was," he replied.

Wen Ning held his breath. Had he heard correctly? Had this business student just solved the mystery? The mystery he himself had spent most of his life struggling to solve? It couldn't be that easy.

Was this what David's dad had figured out?

This changed everything.

David and his friends weren't loose strings that had to be tied up anymore. They could potentially be the solution to his problem. Wen Ning pushed the gun down into his beltline, and let the navy blue shirt hang on the outside of his belt. A trained agent could possibly notice the contours of a gun. But these three were mere amateurs. They had no idea.

No idea what was in store for them.

Wen Ning continued to walk past them. He noticed that they lowered their voices. But none of them looked up. They wouldn't have known who he was anyway. They wouldn't have had a clue.

He was a chameleon.

A man with a thousand faces.

–52–

"If you're correct, if there is a connection between the size of the Giza pyramid and IG Farben's factory at Auschwitz..." David started. They were back in the rental car, heading towards the airport.

"There is most certainly a connection. The buildings have the same ground area. They were both built by slaves. There have been found traces of radiation in them. And we have no good reason why either of them was built."

"...then I might have the missing piece of the puzzle," David continued, leaning closer to Michael and Sophie. "Yossar Devan wired tens of millions of dollars to Turkey in the period between 1970 and 1973. The money ended up in a company he had established there."

"Yes, I remember that," Michael Simpson said. "Gordion Mining. The company never found any gold. It was wound up shortly after Yossar Devan disappeared. Not his most profitable investment, I presume."

David shook his head. "The company never made a cent. Not one single cent."

"But that's not unusual. As far as I remember, Gordion Mining was a pure exploration company. They didn't produce gold. They searched for gold. They didn't even employ any local labour.

All workers were flown in from some low-cost labour country," Michael Simpson said.

"Have you been to their premises?" David asked.

Michael Simpson shook his head. "No. But I've seen pictures. The building is a shame for the area. Not that anyone cares. It is located in the middle of nowhere. But it is just such a waste of money. To build that massive building for a mine that never ended up producing anything."

"Exactly. A massive empty building. A company that never produced anything, but still had an electricity bill equivalent to a small city's."

"What are you saying?" Michael Simpson asked.

"I've got it right here in the notes from the chief investigator of Yossar Devan's disappearance. Yossar Devan wired tens of millions to his mining company, and several of those millions were used to pay massive electricity bills."

"But why?" Sophie asked.

David shrugged his shoulders. "I don't know. But I do know that the company had a different name when it was established. When Yossar Devan set up the company he called it Suiris Mining."

"Sirius spelt backwards," Sophie gasped.

David nodded. "According to the Turkish company register the name was changed to the more anonymous Gordion Mining three days later, but the history never disappears."

"What do you think Devan used the building for?" Sophie asked.

David shrugged his shoulders. "No idea. I'm not even sure it was ever used for anything."

"What do you mean?"

"I think there might be something underneath the building,"

David replied. "Even though the building is huge it would only have cost a fraction of the money Yossar Devan wired to Turkey. If he didn't waste the money searching for gold then he may have built something underneath the building."

"You think King Midas' burial chamber is in the vicinity of the building?" Michael Simpson asked.

"It makes sense," David started. "All the time we have assumed that King Midas' burial chamber was where the excavation collapsed."

"Which is only three kilometres away from his building," Michael Simpson said.

"What if it wasn't the burial chamber itself that collapsed, but a tunnel that led to it?" David asked.

Neither Michael nor Sophie replied.

David pulled out the picture of Dr Kammler next to the young Yossar Devan. "Look closely at the picture. What is it that doesn't make sense?" he asked.

Michael Simpson tried to have a quick glance, but had to revert his attention to driving the car. The traffic was moving fast in Poland.

"I can't see anything special," Sophie said, after having gawked at the picture for two whole minutes.

"Look closer at the clothing,"

"Bad fashion sense?"

David laughed. "That's probably true too. But I was thinking more along the lines of what is the right clothing for what they are about to do?"

Sophie studied the picture again. Dr Hans Kammler was dressed in a uniform and a heavy coat. The young Yossar Devan was dressed in a cotton sweater, long trousers and a beanie. In his hand he was holding a cage with a bird. Dr Kammler held something that looked like a torch.

"I still can't see anything special," Sophie said.

"They are not on their way down into a tomb," David said. "The Tumuli graves in Turkey are large piles of dirt that were built to represent the importance of the deceased. The bigger the pile of dirt, the more important you were. Dr Kammler wouldn't have needed a torch and they would certainly not have needed a canary to enter a Tumuli."

"They're on their way down a mine shaft," Sophie finally said.

"If not a mine, they are at least on their way down some sort of tunnel. That would be the only reason to bring a canary."

"So you believe that King Midas' burial chamber could be located near Yossar Devan's abandoned building? That there could be a tunnel system covering more than three kilometres underneath the factory?"

"How many years has the military been in the area?"

"More than twenty years," Michael Simpson replied.

"Still they have never, ever found anything. King Midas' grave disappeared that day in 1944. Dr Kammler and the rest of the Nazis left Turkey a couple of days later. If there had only been a grave collapsing they would have stayed. They would have tried to find a new entrance."

"But if there was a tunnel system that collapsed, then they wouldn't have had a clue where to start looking. It is possible they had no idea where the actual grave was located," Sophie said.

"According to the local story about the Alchemist, about Yossar Devan, he surfaced in a river several kilometres from the excavation site."

"In the River Paktalos. The river where King Midas, according to legend, washed his hands, and which since has been blessed with large gold deposits."

Sophie looked over at Michael Simpson, who had been surprisingly quiet.

"What's your opinion?" she asked.

Michael Simpson nervously peered into the rear mirror. "It will have to wait. I think we may have a problem. I think someone is following us."

–53–

Wen Ning tried to maintain a decent distance, at least four cars in between them at any time. But he had become too eager, had lost his concentration. Had they noticed him? The driver, the retired physics Professor Michael Simpson, had certainly slowed down. Forced Wen Ning to come closer, to possibly expose himself. Their rental car had been equipped with a GPS tracker, so there was really nothing stopping him from taking the next exit and continuing to follow them via the tracker. He knew they were on their way to the airport anyway. But he wanted to be close.

Wanted to stop them right there and then.

Find out what they knew.

Find out whether David had located king Midas' burial chamber.

It was rather comical. Things had turned out better than expected. Wen Ning had proposed the original plan of using David Dypsvik as bait, a bait to lure him out of his hiding place. But that plan hadn't worked. Instead David, this naïve business student, could possibly have solved the mystery by himself. How was that possible?

Wen Ning was smart. An IQ of 152. He had it in black and white. Done a test ten years ago. He was one of the smartest people on the planet. Could have been a member of Mensa if he wanted. Instead he had used most of his adult life searching for Yossar Devan's secret. He had eventually figured out what the secret was. But that realisation had only led to another, much bigger realisation. A discovery that had changed everything, and had shaped his life the last twenty years.

Die Glocke.

This strange piece of machinery the Germans had built during the Second World War.

Die Glocke – the answer to all his dreams.

Wen Ning had, however, used so much time and so many resources searching for King Midas' burial chamber that he had started to wonder whether the whole thing was a myth.

Then David's dad had arrived. And Wen Ning had been given a new chance.

He could feel he was close now. So close to the grave that had started it all. The grave that would give him all the power he could ever want. How could a simple business student from Norway have solved what Wen Ning had struggled with for so many years? It had to be luck. Pure luck. It had to be.

Come to think of it, it was rather ironic that luck had led to the solution.

Wen Ning eased the pressure on the gas pedal and turned on the indicator. He would take the first exit from the highway. He had been so patient, so patient for so long. He could wait a few hours more.

It wasn't only IQ that was important for success in life. It was the ability to delay the satisfaction of a need. Wen Ning could wait to eat his Marshmallow.

He wasn't a simple American.

"Is he still there?" Sophie asked. It was so quiet in the car that you could almost hear yourself think. Michael Simpson glanced quickly in the rear mirror. Three cars back he saw a black sedan turn on his indicator and take the ramp off the highway. The white SUV that had been on their tail since they left the library was still behind them, though. It appeared as if it was slowing down, but it wasn't going anywhere.

"He's still on us," Michael Simpson said. "I'll try to get rid of him when we get closer to the airport."

-54-

David, Sophie and Michael were sitting next to each other on the plane, talking about what they had learnt during the day. The white car had disappeared ten minutes before they approached the airport, and Michael was no longer sure if they had even been followed.

"There was just something about the way it was hanging back there. Like an undercover police car just waiting for me to go over the speed limit," Michael said.

"It may have been your own imagination," David said. "I've had similar experiences over the last week. Felt that someone was watching me."

"Why haven't you said anything? When did this happen?" Sophie asked.

The outburst came as a surprise to David. He hadn't thought it was important.

"Twice in London, outside the hotel I was staying at. Once when I met Peter Swarkowski. And a couple of times in Turkey."

"Once when you met Peter Swarkowski. Peter Swarkowski who it is impossible to get hold of? A couple of times in Turkey? Didn't you consider this could be important? That Michael and I had the right to know about it?" she asked.

"It was nothing. It was only my own paranoia. I've experienced it before. It is my own mind toying with me, makes me imagine someone is following me."

Michael Simpson nodded. "David is probably right. There was no one following us earlier. We live in a technological world. If someone wanted to keep track of David's whereabouts, then they would have used technological aids."

"Shit. The Kindle reader," David exclaimed.

"The Kindle reader?" Michael Simpson repeated.

"Professor Grossman gave me an e-reader with what was supposed to be Yossar Devan's principles of riches. I've had it on me most of the time. But I think I forgot it in the back seat of the rental car I dropped off in Ankara."

"Was it a rental from AVIS?"

David nodded.

"Let's stop by and see if they have found it when we land. I've got a friend who can check whether it has been tampered with. If it has been equipped with a recording device or a tracker he'll be able to tell us."

"That would ease my mind a little bit. I can't say I love the idea that someone may have been monitoring us," Sophie said.

Ten seat rows farther back an Asian, with black designer sunglasses from Prada and a blue Nike cap pulled down onto his face, was reading the paper. When the airhostess asked whether he wanted beef or chicken for dinner, he gave her a spiteful look. Stupid woman. Beef or chicken? Who cared? He wouldn't taste the difference anyway.

–55–

The CIA director was in a good mood. Finally some good news. The team had located David Dypsvik. He was on his way on a flight from Poland. Estimated arrival time in three hours. The CIA director wondered what David had been doing in Poland. Was it there he was hiding?

They would soon enough get their answers. A team of agents would be waiting for David when he landed. They would interrogate him and find out exactly what he knew and didn't. The CIA director wasn't quite sure where to place David Dypsvik yet. Foe or friend? The picture was still muddy and he had to prepare himself for the possibility that not everything was as it seemed. It was after all he himself who had authorised to involve David Dypsvik. It was the director himself who had put the wheels in motion.

He just hadn't expected that people would start dying. That almost everybody David spoke to would end up dead.

He skimmed through the folder the Agency had prepared on David Dypsvik. Thirty years old. MBA student at Bond University. Clever at school. Maybe a bit too clever. His grades didn't correspond with his career. Two years as a journalist in a financial paper. Two years as a business manager in a large Norwegian bank. Ok salary, but no savings to speak of. Highly geared apartment, and a massive student loan that most certainly would be even greater when he had completed his MBA degree in Australia.

The CIA director shook his head.

He had climbed all the way to the top in the CIA without any formal education. He had worked himself up and forward. He had seen enough of these yuppies with calculator fingers and sharp elbows in the Agency. They thought that a diploma, preferably from an Ivy League school, qualified them for the job. That a diploma was a guarantee that they would do a good job and succeed. It couldn't be further from the truth. Most diplomas weren't worth the paper they were written on.

In the Agency you had to renew yourself every single day. You couldn't afford resting on your laurels.

Never.

He had made up his mind. David Dypsvik, this so-called business student David Dypsvik. It didn't matter whether he was innocent or not. David Dypsvik was about to be taught a lesson in how the real world worked.

-56-

David grabbed his green bag from the luggage belt. With a hunched back he checked the tag, even though he knew it was his bag. He had bought it in Norway ten years ago. It was unlikely anybody else had an identical-looking one.

Farther down the luggage belt something caught his attention. Two tall dark men, appropriately dressed in khaki pants and white short armed sleeves, approached Michael Simpson. There was something strange about them, as if they were trying too hard not to be noticeable. Was he witnessing two nervous passengers, or maybe two undercover agents scouting for potential drug smugglers? He didn't even manage to finish his thought before he felt a strong hand on his shoulder. He turned around and looked straight into the face of a middle-aged Turk with a suntanned face and a strong smell of garlic.

"Mr Dypsvik. Would you please come with me," the Turk said. But it was obviously not meant as a question. In the corner of his eye, David could see Michael Simpson receive the same request from the two guys in khakis.

"What's the problem?" David asked, subtly looking around for Sophie. A female customs officer outside the ladies' bathroom told him she was cleaning herself up.

"Just come with us. Everything will be explained," the Turk said with a big grin.

David put his bag onto the trolley and followed the Turkish customs officer. This was not going as planned.

After ten long minutes of waiting, in a spartanly decorated meeting room, the silence was finally broken by a door being pushed open. David had been going through various scenarios in his head since he first had felt that firm hand on his shoulder. Had he done something illegal? He had of course realised a long time ago that not everything was as it was supposed to be with his assignment. Professor Grossman had disappeared, rumoured to be murdered. And David's friend from Bond University, JC, had told him that the Australian police were interested in talking to him.

And still there was more. The contact in London; Peter Swarkowski, was impossible to get hold of. David's own father had been investigating the missing person case of Yossar Devan and had used 'Die Glocke' as password on his private laptop. David's grandfather had been a Nazi, a physicist who most likely had attempted to help the Germans develop a doomsday weapon. What was it he had gotten himself mixed up in? It couldn't be good. That much he understood.

A handsome man entered the room. He wasn't a customs officer, his clothing revealed him. David had watched enough episodes of Border Patrol to understand that the man in the door entrance was attached to some sort of government agency. Black suit and white shirt. Hair combed backwards. Lightly suntanned face with nice features. An office worker. Not a customs officer.

"Hi David, my name is Agent Uttley. I work for the American government," the handsome man said.

David swallowed. The American government. Did they think he was a terrorist?

"Are you from the FBI?" David asked.

The man smiled. "FBI deals with federal cases in the US. Crimes across US states. I work for the CIA. We handle everything outside the US."

"Have I committed a crime? Have I broken any laws?" David asked. He should probably have asked for a lawyer instead. One of his uncles, not the rich one, had worked for the Norwegian police. He had told David that it didn't matter whether he was innocent or not. The first thing to do if you ever ended up in an interrogation room was to ask for a lawyer. The police force wasn't much different from most other organisations. Everything was about measurable results. And the easiest way to get results was to let the suspect speak. To let the suspect entangle himself in so many contradictions that there was no other way out than to confess to the crime he had or hadn't committed.

The man smiled again, seating himself in front of David. "No, no. Not at all." He shook his head. "You haven't broken any laws. I just want to have a chat. Is that OK?"

We always start the interrogations by saying that you're not a suspect. That you're just a witness. That we just want to have a chat. We act friendly. Almost like an old colleague. And then we let you do the talking. It's almost always this initial chat that becomes the most important part of our case. It's here the amateurs reveal themselves. Not thinking about what they are saying. Telling everything and nothing. David thought back on his uncle's advice. He had never imagined that he would find himself in this situation. That he would be interrogated by the police, by the CIA. To maybe blurt out something that could be used against him on a later occasion. David had decided a long time ago to follow his uncle's advice if he ever ended up in such a situation. To never say a single word.

To be rock hard.

To ask for a lawyer.

"Yes, of course," David heard his mouth say. "I have nothing to hide." And then he started talking.

Agent Uttley walked into the plainly decorated conference room. "Any progress?" he asked. The two other agents in the room shook their heads.

"They've got no idea. Absolutely no idea," one of them answered.

"Fruitcakes," the other agent said.

"First time I've seen so well-educated fruitcakes," Agent Uttley said. "But you're right. These guys are off with the fairies. I wonder what they've smoked. David Dypsvik is rambling on about pyramids and magical gold."

"Magical gold. Is that all? My guy claims they are looking for a time machine," one of the other agents laughed.

"Well, there's no point holding them much longer. They haven't been in contact with him, and it doesn't seem like they have any idea where he is hiding or what he knew."

"Shouldn't we at least hold them overnight? Just as a precaution? The director doesn't land until a couple of hours, and he specifically said it was important that we apprehended them."

"I run the Turkish office. I make the decisions here. These guys are irrelevant. And right now we have bigger fish to catch," Agent Uttley said. "And try to get hold of agent Wen again. I know he reported in sick yesterday, but I need to speak to him urgently."

-57-

"That was a strange experience," Michael Simpson said. "The strangest thing I've ever been through. What do you think they were looking for?" Sophie asked.

Michael Simpson shrugged his shoulders. "Hard to say." He paused, before continuing. "David, they asked if I had been in contact with your father."

"Me too," Sophie remarked, surprised. "It almost seemed like they believed he was still alive," she said, glancing over at David.

David stared at the floor.

"I know," he said, quietly.

"What does it mean?" Michael Simpson asked.

"It means that he may not be dead after all. It means that my life may be a lie," David cried, before walking off toward the exit doors of the airport.

Sophie ran after him and managed to stop him just before he was about to hail a cab.

She managed to convince him to sit down on one of the steel benches outside the airport.

"Breathe slowly. Breathe with your stomach," she said as David seemed to be about to hyperventilate. He had managed to stay relatively unaffected by the questions Agent Uttley asked him. It hadn't started off that bad. But then Agent Uttley had started to ask him questions about his dad. If David knew where he was. It had been as if all the air in the interrogation room had been sucked out in a second. It had felt as if the walls had been caving in to crush him. David's dad was dead. He had been dead for more than a year. Killed in a freak car accident.

Agent Uttley had just nodded to David's comments and continued his questioning. Had David seen something out of the ordinary during the last few days? Had he noticed anyone following him?

Out of the ordinary? David had almost started to laugh. Nothing had been normal during the last several days. It felt like he was walking around in a reverie where nothing was real anymore. Everything he had ever believed in was a lie. Nobody was who he had thought. Not his professor at Bond. Not his grandfather. Not even his dad.

It was as if the gates had finally been opened and all his emotions erupted to the surface. He hardly knew if he wanted to laugh or cry. But in the end it hadn't been tears that had come. It had been something else. Something he hadn't felt for years.

An anger.

A terrible anger.

It was now clear to David that the CIA, and Agent Uttley, believed that his father was still alive. David thought back on his father's funeral. It hadn't been an open casket. It hadn't been a casket at all. David's father's body had never been located. The police report had established that his car had crashed into the guardrail at a speed close to 120 kilometres an hour. It had proceeded straight through the guardrail and flown through the air for more than 200 metres before penetrating the surface of the ocean below the cliff side. The Turkish police had stated that it would have been impossible to survive the crash. David's dad would have died instantly when the car hit the water. The local police had managed to locate and rescue the car wreck a couple of days later, but the body of David's dad hadn't been inside. The police quickly arrived at the conclusion that David's dad must have been thrown through the front window and washed away by the strong currents. It was probably one of the reasons David's mum had been so quick to move to Turkey. She had no grave to visit in Norway.

David's dad was still out there somewhere.

Somewhere out in there in the big blue ocean.

At least that's what he had been led to believe. Until now. The CIA was obviously of a different opinion. They thought that David's dad was still alive. That David's dad might have tried to contact him. Was this the reason David had been involved in the search for Yossar Devan's real identity?

Was it David's own dad who was pulling the strings?

How could David have been so stupid? Of course it was his dad. It could only be him.

David thought back. Professor Grossman, who had played on David's strong wish to find a secret formula for riches; Peter Swarkowski, who had played on David's interest in a possible mystery.

There was only one person who knew exactly how David would react. One person who knew that David would willingly follow the leads that were being laid out for him.

There was only one person who knew David that well.

His own dad.

"What is it?" Sophie asked.

"I feel so stupid," David said. "I feel so betrayed. My dad isn't dead. He is the one responsible for all of this." David rested his head in the palms of his hands. "I thought I had hit rock bottom when I discovered that my granddad had been a Nazi. When I discovered that my granddad had been a war criminal, a mass murderer. And now it turns out my dad wasn't who I thought he was, either. My dad lived a secret life, a secret life where he investigated the disappearance of Yossar Devan and the creation of a doomsday weapon during the war. My dad staged his own death. Who does something like that? Who is my family?"

"Don't make too hasty conclusions," Michael Simpson said. "We only know that the CIA suspects that your father may still be alive. That doesn't necessarily mean that your father is behind what has happened. If your father is still alive, and we have no reason to believe he is, then he may have a reason to be hiding."

David looked up at Michael Simpson, his eyes brimming with anger.

"For at least ten years he knew my granddad was a Nazi officer during the Second World War. Still he has never mentioned it to me. Not with one single word. How can I trust anything he has ever told me? It doesn't matter if he is still alive. To me he is dead," David said.

Sophie gave him a stern look. "You don't mean what you're saying, David."

-58-

Agent Uttley stared at the TV screen as he packed up his equipment. The local news channel was broadcasting an updated report on the murder of the Chinese ambassador a few days earlier. Local police had no suspects even though they had captured CCTV footage of both the murder and the fleeing assailant. The Chinese ambassador had been stabbed to death on one of his nightly jogs. The police had just released video footage of the incident in the hope that someone would step forward with information. Agent Uttley moved closer to the TV screen. There was something familiar about the way the killer moved. It wasn't just the fact that he seemed professional. Even though the murder and the escape had been captured on film it was impossible to identify the killer. But there was something about the way he so purposefully stabbed his victim. So raw and brutal in his movements. And still so elegant. It was evident to Agent Uttley that this was more than a random savage murder. There were emotions involved. Deep emotions.

The presumed murderer was dressed from top to toe in black, and he never faced the camera. It was obvious he was aware that he was being filmed. In any instance it would have been impossible to get close to the ambassador without being captured by a CCTV camera. The embassy row was among the most patrolled and safest areas of Ankara. It was probably why the ambassador had decided to go on a jog without any bodyguards.

But there was something more. A worry that wouldn't go away. There was only one person Agent Uttley knew who could move like the masked person on the TV screen. And that person had called in sick the morning after the murder. A coincidence or something else?

Agent Uttley looked at his watch. There were still a few more hours before the CIA director would arrive at Ankara airport. The director had insisted that Agent Uttley personally pick him up and brief him on the way to the hotel. The order had pissed Agent Uttley off. He was the CIA's chief of station in Turkey. Not some local errand boy. He had deliberately released David Dypsvik and his friends from custody. No big shot from HQ was going to tell him how to run the Turkey office.

The CIA director would have to catch a cab. This couldn't wait. Agent Uttley had to sort this out.

He was most likely wrong, but he needed to know for sure.

-59-

The mood of the group outside the AVIS rental car office was gloomy. David had, only moments earlier, been handed back his Kindle reader. The e-reader he by accident had left in the back seat of his rental car before leaving for Warsaw. Michael Simpson had said that he knew a guy who could pull it apart to check if it had been equipped with a tracking device. Instead, David had taken matters into his own hands, and smashed the Kindle reader into the ground outside the AVIS office. Hidden among all the cheap mass-produced electronics from Amazon, which lay spread out on the concrete, they had found something that didn't look like it belonged. David held up a small chip, the size of a hairpin.

"That's not cheap," Michael said. "That's military-grade equipment. Did your dad work in intelligence?"

"My father was an historian. He worked for a university," David said.

"It may have been a cover. You can't buy that type of equipment over the counter," Michael said, pointing at the tiny chip David held between his right thumb and his index finger. "I think you're wrong, but if it is your dad who has involved you, then he must be working for some sort of intelligence organisation."

"Could the CIA have planted it?" Sophie asked.

Michael Simpson shook his head. "I don't think so. Why would they spy on David? I'm sure they've got bigger fish to catch, with Al-Qaida and other terrorist groups roaming free. I can understand that they may want to have a chat with David if his dad wasn't who he claimed to be, if he was someone else. But they would have no reason to track David."

Sophie stretched her arms above her head. She felt fatigued and dirty after all the travelling.

"I'm tired. Let's just head home. I miss my bathtub," she said in an effort to break up the discussion. They weren't getting anywhere by speculating about whether David's dad was still alive or not. The only thing they achieved was to make David even angrier. She wondered how she would have felt herself if it turned out that her family had lied to her. That they weren't who they had claimed to be.

They all got into Michael Simpson's car and left the parking lot outside the AVIS office. Michael Simpson called his message bank to check for any missed calls.

"No. No. It can't be true!" he cried, a few seconds later.

"What is it," Sophie asked. Michael Simpson was still listening to his messages.

"It's not possible," he cried. "Caroline is dead."

He laid his mobile phone on the mid console and stared out into nothingness. Hearing himself say the words made it even more unreal to him.

Sophie wondered if she should give him some time. Let the shock sink in before asking any questions. But she couldn't resist. "What's happened?" she asked in a worried tone.

"Caroline was murdered two days ago. The police suspect an extreme environmental organisation is responsible."

David thought back on the office barracks of Minutza Mining being blown to pieces when Sophie and he had visited her earlier in the week. Had they finally crossed the line? Had Caroline Summerfield's own prediction come true? Had the greenies made a mistake that had ended up with the loss of human lives?

Or was there someone else responsible?

–60–

"There is something I haven't told you," David said.

Michael Simpson looked at him with sorrowful eyes.

"What is it? I've just been told that one of my dearest friends has been murdered. I'm not up for any more surprises, David."

David nodded. He understood how Michael Simpson felt. But this couldn't wait.

"When I started looking into the disappearance of Yossar Devan in London, I constructed a list of the Oxford University class of 1973. More correctly, I created a list of who had been most successful, who had made the most money." David took a deep breath. "The thought was that someone on that list could have attended Yossar Devan's last lectures."

"What did you find out?" Sophie asked. This was a part of the story David hadn't told her.

"Everyone on the list, all the richest people of the Oxford class of 1973 had, according to Professor Grossman's study, attended the lectures. The problem was that almost half of the names on the list belonged to people who had either died or disappeared in the last year. And none of the ones who were still alive had ever heard of Professor Grossman."

"What does that mean?" Sophie asked.

"I thought it meant that Professor Grossman's study was a lie. That he had never interviewed any of the people he claimed. I managed to get an appointment with a real estate developer in London, John Mitchell...."

"From Mitchell Properties? The real estate billionaire who died a few days ago?" Michael Simpson asked.

David nodded. "He had an accident the day after I visited him in London. I thought it was a coincidence. I checked all the other names on the list, and there was nothing suspicious about any of the deaths. They were all classified as accidents."

"But now you are having doubts?" Michael Simpson asked.

David nodded. "Something is not right. This study about what makes people rich doesn't exist. And everywhere I go people seem to die. I don't know why, but I got the impression that the CIA agent interviewing me suspected I was involved in some sort of a complot. That I was involved in something serious, maybe even murder. It wasn't until I told him about my theory about magical gold that he lost interest." David paused for another deep breath. "I don't think Caroline was killed by this environmental organisation. I fear that she may have been killed by someone stalking me. I fear that she may have been killed by the same person who involved me in the search for Yossar Devan's identity."

"I thought you believed that person was your dad. If it is someone else, what does he want?" Sophie asked.

David shrugged his shoulders. "I've got no idea, but I believe we may be about to find out who it is and what he wants very soon." David pointed to the rear mirror. The black SUV had followed them since they left the airport. In the beginning it had stayed three or four car lengths behind. But now there was only one car separating them.

Michael Simpson turned the wheel and the car screeched before flattening out and avoiding the median strip with only half a metre's clearance. Behind them they heard the sound of brakes and honking horns. David turned around and glanced out the rear window to check whether they had managed to lose the pursuer. They hadn't.

"He's still hanging on," David cried.

"Shit," Michael Simpson exclaimed.

"Should I call the police?" Sophie called out.

"No," David replied. "We can't involve the Turkish police. You saw what happened at the airport. I don't know how your interview went, but I was almost laughed at. They didn't believe a word of what I told them."

Michael Simpson nodded. "David is right. We can't walk into a police station and make accusations when we don't have a freaking clue what is going on."

"So what do you suggest we do?" Sophie asked, stressed.

"We lose him," Michael Simpson replied.

-61-

Michael Simpson had grown up on a farm in England. It had been a hard upbringing with lots of physical work. The hard work was possibly the main reason he had chosen an academic career. Already as a teenager he had been fed up with rising early, working from before sunrise to dawn, and being generally so physically exhausted that he most nights fell asleep before his head hit the pillow. He had missed a lot of the fun and play his friends of the same age had experienced, simply because life was hard for farmers. But one thing he had appreciated with farm life. There had hardly been any police around when he grew up. It meant that he, already as a young kid, had been allowed to drive the family's tractor. At age twelve he had started to bring his dad back and forth from the local pub. And as a fifteen-year-old he had grown into a seasoned driver whom most adults had problems keeping up with. Now, for the first time in his life, he realised that he might actually have use for those skills. For the first time in his life he found himself in a car chase.

"I think our best chance is to get off the highway. We will have a better chance of losing him in the city."

Michael Simpson had barely finished the sentence when he heard the sounds of a siren.

"It's a police car," David said.

"Shit," Michael Simpson shouted. He hadn't even considered that possibility. "This is going to cost me," he said, before tapping the indicator and parking at the shoulder of the road a couple of hundred metres farther ahead.

The black SUV was parked directly behind them with a flashing red light in the front window. Sophie sat in her seat looking straight ahead, while Michael Simpson was trying to locate his driver's licence. In the mirror David saw a short Asian stepping out of the SUV. He was about 1.75 metres tall, and dressed in jeans and a black T-shirt. There was something strangely familiar with his face, but David wasn't able to instantly place him.

"He doesn't look like a policeman," David said, as the Asian approached their car.

The undercover police officer knocked on the window screen of Michael Simpson.

"Was I driving a bit too fast, officer?" Michael Simpson asked with an apologetic smile, as the electric window descended into the door.

The Asian didn't reply. Instead he removed his sunglasses and peered into the car.

"Please turn off your engine, and exit the vehicle," he commanded.

David could sense something was wrong. The undercover officer hadn't even asked to see Michael Simpson's licence. Wasn't that normal procedure?

"Have you got some ID?" David asked, leaning over the mid console.

The Asian undercover officer took a step backwards and reached down into his pocket. He pulled out an ID badge. 'CIA. Special agent Wen Ning,' the badge read.

Michael Simpson looked up with a confused expression. "I don't understand. We've just been interviewed by some of your colleagues."

"Please exit the vehicle. All of you." The Asian took another step backwards.

-62-

Five minutes later they were all seated in the back seat of the black SUV belonging to agent Wen Ning. Wen Ning had first ordered David and Michael to walk around to the back of the car. There he had ordered Sophie to attach white plastic strips around their wrists. David had seen them being used in Hollywood movies. They were almost as strong as hand cuffs. And the more you resisted, the deeper they dug into your skin. When Sophie was ordered to tie their legs together as well, David realised they were screwed.

Agent Wen Ning had repeated the same procedure with Sophie before herding them all into the back seat of his black SUV. Then he had simply gotten into the driver seat, turned on his indicator and gently entered the road again. It was unlikely any other motorists had even noticed the incident. It had all been extremely quick, and only two cars had passed them when they were parked on the side of the road. In the start they had refused to leave the car. Michael Simpson had felt the same way as David. Something was off with the way the CIA agent had behaved. Michael Simpson had therefore demanded that agent Wen Ning contact the local police. Michael now had a bleeding wound over his left eye as evidence his hunch had been correct. Agent Wen had suddenly pulled out his gun and struck him in the face two times. Not hard enough to knock him out, but hard and violent enough to ensure that they would listen to his next order. There hadn't been exchanged too many words after that. Sophie seemed almost paralysed. Michael Simpson was still dazed, and struggled to stay upright. And David was fuming with anger. Angry with himself because he had allowed everything to go this far. Not only had he put Sophie and Michael in danger by not disclosing everything he knew. But he hadn't fought back. And now it was too late. They were tied up in the back seat and had no way of escaping. They were completely at the mercy of this lunatic in the driver seat.

This psychopath who had pretended to be a CIA agent, but obviously was something completely different. Who was he? David knew he had seen his face before, but he just wasn't able to place it.

They hadn't been driving for very long before David understood where they were heading. He recognised the area. They were on their way to Yassihoyuk. He glanced over at Sophie who appeared to have realised the same.

"What do you want from us?" David asked.

Wen Ning ignored him.

"Who are you?" David instead asked.

Wen Ning shot him a quick glance in the mirror. "Everything will be explained very shortly. For now I recommend you keep quiet. Unless you rather want to end up like your friend." Wen Ning turned his eyes back to the road and an eerie silence filled the car.

It was clear to David that the driver wasn't someone who made empty threats. There had been no emotions in his voice as he talked. He almost sounded like a robot. David knew it would take them another half an hour before they reached the site of

King Midas' burial chamber. It would at least give him some time to come up with a plan, a strategy. He had no idea who the driver was. But there was a fairly decent chance it was the same person who had been following David and had left a string of dead persons in his wake. What could his agenda be?

David had started to believe it was his own dad who was responsible for getting him involved in the search for Yossar Devan's real identity. Now he was angry with himself for even allowing himself to entertain that thought.

–63–

The CIA director marched with firm steps through the corridor. He opened the door and burst into the suite at the Marriot Hotel of Ankara. Agent Uttley rose from the couch immediately. He had been busy discussing strategies with the other agents. In the background you could hear the sound of a TV. The match between Besiktas and Galatasaray was in its sixty-fifth minute. Besiktas was up one.

"What are you doing here?" the CIA director asked. "Why aren't you out looking for him?"

"We lost track of him an hour ago. There hasn't been any signal since," Agent Uttley replied.

"There is fuck all chance he is going to walk through the door here, so grab your toys and go looking for him."

Agent Uttley considered delivering a snappy reply, but decided against it. Instead he nodded and signalled to two of the agents on the couch to follow him. Then he quickly left the room.

"So, which one of you imbeciles can tell me what we know so far?" the CIA director asked, sitting down next to one of the three remaining agents. One of the agents looked up from his computer screen with poorly concealed fear on his face.

-64-

It was already late in the evening when they finally arrived at the site where King Midas was believed to have been buried, in the heart of the great Tumulis at Yassihoyuk. To David's surprise Wen Ning just continued past the Tumulis. The grave was obviously not the destination. With horror David realised that the destination would have to be Yossar Devan's abandoned factory.

Another ten minutes passed before the car arrived at the steel gate blocking the dirt road up to the building. Wen Ning exited the car and cut the lock with a bolt cutter. He pushed the gate to the side and re-entered the car. It was dead quiet inside the car as they headed up the bumpy dirt road.

Wen Ning didn't stop the car until he was just outside the entrance of Yossar Devan's old building. He shut off the engine and turned around, facing his passengers.

David thought back on the first time he had been at this place. It hadn't been more than a few days ago, but it felt like an eternity. David had thought the area had seemed spooky then. But it was nothing compared to being there after dark. Handcuffed with plastic strips while some maniac, posing as a CIA agent, was threatening them with a gun. It was now abundantly clear that agent Wen Ning, or whatever his real name was, wasn't working for the American government. There was no reason in the world for the CIA to kidnap David, Sophie and Michael. To tie them up and drive them to this abandoned building in the middle of no-man's land. David thought back on his last trip. He had pondered about what would happen if he had an accident. An abandoned building in no-man's land. Who would ever find him there? Was this the so-called agent Wen Ning's plan? To kill and dump them in this deserted area? No one would ever think about looking for them there.

But why? What was the motivation? Why had they been tied up and driven to Yossar Devan's abandoned building? David wasn't able to think much more about the issue. With a jerk the door was pulled open, and they were all commanded out of the car. Like a chain gang they were forced to walk towards the entrance and into the large empty building. Michael Simpson had lost a considerable amount of blood and seemed rather shaky on his feet. But he managed to stay upright. David wondered how long he would last. He had most likely gotten a concussion and was now struggling to keep his eyes open.

Inside the empty building, Wen Ning ordered them down on their knees. He then raised his gun and out of nowhere he struck Michael Simpson on the left side of his temple with the handle of the gun. Sophie screamed when Michael Simpson's body fell to the ground.

"Relax. He is still alive," Wen Ning said calmly.

David leant over Michael Simpson to check whether he was still breathing. To his relief, he could see Michael's chest moving up and down. He was just knocked unconscious.

"What do you want from us?" David cried. He was fuming with anger.

"I want you to help me," Wen Ning replied, seemingly

unaffected by the violence he had just effected.

"Help you with what?" David asked. He had still no idea what this maniac wanted from them.

"Finding King Midas' grave," Wen Ning answered.

He pointed the gun towards Sophie's head. "Do you think better under stress?"

"I don't understand why you have involved us. We know nothing."

"Maybe. And maybe not. Maybe you have inherited some of your dad's abilities?" Wen Ning said.

"I don't understand what you mean!" David replied.

"You don't know who your father was, do you?"

David didn't respond. He knew the person in front of him was right. David had no idea who his father had really been. Everything he had believed about his family had turned out to be lies. A father who worked as a boring historian at the university, a patriotic grandfather who by accident had ended up on the wrong side during the Second World War. It had all been big lies.

Wen Ning straightened himself up. "I've been searching for Yossar Devan's secret to riches for the last twenty years. I almost started to doubt I would ever find it. And then your father showed up. He discovered a lot of things in the six months he lived here in Turkey. I had already figured out Yossar Devan's real identity. How he as a sixteen-year-old boy helped Dr Kammler to locate the burial chamber of King Midas. But that didn't help me. I still hadn't figured out what was Yossar Devan's secret. What had been the foundation of his vast fortune."

"King Midas' treasure?" David asked.

"Call it whatever you want to call it," Wen Ning said. "King Midas' treasure, the tenth principle of riches. They are all just labels on something you will never understand."

"The principles of riches. It was you who sent them."

"The principles of riches," Wen Ning laughed. "I found your father's diary, and I must say I almost feel that I know you after having read all the things he wrote about you. He wrote about how he had failed as a father. How you were obsessed with becoming rich like your uncle. How you were blinded by money. I think he was disappointed, David."

David looked at him with fire spurting from his eyes.

"It was so easy to manipulate you. Those principles of riches Professor Grossman sent you, did you like them?" Wen Ning asked. "They are almost real. I went to Yossar Devan's lectures. The first nine of them. But he just spoke bullshit. Bragged about how much money he had made. How much he was worth. So I wrote my own principles. Borrowed some ideas from Napoleon Hill. Some from Robert Kiyosaki. Hell, I even quoted Steve Jobs. I was almost a bit surprised you didn't notice. Did you honestly think you would discover the secret to riches? That you could read a few principles and wake up the next day a genius of business? That you were going to become a billionaire because you read a few principles?" Wen Ning laughed loudly.

"But what was the point? Why do you still look for Yossar Devan's secret if all he did was preach bullshit?" Sophie asked.

Wen Ning smiled. "Ah. An attempt on an intelligent question from the unemployed physicist? It was only at the last lecture that Yossar Devan shared something of real value, and I never attended that lecture."

"Why not?" Sophie asked.

"It doesn't matter why I didn't go. What matters is that Yossar Devan had no right to play God. He had no right to only share the secret with those who attended that last lecture."

"Professor Grossman. Is he dead? Did you kill him?" David

asked.

"Professor Grossman killed himself. He was killed by his own greed. He had a gambling problem. Owed the Chinese triad more than a hundred thousand dollars. I gave him a solution to his problems. But he squandered it away. Went for the big prize instead of paying off his debts. The same with Peter Swarkowski. An amateur actor with a gambling problem. A sign of the sick society we live in."

"But why this charade? Why go through so much trouble to get me to Turkey? I don't know anything. Everything I've discovered I've been led to by you. I've got no idea what Yossar Devan said in the last lecture. I've got no idea what the tenth principle is. I didn't even know there was a tenth principle."

"That may be true," Wen Ning remarked. "But your dad figured it out. The tenth principle was simply gold. Yossar Devan discovered King Midas' treasure. He discovered King Midas' gold."

Wen Ning leaned over Michael Simpson and pulled at the plastic strips, ensuring that they were still tight.

"We live in a daze where we are being taught that it is the smartest and hardest-working that succeed. Work hard and you will be rewarded. Survival of the fittest." Wen Ning smiled. "What a lot of crap. Charles Darwin would have turned in his grave if he had learnt about how we misuse his findings. It isn't the strongest individual who survives. It isn't even the most adaptable. Charles Darwin only observed that sudden changes in the environment could give some individuals or species an advantage. This advantage could then increase their chance of survival. A colourful bird could be born with a shade of grey, making it harder to be spotted by predators. A wild cat could be born with bad hearing. To compensate it would have to rely more on its vision. Forcing it to improve its ability to identify prey."

Wen Ning stepped over the lifeless body of Michael Simpson. "The natural selection has nothing to do with skill or strength. It is pure luck that decides who survives. Pure luck that decides which skills are required at a certain point in time. And in the same way it is pure luck that decides who gets rich. Pure luck that decides who is successful. Yossar Devan wasn't clever. He just had luck. That's what he found in King Midas' grave. The source of luck."

Wen Ning smiled again. "That was what I had been searching for all these years, Yossar Devan's secret to his riches. I had even been content with that. But then your father showed up. And overnight the whole world changed. Your father figured out what Dr Kammler and your grandfather had been up to during the war. He found out why they had been searching for King Midas' treasure. Why they had been searching for the gold of Sirius. And then he discovered what they had been doing in the US all those years."

"After the war?" Sophie asked.

Wen Ning smiled. "The Glocke project didn't die with the fall of Nazi Germany in 1945. Dr Kammler and David's grandfather continued their work in the US until 1970," Wen Ning said.

I knew it, David thought, but he kept silent.

"What happened in 1970?" Sophie asked. She didn't really care. But it was the only thing she could do, try to stall for time. Maybe someone had found Michael's abandoned car on the side of the road? Maybe it was the CIA that had planted the tracker in David's Kindle? Maybe it was still transmitting? She vaguely remembered having seen him put the broken chip into his pocket.

"1970 was the year everything fell apart," Wen Ning started. "Yossar Devan had funded a secret hunt for war criminals since the early 1950s. Quite understandably as in 1944 the Nazis had wiped out his entire family at this very place where we stand right now. In 1970 Yossar Devan finally located Dr Kammler and your grandfather Terje Dypsvik. But Yossar Devan wasn't interested in putting them in front of a military court. He simply had them assassinated."

"They deserved it," David said.

"That may be. The problem was that when Dr Kammler died, the US government discovered that not only had he been able to continue the black operation Die Glocke in the US. He had almost been given the same free rein as he had enjoyed in Nazi Germany. Unbeknownst to the American Government, Dr Kammler and your grandfather had managed to deplete a large portion of the German gold deposits in the US, in their continuous failed attempts to get the Glocke machine to work. The American suckers had placed two of Nazi Germany's worst war criminals next door to where they stored most of Germany's gold reserves. Talk about irony."

"That's why the US removed the gold standard," David said.

"It may well be," Wen Ning replied. "The gold standard was removed in a rush in 1971. If it had been publicly known that large quantities of the gold stored in the US were missing, then it could have resulted in a collapse of the world economy. But that's only speculation. What we do know is that the US was forced to remove all traces of Dr Kammler. Yossar Devan was a potential witness. A potential witness to the world's largest fraud."

"Why?" Sophie asked.

"Because not only did he know that the US had been harbouring war criminals for all those years. He also knew that Dr Kammler had plundered the German gold deposits. And the icing on the cake was that Yossar Devan didn't leave empty-handed from the US. After having personally supervised the assassination of Dr Kammler and Terje Dypsvik he brought home a souvenir. He brought home the failed Die Glocke experiment. So the CIA didn't really have a choice. They had to eliminate him."

"How do you know all this?" Sophie asked suspiciously.

"Because he was there," David answered.

Wen Ning turned to face David. "Bravo, when did you figure it out?"

"I recognise you from the Oxford University yearbook. It had a picture of you. You were asked where you saw yourself in ten years' time. I remember you had a very modest answer. You just said that you wanted to become an accountant so that you didn't have to work another weekend for the rest of your life. That's why you didn't attend the last lecture. You worked weekends. You worked weekends in a restaurant."

Wen Ning nodded. "And the reward for working hard. The reward for working harder than everybody else was that I didn't get to know Yossar Devan's secret." He shook his head. "Instead all these spoilt brats were told the secret. Rich kids who had never worked a day their whole life. I contacted Yossar Devan, and he agreed to meet me the very next day. He agreed to tell me everything. Instead I was witness to his death. Five men came and grabbed him. Put a sack over his head and threw him into the back of a van. They tried to kill me too. Ran over me with the van. But I survived. I woke up at a hospital a couple of weeks later. Yossar Devan was missing. And I was alone."

"Why didn't you go to the police?" Sophie asked.

"I did. It didn't help. I spoke to some police chief. But nothing was ever done."

Neill Flynn. Wen Ning had talked to Neill Flynn. That's why the old chief investigator had developed a theory about Yossar

Devan's disappearance. It was all so clear to David now.

"For many years I believed Yossar Devan was still alive. That's what your father also believed in the beginning. He wanted to find out what had happened to your grandfather. A noble motive. But then he had this accident," Wen Ning said.

David attempted a leap towards Wen Ning. But was instead struck down by a hard punch against his shoulder.

"Take it easy. I didn't kill your father. I needed your father. Your father figured out what the tenth principle was. Your father figured out where King Midas' grave was located. He had something I needed," Wen Ning continued. "Your father made his own choice when he drove off that cliff. I didn't pressure him off the road. I was right behind him. So close I could see his face in the rear mirror. He locked eyes with me for a second. And then he simply turned his wheel. He steered the car straight through the guardrail. No one would do such a thing without a plan. That's why I thought he was still alive. The police never located his body. Not in the car and not in the ocean. Nobody disappears. So I assumed he had gotten away. But maybe he was a hero? Maybe he did sacrifice himself? Chose death instead of sharing the secret with me? Well, it was his loss."

David sat as frozen. On the inside he was boiling over with hate. Yet there was nothing he could do. He was handcuffed and Wen Ning held a gun to Sophie's head.

"What's so special about the tenth principle? What's so special about gold?" David forced himself to ask.

"All the participants of the last lecture got a gift, a gift with special powers. They didn't get rich because they were smart or worked harder than everybody else. They got rich because Yossar Devan gave them gold from King Midas' treasure. That's what created their fortunes. That's what made them all rich."

With his spare hand Wen Ning pulled out a black velvet bag from his jacket pocket. Without lowering his gun he poured the contents onto the floor in front of them.

"Sirius gold," he declared proudly.

In front of Sophie and David there were a couple of gold rings, an earring and a gold nugget.

"You stole these from Yossar Devan's disciples?" David asked.

Wen Ning smiled. "You can't steal something that already belongs to you. Sirius gold was never meant for these dilettantes. What did they use it for? To increase their own wealth? To buy yachts and private jets? They never deserved the power Sirius gold gave them. They were of the same sort as Yossar Devan. Corrupted by wealth."

"And what do you plan to use this power to do? To make the world a better place?" Sophie asked in a sarcastic voice. She didn't believe that the pile of gold jewellery in front of them was magic, but her best chance was to play along. To stall Wen Ning as long as possible. Maybe somebody had discovered Michael Simpson's empty car by now. If someone reported it to the police, the CIA might find out about it. Maybe they could use the tracker in David's pocket to locate them?

Wen Ning smiled. "You'll soon understand what I want to do," he said and rose to his feet. "It's time to finish your grandfather's work, David. You should be happy. You will be the first in your family to see how Die Glocke really works."

–65–

The hotel phone was ringing. The CIA director was busy speaking into his mobile and indicated with his index finger that Agent Uttley should answer it.

"Yes. Speaking. What is it?" he asked. Agent Uttley's face gradually turned more and more worried as the conversation progressed. Before he hung up, he instructed the person on the other line to call back with an update ten minutes later.

The CIA director pushed the red phone key on his Blackberry. "This is a fucking disaster. A fucking disaster."

Agent Uttley nodded in silence.

"So? Anything new?" the CIA director asked.

Agent Uttley scratched his chin before answering. "As you know we lost contact four hours ago. We have checked his apartment. Places he frequents. There are no traces of him."

"Friends and family? Have you checked friends and family?" the CIA director asked.

"It doesn't appear he had any close friends outside work. His family lives in China."

"No girlfriend?" the CIA director asked, puzzled.

"No, it appears that he from time to time has booked women from an escort service. But never the same woman. His life outside work has been non-existent."

"How the hell could this happen? One of our agents is a prime suspect in the murder of the Chinese ambassador. How the hell are we going to be able to keep a lid on this?"

"I have more bad news," Agent Uttley said.

"What?" the CIA director exclaimed.

"The phone call I just answered. It was from the team dispatched to his apartment."

"Yes, get to the point."

"It appears that the ambassador may not be the only victim," Agent Uttley said.

"Not the only victim? Are you trying to tell me that we may have a serial killer employed by the CIA? Oh my God." He covered his face with his hands. "This day just keeps getting better. Give me an update. What other victims are we speaking of?"

"They found a list in the apartment."

"A death list?"

"It appears so."

"Whose names are on the list?"

"A bunch of deceased people. A bunch of very rich dead people. The strange thing is that no one has ever suspected foul play in any of the deaths until very recently. They were all initially classified as accidents."

"Check them out. And cross reference his movements with the deaths. If he really is a serial killer then it would appear that his latest killings show normal progression. He has been so successful in concealing his crimes that he has gotten overconfident. The good news is that we can expect him to start making mistakes. The bad news is that he is extremely dangerous right now. He's got nothing to lose. So we need to apprehend him as soon as possible," the CIA director said.

"There's something else as well," Agent Uttley said.

"What can be worse than this?" the CIA director said, staring out of the window of the Marriott Hotel. It was dark outside. Most of the lights were already turned off in the surrounding office buildings.

"It appears that he has been in contact with the Chinese."

"I know he has been in contact with the Chinese. He has killed their ambassador for fuck's sake."

"It appears that he may have been working for them," Agent Uttley said.

The CIA director raised an eyebrow. "And what do you base that on?" he asked.

"The search team found a coat check receipt in his apartment. The receipt was from a well-known Chinese restaurant in the CBD. A restaurant quite popular among the embassy people. The team has just finished going through pictures taken on the day of the wardrobe receipt. It appears agent Wen Ning had dinner with the ambassador that evening."

"Interesting. Follow up that lead. We might be able to turn this into an advantage."

-66-

"I've many times wondered if there was a secret entrance to King Midas' grave, an entrance only Yossar Devan knew about. You have no idea how many times I've been in this building. How many times I've inspected the abandoned mountain gallery. I've also entertained the thought that there might be something underneath the floor here. But where do you begin? Fifty-three thousand square metres is a big area. It would take me a decade to find the entrance. But you solved the code, didn't you? I saw it in your eyes. Back there in the Warsaw Library. You realised what your father had discovered, didn't you?"

"Were you in Warsaw?" David asked, surprised.

"I've been with you everywhere you've been. I've been your shadow ever since you left Australia. You don't need to hide anything from me. I already know everything."

Sophie studied Wen Ning's facial expression. It was evident that he meant what he said. He was clearly delusional, a narcissistic maniac who believed he was better than everybody else.

Wen Ning pushed the muzzle of the gun hard against Sophie's temple. "Now, enlighten us, David. What was it that you realised in the Warsaw Library? What was it your father had discovered?"

David stared at Wen Ning with fire in his eyes. If he told Wen Ning what he knew there would be no reason for him to keep them alive. The very second David told Wen Ning where he believed the entrance was, he would have had signed their death certificates. But he didn't have much choice. If he refused to tell Wen Ning about his theory, then Sophie would be executed. The only thing he could hope to achieve was to stall for time. To look for an opportunity to flee.

"You're correct in that there is a secret entrance. At least my father thought so," David started. "But what's the point of showing you? You'll kill us anyway."

"You have my word, David. If you show me the entrance – if you lead me to Die Glocke – then I won't kill you nor Sophie."

"Die Glocke?" Sophie repeated.

Wen Ning smiled. "It was the reason Yossar Devan was willing to part with some of his gold. He knew he wouldn't need it where he was planning to go. But enough talking. Where is the entrance?"

"I'm not sure. I just have the gut feeling that my dad left me a code on the day he died."

Wen Ning's eyes were almost glowing with anger. "Feeling? You're not even sure where the entrance is? Are you kidding me?" he shouted, waving the gun in front of Sophie's face.

"Take it easy," David said. "I'm certain he left a code. I just need to decipher it."

"What was the code?" Wen Ning asked.

David swallowed. It had bothered him since he had visited his mother's holiday house. The lotto ticket taped to the corkboard behind his father's desk.

A lotto ticket.

His dad never played the lotto.

Never.

But it wasn't just that.

David had had a beginning gambling problem when he was younger. It hadn't been too bad. He had only played lotto. And never with borrowed money, only with savings. But still, he had managed to waste a lot of his savings on something as futile as lotto. The chances of winning were less than one in several million. Still he had, during the first year after graduating with his bachelor degree, used a large portion of his salary on betting. He had convinced himself that it wasn't too bad. He only used money he would have used on other silly things, like clothes or restaurant visits. The problem was that the spending gradually had increased. When in trouble, double, as they said. All he needed was a win. A million dollars would truly change his life. He would have money to invest in shares and real estate like his wealthy friends with rich parents. He would be able to afford to quit his pointless job and start his own business. It had of course all been wishful thinking. And if it hadn't been for his dad, catching on to him, he could have ended up like one of the many casualties of gambling addiction. But his dad had caught him, had understood that something was wrong.

To David's big surprise his dad hadn't been moralizing nor demeaning. Instead he had given David a book and asked him to read it over the next few days.

The book was called Man's Search for Meaning by the Jewish author Viktor Frankl. The book had been a real-life story about Viktor Frankl's time as a concentration camp prisoner in the very camp David had just visited, Auschwitz. Viktor Frankl hadn't survived because he was stronger or smarter than his fellow prisoners. He had simply survived because he had been able to find a purpose for his life. He had started writing a manuscript in the camp and he had wanted to survive to be able to publish it. Fyodor Dostoevsky, the Russian author, had defined a human as 'a being that could adapt to anything.' And he had been right. With a purpose you could handle anything life threw at you.

David had stayed up all night reading that book. In the morning he had decided, there and then, that he would never again waste money on lotto. He didn't need to win a million dollars to be happy. It wasn't money he lacked in his life. It was a purpose.

So he had started to read books. Tried to find a purpose with his life. And life had been good for a while. He had enjoyed his jobs. Felt that he made a difference. But at some stage he had fallen back into his old pattern. Wanting to get rich. Not feeling that his jobs gave him fulfilment.

He simply couldn't see any light at the end of the tunnel. It didn't matter how hard he looked.

And he had realised that he needed to get rich to become happy. He needed to get rich to break out of his life as a slave for his salary. And a lotto win would be the easiest way out.

So he had started gambling again. He had moved to Australia and he had started gambling again.

"My dad left a clue in his office," David said.

Wen Ning squinted. "I've been through his office. There was nothing there."

"He left a lotto ticket, dated the day he died. My dad hated money games. Especially lotto. He would never have spent money buying a lotto ticket."

"So the numbers on the lotto ticket, they represent a code? GPS coordinates?" Wen Ning asked.

"No, that was the first thing I checked. Put the numbers into Google Earth, but nothing relevant came up."

David asked Wen Ning to pull out David's wallet. He had confiscated it earlier when he handcuffed him with the plastic strips. Impatiently, Wen Ning poured the contents of David's wallet onto the grey concrete floor, just next to the black velvet bag. It all spilled out – the coin he had received from Michael Simpson, the Visa card Professor Grossman had given him, his old driver's licence. And next to the picture of a young Yossar Devan, which Peter Swarkowski had given him in London, lay a neatly folded lotto ticket. Wen Ning picked it up.

"So what do the numbers represent?" Wen Ning asked.

"Have you got a mobile phone?"

"Yes."

"Key in the six numbers in the first and second square. Three and three numbers, followed by punctuations."

"An IP address?" Wen Ning asked.

David nodded.

122.132.153.110

There was bad coverage on the 3G net so the downloading of the page took some time. But slowly a webpage materialized on Wen Ning's untraceable mobile.

A blank page with only a small picture up in the right-hand corner. The JPG file was still loading.

"What is this?" Wen Ning asked angrily, holding the phone in front of David's face.

Sophie stared, surprised at the picture. It looked like a picture of a mummy, an Egyptian mummy.

"It's a picture of Khufu, the regent of the fourth Egyptian Dynasty. The regent most archaeologists believe the Giza pyramid was built for."

"And what's he got to do with the secret entrance to King Midas' grave?" Wen Ning asked. He didn't only seem impatient.

He seemed mentally unstable.

"I believe that the picture is a hint for where the entrance is. We know that the Buna factory in Auschwitz, the great pyramid of Giza, and the building we now are in, all had a ground area of fifty-three thousand square metres. I believe that King Midas' grave is located in the same place in the structure as Khufu's burial chamber is in its structure, and that the entrance will be at the same spot as in the Giza pyramid. We are inside a copy of the Giza pyramid."

"Are you saying there is an inverse pyramid below us? An inverse pyramid descending one hundred and forty metres into the ground?" Wen Ning asked.

"I'm not sure if it is an inverse pyramid. We have access to electricity. Dr Kammler had the same in Poland. The ancient Egyptians didn't have access to electricity. Maybe that was the reason they built a pyramid. Maybe the pyramid shape has a functionality we don't know about."

Wen Ning studied David. He seemed unsure.

"So all we need to do is to find the point where the entrance of the Giza pyramid is, and we will find the secret entrance to King Midas' grave?"

"That's the theory, yes." David replied. A bit hesitant. He was starting to fear that he was wrong. But it was the only theory he had. It hadn't occurred to him until they'd sat in the Warsaw Public Library. Michael Simpson had explained that it couldn't be an accident that the Buna factory in Auschwitz and the Giza pyramid in Egypt both had a ground area of fifty-three thousand square metres. David knew about another building that had a ground area of fifty-three thousand square metres, Yossar Devan's old abandoned factory. And suddenly he understood what the picture that had covered his laptop screen, when he was playing around with plotting his dad's lotto number into Google, had meant. The picture of the old mummy had to have a hidden meaning. The picture of an ancient Egyptian mummy. The picture of Khufu.

The lotto numbers were a coded message. An IP address, which in the right hands would provide sufficient information to understand where the entrance was hidden.

David's dad.

The historian.

The statistician.

Always so fascinated by numbers.

Wen Ning bent down and pulled out a jagged knife from a holder attached to his right leg. Instantly he appeared next to Sophie. She almost got a fright. He was so close that she could feel his warm breath against her face. Without diverting his gaze he cut the plastic strips tied around her legs, with a swift movement of his wrist.

"Don't even entertain the thought of trying to escape, David. If you do, both you and your lovely girlfriend here will die."

David didn't respond. He just nodded in silence. Next Wen Ning cut off his plastic cuffs as well. The fact that his legs got a bit of freedom meant nothing though. His hands were still handcuffed. And Wen Ning had a gun and a knife. They were still very much trapped.

"Well, what are you waiting for? Lead the way," Wen Ning said after having freed David's legs, and collected all his things from the concrete floor.

It took them a good hour to mark the different spots in Yossar Devan's empty building. It was a good help that Wen Ning had a smartphone. They were able to look up a website with all the measurements of the Giza pyramid in seconds, and the built-in gyroscope could be used as a compass.

"The entrance should be in here. Inside this room," David said, as they all stood inside a small storage room in the northern end of the building.

"I can't see any entrance. Do we have to go through the floor?" Sophie asked. That was good news. It meant that Wen Ning would have to get equipment from the city.

"No," Wen Ning answered abruptly. "Yossar Devan had plans to travel here after the last lecture. He wouldn't have sealed the entrance. He would have constructed it so that he could have operated it alone. By himself."

David looked around the room. Trying to locate any sharp objects. Something he could use to cut the plastic strips holding his hands together. Something he could use as a weapon. But there was nothing in the naked room. Time was about to run out on them. He had been wrong. His father's lotto ticket hadn't contained a secret code. It had just been one of life's strange coincidences that the numbers on it had coincided with the IP address of a server with a picture of Khufu, the regent of the fourth dynasty in Egypt.

"Is it just me, or is there something strange with this room?" Sophie asked.

"What do you mean?" David said.

"It doesn't feel like we're in a room. It feels like we're in an elevator," she replied.

Wen Ning walked over to one of the walls and knocked on it. It sounded like metal. A smile spread over his face. "Hah! Yossar Devan. That sneaky bastard. Couldn't resist, could he? The best way to hide something is to hide it in plain sight."

"But how do we start it? If this room is an elevator, it wouldn't have been used for more than thirty years," David said.

"I believe someone has used it more recently than that. I think your father was here on the morning of the day he drove off the cliff," Wen Ning said.

It took a couple of seconds before the implications of what Wen Ning had just said hit David. His dad hadn't just solved the mystery. He hadn't just discovered Yossar Devan's secret entrance to King Midas' grave. He had most likely been down in the grave before he died in the car accident. Was that the reason he had made his incomprehensible decision? To take his own life by driving off that cliff? To leave David and his mum without saying goodbye because he was afraid of what he had just discovered could be used for in the wrong hands?

"There is something over here," Sophie yelled out. She was staring at a set of switches on the wall. "Who installs a code lock to regulate room temperature?"

It didn't take long before they all realised that the code lock was the control panel of the elevator. With ten digits there could however be an infinite number of combinations. It was like guessing your own PIN code for an ATM, impossible.

It didn't appear that the problem affected Wen Ning's enthusiasm. With firm steps he walked over to the code lock and punched in a combination of numbers.

The room started moving immediately. It descended so rapidly that David's ears popped. Sophie leant towards the wall to not lose her balance. Their hands were still tied behind their backs and the speed of the elevator made it difficult to stand upright.

After about twenty-five seconds the room started to slow down, and it came to a complete halt only a few moments later. One of the walls slid to the side, and they peered straight into a dark room. David thought back on the time he had visited the Giza pyramids in Egypt with his dad. The room in front of him reminded him of the grand gallery. The hallway where the Egyptians had stored the massive granite blocks used to seal the pyramid. Had Yossar Devan built a true copy of the Giza pyramid? Did they have to crawl through narrow hallways and tiny tunnels to get to the point where King Midas' grave was located?

Wen Ning took a step into the hallway and pulled a switch on the wall.

The fluorescent lamps in the ceiling lighted up.

"Wow!" David involuntarily exclaimed.

Sophie just stood there, frozen, gawking.

What they had thought was a long narrow hall was something entirely different. It was a large gallery. And far inside the gallery something shaped like a bell hung from the ceiling.

"How did you know the code?" Sophie asked.

"I didn't," Wen Ning replied. "But I assumed that Yossar Devan wasn't too worried about somebody hacking his passwords. He did after all disappear back in 1973. When he disappeared, the UK Government, in the absence of a will, assigned a public executor of his estate. The estate spent hundreds of thousands of dollars cracking the code Yossar Devan had used on his personal safe. Eventually they found the combination. It was ridiculously simple. The date, first of April 1944, 01041944. The day he found King Midas' grave. The date his life changed. I assumed the old bugger would be sentimental enough to use the same date for the elevator. It was actually the reason I figured out Yossar Devan had been in Turkey in the first place. I got hold of the code from the estate and understood that the number signified an important event in Yossar Devan's life. I knew from Yossar Devan's features and skin colour that he was most likely of Central

Asian or Mediterranean descent. So I cross referenced the date with accidents, natural catastrophes. Everything of importance in Central Asia and the Mediterranean on that particular date. But I never got a match. The workload grew too big for me to handle alone so I outsourced parts of it. That's how your father became involved. I needed someone to ask about historical events in 1944, and your father was one of the leading experts on the Second World War. So I tasked him with identifying accidents involving any Mediterranean countries and the Second World War. He came through and provided me with the picture of Yossar Devan. I didn't know it at the time, but he had incidentally found something else as well. He had found a connection between Dr Kammler and his own father, your grandfather."

He pointed the barrel of the gun towards Sophie and told David to start walking.

David stared at the bell-shaped construction in front of them. Was this what so many people had died for? Was this what his grandfather and Dr Hans Kammler had executed dozens of innocent kids for? A possible doomsday weapon, a machine that could influence space and time. Nobody really knew what it was. Just that for a brief moment during the bloodstained final months of the Second World War, in a tiny unknown Polish village called Ludokowice, this bell-shaped piece of machinery had suspended all the known physical laws of the universe. Die Glocke had started floating in the air. Some of the scientists had immediately melted like they were made out of wax. And with a massive blue flash Die Glocke had changed the priorities of the Third Reich. The most important task wasn't to make an atomic bomb anymore. Why make firecrackers when you could recreate the big bang? Why become the victors of Europe when you could become Gods?

Now David had led Wen Ning to this machine. This machine that David's grandfather and Dr Kammler had exhausted Germany's entire gold deposits in America to make workable again. The machine that however had never worked its wonders again since that ill-fated day in Ludokowice.

There had been a reason for that. That fatal day the machine had started, the German scientists hadn't used any normal gold. By accident the gold they had used in the experiment had been from the star constellation of Sirius. The same gold that Yossar Devan had found in King Midas' grave. The same gold that Dr Hans Kammler and David's grandfather had spent decades looking for. Now he was here: The Asian Wen Ning, with a couple of gold rings and other jewellery in his hand, made out of the very gold that Yossar Devan had given away in his last lecture. The gold that would make Die Glocke start up again.

"I'm sorry to say, but your trip ends here," Wen Ning said. He asked David and Sophie to kneel down on the concrete floor, close their eyes and face the floor. With a couple of quick steps he was behind them. David could hear Sophie moan as Wen Ning attached new plastic strips around her legs. But she didn't break. She didn't want to give Wen Ning that satisfaction.

David bowed his head and prepared himself for the mercy shot. To his great surprise the shot never came. Instead he could hear Wen Ning's steps fading away. David opened his eyes and raised his head. Through his weary eyes he could see Wen Ning coming to a halt in front of the bell-shaped machine, Die Glocke. David had expected that Wen Ning would execute them. Put a bullet through the backs of their heads. Wen Ning had already shown that he had no scruples nor conscience, no hesitation with taking human lives. And right now Sophie and David were of no value to him.

But they were still witnesses.

Loose threads he needed to tie up.

When Wen Ning pressed the red switch on the control panel of Die Glocke, David understood why Wen Ning hadn't bothered shooting them. Die Glocke started vibrating and a low rumbling started to fill the room. David remembered the story the Polish war investigator had told him. The German scientists who had melted like ice cream bars when they observed the Glocke experiment. Wen Ning didn't need to kill them. Die Glocke would do the job for him.

–67–

ophie wished she was wearing ear plugs. The noise from Die Glocke was deafening. The two drums inside Die Glocke had started to rotate, and it felt like her head was about to explode. "What's happening?" she asked.

Wen Ning stood in front of the machine with a big grin. It was almost as if he was paralysed. This was what he had waited for all these years. He had found Sirius gold. He had finally found Die Glocke. And now he was ready to harvest the fruits of all his hard labour. To finally be compensated for all the sacrifices he had had to make.

Wen Ning pulled out his velvet bag and emptied it in his hand. He hesitated for a second but then dropped a gold coin into the container sticking out of Die Glocke. It appeared it was filled with liquid silver. It had to be mercury, he thought. One of the few materials that was liquid at room temperature.

David glanced over at Sophie. With his mouth he indicated that she should hold her breath. She followed his advice, but oddly enough she seemed to be smiling. She remembered the story David had told her in Warsaw though. The story about the Polish war investigator from Ludwikowice who had told David that the first team of Die Glocke scientists hadn't died from radiation. They had died from inhaling gasses discharged from Die Glocke when it started up. The gasses had caused their bodies to rot from the inside out. Vital organs had stopped working almost immediately and blood had begun to stream out of their bodily orifices. As if with an extreme version of the Ebola virus, the scientists had melted in front of their colleagues.

Wen Ning was still standing in front of Die Glocke. He was standing there with open mouth, gazing at Die Glocke.

Hadn't he sensed the smell of gasses? Didn't he know the stories? David wasn't able to finish his thought. Because in the very same moment Wen Ning turned to face David. And David could see the fear in Wen Ning's eyes when he discovered that David sat with a closed mouth and a bulging face.

The gasses. He had forgotten about the gasses. He had been so transfixed by Die Glocke that he had forgotten that it emitted toxic gasses. Gasses he had no way of detecting.

With a desperate movement Wen Ning dropped the gun to the floor. He covered his mouth and nose with both hands. But David knew it was too late. He could already see tiny effusions of blood building up under the skin of Wen Ning's face. From his fingers a couple of droplets of blood dripped to the ground. First slowly. Then more rapidly. Wen Ning attempted a couple of shaky steps towards Die Glocke and safety. But it was futile.

David quickly glanced at his watch. Forty-five seconds had passed since Wen Ning turned on Die Glocke. David was an avid surfer and had trained his lungs so that he could hold his breath for more than four minutes. But that was under water, in a pool and under ideal circumstances. Humans could hold their breath for almost twice as long under cold water as under warmer water, because the cold slowed down the pulse. Now David was tied up in front of a death machine which slowly but surely was killing

Wen Ning in front of his eyes. David's pulse was probably close to 130. He calculated he had maybe a minute left before he lost consciousness, and wouldn't be able to stop the toxic gasses from entering his lungs.

For Sophie the prognosis was even worse. An average untrained person could only hold her breath for 30 seconds. Sophie was already fifty percent past that.

In a desperate fit of frustration and anger, David jerked his hands as hard as he could, even though he knew the plastic strips would just dig even more deeply into his skin. To his surprise he could feel them giving way. He looked down at the plastic strips holding his legs together. It looked like the plastic was partially melted. The gas from Die Glocke was reacting with the plastic. He yanked harder, both with his legs and arms.

In front of him he could see Wen Ning collapsing in a pool of blood. He seemed to be extending an arm towards David. Trying to form words with what was left of his mouth. "Kiiil mee…Kiiiillll meee." What had once been Wen Ning's mouth dripped down onto the floor like melted stearin.

David didn't let the gross sight distract him. With his last strength he managed to rip the plastic strips holding his hands and feet together. It was not a moment too early. Struggling with dizziness, he got up on his knees. The door to the elevator was thirty meters away, way too far. He wouldn't be able to reach it before passing out. He turned towards Sophie just as she passed out, her head falling to the side, and her body following after.

Professor Grossman's ninth fake principle had been decision.

It was more important to make a decision than not to make one. And David had to make a decision.

The most important decision of his life.

He stumbled over to Sophie, keeping his head low to the

ground. With an exertion of power he lifted Sophie from the ground and staggered four steps toward Die Glocke and the noisy rumbling. He needed to get her to safety. He needed to get her underneath Die Glocke.

But it was too late. He could feel that the last ounce of his oxygen was gone. He recognised the feeling. One of the first times he had surfed outside the Norwegian city of Stavanger he had been knocked off his board and pulled under by the waves. It had been like being inside a tumble-dryer. He had had no idea what was up or down. His body had been bombarded with punches from all sides. He had been completely at the mercy of the forces of nature. And after less than a minute of this treatment, something that appeared like an eternity, he had exhausted his last breath of air. There had been absolutely no air left in his lungs. No strength left in his body. He had stretched out his hands. Longed for the surface. Longed for the liberating air.

But he had felt nothing.

Only calmness.

An overwhelming sense of calmness.

The certainty that he was about to die, that there was nothing he could do to prevent it, had been liberating. And then he had felt it. A hand that grabbed around his ankle. A hand that saved his life.

His dad had seen him struggling, and he had found him at the bottom of the ocean.

His dad had saved him.

But his dad wasn't there now.

The father who had sacrificed himself to prevent Wen Ning from ever locating Die Glocke. The father who had sacrificed his own life for everybody else. The father who had always sacrificed himself.

With the last of his strength David threw his body forward. He landed, face first and arms stretched out, on the hard concrete floor. There was no air left in his lungs to be knocked out. There was no life left.

The pressure in his head threatened to blow up his temples. And through his bloodshot eyes he could see Sophie roll into safety under Die Glocke.

He watched the blue light streaming down from the bottom of Die Glocke, making a play of colours on his fingertips. The fingertips that were stretching out for Sophie.

It was so beautiful.

So blue.

Then it turned darker.

More red.

Then just black.

Only the loud rumble of Die Glocke filled the emptiness.

Then Die Glocke went silent as well.

-68-

Six months later
Bond University
Gold Coast, Australia

The sun was shining above Bond University's small lake. The mood was depressed among the attendees. Sophie had expected something different. She didn't really know what, but something different. Definitely something different. The vice chancellor of Bond University took to the stage. Thirty-some students, all dressed in black, lowered their gazes. This was supposed to be a day of joy. Instead it was a day of sorrow.

They had all known him. Some better than others, but none had a single bad word to say about him.

David's friend, JC, had just left the stage. He had spoken about how much the person had meant to him. How he always would be a role model. Someone they should all aspire to be like. With teary eyes he had said that he had been torn away too early. So brutally and unnecessary.

Sophie thought about how fragile life was. It was something she hadn't given much thought about only a year ago. Why care about something you couldn't influence? We were all going to die one day anyway. It was inevitable. It was one of the laws of the universe that would never change.

But today. In front of all these sad people. Adult friends of David who cried openly, even though they had known him for less than a year. She couldn't keep her tears back. She wiped her eyes.

Damn it. I had promised myself not to do this, she told herself as she tried to quash a sob. She hadn't even cried at her own mother's funeral. She had been the firm obelisk her younger sister could lean on. The one who always kept her cool. Why couldn't she keep her cool now?

She knew the answer.

"We are gathered here today…" the vice chancellor at Bond University started, "to remember a special man. A man who touched many hearts here at this university. A man who will always be with us, in our lives and in our hearts. When you leave these gates today, you will leave with an important lesson. You are not only leaving with a diploma, a fancy degree you can use to negotiate a good job or make lots of money. We are giving you a ballast in your lives. An idea of what you can achieve in your lives, an idea of what is possible…."

Agent Morris Uttley placed his right palm on the Bible. And with a firm gaze he stared at the two judges in front of him. The CIA director was seated next to him.

"Agent Morris Uttley. You are aware that you are under oath today?" one of the judges asked.

"Yes, your honour," Agent Uttley replied.

"Could you give a short explanation of how you discovered that Agent Wen Ning was a serial killer?"

"Based on the way the Chinese ambassador was stabbed, and the murderer's immediate movements afterwards, I began to suspect that agent Wen Ning could be the perpetrator. I had worked with agent Ning for three years and you get to know your colleagues when you work as closely as we do. Agent Ning had also been absent from work since the murder. I followed up my suspicion with a house call. During the following search of his apartment we found a list of names, a so-called death list. Most of the people on the list had died within the last twelve months, and although all the deaths had originally been classified as accidents, it soon became clear that they could be murders. We suspect that agent Wen Ning committed all these murders and that he, using the skills he had been taught in the Agency, camouflaged them as accidents."

"Can you explain why agent Wen Ning killed these people?"

"I am not a psychologist." Agent Uttley responded.

"Tell me your theory," the judge pressed on.

"Wen Ning was a student at Oxford University during the years 1970 to 1973. The last year of his degree he attended some lectures, called the principles of riches, which were held by a self-made billionaire named Yossar Devan."

"The infamous Yossar Devan who disappeared in 1973?" the judge asked.

"Yes, your honour," Agent Uttley replied. "We know that Wen Ning attended nine of Yossar Devan's lectures. The day after the tenth lecture, the one he didn't attend, Wen Ning was hit by a car. He ended up in a coma and we assume that the impact inflicted minor brain damage on him."

"Assume?" the judge repeated.

"Yes, your honour. We don't have solid evidence for this hypothesis, as we haven't been able to perform an autopsy of Wen Ning's brain. But based on the events that have occurred over the last twelve months it is fair to assume that he received brain damage. Latent brain damage."

"Continue," the judge said.

Wen Ning became fixated on this last lecture. There were strong rumours that Yossar Devan had shared a secret with the small number of students attending the last lecture. The secret of how he had been able to make all his money. A secret that everyone could use."

Agent Uttley cleared his throat, and reached out for the glass of water in front of him. "It was of course just a fairy tale. But when it turned out that Yossar Devan disappeared the day after the last lecture, there were so many rumours that even the dean of Oxford University had to come out and publicly deny the story. It appears that Wen Ning never was informed. He woke up from an induced coma several weeks later. After graduation he returned to China."

"How did he get a job with the CIA if he is Chinese?" the judge asked.

"His parents are American and he is an American citizen. He chose however to live with his grandparents in China the first few years after graduation. His background suited the Agency well. And there were never any suspicions that he had psychological problems."

The judge nodded.

Agent Uttley finished the glass of water.

When she stood there in front of all these students, robots in black suits, ready to conquer the world with their calculators and sharp minds, Sophie caught herself thinking about David. How he once had been so single-mindedly focused on riches. As if money would make him happy. As if money was the solution to all his problems. Almost like her ex-boyfriend, the stockbroker.

She herself had never been interested in money. Money was important because it gave you freedom. But she needed something more than that. One of her friends had started a company that eventually was sold for several hundred million dollars. When she had asked how he felt being wealthy beyond his dreams she had received an unexpected answer. Her friend had compared it to having been in a car crash and losing his right arm. Yes, he had received a ridiculously large compensation from the insurance company. And yes he probably would never have to work again. But all he wanted was to get his arm back. All her friend wanted was to get his company back. The money didn't matter.

Wen Ning hadn't really been that different from David, nor most of the suited-up MBA graduates in front of her for that matter. He had just been much more extreme. He had wanted to become rich at any cost. And he hadn't possessed the constraints normal people like David did.

Wen Ning, what a nutcase, she thought. At least he was dead and buried.

Buried beneath several tons of rock and dirt. A groggy Michael Simpson had helped her acquire some TNT after she had managed to get out of Die Glocke and Yossar Devan's old building. Together they had made sure that no one would ever try to start Die Glocke again. It was now just a vague memory that our world probably wasn't exactly like we believed. That our current understanding of physics still had big holes.

Big gaping holes.

"We are gathered here today to remember Professor Evan Grossman," the Vice Chancellor of Bond University said.

Agent Morris Uttley placed the empty glass on the table before continuing. "We believe that agent Wen Ning harboured a hatred for the students attending Yossar Devan's last lecture. He believed that they had made their fortunes using a secret that was meant for him. We are not exactly sure what triggered the escalation. But in December two years ago, Wen Ning decided to do something about the situation. The next twelve months he travelled around, tracking down Oxford alumni, murdering them. He used his CIA training to make the murders look like accidents."

"So he killed all the students who had attended Yossar Devan's last lecture?" the judge asked.

"Not exactly, your honour," Agent Uttley replied. "We have checked the victims' movements, on and around the last lecture. Two of the victims weren't even at Oxford when the last lecture was held."

"What does that mean?" the judge asked.

"Wen Ning created a picture in his own head of who had attended the last lecture, the most successful students. He travelled around and murdered all the richest people from the Oxford class of 1973."

"And the Chinese ambassador, where does he fit into all of this?"

"The Chinese ambassador wasn't a well-planned murder like the others. We believe it was a crime of passion."

"A crime of passion?"

"We believe Wen Ning and the ambassador had a relationship," Agent Uttley said.

"And what do you base this on?" the judge asked.

"We found a coat check ticket from a local Chinese restaurant when we searched his apartment. The restaurant by coincidence one that the local police had under surveillance for an ongoing drug case. We were able to tap into their video footage. Wen Ning had had dinner with the ambassador three days prior to the victim's murder. And Wen Ning was seen leaving the restaurant in anger. We have also interviewed a number of escort ladies Wen Ning had hired over the last two years. He didn't have intercourse with any of them. It strongly indicates he has a different sexual orientation."

"Is this all you've got? It seems very weak."

"We sent out some feelers to the Chinese. Gave them the understanding that we knew about the ambassador's relationship with Wen Ning. Two days later the Chinese reported that they had killed the perpetrator when he attempted to attack another staff member from the embassy. The perpetrator was a twenty-three-year-old Chinese student. The Chinese confirmed our suspicion directly. Two days after we sent our message they came up with a scapegoat."

"But that doesn't mean Wen Ning and the ambassador were lovers. They could have had a different relationship. What was your message to the Chinese?"

Agent Uttley glanced over at the CIA director, who gave a confirming nod. He would handle the question. "I believe it was something along the lines of; we know about the relationship between Wen Ning and your ambassador. For your own best interest, you should put a lid on the case."

"That message could be interpreted in a multitude of ways," the judge said. "Were other avenues discussed?"

Agent Morris Uttley glanced over at the CIA director for support again. The CIA director just looked straight ahead.

Agent Morris Uttley wiped a pearl of sweat from his forehead, before continuing. "We discovered that we had a serial killer employed by the CIA. And we successfully managed to contain the situation within a few days. This happened six months ago.

Not a single rumour has leaked out. I believe that is a good result."

The judge nodded. "And these other murders. None of them can be traced back to agent Wen Ning?"

"We are the only ones who have been inside Wen Ning's apartment. All the evidence has been destroyed. There is nothing linking the CIA to these cases anymore."

The other judge shuffled a pile of papers on his desk.

"Good work, Agent Uttley. I'm sure you will have a very successful career in the Agency," the judge said before rising from his chair. Agent Uttley unclipped his microphone and prepared to descend from the witness stand.

Suddenly the judge stopped him.

"One last matter. This machine, Die Glocke, which was stolen from our American base by Yossar Devan. Where is it now?" he asked.

Agent Morris Uttley looked with begging eyes at his boss, the CIA director, who unwillingly agreed to answer.

"We don't know. But our military had twenty-five years to recreate the experiment of the Germans. They were never even close. So I believe it is fair to say that Die Glocke doesn't constitute a threat. Wherever it is, it is an artefact. It belongs in a museum."

The judge smiled. "And I hear that the Germans have retracted their demand."

The CIA director nodded. "We have renegotiated the deal. We now have fifteen years to return their gold. We have told them that it is not possible to return it any sooner."

"And they accepted that?"

"They had no choice," the CIA director replied. "It's not ideal, but at least it will give us some time to come up with alternatives."

"Thank God for that," the judge said.

David wiped a tear off Sophie's cheek when they wandered back towards the parking lot and their car. It had been a nice graduation ceremony.

David was happy. He gently brushed a hand over Sophie's belly. She smiled and squeezed harder around his hand.

The smile disappeared, however, almost immediately. There was something not right. A soft rumbling sound. A rumbling sound that didn't originate from her belly. She pulled her hand back, fumbled frantically with both hands on her pants. The panic striking her when she couldn't figure out where the sound was originating from. Feeling the nausea coming, the nauseousness she never thought she would ever get used to.

David pointed with his right hand. "It's in your side pocket," he said calmly.

She looked at him with an angry face and pulled up the vibrating phone. I don't want him to be exposed to radiation damage before he is born," she said.

"They've done thousands of tests on that. Radiation from mobile phones is harmless," David replied.

Sophie just stared at him. "Right, thousands of tests. Let's trust that."

David smiled and answered the phone. Her hormones were obviously working overtime.

"Repeat," he said into the phone.

"It's from Golden Casket Lotteries," the voice on the other line said. "Am I talking with David Dypsvik?"

"Yes..." David stuttered.

"Did you play the lottery last night?" the voice asked.

David tried to think. Last night's drawing. It had been the big jackpot. Nobody had won for more than ten weeks and the first prize had jackpotted to seventy million dollars. Had he bought a ticket? Yes he had. He had bought a ticket last Saturday, a quick-pick with random numbers. It had cost him fourteen dollars. He had wanted to get rid of all the coins in his car.

David's mouth suddenly became very dry. He almost wasn't able to stutter out his answer. "Yes, yes," he replied.

The CIA director studied his hands. They were long and knuckly, and they hurt like hell. He often wondered. No, wondered wasn't the right word. He often feared that he would inherit his dad's hands. His dad, who had worked hard his whole life. Toiled for two lifetimes in a butchery as he used to say because he worked so much harder than his colleagues. When he had turned sixty, his hands had been so worn that the tendons had contracted and formed two claws out of what had once been long piano fingers. The CIA director had never worked as hard as his dad. He had mostly had office jobs except for a stint in the field as a twenty-five-year-old. But his hands had started aching the last few weeks, really aching. The CIA director's dad had worn his claws with pride. Viking hands, his doctor had called them, you got them after too much labouring with your hands. The CIA director knew this wasn't true. He had checked on Google. It was genetically conditioned, hereditable. That's why they were called – Viking hands. They were most common up in the cold north, where people drank heavily. And that's why he was concerned. He was both a heavy drinker and had the genes.

Viking hands.

He thought about the young kid who had led them to the serial killer Wen Ning. David Dypsvik, an innocent student who had been used in the insane game of agent Wen Ning.

The Norwegian, the Viking.

The CIA director wondered where this David Dypsvik was

right now.

They were still looking for agent Wen Ning.

David laughed so much that he almost fell down on his knees.

"What is it? What is it?" Sophie asked.

David raised the phone back to his ear. "I'll take the money. You can just transfer it to my account," he said and hung up.

"What is it?" Sophie repeated.

David smiled from ear to ear. "You won't believe it," he said.

It didn't really matter where Wen Ning was hiding. Operation Aurum had been completed, a success.

The CIA director could retire with his honour intact. It had been a close call. It could easily have been a disaster, a scandal of unimaginable proportions. The US had had this precarious situation where Germany had demanded all their gold deposits returned to Germany. The problem was that the US couldn't find it. A German scientist. No, not even a scientist, a German Nazi, a war criminal from the Second World War had used the gold deposits in a crazy attempt to create a doomsday weapon.

What had they been thinking, these politicians who had welcomed Nazis after the war? True, they had possibly helped the US in sending a man to the moon a little more quickly than the Americans could have done by themselves. Perhaps they had helped America to become one of the world's two superpowers, both in military and financial aspects, in record time. But at what cost? At what compromises? The CIA director flipped through the pages of the report. It explained how Dr Kammler and a Norwegian physicist by the name of Terje Dypsvik had been hidden in the US after the war. They had been given almost free rein to further develop a project called Die Glocke, The Bell. A project that Adolf Hitler himself had thought would turn the tide and win the Second World War for the Germans. The project had, however, been riddled with accidents and cost overruns. The claimed capabilities of Die Glocke, that it had the power to influence time and space, had proven to be utter nonsense.

The project had still managed to continue for more than twenty-five years after the war ended, financed as one of the many black projects of the American military.

And then disaster had struck.

Dr Kammler and Terje Dypsvik had been assassinated. Someone had figured out what the Americans had done. That the US had been harbouring wanted war criminals from the Second World War. That the US had been hiding the Nazi general responsible for the construction of the concentration death camps. The incident had the potential to become a scandal of unimaginable proportions. It had to be quashed at all costs. The Military had decided to terminate the Glocke project.

It was then that they first discovered the scandal. Dr Kammler had used up almost all of Germany's gold deposits in his crazy experiments. The gold was gone. To avert a disaster the US had proposed to remove the gold standard, to make the currencies independent of gold.

And they had contained the story. For a long time they suspected that the mysterious billionaire Yossar Devan had been involved in the assassination of Dr Hans Kammler and his partner in crime, the physicist Terje Dypsvik. Yossar Devan had financed similar operations for Israel on prior occasions. He obviously and understandably hated Nazis.

It wasn't until Israel was attacked by Egypt that the US government understood the connection. The Egyptians had believed that Yossar Devan was hiding a secret doomsday weapon in Israel. A doomsday weapon called Die Glocke.

The Americans immediately understood that it was Yossar Devan who had been behind the assassination of Dr Kammler and his American Die Glocke team. It thus had to be Yossar Devan who had stolen Die Glocke from American soil. The US had no other option than to attack, to eliminate Yossar Devan.

The propaganda machinery was initiated, and even though Yossar Devan had been a powerful man there were few who knew about him outside the business world. He even turned out not to be who he claimed he was. He turned out to be a ghost. A man with a fake identity.

The press was gagged and disinformation spread.

Yossar Devan's companies were divided up and anyone asking questions was removed.

Everything went according to plan.

Until Jan-Olav Dypsvik showed up. The young MBA student's father.

Jan-Olav Dypsvik started digging. He started off slowly. Trawled through libraries and old archives hunting for an answer to what had happened to Dr Kammler and Die Glocke. And then two years ago, he had retired and started working full-time on the case. It had become too dangerous. Mr Dypsvik had to be silenced.

An accident-prone road in Turkey had become the solution. The agent in pursuit had called it an accident and the CIA director had thought that would be the end of it.

And then the Germans had wanted their gold back.

"It was Golden Casket Lotteries that called," David said. "They wanted to know whether I had bought a ticket for the draw yesterday."

"Did you?" Sophie asked.

"I did," David replied.

Sophie rolled her eyes. "Why? We agreed not to play, David." She seemed to think for a second before a fright rushed over her face. "It was the jackpot draw. Seventy million in first prize. Did you win?"

David smiled. "That was the funny thing," David said. "They just called to inform me that I had been defrauded. The guy who runs the local newsagent, where I bought my ticket, had cancelled all the games that had been played there over the last week. And run new games in his own name. Apparently he had been under financial strain and thought this could be the way out of his problems. Unfortunately he only ended up winning a few hundred dollars after having bet several thousand."

David laughed. "They called since my playing card had been used on one of the cancelled tickets. They offered me a new ticket in the next draw."

"What did you tell them?"

"I told them I preferred to get my money back."

"Good," Sophie said. "We can't afford to make any mistakes. We can't afford to draw any attention."

She opened the door of the black Ford Mustang Shelby GT 500, which was parked next to the tennis courts at Bond University. Her elegant gold ring sparkled in the summer sun.

She had it made from one of the gold nuggets in Wen Ning's black velvet bag. Wen Ning had never seen it coming. Instead of throwing in some of his own gold he had thrown in the coin Michael Simpson had given David. She had witnessed it just before she passed out, and she had given David the biggest smile she could, but he had failed to understand. And then she had passed out. When she woke up she had seen David lying in front of her, flat on the ground. She had pulled him into safety under the Glocke. David glanced back at Bond University. See you in ten years, he said to himself. He already knew he would be one of those who would look back on the next ten years as the best in his life.

-69-

A freezing gust of wind swept across the cemetery. It knocked down the fresh flowers in front of the grey concrete tombstone. Martha Baumler crouched down, tried to keep the cold out by pulling the collar of her navy blue jacket all the way up to her chin. With shaking fingers she straightened up the flowers before putting her gloves back on. The sky was dark and gloomy. She could sense there was a thunderstorm coming. They should probably get back to the car before the rain started. But she stayed put. She needed this moment. In the background she could hear the sound of her son Oliver's laughter. He was playing with a ball.

She closed her eyes and thought about him. Wished he was there with her. Wrapping his strong arms around her, warming her.

She couldn't relax though. She could sense something was wrong. She opened her eyes, and in fright she rose to her feet. She knew what was wrong. The laughter had stopped. Oliver's laughter had stopped, and been replaced by low chatter.

She started yelling, at first calmly, then hysterically. "Oliver, Oliver wo bist du?"

In the corner of her eye she could see a tall man with a crooked back. He was dressed in an expensive suit and a black coat. He was walking briskly across the cemetery.

And then she saw him.

Hans Baumler.

The man she had loved her entire life. Every time she looked into her son's eyes she could see Hans. It was as if he was still alive. It was as if he was living inside his own son.

"I've told you, Oliver. You're not allowed to speak to strangers," she said with a strict voice.

Oliver looked up at his mum with insulted eyes. "But mummy, he wasn't a stranger."

Martha Baumler waved her index finger at him. "Don't tell lies, Oliver," she said.

"But mummy, I'm not telling lies. He said he was a friend of papa. He said that I should be proud of my papa. That papa was a hero of Germany."

Martha turned around to look for the man in the black coat. But she could only see the back of his coat as he stepped into a black BMW. The car disappeared down the road seconds later.

The sky above Martha and Oliver broke into a massive loud bang. She picked up Oliver and ran towards her car as the sky opened up above them.

Epilogue

3 days later

**The site of IG Farben's old Buna factory
Auschwitz, Germany**

The head of the engineering department of BASF, the company that had been running their operations out of the site of the old Buna Factory for the last forty years, studied the contract in front of him. It was a lot of money. He wasn't only the head of the engineering department, he was also a part owner of the company. He owned two and a half percent of the shares.

He quickly calculated how much his shares would be worth. It was more than he had ever dreamt of. The sum offered would be sufficient to relocate the factory to a new site, to build a brand-new factory and still have leftover funds to grow the business and secure the various owners' retirements.

He studied the well-dressed man in front of him. He was obviously rich. Henrik Waser had understood as much the second he saw the elegant man step out of the black BMW in the parking lot.

He oozed discreet wealth. Old wealth.

But why was he interested in buying the old factory? Why offer them more than double what the building was worth?

"I will discuss it with the rest of the owners tonight. But I'm sure we have an agreement," he said.

The grey-haired man's face broke out into a feminine grin. "Thank you, Mr Waser."

"I have one question though," Henrik Waser started. "What do you intend to produce here? It's an old factory. There is not a lot you can do with it."

The grey-haired man pulled out an old gold watch from his pocket. He studied it a couple of seconds before raising his head and meeting Henrik Waser's gaze.

In perfect German he answered:

"Only time will tell."

Author's note

Thanks for taking the time to read The Last Alchemist.

If you enjoyed the read, and have a few minutes to spare, then writing a review on Amazon or telling a friend about the book would be appreciated more than you think.

Feel free to contact me on eh@erikhamre.com if you have any questions.

Yours truly,
Erik

Erik Hamre

48010973R00238

Made in the USA
Columbia, SC
05 January 2019